MAIALEN

THE KEEPERS OF IMBRIA BOOK 2

J. BARRETT

ANTHEM IN ART

Maialen

The Keepers of Imbria Book 2

Copyright © 2023 by J. Barrett

All rights reserved.

This is a work of fiction. Names, characters, places, and incidents in this book are either the product of the author's imagination or used in a fictitious manner. Any resemblance to actual persons, living or dead, or actual events is purely coincidental.

This first edition published by Anthem in Art

1

The sun burned hotly overhead. The air was prophetically still despite the presence of the King of Samirra, who stood stiffly by my side, watching with a slight frown as I knelt and raked my fingers over the cracked land. I sighed heavily, feeling the depths of the drought reaching far into what had once been fertile soil. The dusty remnants of tattered roots shivered in response to the currents of power that flowed from my fingertips, but even I, the Keeper of Earth and wielder of the Emerald amulet, could not coax the dead land back to life.

"I cannot make the crops grow without water," I told Astraeus, squinting up at my husband through the harsh glare of the sun. I was tempted to ask him if he could conjure at least a slight breeze to combat the insistent heat, but seeing the peevish look on his face I thought better of it and tried not to think about the sticky rivers of sweat that were sliding beneath my gown. I knew, everyone knew, that Astraeus's power as the Keeper of Air was waning and reminding him of it only set off fits of petulant rage.

"This is all her fault," he spat through clenched teeth, his aristocratic face twisting into something garish as he spun on his heel and stomped away from me in a cloud of resentment and dusty earth. I sighed again and lifted my hands from the barren land, wiping them on the hem of my gown. Perhaps he was right, and it was her fault. Perhaps she had muttered a curse before she died that had lingered on these last ten years, slowly killing the kingdom of the man who had killed her. Orabelle, my sister, Queen of the Leharans and the Keeper of Water. It was Astraeus, my husband, who had delivered the fateful blow that had ended her life that day on the battlefield in Veruca. He had taken the last of my family from me, and in return I was left with only him and the shadowy remnants of what I had once foolishly mistaken for love.

"Queen Maialen," the purring voice of Logaire was felt softly near my ear. "We are done here. There is nothing more you can do for him. Let us go back to Kymir and tend to our own problems."

"Samirra's problems are our problems," I said, hoping she could not hear the desperation in my voice. Samirra was the breadbasket of Imbria. All the four kingdoms depended on their crops and grain and for years the unending drought had been choking the life out of the once abundant farmland that stretched beneath the soaring granite cliffs. Rolling fields of golden grain that had shimmered like jewels in the sunlight were now just blistered wastelands. I looked out into the distance, to the north where the mountains pierced the horizon and the snowy peaks melted into streams each spring. There was plenty of water there, and a tantalizing stretch of green at the foot of the mountains, but no farmers would dare to go there anymore. The demons that roamed beneath the mountains had terrified the Samirrans into abandoning the only fertile land left in their realm. It belonged to the blooddrinkers now; the feared half-man, half-beast creatures called the Fomori.

I glanced at Logaire, her coppery hair a fiery halo around her head, tinged with the first hint of age in the silver strands that framed her face. Her full lips were pursed and she tugged at the laces of her fashionable gown, looking as uncomfortable as I felt in the midday heat. I could tell from the glint in her golden eyes that there was no need to point out the real threat that another year of hunger would usher forth, for she knew her cousin well. Blaise, the unpredictable and wrathful ruler of Veruca and the Keeper of Fire. The man who had loved my sister with an irrational obsession that even now could not be dampened though she had died despising him.

"We have to find a solution before Blaise decides to just burn all of Samirra out of spite. Without the promise of enough grain to get the Verucans through the winter, he will find a way to justify the war he has been salivating for," I muttered darkly, feeling exhaustion creeping around me. I could not tell if it was because of the strength I had wasted trying to bring life to the arid, dead fields, or if I was just becoming physically spent from the constant effort of being the one to keep the peace between the realms. Perhaps both.

"Besides," I went on when Logaire did not respond, "I want to see Aracellis. We have come all this way and it has been months since I have seen him."

There was a pain in my chest at the thought of my son. Seven years ago I had given birth, a day that had been the most joyous of my life. I could still feel the tiny weight of him in my arms, the fragile warmth of him against me as I nursed him. Aracellis had been my hope for a better future, the family I had yearned for since mine had been so violently taken from me. I had never been happier than when I had first laid eyes on him and his tiny, perfect face. His big blue eyes stared up at me with complete surrender. But then something happened. Like a rock that cracks from within, I had come apart, unable after that first moment to bask in that wonder again. I had built a wall against him and no matter how much I wanted to, I could not tear it down. When he was three years old Astraeus had come and taken him from Kymir and I had let him. Our son would be raised in Samirra, educated by the finest scholars in the land, reading books from the greatest library on Imbria, preparing to one day be the ruler and successor to his father. And once again I was left with nothing.

Logaire was still silent as she fell into step beside me, walking back to the massive eagles that waited for us impatiently, ruffling their feathers in agitation as the handler tugged on the riding tethers. I knew what she was thinking. The thought she had whispered to me so many times over the years, the thought that her cousin would kill her for voicing. *Give Veruca to me, Maialen, and we will never have to worry about the threat of war again. We can have peace. I am your friend and your ally, together we can make Imbria the world we want it to be.*

"Thank you," I said softly to the handler, buckling my riding helmet under my chin then taking the leather strap from him and swinging myself onto the creature's huge neck. Astraeus had not bothered to wait and I could see the dwindling figure of his own eagle ascending into the distance. The handler bowed low in response to my gratitude and I flicked the tether, the beast lunging powerfully into the open sky. My breath caught in my throat, as it always did when I flew, but after a moment the fear subsided. Logaire lifted into the air beside me and together we soared towards the Samirran palace and the gleaming copper domes that shone like beacons atop its white marble towers. The kingdom stretched beneath us, a vast expanse of dullness mottled with the dilapidated structures of once prosperous farmsteads. Dirt roads churned up great swirls of dust in the wake of plodding horses as we neared the walls that encircled the renowned capital city of Iriellestra, renamed by Astraeus for his dead mother. In former days, the city had been a shining haven of scholars and artists. Now it was overcrowded with people, the farmers having trudged into the towns with their meager belongings to try to find a way to provide for themselves and their families, and the north-erners having fled the presence of the Fomori. What had once been neat rows of stone buildings was now an invasive mess of hastily thrown together shacks. People had used whatever they could find to turn any open space into a shelter. Families were crammed in with their livestock and the once carefully tended streets were covered in grime and flies. We had tried to warn Astraeus of the sickness dangers that the conditions of his city could bring about, but he had curtly told me that he was the King of Samirra and I should keep my focus on my own realm of Kymir. I had to stop myself from laughing aloud at his comment and instead nodded demurely and changed the subject. Samirra was his alone until he needed my help, a circumstance that was becoming all too familiar these last few years.

The city disappeared behind the high palace walls and the eagles landed lightly on the open space between the minarets. I slid down the feathered shoulder onto the soft rugs that had been laid out for our arrival, giving the creature an affectionate pat on the neck.

"My Queen, I am glad to see that you are still alive and have not managed to get yourself killed in my absence," the nettled voice of my Guardian, Magnus, boomed across the polished marble. I cringed inwardly but kept a smile plastered on as I walked to where he and Damek stood waiting for me, both glowering in disdain at my poor choices. Magnus, a Samirran himself, was tall, lithe and grey haired, though still knotted with wiry muscle. He was the former Guardian of Astus, my husband's father, a once brilliant man who had gone quite mad after his reign ended and he had been forced to relinquish his element to his son. Magnus was not the sort of man I would have chosen as my Guardian and protector, but Damek and the others had insisted that he would be the best choice after Gideon had abandoned me.

Gideon.

I hated the memory of that day and tried to push it from my mind, but it lingered distastefully. Gideon, seated in a chair beside my bed, staring out the window, his right arm hanging uselessly by his side and his face drawn and pale beneath his thick beard. Since he had lost the use of his arm to a blooddrinker's bite he had not been the same and his sad countenance had worried me. I had awoken to find him there, staring down at his large, callused hands, opening and closing the left one in a fist as if to reassure himself that at least one of his limbs still obeyed his command. Finally, I had asked him what troubled him and he had turned to me and said in a dull voice that my sister was dead and it had been my husband, Astraeus, who had killed her.

My green eyes had gone wide with shock and I could still feel the knot that had formed in my throat. Orabelle was not dead. I had shaken my head stubbornly at him, for it could not be true and my mind refused to allow it. Orabelle was the most alive person I had ever known, she could not simply be gone from the world.

"It can't be true," I had managed to whisper, twisting the blanket in my fists, not wanting to believe him but knowing from the look on his face that it was true. I had just buried my father, whose death my sister had been instrumental in, and now she was gone too. "When did this happen? How long have I been asleep? I did not even... I don't..."

My voice had trailed off with a hiccupping sob. There were no words that could have been adequate to express what I felt that day. I had lost everyone that was closest to me, my entire family. I was an orphan. I had learned that my sister was a monster, a bastard child of another father and the descendent of blooddrinkers, and now she was gone and I would never know the truth from her. I would never have the chance to understand or forgive her. I would be left with my last memories of her tangled with the murder of my father, a haunting vision that moved through my dreams in a violent, blood-soaked haze.

Gideon had offered me no comfort then or shown any kind of pity for the sobbing that had shaken my whole body. He had simply looked away from me and risen from his chair, walking from my room without another word. He had never returned.

I forced myself out of my reverie and addressed the Guardian who now stood before me. "Magnus, as always I am grateful for your concern. Luckily, we were in no danger from anything but this awful heat. Damek, could you send someone for Aracellis? I would like to spend some time with him."

I pulled off the helmet and passed it to one of the handlers, smoothing the soft waves of chestnut hair back from my face. Another maid handed me a goblet of water which I drank from gratefully. Damek was plucking at his robe as if it were covered in ants, frowning with all the force his gaunt facial muscles could muster.

"I agree, this heat is quite oppressive, my Queen. I will be glad to be back under the trees of Kymir. It is unnatural to be so hot this early in spring. I fear that this kingdom has been abandoned by the gods." The old advisor made no effort to hide his contempt for Samirra. Damek hated anywhere that was not his beloved Kymir. He had a special hatred for Astraeus who he considered a drain on Kymir's resources, which he cared more about than any angry god.

"We will be back in Kymir soon enough, Damek. My son?"

"Aracellis is in the library attending to his studies."

I tried to feel more excited at the prospect of seeing my child and forced a wider smile. "And does he look well?"

Damek wiped the beads of sweat on his forehead with the dark sleeve of his cloak and looked even more discontent than before, muttering uncharitably, "He looks like his father."

I heard Logaire chuckle behind me but I ignored them, stepping past and making my way to the library. At least that was something I could look forward to. The Great Library of Samirra was renowned throughout the four kingdoms. It was the center of knowledge, culture and history, housing all the most important records of the past. The huge space was filled with thousands of books and scrolls, drawings, sketches, ideas, stories, legends, ledgers. I loved coming there, though I had never been as good a student as my sister. Orabelle had been quick to learn, naturally curious, speaking the dialect of the ancients with ease by the time she was twelve years old. I had trailed behind her as she paced the floor, her white hair billowing around her in a cloud and a scroll held open in front of her, speaking magical words that made no sense to me but caused everyone else to nod their heads with approval.

"Mother," the quiet child's voice interrupted my thoughts. I let my fingertips fall from the gilded edge of the scroll case and turned to find my son staring up at me. He was beautiful, with Astraeus's sweep of dark hair that fell across his alabaster forehead and cool, liquid blue eyes. I searched his features for some sign of myself in him, but there was not even a shadow of one of the freckles that were scattered across my nose. There was no familiarity for me to find, no tether to myself that I could grasp onto that might make me feel some maternal affection for him. Instead, I saw nothing of myself and felt only emptiness within me.

"Aracellis!" I exclaimed with fabricated joy. If there was one thing I had learned being Queen, it was how to pretend. I knelt in front of him and opened my arms, grasping him tightly and feeling the threads of his embroidered coat under my palms, so like the ones his father wore. He had grown so much since last I had seen him. "You are looking well, my son."

There was a shuffling behind us and Astus, my son's grandfather, popped his head out from behind a shelf demanding to know what I was doing there.

"Astus, it is good to see you as well," I said, standing and inclining my head in greeting. Astus, mad though he was, had always been kind to me even when I had felt like an outsider in their realm and I was grateful to him.

"Have you seen Irielle?" he asked me, scratching the last whisps of grey hair that clung to his head as I wondered how to reply to his query regarding the whereabouts of his dead wife.

It was Aracellis who answered, his young voice gentle but firm. "No, grandfather, no one has seen her in here today."

The old man wrung his hands in agitation. "Ah, well, I need to speak with her. Important things are coming! Very important things! I have found an auspicious date, an auspicious date indeed! You, servant girl, do you know what it is?"

"Please do not be offended, mother, he does not understand what he sees," Aracellis explained, sounding years wiser than his tiny child's body.

"I understand perfectly!" Astus countered, shaking a finger at the boy. "It is the rest of you who do not understand. The time is coming, mark my words! The awakening of chaos is upon us! She will be here soon and destruction will follow and no one is prepared! We need the child!"

With that he turned and fled further into the interior of the library, his footsteps shuffling rapidly across the polished marble floor. Aracellis was watching the empty space his grandfather had just occupied with a look of quiet contemplation. I thought he would say something more about his grandfather, but he shook his head, turning and reaching for my hand. The warmth of his touch surprised me and I jerked away before I could stop myself, instantly feeling ashamed. I was his mother, how could I not long for his small hand in mine? How could I recoil from my own son?

"I apologize mother, I only wanted to show you my new toy."

"No, no, Aracellis, it is I who apologize. You merely startled me. I would love to see your new toy."

He grasped my hand once again and led me towards the doorway where Magnus stood waiting for us. "I am afraid something has come up that needs your mother's attention, young prince. Do you mind if we steal her from you for a few moments? I promise to return her to you as soon as I can."

"What has happened that is so urgent you would interrupt my time with my son?" I asked irritably as we strode down the hallway and away from the boy who stood alone in the doorway, watching us with eyes much older than they should have been.

"There has been an attack on the supplies bound for Veruca. Nearly everything was lost."

I stopped walking, the blood rushing to my head and making me unsteady on my feet. Magnus caught my elbow and waited a moment for me to regain my composure.

"Does the Fire King know?"

Magnus shook his head. "No, but he will soon."

"Get Logaire and tell her we are going to Veruca. We need to stop a war before it starts."

2

Blaise steepled his fingers and leaned back on the gaudy new throne he had commissioned for himself. It was carved from obsidian rock and was a gleaming, monstrous masterpiece that looked as if hell itself were crawling up from the depths below. Each arm was adorned with the swirling shapes of flames wrapping around howling skulls and the high back boasted an inky black likeness of the Fire Opal surrounded my more burning flames. Torches lined the walls of the cavernous stone room and their flickering light danced over the carvings so that the throne seemed to have a life of its own. Beside the King of Veruca was the sullen figure of his Guardian and adopted son, Akrin, glaring at the scene before him with contempt. He was wearing the crisp uniform of a soldier, his auburn hair shaved close above the high, black collar of his jacket. I avoided the young man's gaze, for I had always found him to be unsettling.

"Well, well, lucky me, an unexpected visit from the prosperous Queen of Kymir," the Fire Keeper mused, smiling at me with all the warmth of a snake about to strike. It had been a long time since we had seen one another face to face and he was still handsome in his own dangerous way, his ruddy complexion now crossed with faint lines that deepened around his eyes and between his brows. His gleaming red hair had no hint of grey and was still thick and curled becomingly around his chiseled features. The muscles of his arms could be seen through the black fabric of his shirt as he folded them across his broad chest. He wore no armor today, and the casualness of his demeanor was at odds with the burning intensity in his amber eyes.

"I apologize for showing up unannounced. I am afraid we have had some unexpected delays with the shipments from Samirra." I decided it was best to just dive right in. Exchanging pleasantries with Blaise was as delightful as petting a rabid dog and waiting for it to bite you. He narrowed his amber eyes and leaned forward on the throne, his cavalier attitude melting quickly at my revelation.

"What do you mean, delays?"

"The ship was attacked. Everything was lost. Several of the crew are still missing and presumed dead and I have ordered the Leharans to search for -"

"I don't care about missing Samirrans!" He practically spat at me. his cheeks flushing with anger under his swarthy tan. "And I do not care about your lost ship. Send another and it better arrive quickly, for we had an agreement, Earth Queen."

"There is not another," I said softly. I let my fingertips touch the amulet that hung around my neck, my power stirring within me. His own power flared across the room in a dance of sparks and Magnus stepped around me, pushing me behind him, his hand on the hilt of his sword.

Blaise laughed at the Guardian and said, taunting, "Give me an excuse to kill you, Samirran. I have no desire to harm the Queen, but you I have no qualms in burning the flesh from your bones as you scream."

"Cousin, please. There is no need for blood to be spilled today," Logaire interjected, her tongue darting over her full red lips nervously as she drew his wrathful attention her way. Akrin stiffened slightly and we all knew that he would love the chance to be rid of Logaire for good. She was his only competition for the succession of the Verucan throne.

"Easy for you to say as you sit there licking the boots of the Kymirrans, your belly full while your own people go hungry," Akrin snapped at her. "You have forgotten who you are, Logaire."

I interrupted before they started an all-out melee. The last thing I needed was those two fighting over a throne that was still occupied. "Samirra is barren land. I have just come from there and even I cannot bring life to the fields without water. The drought continues, there are hardly enough crops from this harvest to feed their own people. Who knows how many of them will starve this winter?"

Blaise stared at me with such ferocity that I had to keep myself from flinching. Magnus's fingers flexed on his sword hilt, and I laid my hand on his shoulder to ease his tension. I let my power flow though the room gently, a soft current that hummed beneath them through the soles of their boots.

"Stop your mind games, Maialen," the Fire Keeper snarled. "If you could actually do something useful and find the Pearl then we would not have this cursed drought to deal with. Better yet, if your idiot husband had not killed my betrothed, then perhaps we would all be enjoying our lives much more right now and not dealing with ten years of the aftermath that he inflicted on us all!"

"It was your war he was fighting!" I retorted angrily. "And my sister would have probably drowned you by now, so yes, that would be a much more enjoyable circumstance for us all!"

As soon as the words had left my mouth, I wished that I could swallow them back. I braced myself inwardly for the other Keeper's rage but instead he seemed to soften at the edges, relaxing back into the throne as a shadow passed over his features. If I had not known better I would have thought

I saw a flash of regret in the gleaming amber eyes. When he spoke again his voice was flat and even.

"You must have something to offer, even you would not come here empty handed. What is it that you have for me, Earth Queen?"

I stilled my hands as my fingers began to nervously fidget with the edge of my amulet. Was I doing the right thing? Would Blaise agree to it? There was no way to be sure how the events that were unfolding would play out but I could see no other option. The Pearl of Water, the amulet that was the conduit to that Element, had disappeared when my sister died. Her Guardian, Damian, had claimed it was still around her neck, somewhere at the bottom of the ocean where she was buried. I had searched for it for years, sailing out to sea with the Leharans and trying to use my power to find her, churning up the ocean floor in our wake. But the Pearl and my sister's body remained hidden. Some had even whispered that she was still alive somewhere, hiding with her bastard child, but I knew her better than that. Orabelle was too proud to have been gone from her throne this long. *Or perhaps she loves her child in a way that you cannot fathom.*

I ignored the thought, bringing my attention back to Blaise and the idea that I was about to propose that I hoped could save us all. "You take your army to Samirra, beat back the blooddrinkers and take back the fertile lands near the mountains."

Blaise's face was impassive as he continued to watch me carefully, waiting for something else, a trick, a contingency, a string attached that would tether him. I lifted my chin and stared back at him boldly, hoping that my plan would not doom us all.

"Well, well," he mused, a flicker of a smile playing at his lips. "Now that is an interesting proposition. Though you must remember what happened the last time we had to confront the beasts."

I shuddered inwardly at the memory he spoke of. Ten years ago, at that same fateful battle, the blooddrinkers had been released on Veruca. They had torn through the kingdom leaving a swathe of bloody carnage in their wake. When they had reached the forests of Kymir I had gone to Blaise, begging him to let us work together to defeat them. I had been to the villages they had attacked, seen the blood and bones strewn through the streets, the mangled corpses they had left scattered about. Blaise had made me kneel before him and swear that I would be his ally and never raise arms against him. I had done it, swallowing the humiliation I felt and ignoring the disdain in everyone's eyes, and we had both kept our word. He had joined me in fighting the creatures, driving them north and into the underground lairs that traversed those cold lands. It had been a long, bloody campaign and we had both lost much. The Fomori did not care to meet on a battlefield, or to face us boldly in one penultimate stance, but instead they fought us at night, in moments we were unprepared for, in small groups whose attacks were so random and unpredictable that we could not anticipate them. So many died. Finally, though, we were winning. I could see it so vividly in my mind, as if I had watched it from outside my own body. I was standing with my green gown billowing around my ankles, my arms trembling from fear and the effort of tearing the ground open to swallow them. A rain of arrows washed down upon them from my archers. Blaise was standing at the edge of the forest, wrapped in a shroud of flame, hurling fire at the grey skinned creatures as they ran, teeth snapping, howling in rage and frustration. I remembered the blood seeping out from his armor where he had torn open the wound on his side. He had been consumed by grief then, wild with it, and he had directed all of it at the blooddrinkers, burning through them like tinder while his black-armored soldiers hacked at the creatures with their swords and battle axes. The Fomori retreated but too late we realized that we had driven them unintentionally to the northern border of Samirra, the weakest of the kingdoms because of the weakness of their Keeper, and thus the safest place for the beasts to take refuge. Now, years later, we were feeling the repercussions of that decision.

"We fought well together," Blaise said, and I knew he was seeing the same memory in his mind's eye. "But there were many losses, and what you are proposing will be even more arduous. It would cost me and Veruca greatly. Tell me, Maialen, what do I get out of it? I already have your fealty so what more could I need from you?"

"You can take the Northern lands and govern them as a province of Veruca."

"Maialen!" Logaire's voice was sharp.

"We don't have a choice and they are useless to us without his help!" I hissed at her. Then, facing the Fire Keeper once again I added my final caveat. "My only other condition is that our alliance will extend to my son, should he ever become Keeper and ruler of Samirra."

"Done," Blaise said so quickly that it took me a moment to realize he had agreed. I blinked, startled, and waited for him to say something more. He was still watching me carefully, as if he were studying an insect in a jar. "I have agreed to do as you have asked of me, Queen of Kymir. I expected you to be more pleased. Perhaps you are merely tired from your journey. I will see that rooms are prepared for you and your companions, and of course you may dine with me this evening."

I mumbled a polite reply and Blaise motioned to Akrin, who led us out of the chamber with a baleful glare at Logaire. He passed us off to another man, a steward of the castle, before stalking off down the corridor without another word.

"Charming lad, as always," Magnus muttered after he had rounded the corner. We were ushered down the same hallway, turning in the opposite direction and ascending a flight of stairs that led to the upper sleeping quarters.

"Are you two dining together tonight? Going to swap Guardian tales of adventure?" Logaire teased him. He frowned down at her but there was a sparkle in his eye. Magnus found Logaire quite entertaining and had always enjoyed her sharp wit and her company.

"I would rather starve than dine with Akrin," he retorted and she chuckled lightly.

The steward opened the first door and motioned for me to enter. "Your Guardian will be in the room just beside you and the lady will be across the hall."

"Lady!" Magnus scoffed. "Maybe you do need to spend more time in Veruca, Logaire, they seem to have mistaken you for someone else!"

"I will spend a moment with the Queen, I can see myself to my room," Logaire told the steward, smoothly sidestepping him and shutting the door between us and the men with a liquid smile. She turned and glanced around the space, the small lines between her brows furrowing. "This castle could use a woman's touch."

I smiled, taking in the austere furnishings of the chamber. The furniture, while massive and made from the finest Kymir-ran oak, was all blunt lines and sharp corners. There was nothing warm or inviting about any of it, not even the canopied bed, whose deep red fabrics somehow managed to look severe despite their obvious richness. There were no adornments in the room, and the only warmth came from a large fireplace along the far wall.

"I don't suppose he welcomes many guests. Can you imagine anyone actually wanting to come here if they didn't have to?" I asked her with a laugh, then stopped abruptly, nearly choking on my own words for I had forgotten momentarily that Veruca was also her kingdom. She had been in Kymir with me for so long that it seemed as if she had always been there. "Oh, Logaire, I am sorry I meant no offense!"

She trailed her long fingernails across the foot of the bed, tilting her head to the side and looking at me sideways beneath her heavy fringe of lashes. "You know you have signed your husband's death warrant, don't you?"

My hands twisted in agitation and I forced myself to still them, brushing down the skirt of my gown. I finally answered in a quiet voice, "I have done all I can for Astraeus. I must think about the rest of Imbria now. Surely, you must see that I have no choice, that if I were to-"

"Maialen, darling!" she interrupted, "I am not admonishing you; I am proud of you. Damek and I have been telling you for years that your frivolous husband is a poor excuse for, well, everything. No, I wanted to speak with you because you have another problem. Magnus."

"Magnus?" I repeated in confusion, having no clue what she was referring to.

Logaire sighed heavily and sat on the edge of the bed. "Sometimes I forget how naive you are, my friend. Surely you know that Magnus is a spy for the Samirrans?"

I closed my eyes and shook my head, feeling the pounding begin at my temples. "No, Magnus is my Guardian, he has always been good to me, protected me."

She laughed, her trilling voice grating on my budding headache. "And why do you think that is? It would do them no good to let you die! Magnus has been telling the Samirrans your every move for years. Damek and I were aware, that is why we convinced you to make him your Guardian."

"You knew?"

"Of course we knew. But better the enemy you know than one you cannot see coming. Before now, there was nothing we needed to be concerned about. So, we let them have their little ruse and Damek intercepted their messages and read them, giving him quite an insight into what was really going on in the north. You'd think at some point they would have figured it out."

I blushed at her disdaining tone, for I had also never figured it out.

She went on, not noticing my embarrassment, or perhaps ignoring it as payment for my scornful remark about her homeland. "Now, however, there is something for Magnus to tell. If he warns Astraeus of what happened here, then you will not be able to control your husband's next move. We all know he is terrified of Blaise, just as we all know that my darling cousin wants nothing more in this world than Astraeus's head on a spike. We can convince Astraeus that the Verucans are coming to help, that this is best, that Blaise will not kill him, but we cannot do that if he learns about it beforehand and works himself up into a frenzy of paranoia. You know how he can be."

"What do you suggest I do?" I asked her, praying that her answer would not be the Guardian's death. I knew that Logaire could be cruel, but I would not agree to that. Whatever Magnus had done, whatever secrets he had shared, they were not enough to justify ending his life.

"I can help you, if you will let me. I can get something that will make him sick and unable to leave Veruca with us. This is the one place no one will help him and he will be unable to send a message, I can make sure of that. However, you are going to have to ask my cousin for help in this little charade. Once we are gone, we will need Magnus to remain here and make a very slow recovery. Blaise can assure that will happen."

"He will kill him."

She grinned up at me. "Not if you ask him not to. Whatever his motivations are, the Fire Keeper has a soft spot for you,

Maialen. He will not break his word to you. Convince him at dinner to help you. He will realize that this benefits him as well and he will agree."

I snorted in disbelief. "Blaise has never kept his word to anyone."

She arched a finely manicured brow. "Hasn't he? When has he broken a promise to you?

I frowned hard, searching my memories for an incident to throw in her face as proof that Blaise was not to be trusted but I could recall nothing specific. The one act that had cemented his reputation as evil was one that I suspected he had nothing to do with. I asked Damek once about Tal's murder and if my father, Chronus, had anything to do with it. Logaire had been the one to plant that seed in my head, to tell me of an angry conversation she overheard where Blaise had railed against Chronus for the murder. Damek had been serving at my father's side since before I was born. He knew everything about him and he would know the truth of this. He became agitated at my query, tugging his robes around him and demanding sharply that I never speak ill of the dead again in his presence. He had practically trembled visibly with indignation and asked me how I could even conceive of such a thought. But he had never once denied that it was true.

"If you really think I can trust Blaise, then I will ask him, but I am worried that this will make me indebted to him. While he may keep his word, he is not a man to give out favors lightly."

She shrugged her shoulders and once again the red lips pulled into a smile. "Perhaps they will all kill each other in the north, and we can be done with the whole lot of them. Now, darling, let us make you as beautiful as possible so that you may charm the wicked Fire King."

3

My shoulder thudded against the side of the wagon as we lurched dangerously along the pitted road from Veruca to Kymir. Logaire was bracing herself across from me, cursing heartily at every bump.

"I am beginning to think my cousin suggested this merely to torture me," she muttered miserably.

"I told you he would want something in return for Magnus," I reminded her, bracing myself yet again as the wagon teetered tempestuously on two wheels before slamming back down on the rough ground.

She gritted her teeth. "I did not think he would take the eagles out from under us! Can't you use your power to make the ride any smoother?"

I banged on the front of the carriage and it drew slowly to a halt, a black-clad soldier opening the door with a worried look. "I apologize, Queen of Kymir, for the road conditions."

"Move aside, I will ride atop with you and help us along," I told him brusquely, lifting the skirts of my gown and stepping down onto the road. He scrambled forward to help me up and it was obvious from his anxious demeanor that it would not go well for him if I were displeased. I thought of Logaire's words the night before, *the Fire Keeper has a soft spot for you.*

I settled on the bench beside the soldier as the other men who made up our escort looked back in curiosity, their horses sidestepping and whinnying in agitation.

"Are you ready, Queen Maialen?" the soldier asked and I gave him a nod, one fist closing around the gold and green amulet that hung from my neck. I felt my power flow into me like a warm current and I sighed with pleasure at its embrace. All around me I could feel the world. The hard dirt, the cold and steady rocks, the pliant grass along the edge of the road, the tall trees in the distance that endlessly stretched their limbs towards the sun at the edge of my kingdom. I felt life, the essence of everything and it was beautiful and peaceful. The dirt on the road shivered and shifted, smoothing over and filling in the holes and ruts. The men threw appreciative looks my way and we started off once again.

"Thank the gods!" I heard Logaire state happily from inside the carriage.

Logaire. She was my friend, my ally, but I could never forget that she was also ambitious and cunning. She wanted Veruca for her own, and I wondered how far she would be willing to go to get it. Perhaps I was being too trusting, perhaps Blaise had been correct when he had stared at me over his goblet of wine, his amber eyes flashing dangerously, and warned me that there was no one on Imbria who did not want something from me. That was the price of power, he had said, and I was the most powerful woman on Imbria.

I had wanted to make a clever retort, to let him know that I did not need his warnings or his wisdom, but the truth of his words had twisted inside me like a snake. He was right, of course, and I was foolish to think that there were people who genuinely cared about what was best for me. I had believed it of both Gideon and Magnus and now here I was, alone again, with no one to protect me except myself.

"You don't need them, Maialen," Blaise had said, leaning back in his chair, his intense gaze raking over me in a way that made me shiver. "We are more than any of them, they can never understand us and they will always want what we have."

I pushed away the thoughts of the Verucan King and focused on the road that stretched out ahead of me. Several hours later we were approaching the border of Kymir, the forests towering in front of us like sentinels. *You are the only Guardians I need*, I thought to them. Soon the road would improve as we approached Par-Anaan, for I made sure that the Kymirran trade routes were well maintained, and I would be able to relax and stop using so much of my power.

As we passed into the forest, the heavy canopy of tree limbs shaded the path with thick summer foliage. Plumed ferns and twisting vines wove throughout the dense thickets beneath the trees and I breathed deeply, the air delicious and heavy with life and growth. My reverie was interrupted by a dull thump and I watched as the leading man in our line slid from his saddle and collapsed in a heap on the ground. I stared for a moment, confused and wondering what was wrong with him, then another man fell. Suddenly the forest was chaos. Men exploded from the tree line, attacking the Verucans and quickly dispatching them as I watched in horror. They hardly had time to reach for their weapons, so quick and brutal was the assault. I snatched the Emerald where it hung around my neck and called my power to me.

Nothing happened.

"Get down!" the soldier beside me yelled, shoving me unceremoniously off the bench and onto the step beneath his feet and dumping his heavy shield on top of me, knocking the air from my lungs. "You must-"

His shout was cut off in a wet gurgle and blood spurted from the wound in his neck, the hilt of a knife sticking out of the tanned skin above his collar. I would have screamed had I been able to draw breath. I gripped the Emerald tighter, the edges of it digging into my palm. I felt a faint tremor, a small current, and I focused on it, willing it to grow. Blood pooled over the shield and dripped onto me as it pulsed from the soldier's body that had collapsed on the bench above me. I reached to try and grasp his sword which was still sheathed on his belt but I was stopped by a warning snarl from the most hideous creature I had ever seen. It stood beside the carriage on all fours and its head was a mottled mass of scars and pink tissue. Part of its lips were missing from the long, dark snout, revealing a row of sharp teeth and it glared at me with one eye, the other an empty, sightless black socket. What should have been ears were gnarled stumps on its head, and its thick, red-brown fur was patchy and mottled with scar tissue. Saliva dripped from its jaws and it growled menacingly, lowering its head so that its one dark, gleaming eye was all I could see. Its muscle tensed as it prepared to leap onto the wagon with me. Panic threatened to overwhelm me and I jerked the sword from the dead soldier's sheath, dropping it with a clatter as the blood-slick hilt fumbled through my fingers. I groped for it frantically, my gaze fixed on the hideous creature that was about to attack me.

"Not so fast, Earth Queen," a woman's voice, lilting and melodic among the screams of the dying men. She wore a heavy cloak and hood and had a cloth tied around her face to obscure her features as she bent over me, tossing the shield aside like it was a piece of parchment. She grabbed the laces on the front of my gown and jerked me towards her. The world exploded into darkness as she brought the hilt of her own sword crashing down against my skull and the last thing I saw was a strange looking man striding up beside her, staring at me curiously. *I know him*, I thought and then there was nothing.

When I came to my head was throbbing, my forehead resting on my folded arms. I took a moment to breathe, remembering what had happened in the woods. We had been attacked, the Verucans killed with such cold efficiency that they had not even had time to retrieve their weapons. And me, useless, unable to call my power. It had happened before; the shock of a moment could startle a Keeper into weakness. It had happened to me when my father died, and to Orabelle when Tal was murdered. Using the amulets required focus and purpose. This time was different though. I should have been able to call it. Even now my Element felt faint to me, as if it were wrapped in a shadow and I couldn't quite reach it. I opened my eyes, my head still on my arms, staring down at the wooden surface of a table. All around me were boisterous sounds, laughter and loud exclamations, curses and jeers. It sounded like I was in a tavern.

I whipped my head up, ignoring the throbbing behind my eyes, and sure enough I was seated in the corner of a crowded ale house. Across from me the hooded woman from the road sat waiting, her countenance still shrouded so that her identity remained a mystery, though she had to be immensely tall, her broad shoulders nearly twice the width of my own. Our table was near the back of the room, enough distance from the other patrons that we would not be heard over their drunken ruckus. The woman pulled the cloth down from her golden face and stared at me with slanted eyes that were the color of a frozen lake in winter and just as cold. She was Leharan.

"I thought you would be shorter," the woman said in her musical voice that I now recognized as the islander's lilt. "Your sister was shorter."

"Who are you? What have you done? Do you know who I am? I will have you hanged for this! And why are we in a tavern of all places?" I was wrapped in a cloak that was not mine, the rough homespun fabric unfamiliar against my skin as I searched frantically for the Emerald around my neck. I was grateful to feel that it was still there.

"Please stay calm, Earth Queen. You are in Par-Anaan, in a place surrounded by people so that you can see we mean you no harm. We have merely brought you here to have a discussion," the woman said, as if this were a normal occurrence and I was overreacting. "I would refrain from screaming or calling for help, it will not help your cause. These people are not exactly heroes. Maybe in another life but now they are just drunkards and opportunists and someone of your stature is quite an opportunity."

"A discussion? You killed all those men! And Logaire! Where is my companion?" I demanded, fear gripping my insides. If they had hurt her...

"The woman? She never came out of the carriage. We left her there. She was not harmed. As for the rest of them, I have no problem killing Verucans, Earth Queen. They have not suffered nearly enough for what they have done." She flicked her fingers in the air distastefully, as if swatting away a gnat.

"I have ordered the Leharans not to attack Veruca! Do you realize what you have done by disobeying me?"

She laughed, a scornful, biting sound. "You are not the Queen of Lehar; you just pretend to be when it suits you."

"Who are you? What do you want with me?" I pressed again, ignoring her stinging words even though I was sure she could see the flush stain my cheeks. Since Orabelle had died and the Pearl and her child had gone missing, there was no heir to Lehar and no way to choose a new Keeper. The succession of the throne had always followed the passing on of an amulet. No one had known exactly what to do and so they had done nothing, leaving me as de facto ruler of the islands because it was the lesser of three evils. The Leharans would never have submitted to Blaise and I was quite sure that one of the fierce warriors would have just killed Astraeus, as he was the one who had taken their beloved Queen from them. I had tried to do my best for them, to honor my sister's memory, but I felt that I had always come up lacking. Colwyn did his best to help me, but I did not understand their customs and ways, their insatiable need for pride and honor, and I would never be her. They would always see me as an outsider, someone to mistrust.

"I told you; we are here to have a discussion. The others will be back soon. Ah, here they are."

She gestured at three men walking towards us carrying mugs of ale. One of them plopped a cup down in front of me, the dark liquid sloshing over the rim and splattering the cloak I was wrapped in. I lifted my chin to glare up at him and saw that it was the man from the road. From the chiseled features I first thought he was Verucan, but he had the pale hair that was distinctive of the Leharans, cut short and sticking up in a wild mess around his head that somehow suited him though it would have looked ridiculous on anyone else. He was not quite handsome but there was something compelling about his face that made you want to stare. His eyes were a startling color I had never seen, deep blue with flecks of pale yellow and accentuated by long lashes. His countenance was so arresting that I found it difficult to look away from him and focus on the other two men who flanked his sides. They were obviously brothers, nearly identical with skin that was a smooth, red-brown ochre stained darker by the sun. Their only distinction was that one had a jagged white scar that cut through his eyebrow and across his forehead. Neither was particularly tall nor short, both dressed in dark leather clothing that looked well made. They both had long brown hair worn loose and their features were a peculiar sort of bland. Unlike their compelling companion, these were two faces you would forget as soon as you looked away. The one with the scar was watching me with eyes that were a very ordinary brown, though there was a sharpness in them that you almost missed if you just glanced over him. Beside him stood the beast from the road and I let out a startled yelp at the sight of the creature, the warm candlelight flickering over its warped features grotesquely. The man with the scar seemed confused and looked down at the beast who pressed against his knee.

"You are afraid of the dog?" he asked me, his voice as bland as the rest of him.

"Dog? That thing is a dog?" I cried, blinking hard as if it would suddenly change shape in front of me and look like a dog.

The man looked at the Leharan woman. "What is wrong with her, is she daft? Did you hit her too hard?"

"I am not daft!" I protested irritably. "You are the one running around with some demon wolf and calling it a dog! And if you don't want me to start screaming then someone needs to explain to me exactly what is going on here."

The woman scooted down the bench to make room for the man with the strange eyes as he sat across from me taking a sip from his mug. "It must be difficult for someone so powerful to feel so helpless. Unable to use the amulet that gives you so much control. But I am getting ahead of myself. I am Thyrr and it is a pleasure to finally meet you, Earth Queen."

He paused as if waiting for something. I shook my head and asked, "Is that supposed to mean something to me?"

Thyrr sighed, one corner of his mouth tilting up in a crooked smile. "No, I suppose not. The two brothers are Seff and Vayk. And our Leharan friend here is Bacatha, do you not recall her either?"

"No... should I?"

"You seem to have a short memory, Queen Maialen. Alas, it does not matter for the past is the past and what concerns us now is the future. You see, I know that you cannot feel your power right now. Don't bother protesting, lies will just waste both our time. You cannot use it because I have prevented you from doing so." He leaned back and took another long sip from his cup. I felt my fingertips tremble inside my cloak where they touched the cold edge of my amulet. I reached for my power but a faint stirring was all that I could call forth, a mere echo of the rush of warmth that I was used to.

"What have you done?" I demanded to know, feeling my large green eyes grow even larger.

Thyrr seemed to enjoy my astonishment. "I have found a way to restore the balance of power. For too long the Keepers on Imbria have been free to do whatever they wish, to destroy lives as they see fit for no reason besides their selfish whims. I can end all of that. With this."

He slammed something down on the table and withdrew his hand just enough so that I could see the stone beneath it. It was smooth and polished, a moonstone, milky and irides-cent where it caught the light. Across the smooth surface was carved a string of tiny symbols I did not recognize. I reached out to touch it and he snatched it back, tucking it inside his shirt and giving me a sardonic smirk, his mouth once again tilting up crookedly.

"No, no, Maialen, you mustn't touch. May I call you Maialen? Earth Queen just sounds so formal. Anyway, you must not touch the stone, I must admit I have no idea what it would do to you. You could lose your power permanently and we would not want that just yet."

"What is it? Where did you get it? How does it work? Does it affect all the amulets or just mine?" I rattled off questions in rapid succession, my heart beating in my chest as I tried not to panic. Was he telling the truth? Was that stone the reason I could not feel my power?

"It is a Warding Stone. Have you heard of it? No? I am not surprised, the Tahitians told me you have never bothered to listen to them," he said, disappointment in me coloring his voice. "The Samains, the historians of the islanders, say that when the amulets were created and the Elements dispersed

among the Imbrians, the Fomori tribes were found to be beyond redemption and so they were banished to the under-
worlds, fated to roam those caves and tunnels restlessly and
with a never-ending hunger. But there was one God who did
not agree with this. There is always one in every legend who
disagrees, have you noticed? But I digress. You see, the legends
say that if a Fomori and a human have a child, the child will
not be a monster, but a thing of great beauty. One such child
was born and she grew into the most beautiful woman that
even the gods had ever seen, but she was raised among the
Fomori, shunned by humans because of what she was. This
god became enamored with her and as a token of his admi-
ration he gave her a handful of these Warding Stones, imbued
with divine magic that can overpower any amulet. He believed
that she would use them to bring balance to the world, but
instead she exploited them for a different advantage, going on
a murderous rampage and killing everyone that she could to
avenge her fallen family. She was finally captured and sealed
away forever in a tomb, the Warding Stones lost and hidden
for centuries. Until I found one."

Thyrr finished with a dramatic flourish of his hand, looking
at me expectantly.

"You must be mad," I told him with a shake of my head. I'd
had enough of the stories and riddles. My head was pounding,
I was hungry and tired, and I did not care the slightest bit
about some ancient woman hellbent on revenge. "You killed
my escorts and probably started a war with Veruca, kidnapped
me, forced me to listen to your ridiculous stories, and for what?
What does any of this mean?"

"We did not want to resort to such measures but you left us
no choice. I want you to give me what is mine," he said softly,
his voice deepening with conviction. "I want Lehar."

My mouth fell open and suddenly that day came roaring
back in my mind. My father, his bloodied body torn to pieces

as I watched. Orabelle screaming at me to run. Carushka, the leader of the Fomori tribe, running towards me with his inhuman face distorted with rage. And the boy. There had been a boy there, watching it all unfold. He had moved towards me with blood-splattered flowers clutched in his hand and I had shrieked at him to get away.

"It was you," I whispered. "I remember you."

A shadow passed over his sublime features as the strange blue-yellow eyes bored into mine. "You are remembering Kymir, the day your father died. I was there. I had come to meet my sister."

My head was spinning and for a moment I thought I would lose consciousness again. I pressed my fingertips to my temples, pulling my gaze from his and staring down at the dark liquid that swirled untouched in my mug. It could not be.

"Orabelle was my half-sister. We shared the same father, the same blood," Thyrr said quietly, as if saying the words out loud was still something strange and new. "He promised Ursula he would never tell, that Orabelle would never know. This was the only way Ursula could still become the Water Keeper. She married Chronus and pretended the baby was his and my sister's true heritage remained a secret. Somehow Chronus learned what she had done, and for a time he used that knowledge as a threat against Ursula, trying to control her and Lehar. Then I was born and Chronus finally made good on his promises and murdered my father, leaving me an orphan."

I felt tears prick the inner corners of my eyes and I kept them downcast, unwilling to look at him, hating the memories he conjured. I muttered miserably, "She is dead, they are all dead, so how do you know it is true?"

"The Fomori. I went north past the mountains to see if I could find the truth there since you all were too wrapped up in trying to destroy each other," Thyrr said. He began to tell me of his journey there, of the long and arduous trek through the cold and how the air had grown thinner as he walked. He had trudged along through that wasteland of snow and rock, his food dwindling and his mind turning against him. Every shadow became a creature, every crevice a cave, only they were nothing and there was nothing but the emptiness. He had never felt more alone than he had in those days, sure that he would die there, wandering hopelessly, with no one left on Imbria who would care. To distract himself from the desolation that threatened to overwhelm him he would imagine what life could have been like had things been different, had Chronus never been part of their story. He would still have his family. He pictured them laughing together while he basked in the overprotective gaze of his loving older sister, his father happy and finally able to smile without the shadows that had always haunted him.

Then, finally, he saw a footprint. Then a second, then a long line of them leading towards a narrow opening in the rock. He stumbled quickly through the snow, tripping and falling in his haste, slipping easily through the opening. Inside the cave the air was still and he nearly cried with joy to be out of the stinging wind that whipped through the mountains relentlessly. He followed the tunnel a short distance and walked into a cavern where several of the dreaded Fomori stared at him in surprise.

Thyrr pushed a hand through his hair and grinned at me. "I don't know who was more surprised, me or them! They almost killed me but one of them knew who I was. They told me I was of Carushka's bloodline, that he was my grandfather."

I shuddered at the mention of the beast's name and tried not to think about how I had hacked his body apart in front of his grandson. "And now you want to rule Lehar, as Orabelle's heir?"

Bacatha, the woman beside him, stirred from the stillness she had cloaked herself in. "At least he has a legitimate claim to the throne, unlike the rest of you. The Pearl is gone but with the Warding Stone he has a power equal to that of the Keepers. Support his claim to the Leharan throne and relinquish your illegitimate authority over the islands."

I looked at the man in front of me, my sister's brother, still so young despite the wear of experience that made his features seem older than they were. There were so many times that I had stood on my balcony in Kymir and stared out at the forest, wishing I could be someone else, anyone else. Wishing I had not been born to be a Queen, that I had not been born into a legacy of pain and death and power. This boy still had a chance. He could be free of it, free to live without the burden that pressed so heavily on my shoulders that every day I thought I would crack beneath it. I said as gently as I could, "You don't want this life."

"I have no other life to lead," was his firm reply. "I have nothing and no one. All I have are the ties that bind me by blood to that throne and I will take it, with or without your help."

There was so much passion in his strange eyes that I looked away, unable to meet his gaze. "And what will you do with your throne? Kill more innocent people?"

Bacatha scoffed and said, "I assure you the Verucan soldiers were not innocent. You have had Lehar for ten years now and what have you done besides weaken us? Nothing. You have done nothing to avenge the deaths at the battle of Queen's End. Remember, it was not just your sister that was killed, but your mother-in-law as well and all you did was take their murderer to your bed! Then you had the gall to come to Lehar, disband the Guard and put a price on the heads of our own, on Kaden and Damian, as if we are so crass that we would betray each other for a few pieces of silver. You do not rule us, you cut off our limbs and leave us to fend for ourselves! Yet you ask, what he will do? He will at least do something, which is more than you have ever done."

She slammed her palms on the table and stood, leaning forward, her lips pressed into a thin line and I wondered if she would try to kill me then and there, so immense was her anger towards me. Thyrr placed a hand on her wrist and she relaxed, folding her long limbs back onto the seat and refusing to look at me again.

"The bounties were the only thing I could do," I tried to explain. "Damian had taken the Pearl and we needed it back, and Kaden disappeared with Orabelle's child, my nephew. I wanted to find them, that is all! I never wished them dead."

Thyrr leveled his strange gaze at me. "If you want to make things right, let us escort you back to Kymir where you can officially support my claim as the heir."

The door to the tavern was suddenly thrown open and my mouth dropped at the sight of an extremely disheveled Logaire standing in the entrance. Her hair was a massive tangle around her head and there was dirt and dried blood on her face. Her skirts were torn and caked with mud, and she looked as furious and miserable as I had ever seen her. Her golden eyes darted around the room till they lit on us. She furrowed her eyebrows, stalking forward and going straight up to Thyrr, slapping him hard on his tanned cheek.

"I should have known it was you, you little bastard," she seethed.

"Nice to see you too, Logaire," Thyrr said, rubbing his jaw as he grinned up at her with his crooked smile. "Don't I get a thank you for not killing you?"

4

I breathed in the smell of the forest, trying to calm the churning in my stomach as I let my fingers trace the carved sigil on the doors to the Council Chamber. It had been a long time since I had descended into those hallowed rooms. Not since Orabelle had been alive. In that moment I remembered her face with startling clarity, her slanted eyes flashing pale and her chin lifted haughtily while her white hair billowed around her. She had looked so much like our mother that sometimes it had made my breath catch in my throat. But she had been more than our mother, Ursula, more than any Keeper who had come before her, the most powerful of them all. It still baffled me that she was gone for I could still feel her presence so keenly, especially here.

"Maialen, darling, are you ready?" Logaire asked gently, her hand on my shoulder. Damek's spindly figure stopped beside her, frowning at her distastefully. Damek hated Logaire, but then Damek hated just about everything and everyone. My father's closest advisor, I had not the heart to cast him out after Chronus's death. His grief was so immense that I was not sure he would survive it without something to distract him and so I had asked him to stay, to help guide me. I needed the help and one thing I could always depend on was Damek being loyal to Kymir above all else.

"This is a bad idea," he stated for the hundredth time since I had told him I was convening the Council. "Though at least we may all get the satisfaction of seeing the Verucan kill that worthless idiot you call a husband."

"Damek, please! Do not say such things," I chided.

"How are we even sure that this usurper is who he says he is? Though if he wants to go wallow on that cursed island with the other savages then I say let him. He is just what they deserve. Oh, and let us not forget that we are inviting all of these imbeciles to Kymir with no Guardian to protect you because you abandoned him in Veruca." He adjusted his dark robes around his skeletal frame and started down the stone steps into the chamber below.

"We have no choice, Maialen, this is the right thing to do," Logaire murmured in her purring voice. I wondered again how much I could trust her. She had convinced me to leave my Guardian in Veruca and Damek was right, it was not a time to be without my sworn protector. But I had no choice, the events that were transpiring had already been set in motion. I had brought Thyrr and his motley crew of vagabonds back to Kymir with me and done as he had wanted. Logaire had encouraged me to capitulate, despite her having kept Thyrr's existence a secret from me for who knew how long. Once I had made up my mind to support his claim, I had sent messengers to both Blaise and Astraeus, asking for a convening of the Council regarding Lehar. I would also be telling my husband that I had granted the Verucan army permission to march into Samirra to fight the Fomori in the north. My stomach twisted again with dread for what the next few hours would bring.

"You look beautiful, they will all be putty in your hands," Logaire murmured with a sly grin on her full red lips. I touched the edge of my hair which was swept up in an elaborate braid and felt my cheeks flush. I hoped that I at least looked like a Queen even though I felt like a terrified girl. I had worn my finest gown, a shimmering green cascade of rich fabric trimmed with gold lace. The Emerald hung from my neck, laying prettily just above the edge of the gown. I clasped the amulet for a moment, enjoying the comforting rush of energy from my power before following Damek down into the chamber.

Blaise was already there, his booted feet resting insolently on the marble table and Akrin standing stiff and sullen behind him. The Verucan King was not pleased and I could feel his anger despite the casual smirk that adorned his ruddy features. He wore a black leather overcoat over a dark tunic and his red hair curled invitingly over the collar. He raised his eyebrows at my approach and the grin widened as he swung his legs down from the table and stood to greet me.

"I am sorry to have called you here," I told him, glad that Damek had thought to remove Orabelle's chair from the room. The last thing any of us needed were more reminders of what we had all lost. "I do not like the memories it conjures any more than you do, but we are Keepers and we have neglected this part of our duty for too long."

His eyes swept over me and I felt a flutter in my stomach that I staunchly ignored. "Our duty? It is a little late for that, Earth Queen. Though I should think that one of your duties was finding out who killed my men on the road to Kymir."

I felt my cheeks flush and I wondered if he knew that we were lying. I had sent word that we had been attacked on the road by unknown assailants, and that only Logaire and I had escaped, making our way through the forest to Par-Anaan to find help.

"These mysterious henchmen seem to have a vendetta against me. First the shipment of grain from Samirra, then the attack on your caravan. Should I be more concerned about your abilities to govern your lands, Earth Queen? Your people seem quite out of control," he continued musing, deliberately trying to provoke me.

"Nonsense. Kymirrans would never attack their Queen!" I countered.

"Whoever it is, I trust that you will find a way to put an end to these little setbacks, and sooner rather than later." He paused, glancing around the chamber. "I see the crowds are already gathering, ready for the debacle."

Blaise sat back in his chair and waved a hand towards the long pews that lined the far wall, teeming with regents and people eager to see what incredible thing had happened to cause the Council of Elements to convene for the first time in nearly ten years. Thyrr was there, the two brothers and the tall Leharan woman beside him. Thankfully, the dog had been left elsewhere for I warned them that bringing the beast to Council would only cause more disruption. Behind Thyrr there was a large group of Leharans and I recognized several of the old Guard and their former Captain, Colwyn. I had seen their ships at the docks the day before but I had been careful to avoid an encounter with them before the meeting today. Colwyn made a gesture of greeting towards me and I nodded back at him. He had softened with age and was balding, the remnants of his fastidiously combed hair peppered with grey.

I walked around to my own chair and slid into it, still feeling like a child wearing an adult's clothing. The chair had always felt like my father's, and I had always felt like an imposter, sitting in a place I shouldn't. Logaire and Damek sat a few feet behind me, Logaire watching the doorway with an eager look on her sultry face. Damek was glowering at the table and avoided looking at anyone, though I noticed that he too was darting glances at the chamber entrance while his long, spidery fingers stroked the papery skin over his chin. I clenched my hands on the ancient, wooden arms of the chair. They were all waiting for my husband, the King of Samirra, to join us. I was not sure he would actually come, knowing that Blaise was present. The Verucan had made no secret of his hatred or his desire to kill Astraeus, and from the look on the Fire Keeper's face, it was quite likely that my husband would be burnt to death as he was entering the room.

"Blaise, please, let us be civil today," I pleaded with him in a whisper.

He laughed, the biting and mirthless laugh that we had all come to fear. "I would be doing you a favor if I killed him."

I ignored the comment and tried to ignore the faint voice in my head that agreed with him. I remembered a time that I had doted on Astraeus, the fair and striking Samirran who I foolishly believed had shared my affections. As soon as we were married I had been cured of all my romantic delusions. Following the hollow ritual that we called a wedding, Astraeus had promptly followed Blaise into battle, that fateful battle that people had taken to calling Queen's End. He had never been the same since. After accidentally killing his mother, Irielle, then slaughtering Orabelle in a fit of rage, he had come home, miraculously alive thanks to his Guardian, Favian. Since that day he barely tolerated the sight of me and after I had given birth to Aracellis he never touched me again.

"He is coming," Logaire leaned forward to whisper in my ear. A hush fell over the crowd and everyone turned to watch as my husband strode through the entryway and into the chamber. His Guardian was beside him and they were followed by a dozen men in gleaming armor. He paused for a moment to glance over the room and stopped short at the sight of Blaise leaning his elbows on the polished marble table.

"Didn't think I would show?" Blaise asked with a smirk. His eyes were so bright that they seemed to glow with amber light. I willed him silently to remain calm, reaching for the Emerald to help soothe the tension in the room.

Astraeus was still as beautiful as ever, tall and stately with a sweep of dramatic dark hair, though there was a coldness now to his patrician features that I had not noticed before. He looked down his long aquiline nose at us and walked to his chair, which I had deliberately placed on the opposite side of the table from Blaise, as far out of his reach as possible. I saw Blaise's hand tremble slightly as he tried to control his volatile temper.

"I hope that we are not here to dredge up the past," Astraeus said with a slight frown. "I should think it has been long enough that we can let that go."

As soon as he said the words I flinched, knowing that it would infuriate Blaise. The Fire Keeper stood with a roar and flung his hand out towards Astraeus, sparking the flint he carried with him. Nothing happened. Instead of the Samirran being engulfed in flames he merely sat there looking perplexed at the empty space between them.

"What is this? What are you doing?" Blaise snarled, whirling to face me.

"It-it is not me!" I stammered, my gaze flying to Thyrr who sat placidly watching the tableaux unfold, the milky moonstone clutched in his hand.

"Who then? Him? Akrin, take that man and bring him here!" Blaise shouted, following my gaze to Thyrr. The young man stood, holding his hands aloft in a gesture of surrender.

"There is no need for violence, Fire King," Thyrr said calmly. His strange eyes locked on Astraeus. He had every reason to want the Samirran dead but for some reason he had saved him, perhaps because of our bargain. "We want the same things."

"I sincerely doubt that," Blaise growled, clutching the Fire Opal. I could see from the shadow of panic that crossed his features that he was feeling what I had felt in the tavern of Par-Anaan. The sick twist of dread that churned within you as you realized your power had abandoned you.

"This is why we are here," I murmured to him, laying my hand on his arm and willing him to breathe deeply and stay calm. Akrin shoved through the gasping crowd and grabbed Thyrr by his collar, dragging him to the Council table. Thyrr did not try to resist and instead bowed his head in greeting as if he had been cordially invited to attend.

I held my breath, waiting to see what Thyrr would say next. This was what he had wanted, no matter how much I had tried to dissuade him when he and his companions had accompanied Logaire and I on the journey back from Par-Anaan. Which was not exactly chivalrous since they had killed our previous escort and given us no other choice. I had ridden beside Thyrr, the huge Leharan woman leading the way before us with her sword and shield strapped ready to her saddle. She would glance back at me occasionally, as if she did not trust me to be in such proximity to him.

"Are you two.... Um, are you..." I asked him awkwardly, gesturing at Bacatha.

Thyrr had laughed, a pleasant sound to hear when it was genuine. "You would be more in danger of the Leharan's affections than I would, dear Queen. Bacatha is merely a loyal protector, and hopefully, with your help, she will soon have the title of Guardian."

A cool breeze wove through the trees, tickling the leaves so that sunlight dappled over us. I breathed in the scent of the forest, enjoying the green sharpness of the pines and the cool tang of eucalyptus as it mixed with the muskiness of the horse beneath me. How could I make him understand that I would give it all up if I could? I would live out here in the forest, away from the lying and the fighting, away from all of them. How could I admit that I wished more than anything to have been born someone else? I could not find the words to express what I felt, the yearning that I had for a different life than the one I had been given, and so I merely said, "It is not what you think it will be."

Thyrr watched the road ahead, his strange eyes staring off into the distance. "It is ironic that you think so, when I have suffered the same fate as you and I was born a nobody."

I was taken aback, realizing that he was speaking the truth. We had more in common than I had let myself believe. We had both lost everyone we loved to a violent struggle that began long before we were even born.

"Despite all your pain, you are still free. You can choose the life you want to live," I said wistfully.

He had given me one of his crooked smiles. "But that's just it, I have chosen."

In the Council chamber, the discord of the crowd echoed throughout the room. Thyrr lifted his hands and gestured for silence, staring around the room, his blue-gold eyes keen with intent. His voice was smooth and assured. "Imbrians! I come here today with the support of the Kymirran Queen, Maialen, to make my claim as ruler of Lehar."

The room once again erupted into a noisy tumult.

"Silence! This is ridiculous," Blaise cried, throwing himself back into his chair and waving a hand at Thyrr. "By what right do you make these preposterous claims?"

"I am brother to the former Queen, Orabelle, and though I have no Element as the Pearl is still lost, I do have this." Thyrr lifted the milky stone he clutched in his palm. "It is called a Warding Stone, created by the gods centuries ago to defend against the power of the Keepers. I should think this would be enough of an advantage to allow me a seat at the table."

Blaise looked as if he were about to murder the younger man, his tanned face flushed with rage, and I leaned towards Thyrr and made a gesture at my Emerald. He gave me a slight nod and I let the calm energy of my amulet flow around the room. Blaise glared at me but I saw his shoulders relax slightly and the tension on his face ease.

"Vile traitor!" to my surprise it was Astraeus, not Blaise, who leapt at the young man. Favian, his Guardian, tackled him to the ground before he could bring down the knife he had swung and make the mistake of breaking the Council Oath.

Damek stood and cried out in indignation, his black robes swirling around him, "Violence is not permitted in the Council Chamber! You violate this sacred place!"

"Please, can everyone just please calm down!" I pleaded. Blaise was staring at me intently and I tried to avoid meeting his eyes.

"You knew about this," he said quietly, and I thought I heard a measure of hurt in his tone.

"This is why I called this meeting," I tried to explain. "If everyone would please stop trying to kill each other then we will tell you exactly what is happening."

Astraeus's face was nearly purple with indignation as he got to his feet and shook off Favian's proffered arm. "He is the reason my amulet has not been working! What have you done to me? I demand that you rectify it immediately!"

It was Blaise who answered him, laughing. "No one needs to do anything to thwart your power, Samirran, you are weak enough on your own and you have been weak for years. No one would be patient enough for that sort of vengeance."

I heard the warning in his voice, the unsaid words *except for me,* but Astraeus was oblivious to it and continued to seethe at the golden-haired young man who faced him calmly, watching and waiting. It dawned on me then that Thyrr had expected what had just happened.

"But perhaps you should try to correct your faults soon, Astraeus, as it looks like I will be the one coming to clean up your mess in the North," Blaise went on, taunting him. "Your wife has granted me permission to pass through Kymir with my army so that I can deal with your little Fomori problem before we all starve because of it."

I wanted to bury my head in my hands but I forced myself to remain upright and be strong. This was not how I had wanted to broach the subject to Astraeus. He narrowed his cold blue eyes and retorted at Blaise, "If you set one foot in Samirra, I will kill you all."

Astraeus then threw me a hateful look and made a gesture to Favian, spinning on his heel and storming out of the chamber without another word, his guards following him in a clatter of armor.

I was about to speak again, to try to bring order to the chaos that this meeting had dissolved into, when a new voice interrupted the proceedings, echoing out from the crowd in righteous indignation. A woman stood, slender and lithe, her long auburn hair pulled back severely from her face. She wore simple, homespun clothing and beside her was a child, a cap pulled low over his face and his eyes downcast.

"That man is not the heir to Lehar!" the woman called out.

"Oh, for the love of Imbria, this is completely preposterous! Get her out of here, along with anyone else who wants to claim a throne and disrupt these proceedings further," Blaise exclaimed, slamming his fists down on the table. I ignored him, staring at the woman and the tiny figure beside her, my heart pounding in my chest and my throat suddenly dry, for I knew who she was.

"Alita." I whispered the name out loud, barely able to make myself say it.

From the corner of my eye I saw Akrin start forward, a look of shock on his face. Blaise caught his wrist and gave a small shake of his head and the sullen young man stepped back behind the Keeper, his eyes remaining fixed on the woman who was his sister.

"I heard there was a usurper to the throne and so I have brought the real heir to Lehar! Orabelle's child, Kaeleb," Alita announced, pulling the cap from the child's head and revealing a shock of white hair over a golden-skinned face.

My mouth fell open and I stood, wanting to do something but instead just standing there stupidly. I felt overwhelmed, the blood rushing too fast and my mind unable to catch up with everything that was happening. I heard someone call my name then there was only darkness.

5

The sun was low in the sky when I came to, lying in my own bed. The doorway that led onto my balcony was thrown open and I tried to relish in the scents of the flora and fauna that drifted up into my chambers. Rich, musky evergreens mingled with the fresh smell of spring as new flowers began to bloom. There was a bite of winter that still lingered on the air at night and a chill danced across my skin as I threw back the blankets. It was not an unpleasant sensation, knowing it was the last of the cold and that the richness and abundance of spring was upon us. I loved Kymir in the spring. My kingdom seemed to come alive, like a gentle beast rousing from its slumber, shaking off the long months of frosty winter. The streets and paths below my lofty manor filled with people and the sprawling houses that nestled among the trees threw open their shuttered doors and windows. Vibrant blooms in a rainbow of delightful colors would drip from every bow, bringing the gentle hum of bees and insects. Laughter and the sweet sounds of new life would fill the air with promise. It was almost enough to make me forget the emptiness of my own existence.

Logaire raised a perfect eyebrow, watching me from the chair she had pulled beside the bed. "Feeling better, darling?"

"Not hardly," I muttered, feeling entirely like a fool and embarrassed that practically everyone on Imbria had seen me collapse. "What happened?"

"You fainted."

"Yes, I am aware of that. What happened after I was unconscious?" I asked with irritation. I stood up from the bed and walked over the open balcony, leaning out into the breeze. I squinted into the distance, beyond the treetops, to the south where the blue-green shimmer of the sea wavered on the horizon.

We were interrupted before she could answer by a soft knock on the door and a maid poked her head in gingerly. "Your highness, the Verucan King is here to see you."

"I will tell him to leave," Logaire said briskly, sauntering towards the door.

"No," I stopped her. "Send him in on your way out. I should like to speak with him."

I wasn't sure why, but I trusted Blaise more than anyone else at that moment. Logaire had always been a good friend, practically a sister, but she had always had her own secrets and ambitions. At least with Blaise I knew exactly what I was getting. I smoothed down my gown and ran my fingers over my hair, thankful that the tight braids still held their shape so at least I did not look as much of a fool as I felt.

"I am surprised my cousin let me see you without a chaperone," Blaise joked, coming in and deliberately leaving the door ajar. He was tense, his eyebrows drawn together despite the easy grin on his handsome face.

"Could we go onto the terrace? I would like some fresh air and the night is quiet," I asked him. He nodded in acquiescence and came to stand beside me, leaning on his elbows and looking down into the woven limbs of trees that nestled us. I admitted that I was quite embarrassed by what had happened in the Council Chamber.

His grin widened. "It was quite the spectacle. I assume from your look of shock and subsequent fainting that you had no idea that Alita had returned?"

I shook my head. No one had seen Alita since before Orabelle had died and everyone assumed that she and Kaden had taken the child to hide it. "Do you believe either of them?"

He shrugged his shoulders and my cheeks flushed as I saw the muscles of his back move beneath his shirt. He went on, not noticing my awkward discomfort. "Neither of them has the Pearl, which means it really does not matter who they are or who they are related to. The amulets determine who rules. Which brings me to another point that your untimely collapse prevented you from hearing. The Leharans, mainly Colwyn, say that there have been sightings of the Sirens near the islands."

I felt my stomach turn. It seemed the surprises of this day would never end. "We all assumed the Sirens died with Orabelle. If they are still here... maybe the rumors are true, maybe she is..."

"Your sister is dead, Maialen, I was there. I watched her die." He turned to me, his amber eyes bright with a look I had not seen in them for a long time. It was sorrow, still there and still so raw after all these years. He had just gotten better at hiding it. "I would be the first to wish that she was still alive, but that is a foolish dream."

I felt a sting at his words and tried to ignore it. I was being ridiculous. Ever since Logaire's insinuations in Veruca I had started to think of Blaise in a different way, one that was both dangerous and foolish. "Damian was the last person with her body. He is the only one that knows where the Pearl is. We must find Damian."

"He will not come out of hiding for no reason, Maialen. Someone will have to go and seek him out."

"And by someone, you mean me? I have tried and I could not find him."

Blaise grinned again, the shadowy sorrow fading from his countenance. "You have dispatched me to Samirra to defeat the evil Fomori for you. I cannot be in two places at once. You will have to be the one to go to Tahitia. Someone there knows where he is and things are different now that the child has returned, perhaps the Guardian will also want to return."

I shuddered, thinking of the forbidding figure of my sister's former Guardian. Damian had always frightened me. "You want to kill him for what happened at the battle that day. That is one of the reasons he remains hidden."

"If he had not attacked me, I could have kept her safe. He is complicit in her death."

I sighed, watching the light as it faded from the sky. Orabelle. It was always about Orabelle. I wondered if she had known that her choices would affect the lives of so many for so long. She probably would not have cared. She had always been self-ish and stubborn and if any of us had mattered she would have just done as she was told and married Blaise instead of starting a war over it. Then I thought of my own loveless marriage, of all the nights alone, and I could not hate her for the decision she had made. If I had known, been less naïve, perhaps I would have done the same. Instead, I was standing here with my husband's enemy and making him my ally, knowing that at the end of it all one of them would be dead.

"This Warding Stone is another problem we need to address, Earth Queen," Blaise interrupted my dark thoughts.

"Yes, of course. The Great Library in Samirra would have been a helpful place to search for any reference to the Stone but I think you have effectively revoked our welcome in the palace."

He chuckled and took a step closer to me. I felt a flush stain my cheeks and hoped he did not notice in the waning light. I could smell him, the earthy scent of rock and dust that clung to him. The dying sunlight danced off his shining red curls and accentuated the angular planes of his face.

"I apologize, Earth Queen, my temper got the better of me."

"Your temper gets the better of you quite often," I retorted, turning away. "I suppose you can let Magnus go now. He will either return to Samirra on his own or I will send him there. After today I cannot afford divided loyalties."

"I will release him. I have also decided to support the brother's claim to the Leharan throne. The best place Thyrr can be is across the sea in Lehar, away from us with that cursed Stone. Once word of it spreads, every thief in existence will be after it and I will, of course, be encouraging them. He will not have time for anything but trying to protect himself, and he has no real power. As for Alita and the child I had them taken into custody and they are being held here, awaiting your decision."

"My decision?" I asked, my green eyes widening in surprise.

"The boy is your nephew, your flesh and blood. Alita stole him. She took him from his family and hid him away from you. It is your right to punish her if you see fit, and it is your right to take the child and raise him as your own."

"Take the child..." I repeated, my mind swirling. Of course, the child was my blood, he was my family. It was my duty to take him. "I am surprised you don't want him dead."

"I did, for a time," the King admitted. "Then I realized that the child is all that is left of her."

"I cannot just take him from his mother-"

Blaise grabbed my wrist, his fingers hot against my skin. "Maialen, think carefully about your next moves. Alita is not his mother, and she is not who you think she is, nor is she who your sister thought she was. She lied to Orabelle, and she lied to everyone. You would be wise to see her dead. Akrin has no love for his sister, he would be happy to oblige you in this matter, just say the word."

I closed my eyes, feeling my head begin to ache as I pulled my arm from his grasp. "I cannot just kill her because you told me a story, Blaise. That is not how we do things in Kymir!"

"It was exactly how your father did things," he snapped back. "Tell me, Maialen, did you know that he was the one who killed your sister's Guardian? Everyone believed it was me, but even I am not that cruel, though you all think I am."

So, it was true, what I had long suspected. My father had been worse than I had ever imagined. I felt tears in the corners of my eyes and wiped at them, furious at myself for crying in front of the Fire Keeper. I had been embarrassed enough for one day. "Leave now. Go to the North and kill the Fomori. I will deal with the child and I will find Damian."

Blaise stood a moment, as if he were struggling with a decision, then he turned and walked from the room, calling back over his shoulder, "Get that boy away from Alita, Maialen. She is poison and whatever she has done to him, you need to undo it."

The door slammed behind him and I felt the tears stream down my face, cold lines of grief chilled by the evening wind. The sun had set, and night awakened the forest around me, teeming with the sounds of nocturnal life. I wondered again why anyone could choose this life.

6

The next morning I paced back and forth in front of the wooden house, the guard staring straight ahead and pretending not to see my obvious agitation. Inside was the child of my sister, a boy that was a stranger to me, and I was now, somehow, supposed to become a mother to. I could not even be a mother to my own child. I had yet to see Alita, or to decide what to do with her. Blaise may have been right that her death would be the best thing for all of us, but I could not justify her murder, especially not when I was about to face the child she had protected all these years.

"I am ready," I told the guard, smoothing my gown and nervously touching the Emerald that hung from my neck. The man opened the door and stepped back, allowing me to enter. The dwelling was darker than I had expected, the windows shuttered and latched from the outside so the boy could not escape.

"Kaeleb?" I called out, trying to see in the darkened interior.

I was answered with a sharp blow to the stomach that made me double over in pain, followed quickly by another blow to the side of my head. I let out a cry and the guard charged in, knocking the child to the ground and kicking away the table leg he had dismantled and used as a weapon. The guard helped me to my feet and I touched my temple where I had been struck. There was no blood and my breath was returning in heaving gasps.

"I am fine," I told him, flush with embarrassment for having just been assailed by a child. "Kaeleb, I do not want to restrain you but if you attack me again, I will have no choice."

I told the guard to leave us but to stay close. When he seemed hesitant I assured him I would be fine and told him to open one of the windows for fresh air. Once he was out of the room I picked up the discarded table leg, looking at the pile of wreckage that had once been the table. I dropped the leg onto the heap then crossed to the window that the guard had unbarred, opening it and flooding the room with light. Kaeleb was not huddled in the corner, cowering, like I had thought. Instead, he was crouched on his feet, balanced to strike, a disconcerting sight to say the least.

"Do you know who I am?" I asked him gently, holding the Emerald and feeling the warmth of my Element wrap around us, hoping to calm him.

"You are one of the betrayers," he said, his pale eyes trained on me, following my movements.

"I am your aunt, Maialen. You are my sister's son. Did you know that?"

He nodded his head. "I know that. My mother was Orabelle, Queen of the Leharans, and I am the Solvrei, sent by the gods to destroy the Keepers."

I felt my eyes widen in surprise and said, "That is quite a burden for a boy your age."

"It is my purpose for being born." He stared up at me, coiled and tense like a snake waiting to strike, his words so at odds with his childish appearance.

I began to pace back and forth, not wanting to stand still and provoke another attack. I felt a pang of sympathy for the boy, imagining what sort of childhood he must have had to make him this way. Why would Alita and Kaden raise him to be the Solvrei? The legendary savior that was part god and part mortal who could unite or destroy the Elements, the decider of the fate of humanity. How could they have thought to put that burden on an innocent child? I myself found it difficult to believe in legends or prophecies. My father had taught us that the Tahitian Samains were fearmongers who told dreadful tales to scare their people into submission. Of course, my father had been an unrepentant liar and murderer so I was no longer sure how much I could trust in his judgment.

"I have a son close to your age, did you know that? You are cousins. His name is Aracellis. Would you like to meet him?"

Kaeleb tilted his head, the shock of pale hair falling over one eye as he seemed to consider what I was saying. "I would like to meet him; I have no qualm with him."

"Tell me where you have been all these years," I coaxed gently, still using my Element to ground him. He sat back on his heels, shaking his white hair back from his forehead.

"Samirra. No one would think to look for us there because the King is my mother's murderer."

I was surprised by his candid answer but then again, he was just a child. I pressed on, "And did you have the Pearl of Water in Samirra? Do you know where the amulet is?"

He frowned at me as if disappointed in my lack of clarity. "If I had the Pearl I would have destroyed it. The Harbonah have shown me that the amulets are a curse, they must be destroyed."

"The Harbonah?" I repeated the name, thinking there was something slightly familiar about it. I had heard it somewhere before but the recollection stayed just out of reach.

Kaeleb pushed himself to his feet and leaned against the wall, rubbing at a spot on the floor with the toe of his boot. He seemed to accept that I was not a threat to him at the moment. "Sister Alita says I cannot speak of the Harbonah."

I stopped pacing. "I see. That is fine, Kaeleb, we do not have to talk of such things now. Are you hungry? Would you like to come with me to my manor and we can see what delicious things the cooks have in the kitchen? Though you must promise not to harm anyone else. No more hitting people with table legs."

"I will not do harm unless I have to," he promised me and I accepted this as a step in the right direction. I reached out my hand to him and he hesitated then took it gingerly. I could feel the rough and calloused palm against my own and I wondered just what this poor child had been doing for the last ten years.

I led him toward my lofty manor in the trees, nodding at the guard to stay at his post as we went by. It was early and the forest was quiet, the leaves and blooms still curled with sleep and a gentle mist blanketing the forest floor. The smell of fresh baking biscuits filled the air and Kaeleb's stomach let out a loud grumble. I silently admonished myself for not making sure that he had been properly cared for the night before, instead of sitting in my room and crying alone.

His rough hand tightened almost imperceptibly on mine and I saw Thyrr approaching with the two brothers, Seff and Vayk. I stopped, pushing him slightly behind me, instinctively protecting him. The hideous dog trotted behind them and I tried to avoid looking it in the eye, focusing on the men instead.

"You do not have to protect my nephew from me, Queen Maialen," Thyrr said in a tone that was mildly chastising. "He will, after all, be my heir to the throne."

"I am the Solvrei, I care nothing about your worldly thrones!" the boy announced defiantly from behind my skirts.

Thyrr raised a golden eyebrow, his crooked smile widening. "Well, then I guess that solves the problem of inheritance, now, doesn't it?"

The two brothers were staring hard at the child, though their faces were void of any emotion. They glanced at each other and one of them shrugged and began to scratch the ugly dog's mangled ear. They seemed to decide that we were of no consequence to them and stood placidly by, looking around as if bored.

"Logaire tells me you will go to seek out Damian, to finally try and find the Pearl," Thyrr said, turning his attention back to me. He motioned to the two men standing inattentively behind him. "Seff and Vayk can accompany you. There are no better trackers in all of Imbria, I can assure you. These two are like a pair of wolves."

"Blaise will march on the northern lands soon, and I cannot say what Astraeus will try to do to retaliate. Finding the Pearl would strengthen our position," I told him. "But I need to know that our alliance is secure."

He ran a hand through his messy hair and laughed. "You surprise me, Queen Maialen. I had not expected you to be such a strategist."

I sniffed in irritation. "And just what did you expect me to be?"

"Weak," he stated bluntly. "A simpering woman locked in your treehouse tower feeling sorry for yourself."

Before I could stop him, Kaeleb shot out from behind me, throwing a handful of dirt up into Thyrr's eyes and grabbing his belt, using it to swing around behind him so that he could kick him hard on the back of his knee, making him stumble to the ground. The boy leapt onto his back and wrapped his tiny arm around the other man's throat and yelled, "Apologize to my aunt!"

"Get your minion off of me, please!" Thyrr cried, trying to stand while Kaeleb held on, kicking him repeatedly. "I meant no disrespect to your aunt, child. We are all family here."

"Kaeleb, stop this at once!" I ordered, though I could not fully suppress the laughter that bubbled up in my throat and I could have sworn the ghost of a smile flitted across the faces of the two brothers. Kaeleb released his uncle's neck and dropped to the ground, circling around him warily till he was once again at my side and glaring at his uncle fiercely.

"I see you have all the protection you will need with this brave warrior," Thyrr quipped, rubbing the back of his leg. "Though I would still feel better if you took Seff and Vayk with you. My claim to Lehar needs your support so I want to make sure you are safe. They can watch over you in the absence of your Guardian."

"Watch over me or spy on me, because it seems lately that those who are meant to protect me do more of the latter. And I am no strategist, Thyrr, I am just trying to do what is best for Imbria and to keep the peace between the realms," I argued with a shake of my head.

He rocked back on his heels. "Sending the Verucans to take land from their sworn enemy is keeping the peace? We all know that will end in war."

"Imbria will starve without Samirra's grain. I had no choice. Astraeus refuses to do what needs to be done."

"As your ally I will support your decision, Queen Maialen," he promised with a bow.

"You need the support of your own people before you can keep any promises to me," I reminded him. "The islanders are not the easiest of people to govern."

He was unconcerned. Bacatha had gone ahead to Lehar to try to rally support for his cause, and with Alita locked up in Kymir there would hopefully be no one challenging his claim, especially not if he named Kaeleb as his heir. The boy was too young to rule, anyway, and this would hopefully seem an acceptable solution to the Leharans. Though it meant Alita was going to need to remain a prisoner until it was all sorted out. The thought ran fleeting through my mind once again that it would be easier with her gone, but I shoved it away. I would not be like the rest of them, I would not condemn her simply for existing.

We took our leave of Thyrr and the brothers, promising him that I would allow them to accompany me to Tahitia and wherever else the search for Damian would take us. Part of me hoped that he would not be found. My heart had never relished the idea of seeing the massive Tahitian again, and I suspected he would not agree with my current alliances. But he was not here, and neither was Orabelle, and I had to do what I thought was best.

Back at the manor I sat Kaeleb at a small round table in one of the parlor rooms, ordering the cupbearers to bring breakfast. They filed in with silver trays laden with food and Kaeleb reached for a biscuit, sniffing it warily while his stomach gave another loud rumble. I motioned for him to eat, taking a bite of my own to show him that I was not attempting to poison him. He waited a few heartbeats after I had swallowed to make sure that I did not keel over dead, then began to stuff his mouth with pastries. His pale eyes widened with delight at the smorgasbord laid before us, sticky crumbs dotting the front of his tunic.

"I have killed, you know," he announced between mouthfuls of warm fritter.

I startled, taken aback by the blunt candor of his words. "What do you mean?"

"I had to hunt and kill a Fomori."

I felt sick to my stomach imagining a small child facing one of those deadly beasts. Surely he was making up stories, trying to impress me. "Would you like to tell me about that?"

He told me it had been in the winter, when snow was on the ground and the land was like a sea of white froth. Brother Kaden had taken him out of Veruca, where they had been for a time, out across the rolling plains and to the edge of Kymir where the tall evergreens soared into the sky like towering sentinels. The former Guard told the child there had been sightings of a Fomori in the area and it was their duty to hunt it down and kill it. Kaeleb had followed obediently, his sword heavy across his back. They walked for several days, the older man stopping and making Kaeleb search for the signs, teaching him how to track the creatures, but in the end it was the beast who found them. It was night and they had built a small fire for warmth, though they both knew it was a dangerous risk, but their toes had started to darken with cold and they had no choice. Sure enough, the Fomori had seen it and come. Kaeleb heard the thing breathing as it approached silently, the snow cushioning its footfalls. He slid his sword from his pack and looked to the older man who had nodded. The boy tucked his pack beneath the blanket where he had been laying and stood slowly and quietly, backing up so that his back was pressed against the cold, icy bark of a tall tree. He listened again. The breathing was closer and to his left he saw the flash of its sickly yellow eyes, followed by the foggy steam of its breath. He kept his gaze trained on the puffs of breath, his hands tightening on the sword hilt which felt immense in his small grasp. He waited, controlling the fear as Brother Kaden had taught him. He wanted to run away, to cry out, to find somewhere to hide, but that was not his destiny. He was the Solvrei, the great warrior, and he would defeat any evil that threatened Imbria.

The Fomori had stepped into the circle of firelight with a snarl, diving straight for the bedding that Kaeleb had just vacated, its clawed hands slashing through the pack that it mistook for the easy prey of a boy. Its head whipped around and Brother Kaden stood ready, his sword in hand, though he made no move to attack the creature. This was to be Kaeleb's kill.

"Are you afraid, Leharan?" The beast had snarled in its eerie, sibilant voice. Kaeleb had never seen one of them so close and the fear threatened to overwhelm him as he stared up at the massive, grey-skinned back of the creature, the broad shoulders and long, muscled arms. Its cracked talons twitched with anticipation as it focused on the older man, thinking this was to be his opponent. The beast tensed, about to strike, and Kaeleb took the moment, the fear nearly paralyzing him but somehow moving despite it. He ran forward, dropping to the ground and sliding between the creature's thick legs, slicing deep into the thigh where the older man had taught him. The creature howled with indignation and fell to one knee, slashing at the boy, its broken talon ripping across his small chest. The pain exploded inside Kaeleb but he fought through it, pushing it away. *Pain is in your mind, Kaeleb. Put it away and save it for later when you can afford to feel it,* he repeated the words that Brother Kaden had taught him. Then he rose to his feet and leapt, swinging the heavy sword with all the strength his child's muscles could muster. The blade bit deep into the beast's neck but he was not strong enough to sever the head. The thing was howling in agony, clawing at the sword that was now piercing its neck. It stumbled away from the boy and Kaeleb lost his grip on the weapon and fell back, nearly landing in the fire. He rolled away and grabbed the knife from his belt, circling the enraged beast warily, searching for the opening. His breath was coming in heavy gasps and each one was like fire across his chest but the wound, though painful, was shallow. He could endure it. *Find the weakness, do not hesitate, for a mere moment of hesitation in battle can mean death.*

Kaeleb saw the weakness, the wide expanse of the rib cage exposed to him as the beast clawed at the weapon in its neck. He darted forward, small and lithe, and shoved the knife up between the ribs, twisting viciously. The Fomori fell onto its side, now whimpering pitifully, its black blood staining the pristine snow that pillowed him.

"Finish him, Kaeleb. We do not let even our enemies suffer unnecessarily. Show him mercy and end his life," Brother Kaden ordered, still standing calmly across the clearing. Kaeleb moved to the beast's side and pulled the knife out from between its ribs. His small hands were gentle as he turned the creature's head to the side, smoothing the dark hair back from the temple before plunging the knife down, killing it.

After his tale I felt a shiver of revulsion run down my spine. Kaeleb was licking pastry from his fingers, his pale grey eyes expectant as he waited for me to voice my approval of his heroic deed, but all I could do was draw in deep breaths and try not to be sick. This was not what my sister would have wanted for her child. They had defiled her memory and her wishes, warped her boy into a monster who took pride in killing. All the times I had imagined the child somewhere, I had never imagined his life had been like this.

"It seems you are quite the fierce warrior, just like your uncle said. I am going on a trip soon to see Tahitia, one of the islands your mother ruled. Would you like to accompany me there?" I asked him. I was afraid to leave him alone and under the influence of anyone else. The safest place he could be was with me. At least I would not drag him out into the wilderness to battle monsters.

"You are going to seek the Pearl from the Guardian? Then I will go with you. We must find the amulet if I am to one day destroy it." He gave me a satisfied nod and then returned his attention to the plates of food, adding, "I have never seen so much food at once, did you not say that people were starving?"

Guilt washed over me and I tried to think how to justify Kymir's abundance to the child. "Kymir is plentiful enough for its own people. It is the rest of Imbria that will go lacking if Samirra does not begin to produce grain once again."

He shrugged and continued eating happily, swinging his feet beneath the chair.

7

Logaire sauntered over to the stables where Blaise and his men were preparing to leave. She watched for a moment as her cousin barked orders at his soldiers, checking the saddle of his horse and adjusting the girth. She enjoyed the looks his men threw at her, the way they tried not to stare at her supple figure swathed in golden cloth. After all these years she still commanded attention and it satisfied her immensely.

"Lost your eagles already?" she asked with a tinkling laugh.

Blaise glared at her over the mare's back. "The Samirran King took them with him when he left."

"Well, darling, now you know how it feels to be banished to horseback yet again. Hopefully you will fare better than we did on the road to Par-Anaan," Logaire said too sweetly, still annoyed with her cousin for having taken the eagles from them as part of his bargain and forcing them to travel the more vulnerable road back to Kymir. It was his fault that Thyrr had finally been able to get to Maialen, when Logaire had worked tirelessly to keep him at bay. The bastard descendent of a Fomori had no right ruling a kingdom and the Warding Stone would have been much easier for her to obtain before everyone knew about it.

"You knew about the Stone already?" Blaise asked, reading her as effortlessly as he always had. "You wanted it for yourself. Tell me, cousin, were you planning to use it to try and take Veruca from me?"

She pretended astonishment. "I would never! I am always loyal to you, after all, we are family."

He let out a sharp laugh, his amber eyes narrowing as he revealed, "I have always known about your schemes to take my lands from me, Logaire, and I have ignored them because they were childish ploys, just like the games we played as children. But make no mistake, if you are a threat to me, I will not let family loyalty stop me from doing what needs to be done."

She felt another flash of irritation. Men had always dismissed her, always looked down on her. If it was not for such a trivial thing as him asking for the eagles they had flown in on, then she would have found a way to take the Stone from Thyrr. She would be the one with the power and the one with the Warding Stone. She would be watching him capitulate, panicked and weak without his Element to protect him. She had waited for years to find a way to stop him, tried everything to undermine him, to usurp his power and influence, and still he lived and continued to rule. Now that he had adopted Akrin she was not even guaranteed succession after his reign ended. It made her want to scream and scratch her long nails down his face. She had put up with Maialen and her simpering weakness for peace, all because she thought the other woman would be the key to helping her unlock Veruca. It seemed now that instead of abhorring the Fire Keeper as Logaire had wanted, Maialen was starting to have affection for him.

"How was your talk with the Earth Queen?" Logaire asked, changing the subject away from her traitorous activities. "I was not aware you two enjoyed each other's company so much."

Blaise glowered at her and slid the bridle over the sleek, dark head. "The Earth Queen is a useful ally, as you well know, since it was you who chose to champion her for all these years. Do not be petty with me because your scheming has not born fruit."

"She is nothing like her sister, perhaps you chose poorly all those years ago," Logaire mused, watching him from under her gilded lashes to gauge his response. There it was, the flush of anger and grief. Just as she thought, he still loved Orabelle, though only the gods could fathom why. Logaire would have to continue to subtly encourage Maialen's affections for her cousin. If he broke her heart, then it would be far easier for Logaire to take the throne. One had only to look at what was happening in Samirra as the Earth Queen prepared to send Blaise in to conquer part of her husband's land. A scorned woman was a thing to be feared, though men were never quite able to grasp that idea. Her only concern was that Blaise would use Maialen to consolidate his power over Imbria. With her under his thumb, or at his side, Logaire would never be able to stop him.

"Goodbye, Logaire," he said dismissively, swinging himself up into the saddle and turning the mare, forcing her to back away quickly.

"I hope you do not die in Samirra!" She sang out after him as he charged away. Maybe he would die there and Akrin with him. Perhaps if both the Fomori and the Samirrans knew when he was coming, and where he would attack, then it would be possible for him to lose. She had her own spies in Veruca, though she now regretted leaving Magnus there. Blaise would surely kill him, there was no way her cousin was stupid enough to let that man return to Samirra and lead the army against him. If he did, she would make sure to use that mistake to her advantage.

She made her way back along the path that led to the Royal Manor, trying to keep her brow from furrowing as she thought over the events that were now unfolding. She had not expected Alita to return with the child. This was something new that had to be considered. She had thought Blaise would want to be rid of the little bastard, as he was the son of Orabelle and her lover, Tal, but instead the Fire King seemed keen on protecting him. She found it difficult to believe that his change of heart was purely sentimental, but whatever he knew about the boy, he was not going to share it with her. Though there was someone else in Kymir who might have answers.

Logaire veered down a different path, now heading away from the manor and out towards the edges of the city where she knew the prisoner was being held. She nodded her head in greeting to the guards who stepped aside as she moved past them. She motioned for one of them to open the lock and they hurried to comply without question, for she was the right hand of the Queen, the persona she had carefully cultivated for so many tortuous years. Night upon night she had spent sitting with the sobbing Earth Queen as she bemoaned the loss of her wretched father and sister. Logaire had stayed by her side, holding her hand, wiping her tears, masking her contempt beneath sympathetic murmurs. She had become the Queen's confidant, her sister, and her closest advisor. Even Damek, who was a master of sycophantic manipulation, could not sway the Queen in the way that Logaire could. It had taken years of listening to Maialen's every word, of absorbing every detail of her simpering personality, but she had done it and earned a place among the royals, though still not as their equal. She had been reminded the last few days that she was still someone who could be left behind to die on the road, dismissed from a room, someone whose ideas could be discarded casually without a second thought. Logaire had gained power and privilege but she was still not one of them, and that was the prestige she craved more than anything.

"Well, darling, you look a bit worse for wear," Logaire said, a smile tugging at the corners of her lips as she entered the room, an austere stone square devoid of any adornment save the narrow openings cut high up on the walls to let light in.

"What do you want?" the woman asked, dragging the chains that bound her across her lap so she could face her visitor. The slant of light from above cut across her face. She was smeared with dirt and her hair had come loose from its bindings. Her slender wrists were already raw from the chains. She had dainty, delicate features with sharp edges, as if she were made of glass and could shatter at any moment. Her brown eyes were large and luminous behind thick auburn lashes, almost disguising the honed intellect that flashed in their depths.

"I have come to officially meet the infamous Alita, of course," Logaire purred, tilting her head to one side as if she were studying an insect in a jar. "You are quite fascinating."

"I know who you are."

Logaire gave a musical little laugh. "Of course you do, darling, everyone knows who I am."

"I do not have the Pearl, nor do I know where it is. You are wasting your time," Alita informed her flatly, but despite her apathetic tone she was watching Logaire with keen interest, her eyes following her around the empty room.

"You are quite cunning, aren't you? Don't bother answering, I can tell that you are. I can see it in your eyes. You don't have to try and hide it from me, it is the Verucan in you." Logaire circled around the slender woman in a shimmer of golden cloth, seeing that her chains were bound to a ring that had been bolted to the floor.

"I hate Veruca and everything it stands for," Alita practically spat, her delicate face twisting with hate.

Logaire laughed again. "That is unfortunate. Do you favor the Leharans more? You are married to one of them, are you not? Kaden, isn't it? There is quite a steep price offered for his head, if you had not heard. For yours too. Stealing the child of a royal family. Tsk, Tsk."

"We did not steal him!" Alita countered. "Damian brought him to us to keep him safe!"

"So, darling, Orabelle did not give you the child herself? Then yes, it seems I am correct and you did steal the baby from the family, and Damian was an accomplice to the theft. It is off that he gave you the baby but did not give you the Pearl as well. I wonder why that is." Logaire could feel the wheels turning in her mind. Why save an heir with no amulet? The amulets determined succession, not birthrights. Damian could have kept the Pearl with him, waiting till the child was of age to give it to him, or he could have hidden it somewhere. Either way, someone else would have to know about it, in case something ever happened to him. He would not allow the Pearl to be lost forever, not while the child lived.

Alita scoffed. "Damian knew that he could not trust the other Keepers or the royal families. Kaeleb would not have lived to see his first birthday if any of you had your way. We took him, and we molded him into the person he needs to be."

"Clearly Damian did not trust you either, darling, since you were not given the Pearl along with the child."

"He was a practical man," the younger woman said with a shrug that rattled the chains that bound her. She shifted uncomfortably and settled her hands on her lap once again.

"You are not what I expected," Logaire murmured, trailing her fingers along the edge of Alita's thin shoulder. "The poor, sad waif from Veruca, lost and helpless, who needed someone to save her."

Alita sneered as she shook off Logaire's hand, then her face softened, her brown eyes widening innocently and her bottom lip trembling as she looked around the room, terrified and helpless. She whispered in a voice that wavered with fear, "Please, don't hurt me. I was only trying to help, to do what Orabelle wanted."

Logaire clapped her hands appreciatively at the little performance. "Quite impressive, my dear. Under different circumstances I think you and I could have been friends."

"I would slit your throat the second you were not watching," Alita said scornfully. "You with your pathetic groveling to the Keepers, doing their bidding while your own people suffer at their hands. You are no better than them. Whatever they sent you for, I will not give it to you."

"It seems I am a better actor than you are, darling, for you have mistaken my intentions. I was not sent here by anyone. I wanted to see you because I had a feeling that our interests are not so different. What if I told you that I had a way to help you bring down the Keepers, starting with my cousin?" Logaire offered enticingly, her full red lips pulling into a sultry smile. She had given the Keepers of Imbria enough time and enough chances, and she was tired of waiting and playing games she could not win.

8

I grasped my amulet tightly in my fist, trying to will myself to believe that it was firm ground beneath me and not the rolling waves of the sea. The ship creaked and moaned and I felt my stomach turn as I gripped the railing with both hands, trying not to be sick.

"Is it your first time on the sea, Queen of Kymir?" Seff, the brother with the scar through one eyebrow, asked me, seeming mildly annoyed with my seasickness.

"No, of course not!" I answered, flushing red. "I have been on a ship many times, though it was in much calmer seas..."

Seff looked out over the waves which swelled gently beneath us, the wind barely blowing. "Yes, this is quite the storm. We will be lucky to survive it."

"I do not need your sarcasm," I admonished him. He shrugged and turned his head to look away, going back to doing what he and his brother seemed to do best. Ignoring me.

Kaeleb was at the rail beside me, his pale eyes intent on the horizon where the first glitter of the island shoreline appeared. The hideous dog sat beside him, his shaggy tail wagging in slow sweeps. Neither the child nor the dog was suffering even a hint of seasickness and Kaeleb had commented that my inferior Kymirran blood was most likely the cause of my troubles. I had thanked him for bringing that fact to my attention and he had beamed up at me, relishing the praise. He was such a strange child and I still had no idea what to make of him. He told me that his training as a warrior had begun at the age of seven, when he was also taught to read and write and to speak the ancient language. This had caught me by surprise and I wanted to question him further on it, for there were not many fluent in that tongue who could have tutored him, but he had already begun to recite to me his daily routine and I was quickly distracted by the traumatic experiences he laid out for me proudly, as if he were putting his favorite toys on display.

To begin, they had taken his boots away, to toughen his feet and make him walk silently. Then he was given a meager cloak to wear all year round, so that he would become accustomed to both the heat and the cold and would not be affected by either. He would be given tasks, long trails to traverse silently and quickly. Steeper and steeper cliffs to climb. In the beginning he would take off running from the start, eager to finish and receive the meager words of praise that were rarely given from Brother Kaden and Sister Alita. He soon realized the foolishness of this after collapsing halfway down a trail and being forced to spend the night alone in the wilderness. He learned to pace himself, to judge the terrain and learn where to expend energy and where to preserve it. He learned to control his breath and his heartbeat. Instead of panting and gasping, he would inhale deeply and feel the world around him, relaxing the burning in his lungs. He became silent and adept at covering any kind of terrain, able to endure long distances with neither food nor water.

"You seem quite in tune with the land. You would make a good Keeper of Earth," I told him with a smile.

His triumphant grin had faltered and he scrunched his face with frustration. "Aunt, I have told you before that I am the Solvrei. I cannot rule just one Element."

"Ah, yes," I murmured, "I had forgotten that."

He had rattled on, telling me about weapons training and how he learned to use a sword and throw a knife, how he had been taught to hunt with a bow and arrow.

"I have heard you are an archer as well, Aunt Maialen."

"That was a long time ago, Kaeleb. I have tried to find more peaceful resolutions to conflicts in these last years. Fighting cannot solve everything," I told him, hoping that over time I would be able to undo some of the damage that had been inflicted on his scarred psyche.

He had looked at me as if I had suggested that he grow another head. I was beginning to think that what had been done to him ran too deep, that there was never going to be a way that I would reach him. Even now, standing on the deck of the ship, journeying towards the homeland of his father and mother, there was no softness to his gaze, no yearning for paternal affection or any sign that he mourned what he had lost. Instead, his pale eyes were wary and calculating, with the only flashes of childlike innocence being the delight he seemed to take in being praised. That and his love for pastries, which I had soon discovered was quite a weakness of his and anytime I was uncertain of his whereabouts he had been found hiding in a corner somewhere, stuffing his mouth with stolen fruit fritters.

"We will soon be in Tahitia. This is where my father grew up?" Kaeleb wanted confirmation.

I felt a pang of guilt for not knowing more that I could share with him about his father. Tal had been my sister's Guardian and the leader of the Leharan army. It had always been obvious that she adored him, and rumors had swirled about them for years, but I had always ignored it, pretending not to see what was so obviously right in front of me. Tal had been a gallant man, not beautiful like Astraeus nor as roguishly handsome as Blaise, but proud and striking in his own way. His presence was one of confidence and strength and I could see, looking back, why my sister had been so drawn to him. He had obviously loved her back, enough that he had given his life for her. I wondered how to explain that to a child, to their child.

"Yes, he was from Tahitia but he left for Lehar after the banishment," was all I said, the inadequate words trailing away on the wind.

"He was the greatest swordsman on Imbria, was he not? That is what Brother Kaden always said."

I felt the urge to stroke his pale hair back from his head and tell him that he could be sad for the loss of his father, but I resisted. "Yes, I believe he was."

Kaeleb turned his attention back to the approaching docks and I felt my heart beat faster in anticipation. I had not been to Tahitia, to any of the islands, since my sister had died, and I was unnerved by how strongly I felt connected to her in that moment. It was as if she were there, as if I could turn my head and she would be standing behind me, her golden skin radiant in the sunlight and her white hair billowing around her in a cloud. I reached out to Kaeleb and he allowed me to grasp his tiny hand in mine, as if he understood that I needed to feel someone present, to connect with something that was real and not a ghost from the past.

"Queen Maialen," one of the men gestured to me after we had been secured to the dock.

I let go of the boy's hand and smoothed down my skirts, still trying to make my heartbeat slow down as I disembarked the ship and walked down the sturdy wooden planks of the pier toward the island.

It was beautiful. The sparkling, turquoise blue waves lapped against the shimmering white sand. The beach near the dock was littered with small boats draped in colorful nets, many of them displaying mountains of gleaming, silver fish waiting to be cleaned. Woven amongst the boats were the Tahitians themselves, tall and majestic with the sun shining off their well-muscled, ebony bodies as they worked tending the nets, cleaning the slippery silver fish, and repairing their boats. Children ran laughing along pathways that snaked up from the beach into the lush tropical forests, hurrying to and from the villages with refreshments and supplies for the hardworking fishermen. I could not help but smile as I walked along, then abruptly fell directly onto my face.

"Aunt Maialen!" Kaeleb cried out, trying to pull me up out of the sand. Seff and Vayk pushed past him, hauling me up unceremoniously between them and setting me less than gently on my feet. I had been so mesmerized with my surroundings that I had not paid attention to where the rough boards of the pier ended and I had stepped onto the loose sand, immediately losing my balance and toppling forward.

Kaeleb made a gesture at my face and I quickly tried to brush the sand from my freckled cheeks which were scarlet with humiliation. The dog was circling me excitedly, barking loudly and drawing even more attention to us.

"Have you never walked on sand before?" Vayk asked me and I shook off his hand, ignoring him and his brother.

"She was too caught up in the beauty of our island!" the warm, rich tone of Cossiana broke through my shame and I found myself looking up at the elderly woman whose wide smile was the most welcoming thing I had seen in a long time. She wrapped her arms around me in a strong embrace. "I heard you were coming to seek out my son."

I lingered for a moment in the maternal circle of her arms, feeling for a few fleeting seconds that I was safe, that I was not a Keeper or a Queen or anything else but a girl wrapped in the arms of a mother.

"I have brought your grandson," I said gently, turning to look at Kaeleb as she released me. Cossiana was the mother of

Damian and the adopted mother of Tal. She was the closest thing, besides me, that Kaeleb had to any family.

Cossiana looked at the boy and her smile faded. She grasped my arm in her hand, her grip tightening painfully. "Why have you brought him here?"

I was taken aback at her reaction and for a moment I just stared at her, uncomprehending. "I... I brought him to see the islands... his family."

"You have made a mistake. Take him away from here at once!"

"Please, Cossiana, I did not mean any harm. He has been through so much, if you would only-"

"Go away, child! Go! Go now!" she yelled at Kaeleb, shooing him back towards the ship with quick motions. I reached to stop her and she knocked my hand away. Immediately two of my Kymirran guards rushed forward and at the same time several of the fishermen on the beach dropped what they were doing and hurried towards us, snatching up their long spears. Before any of them could reach us, though, Kaeleb had whipped out a small knife and shoved me behind him, pointing the blade threateningly at the old woman.

"Kaeleb!" I cried. "Where on Imbria did you get that?"

Cossiana was staring at him as if he had the plague and my guards were pressing forward, their swords brandished at the approaching crowd of fishermen, warning them to get back. The dog was behind me, growling fiendishly.

"What did you do?" Seff asked me, seeming quite bothered by the whole incident as he plucked the knife from Kaeleb's grasp and made a gesture for silence at the dog.

"I did nothing!" I protested, wanting to stomp on his foot. "Please, everyone, let us be calm!"

Seff was checking the belt of daggers that he wore slung around his hips and sure enough, there was one missing. He returned the stolen knife to its place and glared at the boy.

"Steal from us again and I cut off a finger," he warned. He grabbed the boy's shirt collar and began to haul him back down the pier to the ship.

"Cossiana, please, if you would just give me a moment to explain," I pleaded.

She ignored me, watching the boy being dragged along, kicking and shouting insults, the dog nipping playfully at his heels until Seff had carried him out of sight below deck. Finally, she turned her dark gaze back to me. "There are things you do not know, Queen Maialen. Dangerous things."

"Then tell me!" I exploded in frustration. All my life no one had ever told me anything, I was always kept in the dark, treated as if I were too fragile to know the truth even when the truth was destroying everything around me. "All I want is for there to be peace."

"Then destroy that child."

My mouth gaped open. "How can you say such things? He is a child!"

"If you wish to talk then we cannot speak here. Come, walk with me," she offered, waving her hands for the fishermen to disperse. They backed away reluctantly, for they had been denied a good fight and they were disappointed. I told my guards and Vayk to follow us at a short distance and then I allowed her to lead me down the beach. I felt rather ungraceful as I plodded through the sand next to her and she kindly suggested that I remove my slippers and walk barefoot. I did, feeling much relief at the cool touch of the sand beneath me. I almost reached for the amulet that was tucked beneath the neck of my gown but I stopped myself, not wanting to antagonize the situation further. I wanted to speak to Cossiana not as a Queen or a Keeper, but as woman and a friend.

"What has Kaeleb done to make you so angry?" I finally asked her when it became clear that she would not be the first to speak.

"My son, Damian, told your sister of the Solvrei but he did not tell her everything," she began.

"Then tell me," I pleaded with her. "Know that I have never forgotten that you saved Gideon's life from the blooddrinker's bite, dear friend. I will be indebted to you for the rest of my life. Whatever you wish to say, I will listen."

She sighed heavily then she began to tell me the story that had been passed down through generations. The Tahitians were the oldest warrior tribe on Imbria, almost as old as the Fomori. They had been there to see the fall of the world and the rise of the Keepers. They had seen the battles between the gods and the rifts it caused between the people of Imbria. There once lived a woman, a half-breed, who had been part Fomori and part Tahitian. She was an orphan, the only prodigy that blended the two fearsome tribes. She had grown up on the islands, adopted by a kind family and trained with the Tahitians in the ways of the warriors. She had been a valiant fighter, her skill with a sword unparalleled even amongst the men, and her speed and cunning unmatched. But there had always been a darker side to her. She felt a yearning that she could not explain, she only knew that something was drawing her away from Tahitia. One day she left, going to the mainland and trying to seek out this unnamed desire she felt in her heart. There she found the Fomori and learned of her lineage, garnering the attention of the Gods and the newly bestowed Keepers, for her timing was such that she had arrived just before the Fomori were banished to the underworld. She pleaded with the first Keepers to let her go, told them that she was from Tahitia, of the family she had there that had taken her in and raised her. They were afraid of her, and afraid the mixing of the bloodlines would anger the Gods, and so they denied her wishes, banishing her below ground with the rest of them. It was years before she could escape, years the Fomori spent clawing and digging their way out, eating rats and insects and finally each other to survive. Eventually, they made an opening just large enough for her to slip through, out into the world and back into the light. The halfbreed returned to Tahitia, only to find that her family was dead, killed for harboring a Fomori. She went into a rage, attacking everyone around her, blaming them for not protecting her family. The islanders were forced to throw her into the sea to escape her wrath. Somehow, she survived and once again made her way back to the Fomori, freeing more of them from their underground prison and making them into her own vengeful army. She beseeched the help of one of the Gods, using her beauty and cunning to convince him that she would be the one to make the world better, and that the Keepers were failing at the task. He believed her and gave her four stones, to balance against the amulets of the four Keepers.

"The Warding Stones," I murmured. "I have heard some of this from Thyrr, but I still do not understand what this has to do with Kaeleb."

"The Stones were always a myth, no one has seen one before now and so no one believed they really existed. Now that one has been found, we must pay attention to the warnings of the ancients," Cossiana cautioned.

After receiving the Warding Stones, the halfbreed went on a rampage, destroying everything in her path and slaughtering everyone that she could. The Keepers tried to stop her, but she was too clever and too cunning. She eluded them time and time again, until one day they discovered her hiding place in the caves of the North. They went there and defeated her, but she vowed revenge, promising to return and to destroy all the amulets and the rest of Imbria. But to do so she would need the blood of the divine.

I mulled over the wild tale that Cossiana had just told me, still trying to understand how it related to my nephew. I could not shake my father's voice from my head, telling me sternly that the Tahitians were known for warping their ancient tales to suit their circumstances. Perhaps this was what Cossiana was doing. "So, you think that if Kaeleb is the Solvrei, then his blood will somehow be used to end the world?"

She looked down the beach to where the ship was docked. "I do not wish to condemn a child, but I fear that he brings death to the world. A Warding Stone has appeared. This cannot be a coincidence, Earth Queen, and we must heed the warnings. If that child is the Solvrei then he is a descendent of the Gods and has divine blood. He is the only one who can help the halfbreed destroy the world."

I stared at her incredulously. "You would have me kill a child because of a story someone told almost a thousand years ago? And besides that, is it not your legend that also says the Solvrei will save the world?"

"He *can* save the world, Maialen, but he can also condemn it, and from what I have heard of the boy I would not trust him to be on the side of reason. The Harbonah have warped his mind." The older woman frowned, her face folding into deeply etched lines of worry.

"The Harbonah? The child has also mentioned that name, what does it mean?" I asked her, wondering just how ignorant I was to what was going on.

"Zealots," she said with disgust, her dark eyes flashing. "Zealots that despise the Keepers and believe the amulets should be destroyed. Be careful of them, Maialen. They hide in the shadows where you do not look."

"Cossiana," I sighed. "All of this is...well, it is quite a lot to take in, but it is not why I am here."

"Yes, yes, you have come to seek my son." She folded her arms and squinted out to sea. "Damian is not here on Tahitia. You can look if you like, but you will find no trace of him."

I believed that she was telling the truth. There was a longing in her face that I recognized, the desperate hope that you will one day find the thing that is missing. "You do not know where he is, do you?"

She shook her head, her silvery dreadlocks sweeping across her back in slow arcs. "It has been so long since I have seen him or heard anything about him. I do not know if he even still lives."

I reached out and grasped her hand in mine, feeling the warm strength beneath the leathered skin. "If we find him we can put an end to all this, and he can come home."

"Oh, my dear," she answered, turning her dark gaze back to me. "Have you not been listening? This is only the beginning."

9

Samirra stretched below the palace like a dog infested with fleas, a drab swathe of dull brown crawling with scavengers. Astraeus frowned deeply as he looked over the walls at the city of Iriellestra, the beacon of his empire, which was now a swarm of filth and disease. He felt the impotent rage that had been eating at him for years, the unending anger towards the Water Queen whom he wholeheartedly believed had cursed his beloved kingdom. He opened the fist he had clenched tightly and looked down at the sparkling blue stone, the Air Sapphire. It was round and multifaceted so that it caught the light and glittered beautifully with every movement. If only it worked half as well as it sparkled. He closed his eyes, willing the air to move around him, to brush its cool hands over his face and ease the sweat from his brow.

Nothing happened. He closed his fist around the amulet once again and was tempted to throw it over the wall but he stopped himself. The Sapphire, though worthless, was a symbol and one that he desperately needed.

"There must be a Warding Stone in the palace. There must be. Are you sure that you were thorough in your search?" he demanded of the man beside him.

His Guardian nodded his head, not saying aloud the thoughts he could not keep himself from thinking. *If the problem were a Warding Stone it would have to be everywhere with you, not hidden in the palace.* A stone was not to blame, but that was not what Astraeus wanted to hear.

"We have searched the palace several times, there are no signs of any of the Warding Stones," Favian told him, feeling sweat dripping down his narrow face and beneath the long braid of hair that lay along his neck. Wiry and agile, he was still a formidable fighter and the only one of the Guardians left from the time of Orabelle. As he stood beside his King, he wondered again if he should not do as Damian and Gideon had done and just walk away from them all. It pained him to see Samirra this way, sick and gasping for life. The only reason he had not left was that he felt an obligation to the Kingdom, to try and protect what was left of it.

Astraeus pushed his dark sweep of hair back from his forehead and seemed to bristle at his own thoughts. "Has my father found anything useful in the library?"

Favian once again refrained from voicing the thoughts in his head. Instead of yelling at the King that they should have someone besides his addle-brained father, Astus, searching through the records, he merely said, "No, though these past few days he has not been at his best."

"I have not been given an easy lot in this life," Astraeus sighed wistfully, his fingers brushing over the gilded brocade of his jacket, though he failed to see the irony of the gesture. "And, as if I don't have enough to deal with, my wife has given the Verucans permission to march through Kymir. Favian, you know that he will not stop at freeing the north. Once the beasts are destroyed he will come here, to try and take all of Samirra from me,"

Perhaps someone should. "Perhaps now is the time for talks of peace."

Astraeus snorted derisively. "You saw what happened at the Council! None of them are concerned about peace, despite the lies Maialen constantly spins, and Blaise is a tyrant who has always wanted to rule Imbria on his own. My wife is just too stupid to see it. I suppose there is still no word from Magnus?"

Favian shook his head, feeling a stab of worry for the elder Guardian who had been like a father to him. As a young man it had been Magnus who had taught him to fight and taught him what to fight for. Magnus had trained him, doggedly, day after day. It was Magnus who had insisted he learn to read and write, that he be taught the ancient language by Astus. He was the one who had told Favian that part of being a Guardian was to know the difference between right and wrong and to make sure that your Keeper stayed on a righteous path. Magnus had taught him that the Guardian was the only one on Imbria more powerful than the Keepers, for it was the Guardians who were entrusted with their lives. They were the ones who decided who lived and died. He recalled his last conversation with the grizzled older warrior, just before Maialen went to Veruca.

"The time is not yet upon us, Favian. You must hold fast the line," Magnus had told him, gripping his shoulder in a gesture of comradery.

Favian had twisted the knife he held between his hands, feeling the warm ridges of the hilt against his calloused fingers. Guilt and shame were a heavy burden on his shoulders as he confessed, "I do not think that Samirra can last much longer if we do not intervene. The healers say the sickness is spreading and people are dying. The King heeds nothing anyone tells him and he cannot be swayed from the course he has set for himself."

"Aracellis is still too young to rule, so who would you have occupy the throne?" Magnus queried, not really expecting an answer. He folded his thick arms across his chest and waited for Favian to think it through.

"I don't know!" the younger Guardian cried in frustration. "Anyone! His cousin, Zelia? She seems to care more about the Kingdom than he does."

Magnus tilted his head from side to side, as if considering. He scratched at the grey beard that dusted his chin. "Zelia is a good choice, but I fear she does not have the strength it will take to lead us out of this darkness. The people deserve someone who will fight for them. They deserve-"

"Don't say it again," Favian interrupted him, jumping up and pacing the room. "I am no King, I am a soldier."

"So was Blaise," Magnus pointed out. "You could take the throne easily, no one would oppose you, not if you promised to pass it to Aracellis when he comes of age."

"Murder the King and take his throne and you think no one will oppose me?" Favian asked incredulously.

Magnus made a gesture for him to be quiet. "Calm down, my boy, or you will get yourself killed before we even begin. I live with the Earth Queen day in and day out. She has no love for her husband and only wants what is best for her child and for Imbria. She will see that you are what is best."

Favian shook his head. "I can't. I won't do it."

"We will talk when I get back. For now, let me go to Veruca and see what the Fire Keeper will demand for his missing grain. Hopefully you have hidden it well so that the people will not starve this winter."

"It is safe, but we cannot keep attacking and stealing from our own people, even if it is to keep them from starving. The other Keepers will figure it out eventually," Favian warned. Magnus had given him a knowing look and strode from the room. Favian could not help but feel that it was the last time he would see his friend and mentor.

"Favian! Are you even listening to me?" Astraeus's imperious demand broke through his memories and the Guardian shook himself out of his tenebrous thoughts.

"I am sorry, my King. My thoughts were of Magnus. We have received no word of him yet, other than your wife ordered him released back to Samirra. If the Verucan is planning to march on Iriellestra and take the palace as you suspect, then I fear he will not heed the Earth Queen's request and will have him killed. Magnus is a brilliant tactician and leader, the Verucan will know that he stands a better chance of taking this realm without him."

"This is Maialen's fault!" Astraeus seethed, slamming his fist down on the edge of the wall. "He was her Guardian and her responsibility! She could at least have the decency to let us know if he is alive."

Favian did not respond, for he knew that Maialen had done what was best for her, even though it had meant putting his friend's life in jeopardy. All he could hope for now was that the old man was somehow clever enough to escape death in Veruca.

Astraeus spun on his heel and turned away from the wall and the disheartening view of his withering city, stomping back into the interior of the palace and to the Great Library. Favian hurried after him, wondering what foolhearted idea had just occurred to the King to make him hasten to those rooms. Astraeus spent little time in the library, not having much use for what he called dusty old tomes of boring deeds. It was, however, the place where his father could usually be found.

As they entered the arched doorway, Favian was struck as always by the grandeur of the place. The high walls were lined with gilded shelves whose heavy, carved moldings held an impossible number of scrolls and books, and were so tall that one needed a ladder to reach the uppermost shelves. Paned glass windows let in a flood of sunlight that bounced along the marble statues and danced across the painted frescoes of the ceilings before settling on the thick, woven rugs that cushioned the polished floors. Astraeus walked directly over to one corner, where his father was bent over a table, his agitated fingers running back and forth over a line of scroll while he mumbled incoherently to himself. The former king's hair had thinned to fine whisps of white that barely covered his pale head and his jowls hung heavily from his lined cheeks. They were dark smudges around his rheumy eyes that had been there since his wife, Irielle, had died at Queen's End.

"Where is the message I received yesterday?" Astraeus compelled.

"Eh?" Astus squinted one eye up at him and looked confused.

"What message?" Favian asked from behind them.

Astraeus waved him away dismissively. "It was a hawk's message from Kymir I received yesterday."

"What did it say?" Favian asked, surprised that Astraeus had mentioned nothing of it. A message from Kymir right now could mean many things, the least of which held the fate of Samirra in the balance. The Guardian tried not to let his frustration show and took a deep breath, remaining calm as he waited for the King to answer him.

"I do not know, that is why I am looking for it," Astraeus snapped irritably. "I assumed it was Maialen, whining on about something else and trying to justify her betrayal. Now father, where is the message? I left it here, on your table."

The former Keeper grinned up at his son, singing gleefully, "I told you to read it! It was a beautiful song! A bird!"

Astraeus groaned in frustration at his father's mad rantings and pushed the old man roughly aside, rummaging rudely through the papers and scrolls that were littered across the table.

"Oh, you mean this one?" Astus asked, holding up a scrap of paper in his spotted, wrinkled hand. His son snatched it away from him and it was all Favian could do not to grab it from the King's hand.

"Well?" the Guardian prompted, hoping that it held some word of Magnus or a promise of peace. "What does the Queen say?"

Astraeus furrowed his brow as he read, then handed the note over to Favian, a smug smile spreading across his face. "It is not from my wife. It is from Logaire."

10

The return to the mainland from Tahitia had made me just as queasy as the trip there, though I tried not to show it as I endured the condescending stares of the two brothers and their ugly dog. Cossiana had not offered her usual islander hospitality, making it quite clear that we were not welcome to stay. As I departed she promised to send word if she had any news of Damian, but we had both known they were just empty words. I felt a pang of guilt for bringing Kaeleb to see her, but there was no way I could have known that her first reaction to her long-lost grandson would be to call for his death. Kaeleb now sulked below deck, refusing to speak to anyone and I thought that his sullen attitude may have been an unfulfilled longing to see more of his homeland. He had not been pleased when I had said we were leaving, and was even more distempered when I told him it was for his own safety, protesting that the Solvrei did not need the protection of the likes of me.

"It has been hard for him," Seff commented as I walked back onto the upper deck, my stomach not allowing me to stay below for very long. Vayk sat nearby, leaning against the boom of the mast and looking bored. His fingers played restlessly along the hilts of the slew of daggers he wore at his waist and I thought of Kaeleb earlier, his face stern and his eyes cold like steel as he had brandished the weapon.

"Yes, I know that," I answered with a sigh. The sun was warm on my arms and I tried to enjoy the sensation and ignore the heaving of my stomach. The sea swept out around us, beautiful and brilliant, a tumult of blues and frothy whites. I thought of my sister and her flashing eyes that changed color like the sea and I wondered what she would do next. Probably kill someone. That seemed to have been one of her favorite choices when in doubt. For a moment I wished my father was there to help guide me, but then I remembered that he was a murderous liar so I could discard his suggestions along with Orabelle's. When had we become such a violent family? Not when my mother had lived, though maybe even then and I had pretended not to notice. I remembered Chronus, our father, his face crimson with anger and his hand lifting in the air to strike Orabelle. She had stood there, waiting for the blow, her back straight and proud. Even as a child, younger than Kaeleb, she had been defiant, and when he struck her she had refused to cry, sometimes biting her lip till it bled in order to hold in her pain. I begged her to be gentler, to not anger him so much, but now I knew that his anger had never been at anything she had done, it had been her existence that enraged him. All because of my mother's mistake. It seemed it always began with the mother.

I would need to talk to Alita once we were back in Kymir. She was the closest thing Kaeleb had to a mother, though not a very good one from what I had learned. Not that I was in any position to judge her. I had not done much better with poor Aracellis, but I was trying. If Alita could help me find Damian and the Pearl, then we could stop the droughts in Samirra, remove the threat of hunger that loomed over all of Imbria. We could secure Kaeleb's place as an heir to Lehar, teach him that the amulets were not things to hate, but were great gifts, the givers of life. I could undo the damage that had been done to him, and stop the damage that would be done to my own son if I was forced into a war with his father. Alita could be the key to everything.

When we arrived in Kymir I wasted no time, sending Kaeleb to the manor with Vayk and having Seff accompany me to where Alita was being held. The dog trotted along with us, wagging its tale and looking like a terrifying demon from the underworld as Seff occasionally leaned over to scratch his ear as we walked. I was tired but my mind was spinning and too full of thoughts to rest. I needed to see Alita and at least answer some of the questions that were plaguing me since I had spoken to Cossiana.

"Where are the guards?" I wondered aloud as we neared the cluster of stone buildings that served as cells for Kymir.

Seff held out a hand, motioning for me to stop and the dog began to growl, his mangled snout bent low to the ground and the hairs rising along the crest of his back. I felt my eyes widen and I reached for the Emerald, taking a deep breath to remain calm. Seff crept forward, a knife in each hand, moving silently and fading into the shadows as he approached the abandoned structure. The door was unbarred, but shut firmly and he leaned against it, listening. His eyes moved to me and I nodded, clutching the Emerald tighter in my fist. He pushed on the door and it swung open, the dog leaping forward with a horrific snarl and barreling through the opening. Seff swung around after him and then they both backed out, Seff shaking his head.

"What is it?" I hissed, trying to remain quiet despite the panic that gripped my chest.

"She is dead."

I stared at him dumbly, not comprehending.

"Alita. She is dead," he repeated. He slid the knives back into his belt. "She has been dead a while from the look of her."

"Dead? How...what did...I don't understand," I stammered, trying to get my mind to accept what he was saying.

"Her throat has been slit. She bled out," Seff informed me, as if that explained everything.

"It cannot be!" I exclaimed, hurrying forward and pushing past him. He caught my wrist and jerked me abruptly back from the open doorway, but not before I caught a glimpse of the crumpled figure laying on the floor, her slender limbs splayed out like a rag doll drowning in a puddle of blood. I tried again to shove past him and he blocked the doorway with his body, forcing me back and closing the door, sliding the bar into place.

"You cannot help her. She is cold."

I backed up and stared at him, feeling my lips tremble and hating it. The last thing I wanted at that moment was to appear weak. "Who did this? We must find out who did this! Damek! Where is Damek? He will know something; he always knows something. And Kaeleb, what will I tell Kaeleb?"

My eyes were wide and round as Seff led me away from the awful sight, back towards the comfort of the Royal City. I kept gripping the Emerald desperately, willing myself to be calm, letting the gentle hum of the earth beneath me soothe my mind. I somehow made my way through the city without screaming hysterically and when we reached the manor Seff pushed me into a chair and hurried over to speak to the steward who ran the household, telling him to get Damek and to send men to the cells and make sure that no one went in.

I waited in the chair where he left me, seeing the sickening tableau over and over in my mind. There had been so much blood. It had been the same color as her hair.

"Maialen, what has happened?" Damek demanded in a swirl of black robes and seeming very perturbed. "That peasant you sent to fetch me was quite cryptic with his answers."

"She is dead."

"Who? Logaire? I just saw her-"

"No! Alita!" I practically shouted. He seemed genuinely surprised and his eyebrows shot up while the lines of his face folded into a deep frown. I had felt a moment of comfort at the sight of him, but it was quickly overshadowed by the repeating memory of the woman's body.

"Tell me what happened," he said, dragging a chair closer so that he could sit beside me. It was heavy for him, his arms were thin and pale like the branches of a winter aspen, and I wanted to help him but I could not make myself move. I told him about returning and seeking out Alita, only to find her murdered in her cell, her throat cut open in a jagged tear, the guards that should have been posted nowhere to be seen. Damek stroked his chin with his spidery fingers, his frown deepening.

"We must not allow this to go unpunished and we must discover who was behind this. Your father would never have allowed something like this to happen," he chastised. "You refuse to listen to me, Maialen, but I have told you time and again that you must use fear to keep order! You do not have to be a tyrant like Blaise, but you must remind people that you are the one with the power!"

"This is my fault?" I asked in a croaking voice, no longer able to hold back the tears that streamed down my face.

"No, no, child, of course not. It is the fault of whoever killed her," Damek insisted, patting my hand with his papery fingers and trying to be consoling though he was clearly uncomfortable with my display of emotion.

"Damek, do you know what the Harbonah is?" I asked, trying to wipe the tears away and keep my voice from breaking.

"The Harbonah?" he repeated, too sharply. "What has this got to do with them?"

"I was going there to ask Alita about them. Kaeleb mentioned the name before and today Cossiana also spoke of them in passing, though she would not tell me more."

He steepled his fingers and sat back in his chair, glowering. "The Harbonah are idiots. Fanatics that believe the Keepers are an abomination and a scourge on the world. They are a powerless group of fools who run around convincing other simple-minded imbeciles to join them, engaging in pathetic plots and conspiracies that you need not bother yourself with."

"Do you think Alita was one of them? Blaise said something to me about not knowing who she really was."

"I do not know, but I suppose you should ask the Fire Keeper. I can send a hawk with a message, telling him what has happened, though if I had to hazard a guess, I would say he already knows. It would not surprise me if his Guardian, that horrid little runt, Akrin, was the one behind this." Damek practically spat out the name distastefully. "He hates his sister and makes no attempt to hide it. He offered more than once to execute her for us if we so wished it."

"N-no," I stammered stubbornly with a shake of my head. "It was not Blaise, he would not do that to me, not in Kymir."

Damek's eyebrows shot up yet again and he watched me shrewdly. "And why not? Sweet child, do not be so foolish as to forget who that man is. Believe me, he would have no qualms about slitting the throat of a traitor, and that is how they saw her."

I refused to believe it was Blaise but agreed that Damek should send word of what had happened immediately. I knew that it would not help, that Blaise would not come. After all, he was preparing to march to Samirra, an endeavor that would take quite a bit of planning and logistics. He could not come running to me in Kymir just because I was upset, though I found myself wishing that he would.

Seff returned then, informing us that Vayk had gone with the other guards to collect the body. I realized that I had no idea what to do with the poor woman. I did not know if I should bury her, as we did in Kymir, or throw her into the sea as the

Leharans did, or burn her as was the Verucan custom. I could not ask Kaeleb for he was just a boy, and I had no idea how to even begin to tell him what had happened, let alone ask him about burial preferences.

"Kaden!" I exclaimed out loud, startling Damek and eliciting an inquisitive look from Seff. "Kaden will come when he hears of this, especially if we have her body."

"You wish to use the dead woman as bait?" Seff asked, his tone tinged with disgust.

"No, no," I protested. "But she is already gone and when he hears of this it is likely that he will want answers, or that he will come for the child, and we need him. He is the only clue we have to finding Damian and the Pearl. Kaden must know something. He might even be with Damian. Perhaps they have been hiding together this whole time! The Leharans are fiercely loyal to each other, and the Guard was like a brotherhood."

"Splendid," Damek muttered. "That is just what we need, a violent Leharan rushing into Kymir bent on vengeance. I suggest that we do everything in our power to find out who killed that wretched woman before he arrives so that we can have somewhere to direct his hostilities, and I would start with that usurper that you just put on the throne!"

"Maialen!" Logaire burst into the room, interrupting Damek and rushing past him, a startling cascade of sympathy and golden cloth. "I just heard! Darling, are you alright? This is terrible!"

She ran to me and pulled me up, throwing her arms around me and wrapping me in her sisterly embrace. I hesitated for a moment then my doubts of her washed away and I hugged her back, grateful that she was there. For all that I had mistrusted her, Logaire had always been there for me, just as she was here now, and I realized in that moment how incredibly alone I felt.

"You think it was Thyrr?" Logaire asked Damek, letting me go so I could sink back into the chair. I felt fatigue wash over me and suddenly all I wanted to do was sleep and forget the events of the past days for a few brief moments.

"It makes sense," Damek was saying, adjusting the long black robes so that they shivered around his skeletal frame. "She had challenged his claim to the throne, she was a threat to him."

"If she... why would he... how could..." my voice faded to nothing and I could not seem to form a coherent thought.

"Oh, darling. This is too much and you need your rest. I will go to Lehar and see what I can find out about this and if the Usurper, as we are now calling him, had anything to do with it. Damek, you must find the guards who had been posted, we need to know why they were not there."

"I know how to run Kymir, Logaire, I do not need help from you!" Damek snapped at her irritably.

"Please!" I interrupted them. "Do not fight amongst yourselves!"

"Of course, darling. Come with me, let us get you to bed," Logaire soothed. "We will take care of everything."

I allowed her to lead me up to my rooms, grateful for the calming serenity of my own chambers and to have a moment of quiet. I clutched the Emerald tightly in my hand and used the grounding energy of my Element to calm my spinning mind. I could not help but hear Cossiana's words echoing in my head. *This is only the beginning.*

11

The black towers of the Verucan castle pierced the low clouds that hung over the mountains. Men gathered beneath the shadow of the fortress, preparing to march to the North, adorned in obsidian armor that shone even in the dull light from the obscured sun. High above the soldiers as they prepared for war, Blaise was making his way up one of the towers, Akrin following close behind and not bothering to try and hide the scowl from his face.

"I can feel your displeasure without even looking at you," Blaise remarked to his Guardian as they wound their way up the stone flights of steps.

Akrin's lip curled in disgust as he replied, "You keep running to do the Earth Queen's bidding. We are going to war with Samirra at her request, and you would release one of their greatest warriors back to them just because she ordered it done. We should be executing him. Since when is Veruca at the mercy of Kymir?"

Blaise stopped and turned to look down at the younger man, the torch he carried throwing molten gashes of light across his face and his voice held a warning. "You forget who is King here, my boy."

"I do not want to see you made a fool of!" Akrin countered. "The Kymirran woman cannot be trusted, look what she does to her own husband."

Blaise chuckled and started back up the steps. He pictured Maialen, innocent and doll-like, her big green eyes that were too trusting. She was anything but devious. "You misunderstand the situation, Akrin, but that is because you are still young. Maialen is doing what she has been forced to do by circumstance, and she is right to do it. Would you have our people go hungry just because of your pride? Would you waste the opportunity to invade our enemy's land just because the Earth Queen is in support of it? She has given us a gift, do not throw it aside without assessing its value. As for Magnus, he is a valuable source of knowledge on the kingdom we are about to invade. It would be foolish to kill him."

Akrin stayed sullenly silent and Blaise wondered if his young Guardian would ever have the cleverness that it took to rule. The boy was a valuable instrument, and cared about nothing more than pleasing the King, but Blaise was beginning to worry that his lack of insight was not merely due to a lack of experience. If Akrin did not have the cunning that it took to hold one of the most powerful seats in Imbria, then he could never be named as the heir. Which left Logaire, a choice that Blaise did not particularly relish as his cousin was quite the opposite from his adopted son. She was too clever. The second she knew her place in line was secured she would have him killed, and with all her plotting and scheming it would be difficult to know where the blow would come from. Perhaps a drop of poison in his drink, or the blade of an assassin while walking down the hallway. No, Logaire could never have a direct line of succession to the Verucan throne. It would be the end of the rest of them. For a moment he felt the brief sting of nostalgia and wished that things between them were different. She could have been his greatest ally, the one who stood beside him and would carry on the throne after him, but instead she had grown bitter and resentful of his power. She felt that he owed everything to her and in a way she was right. It was Logaire who had helped him that terrible night, when they had dragged his mother's lifeless body to the entrance of the tunnel. It was Logaire who had stood watch while he had picked the lock and who had helped him shove the body through the opening to be food for the blooddrinkers, and it was Logaire who had taken a bucket and rags and mopped the trail of blood away so that no one would know. He remembered sitting beside her in their empty home when it was done, resting his head on her bony shoulder and feeling her coppery curls tickling his cheek. She had been a skinny, awkward girl then, all knobby arms and legs, with no indication of the voluptuous woman she would become.

"I did not mean to," he had whispered to her.

"This way is better, now you will not have to speak of it. We can say that they ran away, that she took Bastion with her and left," Logaire suggested gently.

Blaise had felt his heart twist at the mention of Bastion. His beloved little brother, the one who practically worshipped him. Bastion had been born different, his legs twisting inward so that his life had always been slow and painful, and his mind never quite catching up to his age. Despite this, he had been the most joyous person Blaise had ever met and the two brothers had been inseparable. Their mother, however, saw Bastion as a burden, a curse that had been heaped upon her by their father and his shortcomings. And so, one day Blaise had come home and his brother had been gone, Maritka merely saying that Bastion would not be back. Blaise had seen her hands tremble briefly as she said the words and he knew she had done something terrible. He felt his throat tighten and an ache formed in his chest that he thought would suffocate him, and he had demanded to know where his brother was.

They argued, his mother shouting at him that he was just as worthless as his brother and father and that he deserved to die with them, and then she had struck him. He had stumbled backward, hitting the table and upending it and she laughed. He stood and shook himself off then shoved past her, trying to leave. He pushed too hard and she had fallen, her chest hitting the upturned table leg with a sickening crack and then landing on her face, blood pooling out from her nose. He had only wanted to get away from her, to run from the overwhelming pain of his brother's loss. He tried to shake her, to wake her up, but she had not moved. It was then that Logaire had walked in and found him.

Since that night she had always felt that he owed her something and over the years she changed from the skinny girl he used to play silly games with into the conniving manipulator that she now was. He wondered how Maialen did not see it, though the poor Earth Queen was so traumatized by her life that she was desperate for anyone to show her affection. A brief smile touched his lips as he thought of her. There was something calming in her presence and in the way she affected her Element that he found soothing, a tiny fragment of peace and a feeling that he had begun to crave.

He stepped to the side as they reached the top landing of the tower and Akrin pounded on the door to announce their arrival, then slipped the key into the lock and pushed it open. Inside the sparse room the Samirran warrior sat casually on the edge of the bed, his legs crossed and his head tilted to the side. His grey beard had thickened and Blaise could barely see the smile beneath it.

"So, is this to be the day that I die?" he asked jovially, but the Fire King saw the hard glint in his eyes. He would never go without a fight.

Blaise grinned at him. "Everyone keeps talking about your death, Magnus. It seems that I am the only one who believes you have some worth to me while you are still alive."

"Does my Queen know that you are holding her Guardian captive?" Magnus asked, "I cannot imagine that she would be pleased to hear of it."

Akrin snorted derisively. "And what could the Earth Queen possibly do about it if she did know, old man?"

"She is more powerful than you think, boy. I would caution you not to underestimate her," Magnus warned him.

Blaise moved to stand between them, bringing the older man's attention back to him. "I am afraid that the Earth Queen has decided she is no longer in need of your services, Samirran."

Magnus raised his eyebrows and scratched his grey beard. "So, she has finally had enough of her husband? It is about time."

Blaise noticed that Akrin looked startled by the reply but the Fire Keeper had been expecting it. "She has asked me to go to Samirra and deal with your little blooddrinker problem in the northern territories. We will be marching to your kingdom within the week and she has agreed to forfeit all the northern territories to me once they are freed."

"And you want me to help you?" Magnus guessed correctly. He folded his arms and lounged back against the rail at the foot of the bed. "Now, why would I do that?"

"You are no fool, Guardian. You served Astus when he was the King and everyone knows that it was you who helped his wife rule when he was too mad to tell the difference between a sword and an apple. You know that Astraeus is destroying Samirra, just as you knew his father would before him. You may not want to see Samirra in my hands, but we both know that something must be done."

Magnus seemed to mull over what he was saying. "It is true that I have no love for the current King, but Samirra must be ruled by a Samirran. If there were someone who could take over, someone better, would you be willing to let them keep the kingdom as your ally?"

Blaise chuckled. It was obvious to him that Magnus had already thought this through. It would not surprise him if the wiry old Guardian had already orchestrated a plot against the current Samirran ruler. "I will keep my claim in the northern territories, but the rest of Samirra I care nothing about, other than that whoever rules is it not completely incompetent."

"Let me out of here and I will help you. I will go to Samirra and make sure Astraeus will concede. I know his death is what you really want. It is what you have dreamt of for years since he killed your beloved Water Queen. Let the others in the palace be spared, and I will help grant you your vengeance."

Blaise's amber eyes were bright with emotion. Magnus was no fool, he knew that bringing up Orabelle's death was the easiest way to provoke the Verucan King. Blaise took a breath, dampened his emotions and carefully considered what he said next. "I need to know what power Astraeus still holds, and what is the status of his army."

It was Magnus's turn to laugh. "There is no food to feed an army. If Astraeus can muster a handful of men to defend him then it would be a miracle. As for his power, he has none. His Element is useless to him, though he would never admit it. He is weak and he has made Samirra weak. No one there will rally to his defense, I can promise you that. If you show mercy to the people, they would probably hold your hand and guide you right up the palace steps."

12

Logaire walked around the room, picking up objects and putting them back down again. It was strange the things the islanders collected and displayed. The petrified bones of a fish, broken shells, twisted pieces of driftwood. All gathered and lovingly arranged like beautiful pieces of art, though they were merely just refuse from an uncaring sea. She had arrived on Lehar that afternoon and had been escorted by Bacatha to the lower chamber of the great Citadel, the imposing cerulean fortress that dominated the Leharan landscape. Bacatha had seemed less than pleased with her arrival and the tall Leharan eyed her suspiciously as they walked. Logaire had noticed that the woman was wearing the silver-threaded blue uniform of the Leharan Guard. Thyrr must have reinstated them, and she allowed a small smile of appreciation. She would have done the same. The Leharans were proud people and serving in the Leharan Guard was an honor of unparalleled prestige. It was one of the reasons she had convinced Maialen to disband it in the first place. Bacatha had held the door open for her and then with a last, withering look, she shut it firmly behind her, leaving Logaire alone with the enigmatic new ruler of the island nation. He was watching her as she moved around the room, and as she tilted her head to inspect one particularly shabby looking conch, she let her hair fall alluringly over her bare shoulder, glancing up at Thyrr from under her fringe of gilded lashes.

"Did you come here to look at shells?" he asked bluntly.

She ignored the remark, studying him. He was young and quite attractive, in a strange and compelling way. His wild golden hair had lightened in the sun, making him look more Leharan than before, though it was still obvious that he was not one of them, not completely. He was fit and healthy, with the callused hands of someone who knows how to wield a sword. She had seen the way his eyes passed over her as she walked into the room, the way that even now he could not help glancing at her curving figure. She had noticed it before too, the way he looked at her, in the particular way that men do. It would not be a difficult task to seduce him.

"Alita was killed. Someone slit the poor girl's throat," she said with a slight frown of her full lips.

He started to stand, his eyes widening in surprise. "And my nephew?"

"There, there, darling, no need to be upset. The boy is fine. I am here because the Kymirrans are concerned that you were one of the people who might have wanted her dead."

"Me? Why would I want her dead?" Thyrr questioned, seeming genuinely confused. Logaire wondered if he was telling the truth or just a very good liar. It would be much easier for her if he were just telling the truth.

"She challenged your claim to the throne," Logaire pointed out.

Thyrr scoffed. "That meant nothing, and I have named Kaeleb as my heir. There is no reason I should want her dead. The Sirens are a bigger threat to me than she was."

Logaire's interest peaked. This was something she had not heard about. "The Sirens?"

Thyrr sighed, running a hand through his messy hair then standing to pace the coralstone floor restlessly. "Colwyn claims there have been sightings of them. Some think it could mean that Orabelle still lives."

Now, this was quite interesting. She watched his pacing, like an animal prowling back and forth, and was suddenly quite glad that she had come to Lehar. "And what do you think it means?"

"I do not even know if the claims are true! From what I know of my sister, I believe that she is truly dead. I do not think she could have stayed away from her home for so long."

Logaire pondered the thought silently. She also had no doubt that the Water Queen was dead. Orabelle had been a lot of things, but a coward was not one of them. She would not have stayed hidden in the shadows, especially not when her child was being raised by someone else. If she were alive, she would have been with the boy. But that did not mean the Sirens had died with her. Logaire felt a shiver run down her back as she remembered the first time she had seen the fearsome creatures. It had been in Kymir, the night that Tal had been killed and Orabelle had retaliated for her lover's death by having the Siren's rip apart his murderer in front of everyone. They were amorphous creatures, neither woman nor water, but something in between that ebbed and flowed with liquid grace that was both beautiful and horrifying.

"Even if she is dead, the rumors that she may live are enough to cause a rift among the people, and I need them united," Thyrr went on.

"Then show your support in searching for the creatures and for Orabelle," Logaire suggested, taking his arm and turning him to face her. He was standing close, mere inches away, and she saw the way his eyes flashed and his breath came a little faster. She touched her tongue to her lips and let go of his arm, letting her fingers slide down off his bare skin. "No one can claim that you are trying to steal a throne from her if you are the one seeking her out. Orabelle was quite loved by the Leharans, and they will love you for caring about her."

He narrowed his eyes, taking a step back as if to clear his head. "Why are you helping me?"

"You seem like someone I should help."

He gave a short bark of laughter. "You did everything you could to keep me away from the throne, you did not think to offer me your assistance then. A bastard, unfit to rule, I believe is what you called me."

She shrugged her shoulders prettily. "That was before and this is now."

"You want something from me. You are not here about Alita, you know I had nothing to do with that," he surmised correctly. At least he was no fool.

"Perhaps we can find a way to be mutually beneficial to each other," she offered suggestively.

He stared at her, his strange blue-gold eyes weighing the verity of her offer. "Tell me what you want, Logaire."

"You are new to all this," she began, "but I am not. I know the Keepers and I know how they think and I know what they will do. I also know that someone who shows up with a stone that saps their power from them will not be left alive for long. My cousin will come for you, and Maialen will let him because it keeps her delicate little hands free of blood. You think she is your ally but she cares nothing for you and nothing for Lehar. They are only using you to substantiate their little war in Samirra and when that is done, they will turn on you. Blaise has never been content to just rule Veruca, he seeks to hold all of Imbria under his thumb and you and your Warding Stone pose an imminent threat to his quest for power. The only reason he has not killed you yet is that his thirst for vengeance has waited ten long years and he is blinded by it, but that will only last until the Samirran King is dead."

Thyrr rested one leg on the edge of the table and folded his arms over his chest. She was right, of course, and he had already had to fight off one assassination attempt. The man had come in the night, before Thyrr had moved his living quarters to the Citadel. He had been on the ship that his sister had once called home. The beached vessel had been painstakingly preserved, a task that Colwyn claimed responsibility for and took great pride in. It was eerie to Thyrr, like walking into a mausoleum, a hollow crypt filled with shadows of the past. He had thought that by establishing himself there he would enhance his legitimacy in the eyes of the islanders, but he could not stand being there. At night he would lay awake, hearing the past whisper to him like an angry ghost. He was awake the night the man came, listening to the rhythmic beating of the waves against the shore and wishing for sleep when he heard the sound. He had sat up in the bed, his senses alert. At first he thought it could have been Bacatha, for she was in the captain's quarters on the foredeck, but the sound had come from the other end of the ship. He listened and there it was again, a soft footfall, barely discernible over the sounds of the ocean breeze rustling through the palms. Thyrr slid out of the bed, reaching for the closest weapon, the curved sword that hung from a hook on the wall, a deadly and beautiful decoration of Leharan silver. His sister's weapon. He had gripped the hilt, feeling a strange connection to her. This was the sword she must have been holding when she died, the weapon she had fought with in that final battle that took her life.

The curtain that hung over the doorway shivered with movement and Thyrr swung the weapon, tearing the gossamer fabric in ragged shards and slicing deep into the arm of the man who had been reaching to push it aside. The man cried out in pain and stabbed at Thyrr with a wicked dagger, almost gutting him had he not spun out of the way quickly. Thyrr grabbed the edge of the dangling fabric and looped it around the man's wrist, jerking it against the doorframe and causing the knife to fall clattering to the floor. The man reached behind him for another weapon, an axe that he had strapped across his back, and Bacatha appeared then, her sword biting deep into the man's neck with a spray of blood that washed over Thyrr in a crimson cascade. The dead man toppled to the floor in a heap.

"Sorry," she said with a grimace, gesturing at the wash of blood that coated his face.

"I was trying to keep him alive!" He wiped ineffectually at the blood with the sleeve of his tunic.

"I was trying to keep you alive," Bacatha countered. She kicked at the body with her boot, rolling it over so they could see his face. "Do you know him?"

Thyrr glanced around at the ruined quarters. Colwyn would not be happy. "No, but I am sure that he will not be the only one. Perhaps it is best if we moved to the Citadel, we will be safer there."

He had been right, and the Citadel had been safer, the newly reinstated Leharan Guard taking great pride in keeping the fortress secure. But it only took one moment, one mistake, and then he would be dead. Logaire was someone that he would much rather have with him than against him, at least it would be one less assassin's blade he would have to worry about for the time being. He also wouldn't mind having her in his bed and if her sultry looks towards him were any indication then she would not be averse to that idea either.

"What would you have me do, if I were to take you up on your offer of wise council?" Thyrr asked her with a raised eyebrow and one of his crooked smiles.

"First of all, darling, I would suggest that you keep me close," she purred, reaching out to let her long nails trace the muscle of his thigh. "Secondly, I would stay out of the war in Samirra.

They may want your help, and you would be wise to agree to give it, but stay away from the north. Find excuses not to come. Lost supplies, a problem with the ships, whatever reason is needed to postpone sending them aid. Let their battle play out as it will."

"You think they will lose," he surmised.

"It is a possibility," she countered. "And one that can be made more likely with your help."

"I have no plans on joining them in Samirra," Thyrr confessed, "but I am not enthusiastic about betraying the King of Veruca and incurring his legendary wrath."

Logaire frowned, her lips folding into a soft pout. "You do not strike me as a coward. Besides, you would not need to do anything and whatever the outcome, they will never even know that we spoke of it. It will be our little secret, darling. Telling them would be signing my own death warrant along with yours and I should like to keep my head where it is. All I need from you is to know how to find the Fomori."

"Why would you want to know..." Thyrr paused, his brow furrowed. "Oh, I see. You would warn the Fomori that they are coming."

Logaire's golden eyes glittered with anticipation. "Yes, and any other knowledge my spies can gather about the forthcoming attack. The Fomori will not be so easy to dispatch as my cousin believes. You are one of them, surely you do not wish your people to be slaughtered."

Thyrr let out another laugh. "That manipulation will not work on me, Logaire. I have no feelings of familial warmth for those beasts. One of them raped my grandmother, that is how my father came to be born. It was not a tale of star-crossed lovers. That they let me live in the north was mostly due to my ability to talk my way out of it, less to their mercifulness."

"Fine then, use the opportunity to destroy your enemies, be rid of the ones that discount us at every turn, and together you and I can lead Imbria." She molded her curves against him, wrapping her hands around his neck and bringing him close. "We will start a new legacy."

13

In the days that followed the murder of Alita I walked around in a haze. I could not seem to shake the image of her lifeless body from my mind. Damek had interrogated the guards, learning that there was one named Yosef who had come by, telling the others they were needed elsewhere and that he was to take over their post. Since then, Yosef had disappeared, probably to somewhere far away and with a pocket full of silver for his betrayal. I had ordered Damek to put a price on his head, and all I could hope for was that someone would recognize him and lead us to where he was. Aside from that we knew nothing and were no closer to finding out why someone had cut her throat so brutally. Damek continued to insinuate that the Usurper was to blame, and I had dispatched Logaire to Lehar to learn what she could, but I doubted strongly that Thyrr had anything to do with the murder. The brothers had been with me on Tahitia and his other companion, Bacatha, did not seem the type to murder a bound and helpless woman, nor did she seem the type to follow a man who would sanction the murder of a defenseless woman.

The two brothers had been quiet about the incident, but then again, they were quiet about everything. I wondered sometimes if their aversion to conversation extended to everyone or if it was just me that they did not care to speak to. It was very likely that it was just me.

I sighed thinking about it, setting down the parchment I held in my hands. It was a tally of Blaise's forces and a list of supplies that he expected to collect while passing through Kymir. Damek had practically purpled with rage when I had shown him, spittle foaming on the corners of his thin lips as he raved about the worthless Verucans. In the end I had used my amulet to soothe him, saying that we would do everything we could do to help the Verucans in their endeavor. He had stalked away, muttering under his breath about what my father would have done.

I caught a flash of something pale from the corner of my eye and I jerked in startled response to seeing Kaeleb sitting across from me, swinging his legs under the chair and watching me intently.

"When did you get here?" I asked, looking around in bewilderment. We were in my chambers, sitting in the plush chairs that faced out over the open terrace. I had not heard nor seen him come in, he had just appeared across from me like an apparition.

He smiled happily, pleased with himself, the intensity melting away. "I was taught to hunt quietly."

"I am not prey, Kaeleb, do not sneak up on me!" I admonished him.

"It is not my fault you are a Kymirran and therefore unobservant. You should be more aware of your surroundings, aunt. I would not want you to be murdered as well." His tone was chastising, as if I were the child and he were correcting me.

"Kaeleb! Do not speak of murder or killing!" I pressed my fingertips to my temples, once again flooded with the memory of Alita.

Kaeleb looked mildly chagrined and bit his lip, lowering his chin so that his shock of white hair fell over his eyes. "I did not mean to upset you. Has Brother Kaden come yet?"

"No," I said gently, wondering if the boy felt any sense of loss for the woman that had raised him. When I had informed him of her death he merely stared at me, waiting for me to say more. I had been confused, not sure what he wanted or what else to say, and so I had tried to embrace him in a comforting hug, which I quickly learned was not the sort of thing he had grown up accustomed to. He leapt away from me, demanding to know what on Imbria I was doing.

"I am trying to comfort you," I had told him.

He had looked at me as if I were mad and shaken his head. "Death is not the end. I am not sad for her. She is with the gods now, for she has served them well."

"Did she serve them as a Harbonah?" I asked carefully. I felt a pang of guilt for using her death to manipulate him but I shoved it down, telling myself that it was more important that I get answers about what was happening.

He squinted his grey eyes in a suspicious manner and nodded his head, wondering whether I would press him for more information. I had merely nodded, not wanting to push him further into retreating from me, and offered him a pastry. He had taken it and gleefully stuffed it into his mouth, forgetting all his troubles in a moment of childish delight that I quite envied.

Now he sat across from me again and I could not help but wonder what he knew. It should not be so difficult to talk to a child. Perhaps I could have practiced more with my own son, instead of complacently handing him over to his father.

"He will not come," Kaeleb said finally, as if he had made the final decision on the matter.

"Kaden? Why do you say that?"

"He would have been here by now if he were coming. When we left he told us that he was leaving for good, and that he had done his duty to my mother and to me and he wanted no more to do with what was happening."

I was once again startled by him, this time by the unexpected rush of words. I tried to think what to say next to keep him talking. I wished Logaire was there with me, she had always been better at coaxing secrets out of people than I was.

"Was Kaden not married to Alita?" I queried. "I should think husband and wife would want to stay together."

"You do not stay with your husband," he pointed out with his childlike practicality, making my cheeks flush red. "No, they were not married. They hated each other."

"Really?" I felt my eyebrows raise up. "Did they fight often?" He nodded enthusiastically.

"That must have been difficult for you," I sympathized.

"Not always. Brother Kaden and I went on many adventures together, so that he could get away from Sister Alita. He said he had sworn an oath to protect me and would not break it, no matter what she did. He was nicer to me than she was. He told me stories of my mother and father and of you. He said you always tried to be a good Queen."

I smiled even though tears pricked at my eyes and guilt welled up within me. I had put a bounty on Kaden, forced him to hide in the shadows, and all the while he had defended me to my nephew. If I did ever see him again, I would do whatever I could to make amends for what my family and I had put him through, though I was not sure how to begin to make amends for ruining someone's life.

"What else did Kaden say? He sounds like a very wise man."

Kaeleb shrugged, still swinging his legs back and forth over the edge of the chair. "He said that my duty was to all the people of Imbria, to help protect them and keep them safe."

"From the Keepers?" I prompted when he fell into silence. He seemed to think deeply about the question and finally shook his head.

"No, that was the Harbonah. Brother Kaden said he would only teach me to survive what was coming."

There was that name again. The Harbonah. Whoever they were, they had something to do with everything that was happening. I felt a little flutter in my stomach and wondered if I would finally have some answers. "The Harbonah taught you that the Keepers were your enemies?"

"Yes, he said because you have abused your power and angered the Gods. The Solvrei is sent to destroy the corruption," Kaeleb began then abruptly changed the subject, asking me if I had any of his favorite fruit fritters. I told him I would have some sent up and tried to steer him back to the topic of the mysterious zealots, but he would not speak more of it, stubbornly crossing his arms over his chest and glaring at me.

I had gotten no more out of him that day and he had been in a foul mood ever since, as if he were angry with me for coaxing even those meager facts from him. I could not claim to be in a better state of mind myself. I had sent the wagons laden with supplies to Blaise as his soldiers marched through the northern border of Kymir and received a curt note of thanks in response. I tried not to be stung by his bluntness, knowing that he was marching to a war and that was a far more pressing matter to occupy his thoughts than worry over my feelings. Logaire had sent word that she needed more time in Lehar and though I was surprised, I had decided to trust her and so I did not question the decision. If she thought it best to remain there, she would have a good reason. I, however, was once again left alone in my lofty manor in the trees, while our fates were decided elsewhere on Imbria. I remembered another time I had been left behind, at the battle of Queen's End, and in the aftermath I had wished more than anything that I had been there. Maybe I could have changed what had happened, but instead I was always watching from a safe distance, never close enough to affect the outcome. There was nothing I could do now but wait and pray that Blaise would defeat the Fomori quickly. Then...

I let the thought trail off. In my heart I knew what would happen next, but it was not what I wished for. What I wished for, though I hated to admit it even to myself, was that he would defeat the Fomori and then come back to me. I wanted nothing in those days so much as to see his ruddy face again, the careless grin and flashing amber eyes. What would actually happen was that he would defeat the Fomori and then he would march on Samirra, to kill my husband. At least I had secured his promise to spare Aracellis. Astraeus had been doomed a long time ago, but my son would not have to suffer for what his father had done.

Days dragged on as I waited. I constantly pestered Damek to see if he had any word as to what was happening. Had they reached the north? Had there been any battles? Were they winning or losing? But there was nothing and no news. Neither had there been any word from Samirra. I knew that Damek had spies everywhere, but he claimed that they had been silent, and that he too had received no word. I started to lie awake at night, thinking of all the horrible things that could be happening, seeing the hideous Fomori beasts with their snapping jaws and poisonous fangs, sinking their teeth into Blaise's neck, tearing him limb from limb. The only time I found comfort in the waiting was when I went to practice with my bow. It had been years since I had picked one up, and Seff had graciously watched over me as I found a quiet place in the sprawling gardens around the manor to set up my little pieces of fruit that would serve as my targets. He would stand by, looking bored and unassuming, while I notched the arrow and drew back the taut string, trying to focus my mind, feeling the rest of the world fall away. At first my aim was unimpressive, but then it came back to me, like an old friend who had never left. I remembered Gideon's words as he had first taught me.

"To be a truly exceptional archer you must have the perfect grip," he had said, his gentle baritone voice rumbling in his chest. He was dressed in the leather armor of the Kymirran archers, his beard thick below his soft eyes. He had been a massive, brawny man and a brave fighter, my Guardian, but he had a sweet soul and was always patient and kind to me.

He had lined up my hand, shown me where to put pressure on the line that ran from the center of my palm to my thumb. He made me practice gripping the bow over and over before he ever allowed me to try to notch an arrow. Once I had perfected my grip to his satisfaction it was time to anchor. The tip of the nose resting near the string, the release hand resting along the bottom jawline.

"Now draw and hold," Gideon said, watching me carefully to make sure that my form was perfect. "Keep holding!"

"Should I release it?" I wanted to know, worried that I had done something improperly.

"No, keep holding," he ordered.

I had done as he commanded, fighting to keep the arrow on center, my muscles in my arms beginning to scream. *Keep holding.* He had repeated it over and over until my arms were shaking with the effort and I could not hold any longer, releasing the arrow wildly into the trees.

"Well done, Princess," he had smiled at me. "You must learn control, and to hold the bow. Your enemy will not always be standing in an open field waiting to be killed. You must be strong enough to remain ready. Keep practicing."

I smiled at the memory and glanced at Seff before recentering my focus and letting the arrow fly. It sliced into the glossy red apple, nearly splitting the fruit in two. I let out a cry of triumph and Seff nodded his head, a largess show of appreciation on his part. He seemed about to say something, then changed his mind and took out one of his knives, flinging it with a flick of the wrist at the apple so that the two pieces of the fruit fell apart, sliced cleanly in half.

I grinned at him, and it was my turn to nod in appreciation. I would not have thought that I would be bonding with one of the brooding brothers over an array of tortured fruit, but here we were and it was the first time in a long time that I felt I could actually do something and do it well.

We were weaving our way back from the gardens to the manor, silent and content with our feats of skill, when I heard my name being yelled out. I was startled and about to run towards the sound when Seff caught my arm in a vise-like grip, giving me a quick shake of his head. He motioned for me to lift the bow and be ready, then he waited, listening. A man yelled my name again and Seff leapt towards the sound, hurtling out of the dense foliage and barreling into a very sturdy and very surprised Kymirran woman.

She cursed him heartily, shoving him off her and heaving herself up from the ground. Nearby a man was staring at us with wide eyes, his face and clothing coated with dust and grime.

"Queen Maialen!" the man exclaimed in relief upon seeing me. "I have a message for you. From the north."

I ran forward while Seff tried vainly to apologize to the poor woman he had mistaken as a threat. I snatched the tiny parchment case the man had pulled from beneath his tunic. My fingers shook and I could not get it open while still holding the bow, so I shoved the weapon into the man's hands, tearing open the case and unrolling the slip of parchment. Blaise's scrawling hand was instantly recognizable and my first thought was a sharp stab of relief that he was still alive. Or at least he had been when he had sent the message. The edges of the parchment were smudged with bloody fingerprints and I tried to calm the quaking fear that rose in me as I read.

Samirra has betrayed us. We cannot last without reinforcements. I need you.

"What has happened?" I demanded in a shrill cry. The dust covered man shook his head and lifted his hands as if to show me that he had no part in whatever had occurred.

"I do not know, my Queen. I was merely passed the message along the road and told to bring it to you as quickly as I could," he explained. "The man who gave it to me said it was from a Verucan soldier and that it had to get to the Queen as soon as possible. I rode as fast as I could."

I took a breath, shoving the paper into the pocket of my gown and taking the bow back from him with trembling hands. "Thank you, your bravery will be rewarded. Please, go into the manor and tell them I sent you for a bath and food."

Seff had somehow pacified the robust woman, or more likely she had been distracted by the sight of her Queen receiving an urgent missive from the battlefield and had left off yelling at him, turning her attention towards me with curious eagerness. Soon everyone would know there had been news, for there was nothing as efficient as gossip for spreading the word.

As I ran to find Damek, I kept seeing the scrawling bold letters of his writing, the bloody fingertips that had touched the page, and the simple words, *I need you.*

14

The hooves of our horses beat like drums on the hard earth as I rode to the north, the two brothers close behind me and a cavalry of archers following them. I glanced back and saw that the dog was still happily draped over the front of Vayk's saddle, his tongue lolling blithely as he was galloped along.

"What are you doing?" I had asked Vayk that morning as I had swung myself up on my own horse, a strong Natali mare from the plains that I knew could make the hard ride ahead. He frowned at me, adjusting the long swathe of cloth he was draping like an oversized sling around his chest.

"For the dog," he said in his bland voice as if I should have been able to discern exactly what he was doing.

"The... you are taking the dog?" I had balked, incredulous.

Seff had given me a withering look as he lifted the massive creature and slung him into his brother's arms with a grunt of effort. "Why would we go to war without the dog?"

I shook my head, unable to think of a reasonable reply. If they wanted to take their dog to the battle, I was not going to stop them, and arguing would just waste time. It has already been a day since the bloodied message had come from Blaise and I was anxious to get going. Damek had begun to organize the legion of archers and they would follow behind, for it took much longer to move an army than it would for a few of us to get there, riding fast and light on horseback. He had insisted that I take the Cavalry of Archers with me, for they could easily keep up and carry their own supplies.

"We have heard nothing from Samirra about their army moving north, the only thing my spies in the palace have reported was that the sickness in Iriellestra is spreading and they are rounding up the infected into camps to contain the illness. Oh, and your idiot husband is still hiding safely within his palace walls," Damek told me, disgust coating his words.

"And Thyrr?" I asked, choosing to ignore his churlish tone.

"I have sent word to the Leharan Usurper that you claim is your ally. Logaire is still on the island, she should be able to convince him to happily send his Leharans to the battle. After all, fighting is what those savages love more than anything. If you will not wait for the Leharans or for our own legion to be ready, then you must at least take the cavalry. It would be foolish of you to go barreling onto a battlefield with no one to protect you but those two mercenary ruffians, whom we barely know. It is the prudent thing to do, my Queen," Damek had argued. I agreed, but only as long as they could be ready within a day.

He had rushed to follow me around my room as I stormed through the wardrobe cabinets, throwing aside gowns and gilded fabrics until I cried in exasperation, "Where are my leathers?"

"I will see to it that you are properly attired if you will please stop destroying the manor now. The maids will not be pleased to see this mess you have made of your chambers," he chastised, frowning distastefully.

"I do not care about the opinion of the maids when he could be dying or dead!" I had exclaimed, my face flushing instantly at the admission, knowing that my shrewd advisor would undoubtedly read the meaning behind my words.

"Do not be naïve, child," Damek cautioned, his eyes narrowed so they were barely slits above his gaunt cheeks. "You do not owe the Verucans or their King anything. Your duty is to Kymir."

"I have a duty to Imbria," I said in response. "We must take back the fertile lands, and if Blaise needs my help to do it, then he shall have it."

"He does not deserve your loyalty, my child," Damek had muttered bitterly, stalking off to do as I had asked of him in a flurry of black robes and spidery limbs. He had tried several more times to dissuade me from going but I was resolute. I knew the damage the Fomori could inflict, and I knew the cost of fighting them. I was a Keeper. There was no one who could turn the tide of war more quickly than I could, and I could not abandon Blaise after reading those three simple words. *I need you.*

We had ridden out that next morning, properly attired as Damek had promised, in the supple leather pants and vest that I had once used for archery competitions. My feet were encased in sturdy boots that would be good for riding and for chill of snow in the north, and I had a heavy leather overcoat rolled into my saddle pack. I had set a grueling pace out of the Royal City, the men keeping up without complaint though I could tell as the day waned that the journey was taking its toll on the horses.

"Maialen!" Seff shouted from behind me. I turned to look and he was motioning for me to halt. I tugged gently on the reigns and my horse slowed to a walk so that he could come up alongside me. "The horses need rest. So do the men. There is a river nearby, it will be a good place to camp."

I knew he could see the emotions that were fleeting across my face as I looked past him at the men of the cavalry, their mounts panting and covered in sweat. He was right, they needed rest, but every moment we wasted could mean more deaths in Samirra.

"We will be no good to them if we are not fit to fight, or if the horses tire out before the journey is completed," Seff warned.

I sighed and nodded in agreement. "We will make camp for the night but we leave again at first light."

Seff nodded back and took the lead, turning from the road and picking his way through the forest with what seemed like aimless abandon. Soon the land sloped down along the river-bank and we reached a clearing and I could not help but smile at the incredible sight that lay before us. A rocky outcropping at the bend of the river sheltered a glistening green pool, overhung with thick moss and crawling vines. A tiny waterfall cascaded from above into the pool and the fading sun dappled across the surface of the water. It was the perfect spot for a camp, away from the road and the rock sheltering us from other travelers and from the weather.

"How did you find this place?" I asked them, sliding down the sweating flanks of my mare and leading her towards the water to drink. The cavalry archers spread out around us, unrolling their saddle packs and tending to their own mounts, splashing the cool water on their dusty faces. The dog waded happily into the little pool, shaking himself off with gleeful abandon and showering the rest of us with droplets of water.

"We have spent much time in the forest," Vayk answered me, settling himself on a large, flat rock and laying out his belt of knives so that he could inspect them. "The dog likes it."

As so often happened when the brothers spoke, I could think of no suitable reply and so I left off the conversation there. Seff set about making a fire and preparing food, the cavalry men doing the same, and I relaxed back, trying to focus on the beauty of the landscape that surrounded me and not on what lay ahead.

War.

Blaise's message said they had been betrayed by Samirra, but Damek had sworn that an army had not been sent. Had Astraeus warned the blooddrinkers that the Verucans were coming? Made a pact with them, as Blaise and my father once had? It did not seem like something my husband would do. He was too prideful to debase himself to those beasts. I wished for the hundredth time that Blaise had been less cryptic in his desperate plea, and that I had some idea as to what I was running toward. But at least I was running towards something and not hiding in the shadows of Kymir. Most of my life I had been treated like an ineffectual doll. A pretty thing to be shown off but of no real use to anyone. The only person who had ever made me feel like I was strong, like I was worth something more than my title, was Blaise. I remembered standing beside him the last time we had fought the Fomori together, feeling as his equal, not as a pet or a child. Terrified, but bolstered by his lack of fear for me. He had not coddled me or tried to protect me, he had let me stand on my own and I had survived. Before, I had thought that it was merely due to his lack of caring about whether I lived or died, but now I saw that it was because he had believed in me, in my strength as a Keeper, and expected more from me than anyone else ever had.

"Are you prepared for what is coming?" Vayk asked me with a sideways glance, fingering the sharp point of his dagger.

I was surprised that he had spoken to me unnecessarily, and confessed, "I wish I knew more about what we were facing."

"You underestimate the Fomori. This is why you question what will happen. To know your enemy, you must become your enemy, but you have not bothered to know those you seek to destroy," Vayk said, sliding the dagger back into its sheath and plucking out another. Firelight flickered across the blade and danced around the shadows of the rocky outcropping like demons swaying at the edges of my vision. A knot twisted in my stomach, for I could hear the doubt in his words as he went on, "You treat them as beasts, and some of them are, but you forget that for hundreds of years they have been one of the most feared tribes on Imbria. You forget the cunning of the ancient ones like Carushka. Your power as Keepers has made you arrogant, and arrogance does not win wars."

The dog trotted up and laid silently on the ground beside him, turning its head so that its one eye looked up at me with unsettling directness as I responded, "You are quite young to have seen enough war in your lifetime to council on it."

"We have learned from the lessons of the past," he said with a glance down at the mangled creature who lay at his feet and I wondered if he was referring to his brother or to the dog.

"So what would you have me do?" I asked, feeling my anxiousness creep into my voice.

He shrugged, folding the sheaf of knives and setting it aside. "I would not tell you what you should do, you are a Queen and a Keeper, you will make your own choices. What I will tell you is what I have already told you, do not dismiss other beings as mindless beasts just because you do not understand what they are. Do you know why the Fomori began to drink the blood of their victims?"

I shook my head, a chill trailing down my spine as I vividly recalled the time one of them had bit deep into my Guardian's arm, its eerie icterine eyes alit with ravenous hunger. Gideon had howled in pain and the creature had lifted his jaws to howl back in triumph, the long fangs dripping with my Guardian's blood.

"Long ago, there were many whose bloodlines had mixed with the divine. The Gods came often then, to see how their progeny fared, and it was easy for them to fall in love with the humans, whose brief lives created a passion for living that the Gods had not known. Mortal children were born who had the blood of the immortals coursing through their veins. There was one Fomori, the half-breed, who the first Keepers tried to enslave, for they feared her power and her vicious warriors, who called her Mother and obeyed her every command. She was the one who carried the Warding Stones. During one of the battles to capture her they had managed to bind her hands and in a desperate attempt to save herself she bit the neck of her assailant, tasting the blood of a descendent of the Gods. She found it exhilarating and realized that it made the power of the Stones stronger. She escaped that day, and it was because of her that the Fomori began the tradition of drinking blood, in their search for the strength of the divine bloodlines."

I sat watching him for a long moment with wide eyes, wondering how on Imbria his tale was supposed to help me win in a fight. "I have heard some of the old Tahitian legend of the half-breed from Cossiana, but my father taught me that they were just make-believe stories, scary things to tell children to keep them in line."

Vayk shrugged again and stood up, stretching his arms to signify the end of the conversation. Night had fallen and everyone needed to get as much sleep as they could. As he walked to where his brother had spread their thin blankets on the ground, he said over his shoulder, "Until Thyrr found one, everyone thought the Warding Stones were make-believe tales as well."

I narrowed my eyes and glared at his back, not liking the simpleness of his logic. The dog was still looking at me from its one eye and I glared at it too, until it got up and trotted away, leaving me to a restless night of tossing and turning through nightmares of an ancient, evil hag bent on destroying all of Imbria.

The morning could not come soon enough and though I had barely slept, I jumped up from my makeshift bed as soon as the first grey shimmer of the approaching dawn touched the sky. I was ready to rouse the others and get moving as soon as possible.

"What on Imbria!" I cried out, stumbling backwards and nearly toppling into the pool of water. Kaeleb sat in front of me, his arms folded over his chest and his steely eyes narrowed so that his pale brows almost touched.

"You would go to battle without me!" he accused. Several men had roused at my cry but I waved them off, gesturing at the boy. Seff and Vayk had also awoken and seemed not the least bit surprised to find my ferocious nephew squatting in our camp.

"What are you doing here?" I demanded of the boy, wondering just how he had found us.

"Your trail was not hard to follow. A herd of pigs would have been less obvious than you all," he muttered disdainfully as if reading my mind. He had a bow and a quiver of arrows that was nearly the length of him slung across his back and a short sword resting across his knees.

"Where did you get those weapons?" I continued to try to demand answers from him despite his growing exasperation with me.

"Your legion," he finally answered with a defiant lift of his chin. "Everything was just lying about, I did not have to even try and steal it."

"That is because in Kymir people do not steal from me!" I retorted shrilly. "You are the most infuriating child I have ever met!"

"I am the Solvrei!" he shouted back at me, his cheeks turning pink with emotion.

"I do not care! Vayk, take two of the cavalry men with you and take him back to Kymir," I ordered, turning to the closest brother.

"I do not think-" Vayk began but I silenced him with an angry gesture.

"I did not ask what you think! This is not the place for a child, even one who is a violent, savage little thief!" I exploded. "And now you have cost me three men who will not be at my side in a battle because you could not do as you are told!"

Kaeleb's chin quivered as he stood, throwing the sword down in the dirt and flinging down the quiver of arrows and the bow on top of it. "Brother Kaden was wrong about you!"

"Then go and find him and leave me alone," I snapped. He stormed off, and the two brothers exchanged a long look before Vayk jogged after him, snatching him by the collar and dragging him to where the horses were tethered while he writhed angrily in his grasp. I felt a pang of guilt for losing my temper and being so harsh with him, but being reasonable did not seem to work and the last thing I needed was to worry about the safety of my sister's homicidal child. I had my own child to worry about, in the Kingdom that we were marching towards. In that moment I felt a wash of hatred for my sister that surprised me with its vehemence. Orabelle had left all of us shattered and broken, the pieces of our lives scattered across Imbria. Everything that was happening was because of her and her selfishness. I started to reach for my amulet, to use the serene energy of my Element to calm me, but I let my hand fall back down. I did not need to be calm, I needed to be ready.

"Make haste to ride out," I ordered the men curtly. "We have wasted enough time already."

15

Logaire waited, her head resting on Thyrr's warm chest, her coppery hair spilling across his tanned skin. She listened to the rhythmic pulse of his breathing and she was tempted to run her long fingernails over the thigh that was entwined with hers but she kept still, wanting to make sure that he was soundly asleep. She had waited for so long, she would not ruin her chance now.

The message she had been anticipating had come from Kymir earlier that evening. The hawk had circled the Citadel, screeching out like a banshee, and the Leharan handler had rushed out, lifting his leather wrapped forearm into the air and calling to the bird. It landed obediently, tearing into the morsels of fish that the handler had ready to reward it. Logaire had waited behind the others, seeming demure and patient, fading into the background, while her whole body had thrummed with anticipation. This could be the message she had been waiting for. In her mind she unrolled the small parchment and read out the myriad possibilities. *Blaise was dead and the Verucans had been defeated*. That was the best possible outcome but she doubted she was that lucky. Her cousin was like a lizard that kept growing its tail back after it had been cut off. The best she would allow herself to hope for was that the Verucans were overrun and needed the Leharan's support. Which would, of course, be promised, but would never actually arrive. Logaire could not be sure that Thyrr would keep his word to stay out of the fight, for men could be vainglorious and the islanders had an unquenchable thirst for combat, but she would do everything in her power to keep them away from the north.

Thyrr had bent his head close to Bacatha's, speaking urgently, his eyes flicking to Logaire. He would come to her soon, tell her what the Kymirrans had sent, she would not need to ask. She had done well with him, ingratiating herself so quickly into his life that he now sought out her council before making any decision. She guided him through the complexities of ruling, making suggestions that would endear him to the Leharan people. While everyone had been taking her for granted all these years, she had studied the people of Imbria and the four realms. She learned their customs, their traditions, their motivations. She knew their commerce and their trade, what resources each of them had and what made them dependent on the others. The Keepers could run around with their amulets, showing off with flashing displays of Elemental power, but she had learned where the real power lay, and finally, soon, she would show them all that they had underestimated her.

Thyrr sent for her that night after the message had arrived, as she expected, and she had come to him, her sultry body draped in a golden silk gown that clung to her curves invitingly. She had spent nearly every night with him since arriving on Lehar, and she thoroughly enjoyed the younger man's enthusiastic company and surprised herself by finding that she also enjoyed his quick wit and his intellect. She looked forward to their banter as much as to their lovemaking, recognizing the kindred streak of bitterness that ran within them both.

"It is as you predicted," Thyrr told her, pouring her a goblet of wine and taking one for himself. She smiled, looking up at him from under her lashes as she sipped the crimson liquid.

"My cousin does not fare well in the north?"

"Damek has asked us to send reinforcements to Samirra, and specifically to send the Tahitian healers," Thyrr said, setting down his goblet and moving to the window to stare out at the black sea that sparkled in the moonlight. He seemed pensive and she worried again that he would not keep his word to stay out of the conflict. She slipped her hand into the bosom of her gown, lifting the tiny bottle of liquid she had hidden.

"Do you think the Tahitians would go without consulting you? It is possible that Maialen has already sent word directly to Cossiana, though with my being here she will probably think there is no need, that I will leap to do her bidding and rally the troops behind them," Logaire said sardonically.

Thyrr was still staring out the window, probably pondering all of the glorious killing he could be doing if he disregarded her advice. She tipped the liquid quickly into his goblet and hid the bottle behind the table, swirling the herbal concoction and joining him at the window, pressing the cup into his hands.

He took it from her, saying, "Who knows what the Tahitians would do. They have pledged loyalty to me but every time something happens on Imbria they have a new legend and a new prophecy to influence them. Their superstitious storytellers, the Samains, hold more sway over the people than I would like. I could ask the elders, seek their counsel on joining the others in the north."

"That is a bad idea, darling. You are the ruler of Lehar and all its islands and you do not ask permission before you make decisions. The Leharans and the Tahitians both detest weakness so you must be decisive. You may want to be brave and ride off to the battle, but you must do what is best for Lehar and leave this war to the others," she reminded him, pleased when he took a long drink. She needed him to sleep soundly that night.

"Is letting the blooddrinkers live really what is best?" he questioned, his brows drawn together.

"Of course not," she purred, reaching up to rub the tense muscles in his neck. "The blooddrinkers can be dealt with later. They are a nuisance, nothing more, and they pose no threat to Lehar. What is best for you is to weaken the threat from Veruca. Blaise will never let you live, not while you have the Warding Stone."

He cast a fleeting glance at the bed that dominated the center of his chambers before turning back to the unforgiving sea. She felt a thrill of satisfaction. So that's where he was keeping the Stone, somewhere near the bed. It was a wise decision, that way it could not be stolen in his sleep. Not by a hired thief, anyway.

He sighed heavily. "Maialen is going to the north to join the Verucans. Are you not concerned for her safety? You have been her companion for so many years, how can you not want to help her?"

"Maialen is not your family," she said sharply, causing him to flinch at the harshness of her tone. She forced herself to soften before continuing, "You are the bastard half-brother of a sister who she has never forgiven. She still blames Orabelle for taking her father from her, even though she will not admit it. I told her that Blaise was the one who had the pact with Carushka, and still she harbors resentment and anger for her sister while she trails after Blaise like a lovesick puppy despite what he has done. I know her better than anyone, darling, and believe me when I tell you that Maialen does not and will not ever see you as part of her family. The Earth Queen is not as fragile as she appears to be, remember that she is a Keeper, one who has used her power to strengthen her own kingdom, letting the islands practically fend for themselves. She does not care what happens here."

He nodded, believing the lie, as she continued to knead the tension in his back. Maialen cared about the islands, she cared about all of Imbria, that was her problem. If not for Damek and Logaire she would have bled Kymir dry trying to save the other realms. And now, thanks to Logaire's gentle manipulation, she cared about the Fire Keeper too.

"Come, darling, that is enough worry for tonight. I will make sure to send word that we are coming to help, and I will also make sure that we cannot come. Tomorrow I will take care of Imbria, but for now, let me take care of you."

They had gone to bed and she had done her best to tire him out quickly, the herbal concoction helping her along. Now she waited, not risking that he would awaken before she had accomplished what she had set out to do all along. His chest moved up and down, his breath warm in her hair. She untangled her limbs from his and paused again, waiting. His breathing continued undisturbed and she slipped out of the bed, shoving her mane of hair back from her face and giving him an appreciative look. He really was quite compelling, and she was going to miss him when she was gone.

Logaire bent and peered under the bed, reaching her hand up to feel along underneath the boards. There was nothing. She tried to look behind the massive headboard, but the sliver of moonlight was not enough for her to see back there so she pressed herself flat on the wall, once again feeling along with her fingertips for anything out of the ordinary. It had to be there. She had seen the way his eyes had flicked to the bed when she had mentioned the Stone. She ran her hands over the pillows, carefully not to disturb him too much. There was nothing. She felt irritation bubble up within her and she wanted to smash the bed into a thousand pieces. Everything had come down to this moment, and to her being able to find the Stone. She gripped the post of the headboard, wishing that she could break it off and bash it against the wall till it was nothing but splinters. She paused, her golden eyes widening in pleasure. There, under her thumb, a tiny fissure, so fine that had she not been gripping it as hard as she was, she never would have felt it. She twisted the post and after a moment of effort it began to turn, and as she lifted the disengaged piece she saw a flash of silver. She set the post down gently and reached in, drawing out a silver ribbon that had been wound around the milky moonstone. She unfurled the ribbon, stuffing it back into its hiding place and replacing the post.

The Warding Stone. Finally, it was hers. She stood naked in the moonlight, the pale, opalescent orb glistening in her palm. Her thumb passed over the string of runes that were carved into the glossy surface and she felt a strange sensation wash over her. It was not the hum of power that she had expected from watching the Keepers and their amulets. This was an entirely different feeling, like a bottomless emptiness, the absence of everything. She shuddered and quickly shimmied into her gown, sliding the stone between her breasts to hide it.

At the doorway she gave a last, fond glance at the man who lay sprawled in the bed and then left, closing the door gently behind her. The hallway was dark as she made her way to the staircase and started down it carefully, not wanting to draw the attention of the Guard who patrolled the Citadel throughout the night.

"Logaire," the melodic voice of Bacatha caused her to halt with a startled gasp. The woman was coming up the stairway, her broad shoulders and severe features lined with moonlight that crept in through the balistraria, the narrow arrowslits that encircled the citadel where archers could launch arrows down on their enemies below.

"Bacatha," Logaire inclined her head in greeting, moving to slip past the Guard but the woman blocked her path. Logaire swallowed her annoyance and forced a smile. "Am I not allowed to return to my chambers?"

"I know what you are doing. You may be able to fool Thyrr and the others, but I am not so easily duped," the Leharan said, still refusing to let her pass.

"Perhaps we should have invited you to join us, then," Logaire offered suggestively.

Bacatha scoffed. "I do not need a man's help to please a woman. What are you doing out here?"

Logaire contemplated her next move. If Bacatha made a scene and woke any of the others, then it could be discovered that she had taken the Stone, and Thyrr could have her banished, or worse, and she would have nothing to show for all of her efforts. She decided to take a risk, and instead of lying, she said boldly, "I have taken the Warding Stone."

Bacatha was so shocked by her admission that her mouth fell open in surprise. Before she could regain her composure Logaire hurried on, "I did not harm him, merely helped him to sleep deeply through the night. Do not call for help, listen to me first. You are honorable, you want to serve your new ruler and Lehar and the best way to do that is to let me take the Stone."

Bacatha's eyes were like icy lakes. She had heard the rumors about Logaire and her herbs, the gossip that circulated as to the mysterious deaths of the woman's first two husbands. "Go on."

Logaire licked her lips, leaning in close to the woman. "The Warding Stone has given him the throne that he sought, but it will also bring him misery and death. The assassins have already come, and they will not stop coming. My cousin will never allow him and the Stone to exist, it is too much of a threat. If the Fire Keeper comes back from the north the next place he will look to is Lehar. He will decimate these islands, and he will not stop until Thyrr and everyone who followed him is dead."

"We can protect Lehar-" Bacatha began to protest.

"No, you cannot!" Logaire hissed. "The famine in Samirra will drain everyone's resources on Imbria. The islands can sustain themselves for a time, hopefully until we can repair the damage the Keepers have caused, but a war with Veruca will be costly and deadly. It will cripple your kingdom. You are not a fool, as you have already pointed out to me. You must know that I am right. Taking the Stone is the best way to protect Thyrr and Lehar even though he will not see it that way. If saving your kingdom is not enough incentive to let me leave here, then I can offer you more than that. I know who the traitor is among the old Guard, the one whose treachery stopped your people from winning the battle at Queen's End. The traitor who caused Orabelle's death. Surely this is something you wish to know, something that Brogan, your dear father, would want to know, as it was his friends who died that day. I will tell you, once I am safely away from here with the Stone."

"And what will you do with it? Are you not worried the Verucans will come for you?" Bacatha asked. She could see the truth of what Logaire was saying. Her duty was to keep Lehar safe and perhaps the woman was right, and this was the best way. Thyrr had the throne, he would not need the Stone to hold it, not if the threat of the Stone came from somewhere else. She also knew that her father would want to know the answers to what had happened at Queen's End, and even though Bacatha did not trust the Verucan woman, she sensed that she was telling the truth about this.

"No, I am not worried about the Verucans," Logaire whispered with an acidic smile. "While my cousin is playing games up in the north and distracted by his incessant need for vengeance, I will be using our little Warding Stone and taking the kingdom right out from under him. Once I have, Lehar and Veruca will be the greatest alliance that Imbria has ever seen."

16

We reached the bodies before we reached the war. It had been easy to follow the route Blaise had taken once we were in Samirra, for an army left quite an impression on the landscape and on the unkempt roads. The first sign that we were nearing them was a brown haze that choked the air, as if the sky itself had died was now as dull and lifeless as the rest of Samirra. We had slowed our approach, moving carefully across the valley towards the mountains. The dog trotted beside me and as his one eye lolled up at me occasionally, I would smile back down at him, unexpectedly grateful for his company and the alertness of his mangled ears. He would not let us be set upon unaware.

The chill was biting and at first I thought it was snow that was falling on us, timid flakes of leftover winter floating down from the clouds. Then I wiped at one and a smear of sooty residue stuck to the fingers of my glove. Ash.

The stench followed the ash, so pungent that I nearly gagged, gripping my amulet to try to calm my heaving stomach, feeling the grounding energy of my Element flow through me. One of the cavalry men was sick, leaning over the side of his horse and vomiting onto the ashen ground. The smoke thickened, ripe with the odor of burning bodies and my eyes stung from it. I pulled out a scarf from my saddle pack, seeing that the men were doing the same, and wound it around my face, covering my nose and mouth. The landscape was an eerie, silent wasteland. Then I saw them. Piles of blackened corpses, the fires still smoldering on some of them with horrible hisses and pops. I was horrified, unable to tell if the charred remains were Verucan or Fomori. Some of the bodies looked particularly small, not like the full-grown men who would be fighting a battle or the massive Fomori. I stopped, sliding down from my horse and moving towards them, my eyes fixed on a blackened, outstretched hand that reached towards me in deadly stillness.

"Do not touch them!" Seff shouted at me. The dog snarled, jumping and biting the edge of my thick leather overcoat, pulling me back. "Something is wrong with them."

"What do you mean?" I asked, hastily backing away from the pile of corpses. The dog released me and began to growl, shaking its body in agitation.

"Look there," Seff said, motioning ahead where the dark silhouette of a man could be seen walking through the carnage towards us.

"Get back on your horse!" the man croaked. He stopped some distance away and through the fog of smoke I could see that he was sweating profusely, his face red and there were deep purple smudges under his eyes. He was several yards away from us, panting with exhaustion. "You must get out of here. Go forward, they are at the base of the mountains."

I hurried to get back on my horse, swinging up into the saddle and wondering what on Imbria this man was doing out there, wandering through burnt corpses. "What happened here?"

It was Seff who answered me, as the man doubled over coughing, thick sputum running down his chin. "They have the sickness. Plague."

"The Samirrans," the man managed to gasp through fits of coughing. "They gathered up the sick ones, marched them here and left them to infect our army. We tried to help them but what could we do? They were dying anyway and our soldiers began to fall sick..."

I had never felt such complete revulsion and horror in my entire life. I stared around at the bodies, my eyes watering from the smoke and from tears as I remembered Damek's claim that the Samirrans had been rounding up the sick to put in camps. Not to treat them or isolate them, as we had thought, but to use them against his enemies. I tasted vomit in my throat and forced myself to swallow it down, keeping my eyes fixed on the man, trying not to look at the small bodies that I now knew were women and children.

"You are infected?" I asked him, pity coloring my voice.

"Those of us that showed signs were left behind. The King, he offered to end us quickly, and some of them accepted, for it was a better way to die, but I offered to wait for you, to make sure that you would not linger here where it was not safe."

"Is there no chance you will recover?"

He shook his head. "There are some that do, but that would have happened already. I am too far gone; this will be my end."

"I can end it for you," Seff offered him, "I can give you the warrior's death that you have earned."

The man paused for a moment to consider, fear and relief fleeting across his tortured features, then he nodded in acquiescence. Seff drew a knife from his sheath, lifting it in his fingers to throw, but I stopped him.

"No!" I ordered. "I will do it. I will not miss and I owe him that mercy."

"Taking a man's life is no easy thing to live with," Seff warned, but he slid the knife back into the belt.

"I am not weak," I said to him through clenched teeth. I reached down to pull the bow from where it was strapped against my saddle and I plucked an arrow from my sheath. I did not understand in that moment why I was compelled to act, why I had to be the one to notch the arrow, draw it back, see the brave, sad resolve on the man's face, and then release it. It pierced his heart and he crumpled to the ground, his misery ended. My body trembled as I tried to hold in the grief that welled in me, and I thought I would break in two, so immense was the pain that I felt for the hundreds of dead that lay strewn across the valley. Later, I would realize that I had needed the pain, that I had needed to sever that final tie that held any sort of compassion for the father of my son. I needed to be broken, so that I would have no doubts that Astraeus deserved what was coming.

"You two, go back to the border of Kymir and wait for reinforcements there, make sure that they know what is coming and to stay away from the bodies," I commanded, my voice wavering but still able to form the words. Two more of my cavalry gone. Hopefully, the legion of archers would be there soon.

Seff turned his horse to come up beside me, his ordinarily bland features taut with anxiety. Bits of ash clung to his long hair as he pulled down the scarf that covered his face to say quietly, "We should go back. The rest of the Verucans could be sick, the sickness could still be spreading through their army."

"No," I shook my head. "Blaise would not have brought us here if he was not sure that he had contained it. We will keep going. If you do not wish to go on, then you can leave and wait at the border with the others."

He looked surprised and glanced at the dog who was circling our horses, his tail wagging. "We will stay with you."

We rode on until evening was settling over the valley, darkness coming quickly in the shadows of the peaked granite monoliths that were the northern mountains. A whistle pierced through the silence. The smoke had begun to clear once we had left the desolate graveyard of burnt bodies behind us, and I saw a group of black-armored men up ahead, their arrows fixed on us.

"I am escorting the Earth Queen," Seff shouted to them. I reached for my amulet and let the power wrap around me, feeling it more keenly than usual, as if the very land here had been scarred and beaten. The ground rumbled beneath the soldiers and the rocks and pebbles lifted into the air before settling back down, undeniable proof of who I was.

The Verucans lowered their weapons and even from the distance I could see the relief on their faces. They motioned for us to follow them and we wound our way to their camp at the edge of the mountains, where the huge slabs of granite pierced through the ground and soared towards the sky. The camp was a sprawling swathe of conical tents dotted with firepits and crawling with men. In the center was one large, circular tent enclosed within a wall of timber and surrounded by a trench into which the Verucans had sunk sharpened stakes, hardened by fire and fixed in rows five deep. Another trench was being dug at the northern edge of the camp and over it all fluttered the black flags of Veruca.

The men led us to the large tent within the imposing wall of deadly spikes, and I dismounted, motioning for the others to wait outside while I went in, pushing aside the heavy fabric that sheltered the doorway. Inside was more lavish than I had expected, though still in the stark, austere style that Blaise seemed to favor. There was a large table set up to one side, littered with maps and parchments, and beside it a rack that held weapons and a round shield. Opposite the table was the bed draped in thick blankets and a wooden chest, and all around the tent were tall, standing candelabras, coating everything in a warm glow. In the center of the room stood Blaise, wearing his shining obsidian armor, his head bent in conversation with one of his generals and the Fire Opal gleaming around his neck. The men looked up at me as I entered and the Fire Keeper motioned me forward, dismissing the other man from the room.

I stood in front of him, staring up at the strong planes of his face and his burning amber eyes, not sure what to say first. He was alive, and upon seeing him I felt an immense wash of relief, but there was nothing comforting in his agonized demeanor.

"Where are the others?" he asked me.

"Damek is sending a legion of archers, they will arrive soon, and the Leharans have promised help and healers from Tahitia. Blaise... what happened?" I asked, reaching to touch his arm. He stepped away from my outstretched fingertips, walking over to the table and throwing himself down in one of the chairs.

"Your husband happened," he replied curtly and a haunted vision passed over his eyes.

"I found the man you left to warn us. I know what Astraeus did. I cannot imagine-"

"No, Maialen!" He interrupted me with a snarl. "You cannot imagine it! He marched them here, anyone he could find, men, women and children, old women, sick and dying, and he left them at our backs with no food and no supplies. At first we did not know, we thought they were his army and we prepared to fight, then as they drew closer we saw them, shambling at us pitifully like walking corpses, crying out for help. There was one I cannot stop seeing, a mother holding her dead baby. It must have died on the way but she kept holding it, asking us to help her dead child. He used his people as weapons and I, I had no choice! I had to... I had to... "

"You killed them," I finished for him when he broke off and could not form the words. I had never seen him so furious or so tortured. He looked as if he would shatter at any moment, that the slightest touch against his trembling hands would cause him to fall apart.

"I have done my share of killing, but not like that," he muttered, his haunted amber gaze fixed on the memory. "Never like that."

"What will you do now?" I asked him softly, afraid that even the sound of my voice would be too much for him to bear in that moment. I reached for my amulet and saw a flicker of gratitude on his face as I let the calm, grounding serenity of my Element flow across him.

"I will finish this. We will kill the Fomori, and then I will find Astraeus and rip him limb from limb. But we must wait for your legion. The sickness has decimated our numbers, though thankfully it seems that we have been able to stop the spread within the army."

"And the Fomori? Have you encountered them?"

"They came after we... after it was done, probably drawn by the scent of death. They seemed different than I remember from before, more organized. It was almost as if they were testing our ranks. We followed them into the valley, driving them back to the mountains through the bottleneck, but we lost more men that I had anticipated. We were exhausted and worn down from dealing with the plague. It was a good time to attack, and it seemed they knew that."

"You think they will come again?"

"Probably," he conceded. "The numbers that we faced would not have been sufficient to drive all the northern dwelling Samirrans from these lands. There must be more of them. I will feel much better when your Archers have reached us and we can be back on the offensive. Thank you for coming."

I felt my cheeks flush crimson and I looked away from him, hoping he did not notice and praying that the legion would be here soon and we could leave this land of horrors behind us. I had already seen enough atrocities and we had not even been here a day. Though I would never say it aloud, I feared what else was coming for us.

17

They came that night. It was not as if we were unprepared for a night attack, for we knew well the way the Fomori liked to fight. The last time we had forced them from the other kingdoms we had fought them under the blanket of darkness many times. Blaise had posted guards and scouts to patrol at all hours, set up tripwires along the northern edge of the camp and started to dig the spike-laden trenches there. We were prepared for them to try and come at night, but what we had not been ready for was the number of them that came. The beasts had poured down from the mountains like a monstrous avalanche, crushing the defenses and tearing through the sentries like they were paper dolls. There were mere seconds between the first clang of bells that sounded the alarm that intruders had invaded the camp, and the cacophony of the destruction that followed in their wake.

I tore myself from sleep at the first peremptory peal of bells that shattered the still night, shoving my feet into my boots and grabbing the bow and my quiver of arrows before leaping out of the tent. Seff was already there, his body shielding me. The ugly dog was standing watch beside him and a group of Verucan soldiers were clustered around us, sent by Blaise to protect me. The smell was overwhelming, worse than the burned bodies we had left behind us. It smelled of death, of rotting meat and putrid flesh.

"What is happening?" I demanded, strapping the quiver across my back and pulling on my long leather gloves. I wondered how long I had been asleep, for it felt like mere seconds had passed since I had laid my head on my folded arms and closed my eyes, and night still hung heavy over the valley.

"The Fomori are here." Seff's face was set in grim lines and his eyes flicked over the chaotic scene that unfolded around us. The scar that ran through his brow stood out like a pale gash in the moonlight. The dog bristled beside him, a low growl forming in its throat and saliva dripping from its fangs and out of the mangled jaw, looking so much like a demon that I was grateful it was on our side.

"Blaise!" I cried out, seeing a huge arc of fire explode into the night sky in the direction of his tent. I ran towards it, Seff and the other soldiers hurrying to keep up with me.

The Fomori were everywhere. They were slashing through the tents with razor sharp talons, kicking the firepits over in showers of sparks, and tearing through the Verucans with wild abandon. I called my power, shifting the ground beneath the beasts so that they stumbled and fell, but afraid to open the land to swallow them, for fear of taking our own soldiers down with them. A man screamed in front of me as one of the creatures bit down into his forearm and I let an arrow fly, piercing its shoulder and eliciting a howl of rage from the beast. It dropped the man's arm, lifting its eerie yellow eyes to me, a grotesque smile spreading across its face.

"There you are," it hissed. It threw its head back and howled, the sound undulating through the night. Then it grasped the arrow and ripped it from its flesh, starting towards me. I lifted another arrow but the beast toppled to the ground before I could release it, a long knife protruding from its eye socket. Seff ran to it and yanked the knife out, the eyeball coming with it, and he flicked the blade, sending the bloody yellow orb bouncing across the dirt where the dog promptly snapped it up, swallowing it in its distorted jaws.

"I think he called for help," Seff warned me, as more of the beasts descended on us. The dog ran to where I was and circled around me, still growling and snarling. The Verucan guards fell upon the onslaught of beasts, I could see my cavalry archers fighting in the distance, and everything was blood and carnage around us. I kept moving towards Blaise's tent, grateful that I could still see the fiery orange glow from his attacks. He was alive. Seff was in the tangled melee of beasts and Verucans, slashing furiously with his knives, and I hesitated to leave him, seeing a clear opening where I could get to Blaise's tent. Together, we were more powerful, we could stop the attack. I had to try and reach him. I ran forward, the dog loping along beside me, barking in alarm. One of the beasts sprinted towards us, blood dripping down its inhuman face, and the dog turned, letting out a sound that was so terrifying it made me shudder. The blooddrinker cried out in fright and spun away, fleeing, the dog close on his heels. I kept running.

"Blaise!" I screamed, halting at the edge of the spiked trench that encircled the Fire King's tent. The air was thick with smoke and I could hardly see, trying to find the opening of the barricade without impaling myself. Frustrated, I gripped the amulet, pushing the wicked spikes out of the dirt to make a new opening and rushing through it, not thinking in my haste to close the barrier back behind me.

He was there, and my eyes widened at the sight of him and his power. I had seen him fight before, and it was impressive, but he had been distracted then, younger and more emotional, tormented by my sister's recent death. Now, he was incredible to behold, masterful in the way that he manipulated his Element, moving with a savage grace that I had never witnessed. His face was set, his jaw clenched and sweat dripping down him, the bright amber eyes flashing. The beasts were funneling in through the opening of the defenses, and others were trying to clamor over the spiked barricades, using the impaled bodies of their brethren as leverage. One of them leapt at Blaise, its jagged talons slashing through the air and the flint sparked in his hand, the creature exploding in a shower of embers.

"Are you just going to stand there?" he shouted at me. I turned to face the main onslaught and the ground fell away beneath them, the dirt sifting like flour around their feet so that they sunk down in it nearly to their knees. Then it hardened like rock, trapping them where they stood. A plume of flame raged over them as they struggled to free themselves and they shrieked wildly as they caught fire. More were coming, howling with frenzied hysteria. I felt a stinging pain in the back of my head as one of them grabbed my long braid, jerking me backwards and clawing at my neck. They were pouring in behind me through the opening I had made in the barrier and they were forming a deadly circle around us. I shook the ground beneath them, throwing off the one who had gripped me. Blaise was still fighting them off but I could tell his energy was waning, he had yanked his sword from its sheath and was using the weapon instead of his Element. There were so many of the beasts, too many, and they kept circling us, drawing us closer together and forcing us out of the defensive barricade into the open camp.

I tried to push through them but they shoved me back, an impenetrable wall of eerie, icterine eyes and grey hide.

"They are herding us!" Blaise cried, beginning to hack at them desperately with his sword, their black blood spraying over him. Still they kept coming, a never-ending tidal wave, surrounding us, pushing us toward the mountain.

Blaise turned to me, gripping my wrist tightly and forcing me to look at him. "When I say run, I want you to run."

"And go where?" I demanded incredulously.

"The men are being slaughtered, get them out of here! Find Akrin and tell him I gave the order to retreat," he said through clenched teeth. Then he flung his sword at one of the beasts and fire sparked along the blade, the flame swelling into a maelstrom that tore into the Fomori that encircled us. "Go! Now!"

I started to run, following the path of his storm of fire, seeing what he wanted me to do. I dove between their burning bodies, sliding on the ground between their feet, then using my Element to push myself upright again, ready to sprint away.

"Not so fast, Earth Queen," one of them hissed, locking its thick arm around my neck. I could feel the heat and sticky flesh where Blaise had burned the creature but it seemed impervious to the pain. The strong muscles of its forearm pressed against my neck and I gasped for air, scratching desperately at it.

"Maialen!" Blaise shouted as the beast dragged me back into the deadly circle of its brethren.

"Move with us or she dies," the one holding me commanded. Blaise hesitated and the grip tightened on my throat, the beast's jaws gaping open near my neck while the burnt flesh of its face stuck to my cheek. Blaise stepped back and the circle of blooddrinkers began to move, keeping us within it and shepherding us away from the battle until we could no longer see or hear the sounds of fighting. They finally stopped, drawing more tightly around us and pressing me close against him.

"Are you alright?" he whispered. I nodded and the beast jerked me back, the Fomori changing their formation so that we were the tip of an arrowhead. It pulled me into a crevice in the rock and suddenly there was only darkness. I stumbled along with the thing, hearing the other Fomori following, searching for any sound of Blaise to know that he was still with me. I called out his name and the creature that was holding me cackled gleefully in my ear.

"Do not worry," it hissed in my ear, "We will not leave him behind."

I tried not to panic as we moved further into the cave, the air startlingly cold. The Fomori were draped in thick pelts of fur, but I only had on my tunic and vest, the heavy leather overcoat folded neatly beside my bed in the tent where I had left it. I shivered and reached for my amulet but the creature swatted my hand away.

"Use it and he dies."

I obeyed it, for I had not really known what I could do to help us anyway. I could not see in the all-consuming blackness of the cave so any attack I attempted was as likely to be inflicted upon Blaise as it was on the Fomori. Gripping the gleaming, green gem was more a habit than a necessity, for I could use my power as long as it lay against my heart, but holding it brought me comfort.

"What do you want with us?" I asked the creature, still unsettled by the complete and utter blackness that surrounded us. If they could see in this dark nothingness then it was no wonder they preferred to attack at night. It was quite the advantage.

The beast cackled again, the laugh choking off into a cough of pain from its injuries. "She has asked for you."

"She?" I repeated.

"The Va'Kul," the beast answered, its sibilant voice whispering the word almost reverently. I wanted to question it further but I stumbled suddenly and toppled forward, landing hard on my knees with a cry.

"What are you doing? If you hurt her-" Blaise started to shout and I could hear him struggling. There was a thud and he cursed heartily.

"Do not harm him!" the one who held me shrieked back at them, hauling me to my feet. "We still need them both. We have reached our destination. Use your magic, Fire Keeper, since you pathetic humans cannot find your way in the dark."

A warm glow spread out from behind me and I gave Blaise a grateful smile before the creature prodded me to keep moving forward. I turned and let out another startled cry at the sight that lay before me in the illuminated chamber.

I realized then that I had never seen a female Fomori. I remembered Vayk's words in the forest, that I had not bothered to know my enemy, and he had been right. Looking around it was obvious that the women of the Fomori tribe were the ones who wielded the power. The males served them, doing their bidding like drone bees serving their queens. There were a dozen of them in the cavern and they all wore thick pelts, but these were not the haphazard scraps of fur that the fighting Fomori wore, instead these were complete skins, heads and all, immaculately preserved and draped over their grey-skinned bodies luxuriously. They all wore their black hair long and straight, and their strange, grey features were an unsettling blend of femininity and savagery.

Behind them the chamber ended in a wall, the surface smooth and polished like glass so that I could see the entire cavern reflected on it, making it seem as if the scene before us stretched on, never ending.

One of the females came forward, not with the graceful walk of a woman, but with the prowling ferocity of a hunter stalking its prey. She stopped before us, towering over me, her yellow eyes glowing with satisfaction. When her lips parted they revealed a row of sharp fangs, stained pink with blood.

"You have done well," she hissed at the ones who had captured us. They delighted in her praise, making tender sounds of pleasure. This must be the Va'Kul they had spoken of. She reached out with her taloned hand and hooked one claw around the golden chain that held my amulet, lifting the Emerald so that it sparkled in the glow of Blaise's firelight. Then she dropped it abruptly, so that it hit my chest with a thud, making me wince. She seemed pleased by that and her savage smile widened.

"Go to the wall and break it open," she commanded.

I shook my head and she looked annoyed, clearly not accustomed to disobedience.

"Do not make me go through this tiresome reprieve of constantly threatening you. You are at our mercy, and you will behave as such. Or I can take a bite from the Fire King to prove my point," she offered. "You have seen what our bites do to your weak, human flesh, have you not? It is a slow and painful way to die."

I glanced back at Blaise who was watching the tableaux unfold with burning intensity, his eyes roaming quickly around the chamber, searching for a weakness. His gaze settled back on me and he gave me a slight nod. I walked forward to the end of the chamber, past the daunting Fomori women whose heads turned to follow me as I walked. I reached out my hand, letting my fingertips slide over the mirror-glass surface. There was something behind it, obscured by the shining boundary. I closed my eyes and called my power to me, feeling the warmth of it wrap me in its comforting embrace. I breathed in for a moment, suspended from time, fully enveloped in the power so that there was no fear, no loss, no war, no Fomori. Just the land beneath me, the steadfast rock of the mountain above me. I felt the polished surface again and let out a soft gasp, realizing what it was.

"Diamond," I murmured. An impenetrable barrier, one that the Fomori could never break through. Whatever it was that they wanted, it was obvious that Keepers had been the ones to deprive them of it. Only the Keepers had the power to create such a prison, and whatever they had trapped in there was meant to remain there forever. I squeezed the amulet in my hand and in a moment of foolish bravery decided to risk everything, calling on my power to pull down the mountain above us. Blaise was still near the entrance of the chamber and if I could destroy the revered women who stood between us then perhaps the males would panic, giving him an opportunity to escape in the confusion, though I would be leaving myself trapped with no way out.

Nothing happened. I felt it again then, the bottomless well of emptiness that the Warding Stone caused. The Va'Kul slashed out, knocking the amulet from my hand. Blood welled up where her talon had cut through my leather glove and sliced across my palm and I saw the Fomori lean forward collectively towards the scent.

"Do you think we are fools?" she seethed at me. "You think that we would bring you here if we could not protect the Mother? I should rip your hands off for your disobedience!"

"Maialen, do what they want!" Blaise yelled in frustration, drawing her wrath away from me while I tried to press the cuff of my tunic against the cut, trying to stop the blood from oozing out and enticing the creatures who watched me with ravenous glee.

"You do not give orders here, human," the Va'Kul snapped at him. She made a motion with her hand and they dragged Blaise forward, shoving him to his knees in front of the shining barrier. She turned to me, licking her fangs with the tip of her pink tongue. "This will be the last time you see him in one piece unless you open it. I can start with something small, perhaps an ear?"

I pressed my hands against the mirrored surface, seeing my gaunt face staring back at me. My eyes were wide and frightened, the freckles across my nose standing out starkly against the pale skin beneath. I could see bruises already forming on my neck and I was smudged with soot and ash and splattered with black blood. I breathed in and felt my power return, and I pushed it into the wall, willing the surface to break apart.

It splintered with a sharp crack and fissures spread out from beneath my hands like spiderwebs. Shards begin to fall to the ground, revealing a second barrier, a cold, impervious wall of ice.

"Get back!" the Va'Kul ordered and as she shoved me aside I could feel my power leeching away again. "It is his turn."

Blaise stared into the ice and then turned back to look up at her. "No."

"Free her!" the Va'Kul screamed. She snatched my throat, her talons digging into the soft flesh of my neck. Droplets of blood welled up and the Fomori behind me inched closer, breathing in the scent while saliva dripped from their fangs. "Free her or the Queen gets ripped apart in front of you."

Thyrr's words rang out in my mind, like the clanging bells of the battlefield. *She was finally captured and sealed away forever in a tomb.* The half-breed. The legend that was so intertwined with that of the Warding Stones. The evil that would destroy Imbria.

Blaise was on his knees at the wall of ice and the glowing orb of fire that he had been using to light the room grew larger, spreading across the frozen surface in a blazing spectacle of dazzling sparks. Water pooled out from the wall as it melted away, spreading around him.

"Keep going!" the Va'Kul commanded when the fire began to dim. He squared his shoulders and got to his feet, spreading his hands in an arc, the fire curving to obey his command. I was staring past him at the melting ice, watching with a sick sense of dread. There was a tremor of movement behind the thin sheet of remaining ice and then suddenly a dark shape tumbled towards the ground, the female Fomori running forward to catch it and shoving Blaise aside in their haste. He turned, and I saw the flash of something in his hand, a shard of broken ice with a deadly point on it. He made a motion with his other hand for me to duck and I flung myself to the ground, the Va'Kul's claws leaving bloody gashes down my throat while she stood transfixed by the sight at the wall, her face exultant. Her eyes widened in surprise and she collapsed to the ground beside me and for a moment I thought Blaise had flung the ice at her but the shard was still in his hand and there was no way he could have thrown it hard enough to impale her. Then I saw the axe buried in her back and I whipped my head up to find the cold, wet snout of the dog in my face, Seff standing behind him, and a pile of dead Fomori cluttering the entrance.

"We should go now," Seff suggested, waving for me to come. Blaise sprinted towards us, flinging an arc of fire behind him at the rapt Fomori. They shrieked in protest, throwing them-selves on top of the thing that had fallen from the ice. The dog lowered his head, growling at the thick pelts of fur that were writhing on the cavern floor. Suddenly the chamber seemed to come alive, a scream echoing so violently through it that I had to stop, pressing my hands over my ears. Blaise grabbed my arm and hauled me out of the chamber.

"Stop them from following us," he said.

I grabbed the Emerald, turning back as we passed through the archway. I could feel the energy of my amulet like a rush of warmth from the sun. It must have been the Va'Kul who had wielded a Warding Stone and now that she was dead my power had returned. I was about to collapse the archway, sealing the chamber like a tomb, when I saw the dog, still inside the cavern and furiously attacking the enraged Fomori, keeping them from following us.

"Dog!" I shouted at it. The beast turned its one eye to me, then the horrible scream once again filled the chamber and the protective wall of Fomori parted, revealing the dark, damp hair and terrifying face of the woman who lay beneath them. She opened her eyes, beautiful and awful, black like the night sky with shards of yellow, a bottomless abyss of rage and pain.

"Fenris!" she ground out the name through clenched teeth, her voice hoarse and grating. The dog snarled at her, then Seff was beside it, grabbing the animal and shoving it towards us. It skidded across the floor, howling in protest, and I snatched a handful of its fur, dragging it out as the Fomori fell on Seff in a sea of grey-skinned death.

"Now!" Blaise shouted.

"I can't! Seff is still in there!" I cried, shaking my head.

"He's gone, Maialen, we cannot help him now!"

I felt like I would tear in half in that moment and I grabbed the Emerald so tightly that the edges of it cut into my already bloodied palm. "I can't, we have to wait for him!"

"Do it now or we all die!" Blaise's voice was desperate and I knew that he had overused his power, that he was exhausted. If they came for us now they had no reason to keep us alive and we would not be able to fight them all off. One of the Fomori was lurching at us, her hands outstretched, claws slicing the air. A few more seconds and she would be upon us, the others close behind her.

The archway collapsed in a cascade of dirt and rock. I let out a wail, a sound almost as horrible as the one that had emanated from the chamber moments before. The dog leaned back on his haunches and howled with me. Blaise stood in front of me and took my face in his hands, his amber eyes burning into mine.

"We can mourn later, Maialen. Right now we need to get out of here."

I nodded my head, my face wet with tears and Blaise wiped them away with his thumbs then stood back, looking at the maze of tunnels around us. I had no idea where to go, I couldn't think about anything but the man I had trapped in there with the ravenous beasts. The man who had come to save us, who had become my friend and I had just condemned to a horrible death. The dog whined softly and padded over to stand before one of the dark passages, as if waiting for us to follow. And so we did.

18

It seemed like we spent an eternity beneath the mountains. In the dark, we had no concept of time passing, no way to know when it was day or night. We had followed the dog, stopping only when we were too physically exhausted to go on. Blaise had used his power to keep us from freezing to death, but I could see the toll it was taking on him, the constant strain he felt, though he never spoke a word of complaint. He melted the ice that coated the cave walls so that we had water to drink, but there was no food to be found anywhere and the incessant cold and hunger gnawed away at us. We were lurching along yet another passageway that looked no different to me than all the others we had already traversed, when the dog let out an excited bark and began to run. I felt hope flutter in my chest when I saw the bright, glorious, wonderful beam of daylight at the end of the passage. The dog spun in a circle of delight, wagging his tail, the gash of daylight throwing bright streaks across his brindle fur. The opening was not large enough for any of us to fit through and as I grasped the Emerald in my shaking hand, I prayed that I would have enough strength to save us.

The ground shuddered and the walls of the passage groaned in protest. Dust floated down around us and I grimaced in frustration, blinking hard to try and focus all of my energy on that bright spot of hope. I kept seeing Seff in my mind, the swarm of grey-skinned bodies surrounding him. We had left him. We had not even tried to help him. He had gone back to save the damn dog, doing more for his pet than we had done for him, and now I would probably bring the whole mountain down on top of us so what had it mattered anyway?

Blaise drew my attention back to him. "Try to concentrate, Maialen. Just think about the power, see if flowing from you to the rock, see the rocks move as you command them to."

I nodded and bit down on my lip, trying again to focus. The opening widened and the dog darted through it, yipping gleefully. Blaise grinned at me, covered in soot and filth, with dark smudges under his amber eyes and dried blood staining his clothes. I smiled back at him and he took my hand, his callused fingers rough and strong, leading me out into the light.

"I have never seen anything so beautiful," I murmured, pulling myself out through the opening and turning my face up to bask in the sunlight. I spun around, throwing my arms out wide. I quickly became dizzy and stopped, the lack of food and sleep painfully apparent. I sat down in the tall, weedy grass, extremely grateful that the dog had led us south and not further into the icy wilderness of the north.

"We need food," Blaise pointed out needlessly, looking around us. We had traveled so far through the underground tunnels that the mountains were a dark swathe painted on the horizon. "We must be close to the border of Kymir."

Kymir. The thought of my home brought tears to my eyes. I had thought I would never see my land again, that I would die trapped in a cold, barren underground tomb. Now, the thought of being home, of being in the rich forest teeming with life, was almost too exquisite to bear.

I pulled off my gloves, spread my hands out on the ground and closed my eyes, searching. The dog trotted away, probably going in search of his own meal, and I felt his soft footfalls on the dirt, the way the grass bent beneath his paws. I reached further, seeking, then I found what it was I had been after. The vine twisted and crawled along the ground, answering my beckoning call. It bloomed beneath my fingertips and I coaxed it further, the buds drying up and replaced by glistening, purple berries, fat and ripe with juice. I stopped and looked up at the Fire King who bent down next to me and popped one of the berries in his mouth.

"Well done, Earth Queen," he said with a grin.

"We cannot survive on them, but it is something. We used to eat these when we were girls," I smiled, stuffing a handful of berries into my mouth, letting the sweet juice trickle down my throat. We sat there for a while, enjoying the sun, the feel of food on our tongues, forgetting the horrors of the last few days for just a moment.

"We should get moving," Blaise suggested. "I would feel better putting more distance between us and the caves before nightfall."

I stood, wiping my hands on my leather breeches, the dark juice of the berries mixing with the splatters of blood. Blaise looked at me up and down and started to laugh, not the mirthless and biting sound I had been accustomed to, but a real laugh from deep in his throat.

"You look absolutely terrible," he told me, shaking with humor.

I felt my own laughter bubble up in my throat. "You should see yourself."

"Not quite the dashing vision of your dreams?" he asked.

I felt my cheeks flush deep crimson and I looked away from him. In the time that we had been trapped in the tunnels we had foregone all sense of dignity and modesty, but nothing had embarrassed me quite as much as the idea that he knew I had dreamt of him. He was only teasing, of course, but I still could not help but feel that he knew it was true.

He whistled for the dog, and when it didn't return we started walking, knowing it could easily follow our scent and find us. We walked as far as we could before neither of us had the strength to go further. A tiny stream trickled down and snaked through the tall grass, and there were small groves of trees that would provide some shelter and, if we were lucky, some food, for wild mushrooms often grew in the shade of trees. It was not the worst place to camp.

I washed myself as best I could in the cold trickle of water, scrubbing fervently at the blood and grey flesh that still crusted the side of my face. Blaise did the same, a bit downstream from me, but it was mostly a futile effort and I wondered if I would ever again feel clean. The cut on my hand was red and angry and I gathered a handful of yarrow leaves to crush in my fist, making a poultice and hoping that would suffice. As the sun settled into the horizon I whispered to the ground and soft moss sprung up at my command, making a bed beneath the trees. Then I carved out a shallow bowl for a fire, my fingers trembling with the effort.

"You have done enough," Blaise said, noticing the trembling. He broke off a few low branches and tossed them in the pit, igniting them with a snap of the flint. I sat on the makeshift moss bed, holding my hands out to the fire to warm them. I heard a sound behind me and whipped around to see the dog trotting up to us, a squirrel carcass hanging from its mangled jaws. It dropped the dead animal unceremoniously at Blaise's feet and stared up at him expectantly with its one good eye. Blaise looked around and found a splintered piece of wood, dipping the sharp end of it in the fire to harden it and using it to crudely dress the dog's kill. My mouth salivated as the meat was cooked, the ugly dog laying on the moss beside me while I stroked its scar-pocked fur.

We sat, grinning at each other over the firelight, tearing into the meat with feral hunger. The warmth of it nestled comfortingly in the pit of my stomach and I plucked wild mushrooms from beneath the cool shade of the tree, adding to our meal. Afterwards we lay back on the mossy bed, the dog between us, curled so that his nose was tucked under his bushy tail. Night had fallen and the stars twinkled through the tree limbs.

"Do you think the others are alive? Akrin and your men? The cavalry?" I asked Blaise.

He sighed heavily. "I hope so. Akrin is not particularly clever, but he is a good soldier. He would have known to fall back and regroup. We can only hope that they made it back to meet your legion."

A thousand possibilities raced through my mind. I hated that I was not there, that I had no control over what was happening. Had the legion marched into the north to find me? Had they defeated the blooddrinkers? Had they all been killed? Would we find them out here in the wilderness, struggling to survive and get back home like we were?

And then there was the thing that had been trapped in the wall. Who was she? Was she the halfbreed of the legends? Was she trapped again, enclosed in another tomb that I had created for her? There were too many questions and I had no way to know the answers. We had expected some of the Fomori to come after us in the tunnels, but none had. It was possible they were all too busy trying to free that thing from the cavern I had trapped her in, and I shuddered to think what she would do if she escaped.

"What do we do now?" I whispered.

"Keep moving south. I know a place where we can find help, if we are where I think we are. We can reach it by the end of day tomorrow." He shoved a hand through his red curls, his brows drawn together, then he let his easy grin spread across his face and said, "The first thing I will do when we return is have a warm bath."

"Ohhhh," I murmured longingly. "The hot springs of Kymir will be glorious. After that, I shall eat a thousand pastries."

He chuckled. "You will have to fight the boy for them. I heard he is quite fond of Kymir's pastries."

I felt my mood sour at the mention of my sister's child. "I do not know what to do with Kaeleb. Do you know that Cossiana suggested that I get rid of him? She said the Tahitian Samains say that there is an evil halfbreed Fomori who will awaken to destroy the world and that Kaeleb will help her do it. If that is who we awakened in the cavern..."

"You cannot listen to such nonsense," Blaise said, lifting himself onto his elbow to stare at me over the sleeping dog. His amber eyes were burning with intensity. "You cannot kill her child; he is all that is left of her."

I let out a bitter laugh, hating the way my stomach twisted at the sound of his voice when he spoke of my sister. "I always thought you would have wanted him dead more than anyone."

"He is a child, a boy, he did not choose this life, or to be born into it, and he should not be punished for it," he said, his voice quiet but adamant. "Promise me you will not harm him, Maialen, no matter what prophecies or wild tales the Tahitians tell."

I was quiet, part of me angry at him for still caring about Orabelle and her child, and part of me angry at myself for caring about him. I was being foolish. I did not know then that Blaise was thinking of his brother, of the sweet, innocent child that his mother had sacrificed for her own ambition, to ease the burden of his existence. The silence seemed to stretch forever between us and I felt as if I were across an ocean from him, instead of just a mere arm's length away.

He laid back down, settling his head on his folded hands and surprising me by saying, "Do you know what I miss? Festivals."

"Really? I thought you hated the festivals! You never came, not after Queen's End..."

"That was only because I did not like all of you, not because I did not like the festivals," he admitted ruefully.

"Then perhaps you should attend the Solstice in Kymir this summer season. It has been a long time since I have danced, it would be nice to do so again," I admitted, thinking of the old days, when there had been so much music and laughter, when I had looked joyously to the future, believing that only happiness lay in store for me.

"Are you asking me to dance with you at your festival, in sight of all the realms and their regents?" he teased.

I almost said aloud the dark thought, *if we live that long*, but I swallowed it back and simply smiled, trying not to think too much of what the future held. I scooted closer to the dog, wrapping around him for warmth, my hand brushing against Blaise's chest. He turned to look at me and I felt my heartbeat quicken at the look in his eyes.

"You are not what I expected you to be, all those years ago when we still danced at festivals," he said quietly. I let my hand travel over the muscles of his shoulder, feeling his strength beneath my fingertips. He reached up to take my hand, holding it in his warm grip. Then he abruptly let go and I looked away, once again blushing furiously and withdrawing my hand. We stayed that way throughout the night, close enough to hear each other's breath but with that ocean of space still somehow between us.

19

Logaire stood facing the throne, her eyes shining with triumph. She was beautiful, dazzling in a spectacular gown of gold, a cascade of rubies hanging from her neck, their blood-red facets dancing in the torchlight. Her copper hair was pulled back from her face with a gold circlet and she smiled, her full lips parting as she ran her hands over the obsidian arms of the gaudy throne.

Behind her was a gathering of Verucans she had summoned to the castle that included the most important and influential regents, the most revered commanders that had not been marched to the north, and, of course, all of those whose allegiance she knew she could count on. The time had finally come. Her cousin had disappeared in the north, captured by the Fomori and most likely dead. She felt twinges of regret creeping over her but she pushed them down, refusing to feel responsible for Maialen, who had been nothing more than an unwitting pawn caught in the crossfire of her ambition. Whatever happened to the Earth Queen, she had made her own choices. It was her idea to begin that fiasco in the north, she should have known there was no way it would end well. Logaire had tried to warn her but Maialen had refused to listen, so she would not waste any more time feeling sorry for the naive Queen. What mattered now was not what had happened in the north, but that there was no one left to stand in Logaire's way, no one left for her to coddle and bow to.

"Thank you for coming at my humble request," she said, turning to face the curious crowd. Some of them knew why they were there, and others waited impatiently to find out. "There has been word from the north. The army has taken heavy losses and are retreating back to Veruca, but the King has gone missing."

The room rumbled with surprised exclamations and shouted questions. Logaire lifted her hands in a pacifying gesture, calling for them to quiet down.

"This is a dark time for our kingdom, and a dark time for Imbria. We have no idea what has become of the Fire Opal or the King, and now there are two amulets missing. Amulets whose power can destroy kingdoms. We must keep Veruca safe before all else," she paused for dramatic effect, staring around the room with her chin held high. A few were nodding in agreement and she went on. "I have come here not to rile your fears or to create a panic, but to bring you a solution. I now possess the Warding Stone."

There was an uproar and once again she lifted her hands, urging patience.

"The gods created the Warding Stones to protect people from the power of the Keepers," she went on, her purring voice thick with influence. "They saw that an unfair balance had been created, and now we have a way to correct that balance. I promise that I will use the Stone to protect Veruca, to put Veruca before all else, to make us the most powerful kingdom in the four realms! We have bent the knee to the others for too long. I have been forced to serve the Kymirrans, to be a puppet to their Queen, but no longer. They treat us like we are their dogs, tossing us scraps to appease us while the rest of them grow fat off their bounty. Tell me, what would the other realms do without the silver for their swords? Or the metal for their armor? What would the Keepers do without our gold chains to hang their jewels from?"

The gathered crowd roared in response, the soldiers in the room beating their swords against their shields. Logaire thrilled at their enthusiasm, feeling the power, the real power of being a ruler, flow over her. They would worship her.

"Your King went north to fight the Fomori for the glory of Kymir, and for his vendetta against the Samirrans. His judgement is clouded with his emotions, but I can see clearly. I will not send Verucans to die for the other realms. I will bring Veruca into a new age! An age of prosperity and wealth! We will be revered by the other kingdoms, coveted by their people. We will be the beacon of light in these dark times!" She paused again, waiting for the din of their discord to die down. It was time for the final caveat. "All I ask in return is that you pledge your loyalty to me here and now."

She reached back, touching the polished arms of the throne and sliding into it with a smug sense of satisfaction. It was Akrin who had sent word that Blaise was missing, so the little upstart was still alive and she had no doubt he was on his way home to make a bid for the throne. She needed to put an end to his ambitions here and now, to root out those who would be against her if he challenged her place. Besides, Akrin had no business trying to rule, he did not have the gift for it that she did, nor the wits that were required to hold the throne. She pictured his sulking face with his beady, baleful eyes and knew that he would be a cruel ruler, a true tyrant. She could not allow him to have that much control, there was no telling what sick designs he had in mind. She was also quite sure that killing her was one of those designs, for even dimwitted as he was, he knew that she was a threat to him, and he did not seem the sort of man to grant her the mercy of a quick death.

Several of the regents came forward, taking the knee as planned. She had met with them earlier, when she first arrived in Veruca, making sure that they would lead the others to submit. In return she had promised them privileges that the Fire King had long denied them, for they were the ones that had fallen out of his favor years before, and her cousin held a long grudge. Others began to follow suit, whispering to each other and hesitant at first, then more emboldened at the sight of their peers rushing eagerly to her side. She smiled. It was working perfectly.

One man turned on his heel and stomped out of the room and she made a miniscule motion with her finger, the unassuming scribe in the corner taking note. Several others followed after and she felt her smile slipping but she forced it to stay in place. She had known there would be opposition, it was not unexpected, though each body that passed through the doorway grated on her nerves.

When it was done she presided over her room of loyal subjects, inwardly gloating at her triumph. She had the strength and the numbers that she needed; she could hold the throne. She thanked them for their loyalty, giving them another stirring speech about the greatness of Veruca, then she excused herself, flicking her wrist at the scribe so that he rushed after her.

"This is all of them?" she asked him, fingering the parchment he held in his hands.

"Yes, everyone who did not submit," he assured, passing the list to her. She took it from him and dismissed him, continuing on towards the tower, hurrying up the spiraling steps and cursing her cousin for not holding his prisoners in a dungeon like everyone else.

She unlocked the door at the top of the stairs and threw it open, panting with the exertion of her climb, and looking at the bemused and grizzled face of the old Guardian, Magnus.

"So, you have done it?" he asked.

"No thanks to you, you old goat," she answered, still trying to catch her breath. "But now that I have done my part it is your turn."

She remembered sitting across from Magnus the last time they had been in Veruca, sipping wine and sharing their frustrations while Blaise and Maialen dined together in another room. Logaire had laughed heartily at Magnus's impersonation of the ineffectual Samirran King, fanning herself to calm the flush of humor that stained her cheeks.

"We could do things so much better than they have done," she said, clinking her goblet against his, acting as if the words were merely a jest, even though it was a jest that was treason and could cost them their lives.

"You think so?" Magnus had asked, raising his grey brows and leaning back to assess her. She noticed again that he never looked at her with lust or greed, the way that most men did, but merely regarded her as an equal.

"Anyone could do better than Astraeus," she had smirked.

"Ah, well, I cannot argue with that," the old Guardian conceded. "It is difficult to be Samirran in times like these. Difficult to watch your beloved kingdom crumbling, knowing there are better men for the task, but unable to act."

"But what if you could act?" Logaire had whispered, leaning close to him.

"How do you know I haven't tried?" he countered and it was her turn to raise her perfectly arched brows.

"My, my, Magnus, you are a man of surprises. Perhaps the problem we have both faced is that we have been going it alone."

He seemed genuinely interested, his gaze sharpening as he bent his wiry frame towards her conspiratorially. "Are you suggesting a partnership?"

She laughed, pulling out a small cloth packet of herbs she had tucked into the bosom of her gown. "I am afraid what I had in mind won't be so pleasant for you."

"Planning to poison me, Logaire?"

"Not hardly, just a little something to make you unfit to travel. You are more useful here in Veruca," she said, tossing the herbal concoction onto the table between them. "And do not worry, I have the Earth Queen's permission. She has also assured me that she will ask Blaise not to kill you while you are here."

Magnus sat back and eyed her appreciatively. She was like a viper, always plotting and scheming a way to swallow her prey. She would make a good ally, if he made sure that their interests continued to be aligned.

They had stayed up late into the night making plans, and Logaire had known it was a gamble but she had decided to take a risk and trust him, just as she was trusting him now and releasing him from the tower. She handed him the parchment the scribe had given her, scrawled with a list of names. He glanced over it, stroking his long, grey beard. "More than I expected."

"They will soon learn the error of their choice. We need it finished before Akrin returns and rallies more to his side. There must be no challenge to my succession to the throne. I do not wish to waste years fighting a civil war amongst my own people, not when I am trying to save them from the disaster that his reign would be."

"And you are sure that Blaise is dead?" Magnus questioned. The last thing they needed was the Fire Keeper returning in a rage to find his throne occupied by another.

Logaire shrugged her shoulders. "He is missing, the Fomori were seen taking him. Surely they would not have let him live."

Magnus shook his head. "I would feel better if we had his body. What does Maialen say about all of this?"

Logaire hesitated, once again feeling a wave of guilt and once again shoving it away. Magnus did not strike her as the sentimental type. He was, after all, trying to have his own King in Samirra assassinated, and she hoped that he harbored no ridiculous sense of duty or paternal affection for the Earth Queen. Logaire preferred to keep his loyalty to her own cause unshaken.

"She has also gone missing, taken with Blaise. I did not share this with the assembly. There is enough chaos right now and I did not want to create a panic among the regents. Two missing amulets is bad enough, but I can balance that with the Warding Stone. Three missing amulets is a much bigger problem, especially when the only remaining one belongs to the Air Keeper and he cannot even blow over a dandelion with it. It is more important than ever that we make sure that Veruca is united."

To her relief, Magnus seemed unperturbed and he continued to stroke his beard thoughtfully. "We are lucky that the full-blooded Fomori cannot wield the amulets. Losing the two Keepers in the north could be a blessing in disguise. As for Astraeus, he will not be a problem for much longer. Once your place here is secure, I will go to Samirra and take care of him once and for all, and make sure that Favian takes the amulet. He is the only one who we can trust to do what is best for Samirra."

Logaire felt another thrill of exultant satisfaction as Magnus moved past her, taking the list with him. She called down the steps after him, "Enjoy your freedom, old man!"

His chuckle floated back to her as he continued on and she took a moment to savor her victory. Tonight, Magnus would make sure that anyone who had refused to acknowledge her would be dead by morning. It would be a bloody night in Veruca, but it was a better than a drawn-out conflict of Verucans fighting each other over divided loyalties. It was not her fault they had chosen the wrong side.

She smoothed her hair down and started back down the stairway after Magnus. She would need to settle things with Thyrr soon, before he did anything foolish. She wanted Lehar as her ally, and if Magnus was successful in his little coup in Samirra, then she would also have Favian on her side. The only variable that she had not accounted for was Kymir. She was not expecting Maialen to go missing and she wondered again what those idiot cavalry men of hers had been doing to let the Queen actually join a battle with the Fomori and get captured. Now Logaire would have to decide what could be done about the Earth Queen's realm. Logaire knew Kymir better than anyone, she was the obvious choice to take control, and Kymir shared a border with Veruca. It would not be difficult for her to rule them both. She wondered just what she would need to do to convince Thyrr and Favian. She had some ideas for Thyrr, but the Samirran Guardian would be more of a challenge. She had often wondered if Magnus's unfettered insistence that Favian should take over after Astraeus was because perhaps there were stronger feelings than friendship between the two of them.

Logaire crossed back into the throne room, the torches flickering over the now empty space and making her gown shimmer like molten gold. She slid into the monstrous chair, luxuriating in the feel of it. She had been born to rule, and it was finally her time. Now she just had to sit back and wait for Akrin to show up, so she could promptly remove his head.

20

We had been walking for an eternity. My mouth was thick and parched with thirst and my stomach groaned in protest of its empty state of being, the mushrooms we had for breakfast long gone. The dog trotted beside me, but he had not bestowed any more gifts of nourishment upon us.

"We are almost there," Blaise said, aware of my state of abject misery. He seemed to have an unending well of strength and I was pushing myself to my limits to keep up with him. He had told me there was a cabin out here, a remote place whose inhabitant did not care to be bothered and wanted to remain as far away from people as possible. He had said it was nearby but that had been hours ago and I was starting to doubt that he knew the meaning of that word, for I had a very different idea as to what nearby meant.

"Who would choose to live out here?" I muttered, though I supposed I should be grateful that someone did, otherwise I did not know how we would make it further. The trees soared around us, evergreens mingled with beech and maples, and beneath their limbs the forest floor was cloaked in new, green growth. I tried to help clear a path for us, moving aside the worst tangles of brush and thorns, but I was still too weak to use my Element very effectively and we moved at a plodding pace.

"He would," Blaise said softly, stopping. I whipped my head up and found myself gaping at the giant woodsman that had once been my Guardian. Gideon.

"Do not come any further," Gideon warned, brandishing an axe in his good hand while the other arm still hung limply by his side. His beard was longer and thicker, so was his hair which was tied back from his face, and there were creases around his eyes that I did not recall being there. He was still huge and imposing, and there was nothing friendly or welcoming in his face. He was wearing simple, homespun clothing with a leather coat, the collar trimmed in fur and a tiny yellow flower tucked in one of the laces of his tunic.

"Gideon!" I exclaimed, thinking he must not recognize me in my disheveled state. "It's me, Maialen."

"I know who you are, and I know who he is. You think I could forget any of you? What are you doing here?" he asked with wary distrust. I felt his words like a dagger to my heart. Gideon. My best friend, my confidant, my fiercest protector, a man I had grieved the loss of for ten years, and he acted like I was his enemy.

Blaise spread his hands out showing he was unarmed. "We were fighting the Fomori in the north and we were separated from our people. We have been walking for days. All we ask is food and water, shelter for one night, then we will leave you alone and never return."

I still could not wrap my mind around what was happening, that it was really Gideon who stood there, eyeing us distrustfully.

"You knew he was here," I said to Blaise, unable to help the hurt that colored my voice. "You knew and you never told me? Why? How?"

"Leverage," he answered with a frown, still keeping his gaze fixed on Gideon as if he expected the brawny woodsmen to hurl the axe at him at any second.

"Leverage against what?" I demanded.

"Against you."

Gideon interrupted us with a disgusted grunt. "I see nothing has changed. You are the same as you always were. Go, leave here now, and do not come back."

"Gideon, please," I pleaded. "Please, we need help. If you ever cared about me, then help me now."

I saw the emotions marching across his face as he hesitated, struggling with the decision. Tears slid down my cheeks and he sighed heavily at the sight of them, turning and motioning for us to follow. I hurried after him, the dog letting out an excited yip, and Blaise trailing after us, not entirely trusting our welcome.

Gideon meandered through the forest till we came upon a clearing. In it was nestled a cozy cabin, built of rough timber and topped with a thatched roof, encircled with beds of herbs and wildflowers. Another, smaller structure was near the main cabin, a stack of firewood leaning against the doorframe and the smell of smoked meat wafting from inside. Across the clearing was a rather haphazard looking barn with a mule sticking his head out of the open doorway, munching lazily on fresh clover. A few pieces of clothing were hung over branches to dry, and I could hear the gurgle of a river nearby. I noticed some of the clothing was tiny, much too small for a grown man to wear.

"Do you have a child?" I asked. He stopped and followed my gaze to where the small tunic hung, frowning beneath his thick, brown beard.

"Papa! A dog!" As if in answer, a child came tearing out of the cabin, practically throwing themselves on the dog who howled in indignation, trying unsuccessfully to shake himself free. I was startled, wondering how the child was not afraid of the beast and his mangled visage, but they seemed unbothered by it and continued to nuzzle their face into the soft fur of his neck, making delighted sounds of affection. Gideon grabbed the small hand and dislodged it from the tuft of fur, pulling the child to his side. It was a girl, her hair covered in a bonnet and a chain of yellow flowers around her neck to match the one Gideon wore. She buried her face in his leg, not looking up at us, but still reaching out her hand, blindly beckoning the dog who refused to be enticed closer to her.

"Go inside, Eolande," Gideon ordered her. She made a disappointed sound that was muffled against his pant leg and turned, fleeing into the cabin in a blur. Blaise stared after her with such acute intensity that I was slightly unsettled and wondered what it was that had disturbed him so much about the precocious child.

"Is your wife here too?" Blaise asked Gideon, shaking off whatever had bothered him and displaying his easy smile.

"My wife is dead," Gideon said bluntly. "You can sleep in there with the mule, that is the best that I can offer. I will bring you food and some fresh clothes and you can bathe in the stream, but I want you gone by tomorrow. And stay away from my daughter."

With that he spun on his heel and marched into the cabin after the child, slamming the door soundly behind him.

"I don't think he was happy to see us," Blaise said with a shallow laugh.

"Can you blame him?" I muttered, still feeling the sting of his rejection. I had imagined finding Gideon so many times, and I had always prophesied a happy reunion, full of joy and warm embraces. I had certainly never imagined the cold reception and begrudging offer of shelter that we had been given. "Perhaps if I could just talk to him-"

"No, Maialen," Blaise interrupted me. "Let him be."

We stood waiting until Gideon came storming back out of the cabin, practically throwing a pile of clothes at me.

"They were Filomene's. My wife. They should fit you," he said, then glared at Blaise. "I have nothing for you."

He once again stomped away and we followed the path down the edge of the river where it flowed over the tumbled rocks in tiny waterfalls. Blaise threw off his leather armor and tugged his black tunic over his head and I spun away, my face flushing scarlet. I heard him chuckle and then there was a splash of water as he dove into the deepest part.

"It is quite cold, Earth Queen, perhaps you should come and warm me up," Blaise called, apparently enjoying my discomfort thoroughly. I snuck a glance back and saw the tanned lines of his chest and torso, water dripping down him and his red hair was plastered around his face. The Fire Opal shone like a glistening wound against his skin.

"I would rather freeze to death myself!" I retorted back, clutching the pile of fabric Gideon had handed me close to my chest and hurrying downstream, away from him. I heard his laughter trailing after me until I found a copse of shrubs that obscured him from my sight and I set about carefully peeling off my own layers of filthy clothing. I hurried into the water, stealing sideways looks to make sure that he could not see me, gasping at the icy chill of the river against my bare skin. I reached down to the riverbed beneath my feet, pushing aside the worn stones and grabbing a handful of sand to scrub myself with. I did not think that I would ever feel clean again, but I practically scrubbed myself raw trying.

I came out shivering and hurriedly pulled on the simple frock that Gideon had given me, a long-sleeved gown of buttery yellow with no adornments save one deep pocket in the front. It was a tiny bit snug across my hips but it smelled of fresh herbs and was not crusted in dried Fomori blood, so I was quite pleased to have it. I walked back towards where

Blaise had been, shivering and wringing the water out of my hair. He was kneeling on the riverbank, warming himself over a small fire, completely naked.

"Must you be like this?" I cried in exasperation, turning away once again.

"I had to wash my clothes. They are not dry yet," he said, and I could hear the amusement in his voice. I stormed past him, refusing to look his way, and followed the path back up to the barn.

"Seff!" I cried out in shock, seeing the bland countenance of the man I had left for dead leaning against the barn, scratching the dog behind the gnarled stumps of its ears. There was not a mark on him and I just stood there, gaping at him, not knowing what to do or say. How did one begin a conversation after what we had been through? *So sorry that I left you to die in a room full of carnivorous beasts and their ancient evil mother that we awakened from centuries of imprisonment.*

"He is not pleased we are here," Seff informed me with a wave at the cabin where I could hear an infuriated Gideon banging and slamming things around.

"Er.. no... he was my Guardian before, a long time ago, and I don't think he wanted to be found. Not by us anyway," I answered sadly, still feeling the sharp pain of the reunion deep in my chest. "Seff, how did you get here? How did you find us? How did you escape? Did that thing get out?"

He looked uncomfortable and stared down at the dog who was panting happily, its long tongue lolling out of the side of its mouth. "I do not know, I just woke up in the woods."

I wanted to scream or throw a rock at him but instead I just stood there, my mouth gaping open once again. "How do you not know?"

Seff shrugged. "I was in the woods. I came back for the dog."

I felt frustration bubbling up in me like a cauldron, and I grabbed my amulet, letting the calm energy flow through me.

Blaise came sauntering up the path just then, thankfully with his clothes on, and he lifted one of his auburn brows at the sight of the other man.

"I did not expect to see you again," he commented with an offhand flippancy, but I could see the glint in his eye and his wary glance around the clearing.

"I did not lead them here. I was not followed," Seff told him, for he also noticed the wary glance.

"How could you possibly know that?" I exploded in frustration, so loudly that the mule flicked its ears and lifted its head to see what the commotion was. "You do not even know how you got here! You just magically showed up in the woods, right where we happened to be!"

"Maialen, calm down-" Blaise began and I turned on him.

"Do not tell me to be calm! I have been perfectly calm but I am sick to death of all of this! No one ever tells me anything! You knew where Gideon was this whole time and instead of telling me you hoarded that knowledge away in case you could use it against me one day! And now this one shows up here out of nowhere and you will not tell me what happened either! I am tired of always being kept in the dark! I am not a child, I am a Keeper!" I was practically shouting by the time I had finished ranting at them and they were both staring at me with wide eyes, a smile creeping at the corners of Blaise's lips.

I shoved open the barn door, the startled mule scurrying out of my way, slamming it shut behind me before the tears started to fall. The last thing I needed was for them to see me cry. They already thought I was weak, too weak to ever know the truth about anything. Too naive to ever be trusted. I thought of Orabelle then, how she had kept so many things from me too. No one had treated her this way, they had respected her power, feared it even. She had been selfish and stubborn and reckless and everyone had revered her for it. It was not fair and I once again felt the hot torrent of hatred towards her flow through me. I clenched my fists and breathed in, willing it to pass, hating myself as much as I hated her for deep down I knew that she had loved me, but her love had not been enough to save me from hating her.

I heard the muffled voices of the men outside but I stayed where I was, trying to make the tears stop raining down my cheeks. The door opened and Blaise entered, lifting his hands in a gesture of surrender against my anger. "Seff declined to stay in our lovely barn and says he will sleep in the woods with the dog. Most likely to avoid being trapped anywhere else with us and I can't say I blame him. Gideon gave him some smoked meat and he brought food for us as well. It is right outside. I can bring it in here but the smell is not very appetizing."

I couldn't help but laugh, a small, hiccupping sound amongst my tears, which I was hastily trying to wipe away. "It smells like a goat but there are no goats."

"Perhaps there was at the beginning of winter," Blaise said with a grimace of sympathy for the departed goats. I followed him back outside and there were two wooden bowls sitting on a rock, filled with steaming liquid. The mule was eyeing them curiously and Blaise shooed him away, folding himself down onto the patch of clover and gesturing gallantly for me to join him. The sun was getting low, hanging like a heavy red orb over the treetops that encircled us. I sat down, taking the bowl he had passed and sipping the rich stew. I closed my eyes in pleasure, the anger and frustration flowing out of me as I savored the delicious meal.

The pluck of a lyre floated across the evening air from the window of the cabin where a muslin curtain fluttered gently in the breeze. I stopped, my breath catching in my throat at the sound. It was a tone that was as familiar to me as the sound of my own voice. Gideon had always loved to play and I used to listen to him for hours. Even though he hated me, it warmed my heart to know that he still played the stringed instrument.

Suddenly a wash of guilt crashed over me and as I looked around at the simple, idyllic life he had created for himself, I understood why he did not want us here. He had found something beautiful, carved out a tiny piece of happiness for himself and his child, way out here, away from all of us and the ugly tragedies that our lives had become.

The notes floated out and his deep baritone rumbled gently along with them, a sweet, sad song with an aching melody. I finished the stew and set the bowl aside and Blaise stood, reaching for my hand. I looked up at him, confused.

"You promised me a dance, Maialen," he said with his easy grin.

I hesitated and for a moment in my mind it was Blaise as I had known him all those years before. The callous and dangerous man who would do anything to get what he wanted, the man who had known where to find Gideon and never told me. The man who had started a war over my sister. Then I saw him in the glow of the battle fires telling me to run, willing to sacrifice himself to save me. I saw him in the cave with the Fomori when he had grabbed my hand and pulled me out, and in the tunnels when he was weak and starving and used the last of his strength to keep me warm while he shivered through the night. I saw him in the sunshine laughing, in the forest laying on the moss next to me, by the river teasing me. I saw him and I took his hand, allowing him to help me stand, staring up at his amber eyes and the strong planes of his face and feeling like I would never breathe again. He wrapped his other arm around my waist and pulled me against him, spinning me in a slow circle while the solemn song enveloped us. My heart was pounding in my chest and I wondered if he could feel it, the way I felt his warm breath on my cheek. His eyes were bright and fixed on mine, his jaw stern despite the casual smirk. I felt his fingers splay against my back and my breath quickened. From the cabin the high-pitched soprano of the child wove itself into the song, innocent and clear and bright. It was beautiful, the way they sang together and as the song ended I found myself wishing we could stay there in the forest with them forever, just living, everything else a distant memory.

We stopped moving in the silence that followed, still holding each other, neither of us wanting to shatter the moment. I started to pull away and he released me then seemed to change his mind, pulling me back with a shake of his head, his hands holding my face and his lips warm against mine as he kissed me. I felt like I had never been kissed before in my life, and I never had, not in that way. It was as if he were suddenly everything, that nothing existed outside of him and nothing mattered but the feel of him against me. I could feel the hot edge of his power, the strength of him, the intensity, and I wanted to lose myself in it.

He finally stepped back and his release was like a rush of cold air. A chill danced over my skin and I shivered in the cool night as he took my hand and led me inside the barn, finding a soft pile of hay and pulling me down beside him. He tucked his arm around me, holding me close, but hesitating. Moonlight slanted in through the cracks in the barn, silhouetting him in a silver glow.

"Maialen, I can't be what you want me to be," he said, his voice soft but warning. Logaire had been right, at least he would not lie to me.

"All I want is for someone to see me," I whispered back, feeling my face flush at the confession.

He chuckled, running his finger along the edge of my lips before he kissed me again. "I see you, Earth Queen."

21

When I first opened my eyes I thought the night before had been a dream, that I had imagined it all as I slept. Then it came rushing back to me, the exquisite memory of him, too poignant to have been imagined. I lifted myself on my elbow, reaching for my gown as the night air danced across my bare skin. There was a scraping noise and the muffled sounds of movement next to me and I pulled the gown over my head and squinted into the darkness, trying to use the last shred of moonlight to see, thinking with a sinking feeling in my stomach that it was Blaise, filled with regret and trying to get away from me.

In the darkness I saw a large, blurred shape rolling across the floor of the barn and I then wondered if Blaise was having some kind of nightmare, though until now he had slept peacefully still and serene every night.

"Maialen!" the strangled cry broke the stillness of the night just as a shower of sparks flung across the room, briefly illuminating the brawny figure of Gideon, his axe buried deep in the dirt floor where Blaise had been sleeping and his hands around the Fire King's neck. Blaise was naked, and there was blood from a gash on his forearm that had smeared across his torso. He must have rolled out of the way just as Gideon had tried to bring down the axe.

I jumped up and shoved at Gideon and he flung me aside like a ragdoll, sending me sprawling in the dirt. Blaise took advantage of his momentary distraction to deliver a sharp blow to the underside of his chin, his other hand jabbing at the woodsman's ribs.

"I'm not going to hurt her!" Blaise croaked, turning his body and tucking his leg so that his foot could shove into Gideon's hip, pushing him back and breaking the hold on his neck.

"I know what you are! You will destroy her!" Gideon was seething, his gentle face set in grim, determined lines.

"Gideon, he saved my life!" I yelled out, pleading with him to stop. He ignored me, still grappling with Blaise who was able to roll aside, twisting out from under him and causing Gideon to collapse onto the hard dirt. The woodsman grunted in frustration and swung his huge fist, hitting Blaise on the side of the head twice and sending blood splattering across the room. The Fire Keeper rolled onto his back, stunned from the blows, and tried to get up but Gideon was faster, jumping to his feet and wrenching the axe from the ground. He stood over Blaise and lifted the weapon.

"I don't want to hurt her," Blaise was repeating, struggling to clear his head. "I want to protect her."

"You are all poison," Gideon spat out. "You poison everything you touch. You should not have come here."

He started to swing the weapon and I screamed, the earth buckling underneath him and throwing him backwards. He stumbled, trying to regain his footing on the shifting ground before he toppled forward, and the weight of him hitting the dirt reverberated through the room. I waited, eyes wide with horror, the shifting ground settling in the eerie stillness that followed.

"Gideon?" I whispered when he did not move. "Gideon!"

Blaise had gotten to his feet, one hand pressed to his ribs, and he bent over the brawny figure, pushing Gideon's head to the side to feel along his neck. He sighed heavily and said, "He is dead. He fell on the axe."

I felt like the ground had melted away beneath me and I was falling, falling forever, into a bottomless abyss of sorrow that I would never reach the end of. A wail escaped my mouth and I bit down on my fist to quiet myself, thinking of the little girl who slept not too far away. I stared at the back of Gideon's body in shock. My Guardian, my friend, my champion, the man who would have given his life for me, the man who sang songs with his daughter, and who only wanted to be left alone. I had just killed him.

"What have I done? What have I done?" I kept repeating in a hoarse whisper.

Blaise winced as he pulled on his clothes, still favoring his right side. I realized it was the same place as the old wound my sister had inflicted upon him when she had stabbed him on the battlefield in Veruca. Gideon was right, we were poison. Look at the things we did to each other. He would have been better off had he never met any of us, if he had turned away from the contest that day, if his horse had stumbled and gone lame and he had missed the tournament that had made him my Guardian.

I kept seeing that day in my mind, for that was the pivotal moment that had changed everything for him. It had been the Solstice Festival, and my father had thrown a lavish celebration that year. My mother was dead by then, and Chronus had named me as his future successor. I remembered the feel of the sun on my skin, dappling through the trees to scatter amongst the freckles that charmed my face. Bright colored ribbons were draped among the trees and children ran beneath them, twirling and spinning with glee. Orabelle was there, glaring rebelliously at everyone with pale eyes while her Guardian, Tal, stood proud and silent beside her. I had been so excited to choose my own Guardian, for it was a rite of passage to me. Having a Guardian solidified the fact that soon I would be Queen of my beloved Kymir, the best Queen that had ever ruled the forested realm. I still believed in the fairy tales then, in the happiness that I had been promised all my life by my father. I remembered when Gideon had walked into the arena, his huge woodsman's axe held almost gingerly by his side.

"I like this one," Orabelle had leaned over to say in my ear, her smile pulling at the corners of her lips. "He has kind eyes."

"He has a reputation as a skilled fighter," Tal added with a nod of approval.

Gideon had won every round easily. No one was able to even come close to defeating him. He had been so young then, his beard not quite full and his hair worn long and loose, and his eyes were clear and warm. He had smiled, sweetly and a little shyly, glancing around at the cheering crowd of spectators, as if not quite believing that they cheered for him. I could not get the image of that sweet smile out of my head. I could not help but compare it to the grimace that death had preserved forever on his face. We had broken him, stolen the innocent smile from the boy that he had been, and I knew I would never forgive myself for it.

"Maialen," Blaise said, his voice steady and even. "It was an accident, he fell."

I shook my head, my guilt and grief too much to bear, my face wet with tears. "No, I did this. I did this to him and he was only trying to protect me."

"We need to find the child, to stop her from coming in here. I can burn the barn-"

"No!" I shrieked at him. "No, you will not burn him! He is... he was my Guardian. He deserves a proper burial. His daughter deserves to say goodbye."

He shoved his hand through his red curls and paced the floor for a moment, thinking, then he marched out of the barn and straight for the cabin. I stumbled after him in confusion.

Was he going to tell the child what had happened? I heard him moving through the small rooms and I stopped on the threshold, unable to force myself to go inside. How could I go in and look upon the life that I had just taken away from them both? How could I see the places where they had smiled and laughed and loved each other? I could not bear it. I spun away from the door, collapsing to the ground and feeling my whole body tremble with the shock of what I had done.

"She is not here," Blaise muttered, coming back outside, his frown deepening as he scanned the tree line around us. There was a soft whine and I saw the single gleaming eye of the dog in the forest, the little girl pressing her face into his soft neck and making whimpering sounds. Seff stood beside her, watching us, one of his knives in his hand.

"She is coming with us. He did not want you to have her," Seff told us, an edge of warning in the words.

I wanted to say something, to stop them, to make it better, to take back what I had done, to bring Gideon back to us all, but I couldn't. All I could do was sit there with my hands in the dirt, sobbing, feeling as if I were being ripped apart from the inside out. Blaise took a step towards them and Seff flung the knife, not at the Fire King, but at me, the blade slicing through the night and impaling itself in my hand where it lay outstretched on the ground. I cried out in pain and Blaise hesitated for just a moment, his gaze flicking between us, then he ran over to me, jerking the knife out and grabbing a piece of my skirt to try and staunch the wound. When we looked up they were gone.

"Come inside, we need to find something clean to dress it."

I shook my head. "No, I can't. I can't go in there. Just burn it. Burn the wound and burn the house. Burn all of it."

The child was gone, there was no need for a burial and I could not face what I had done for one more second. I wanted it gone, gone from my sight, gone from existence. He took my hand in his and unwound the butter-colored scrap of skirt, dropping it in the dirt.

"Burn it!" I yelled when he hesitated once again. However much it hurt, I deserved that and worse. He turned my hand over and sparks of flame danced over the skin, cauterizing the puncture. I howled in pain and with the wild abandon of grief. In the woods I heard another howl echo to match mine, acknowledging my pain, telling me that it understood, and somehow I found that sound from the mongrel dog more comforting than any words that Blaise could have uttered.

Moments later we stood side by side at the edge of the clearing and watched as the red tongues of flame demolished everything we had come near, Gideon's words repeating over and over in my head. *You poison everything you touch.* We stood there until it was nothing but ash and smoke and memories, and then we began to walk, neither of us saying a word for there were no words to say that could make it better.

22

Favian lifted his hand to shade his eyes, peering out at the horizon as if seeing what was coming would make a difference. It did not matter if he could see them, nor would it matter if he knew when the inevitable onslaught would begin. The scouts had reported thousands of Fomori flooding towards Iriellestra, and between the plague and hunger, there weren't nearly enough fighting men and women to hold them off. The walls of the city would keep them out for a while and give the Samirrans a brief defensive advantage, but they would not be able to hold out for long in a city that was already starving. How long would men fight for a kingdom they knew was already lost? Favian tugged on his long braid of dark hair, a nervous gesture he had tried to break the habit of, but he allowed himself to indulge the compulsion in that moment.

"Are there any new reports from the scouts?" Astraeus, King of Samirra, asked from beside him as he squinted into the glare of sun. His perfect visage was so noble, so aristocratic that it was hard to believe that he was as completely inept as he was. "I saw that the eagles have returned. Perhaps the Fomori have changed direction?"

Favian sighed heavily, not bothering to try and hide his exhaustion with his ruler. "Where else would they go? There are thousands of them, an army of beasts, heading straight for us. They would not suddenly turn and take another route."

Astraeus bristled at the response and looked quite displeased, flicking an imaginary piece of lint off of his embroidered coat in agitation. "Then we shall defeat them once and for all and be done with this whole nuisance."

"We barely have enough riders for the scouting eagles, how can we defend the entire city? There are innocent people down there that will be slaughtered," Favian pointed out, wondering just what Astraeus told himself every night so that he could sleep soundly despite his failings as a leader. Maybe Magnus had been right, and he should have taken care of the problem before it had gotten to this. But he had not, and he would have to live with his part in whatever came next.

"Send the eagles to your wife, ask her for help, she will not refuse," Favian suggested.

Astraeus threw up his hands in exasperation. "You have just told me that we do not have enough eagles, now you want me to send them to Kymir? It will leave us defenseless!"

Favian silently counted in his head, a calming ritual that he employed often when dealing with his ruler. *One, two, three, four, five...* When he reached ten he said aloud, "There are not enough riders but there are plenty of eagles. If we send those eagles to Kymir and they come back laden with archers, then we have more resources with which to mount a defense."

"Then do it," Astraeus said crisply before his voice turned petulant. "I cannot believe they are coming here! After everything we did for them, we warned them about the Verucans coming!"

Favian felt guilt settle over him like a dark shroud and he thought again that he should have listened to Magnus. He had been against Astraeus's plan to aid the Fomori, and he had been horrified with the way that it had been carried out. Astus, the King's father, was the one who had planted the idea in his son's head, rattling off on one of his mad rants about an ancient battle and using the sick as weapons. Astraeus had not hesitated for a moment, seeing the disgusting solution as a way to solve several of his problems. Favian had almost left the palace then, but his loyalty to Samirra had stopped him. He was the Guardian, and his ruler was his responsibility. He could not walk away and abandon his kingdom.

"They are the Fomori, they are not our allies and they are certainly not our friends. I warned you not to help them, and not to trust Logaire," Favian could not help but say. He had stayed silent for far too long and was finding it harder and harder to hold his tongue as the army of beasts drew closer. He tugged on his long braid again.

Astraeus waved his hand dismissively, for nothing would ever be his fault. "Then it would be an army of Verucans descending upon us."

"I will dispatch the eagles for Kymir at once," Favian said, refusing to acknowledge the remark. The King was probably right, but at least with the Verucans they would have had the option of diplomacy. Maialen would never have allowed Blaise to wantonly slaughter the Samirrans. He hesitated before adding, "I can send Aracellis with them. He will be safer there."

Astraeus clenched his fists and Favian could see the lines deepen between his brows. "Aracellis is the future King of Samirra. He will not run away at the first sign of danger."

"He is just a child," Favian argued, thinking of the boy's solemn face, so like his father in appearance but thankfully not in mannerism. Aracellis was quiet and contemplative, happiest when his nose was buried in a book. He had none of his father's grandiose and misguided heroism.

"What does that matter? He is my son, he was born into greatness!" Astraeus boasted and Favian once more breathed in slowly and counted to ten.

"His mother will-" the Guardian began but Astraeus rounded on him, his blue eyes flashing.

"I will not have him corrupted by his mother! It is bad enough that he is tainted with their cursed bloodline, the least I can do for him is to limit her influence. She is the one who allowed the Verucans to march here and she is the one to blame for what is happening now! This was all her doing."

Favian just stared at him, wondering how he could not see it, why he refused to see it. It never occurred to the King of Samirra that the downfall of his great kingdom was because of him. It was always someone else. He would never see that what the other Keepers had done was to try to save the dying realm, and that by betraying them he had destroyed their last hope for redemption.

The Guardian tried to remember a time when it had been different, tried to recall some vestige of memory that would allow him to believe that there was still a chance for them, that Astraeus would be the man he should be. Perhaps when his mother, Irielle, had been alive. She had a gentle but firm hand in guiding the King, just as she had done with his father, using wisdom and compassion to decide the best course. After she had died, Astraeus had sunk even worse into his denial of all responsibility. Irielle had died by his hand, because he could not control his Element, but he refused to see it that way. At her lavish funeral, Astraeus had cursed the name of the Leharan Queen and anyone else who had been at the battle of Queen's End. He had never stopped to consider his part in any of it, or the feelings of his young wife who had stood pitifully by his side, her big, green eyes wide with shock and her face pale. He had railed on against her family, not noticing when she winced at his harsh words. Favian recalled her looking over at him, her beautiful doll's face with the smattering of freckles that made her look even more innocent, and her eyes had been so tortured that he thought surely she had been broken inside.

"Are you listening?" Astraeus snapped, jerking the Guardian out of his memory and back to the present.

"I'm sorry, I was just thinking about something," Favian inclined his head in apology. "What were you saying?"

"Be sure that my eagle is ready on the landing at all times. When the Fomori get closer I will take a flight around the city. My people need to see me, it will comfort them."

One. Two. Three. Four.... Favian counted again, focusing on his breathing and praying for patience. What the people needed was a Keeper who could actually use his Element, not a worthless figurehead whose defining trait was his own vanity. "I will see it done."

Astraeus waved a manicured hand at him in dismissal and Favian spun on his heel, making his way through the maze of the palace to the garrison at the inner wall. As he passed through the rooms filled with opulent furnishings and exquisite, ancient tapestries and frescoes, he could not help but feel sick to his stomach with worry. The Samirran palace had stood for centuries, one of the first monuments to the Keepers that had ever been built. It was the beacon of light, the shining, golden monument to the greatness of its rulers, and the Guardian feared that for the first time ever, it would fall.

"Ah, Favian! I have been looking for you," a man came hurrying towards him. Hovard was one of the palace guards and a good man and even better friend. He was a typical Samirran, lean with short dark hair and lake-blue eyes. A dusting of beard coated his chin and he tried to smile but it faltered into a peculiar sort of grimace. He and Favian had once been more than friends, but that brief affair had ended with neither of them holding any ill will towards the other and as a result the

Guardian knew Hovard's particular facial expressions quite well.

"What has happened?" Favian asked immediately, dispensing with formalities and small talk. "Any news from Veruca? Or from Magnus?"

Hovard shook his head, squinting against the bright glare of the sun off the white stone walls that encircled the palace. "Not yet, but we have another problem. The men are deserting. They have heard the Fomori are coming and they are stealing away, taking horses and eagles with them. Between the deserters and the plague..."

Favian cursed heartily and tugged on his long braid of hair. "Post guards, men that you trust, at the stables. We need to send the remaining eagles to Kymir as soon as possible to ask for the Queen's help. If she could send them back with archers then perhaps we will have a chance."

"Have you not heard? Maialen and her legion marched north to help the Verucans."

Favian felt as if the ground was dissolving beneath him, his world teetering on the brink of ruin. The Earth Queen had been his one hope to withstand the Fomori. He had not known that she would be in the north, if he had he would have tried harder to stop what Astraeus had done. He wondered if his King had known she would be there, if that was part of what motivated such a vile attack. Astraeus hated being married to her, perhaps he had seen it as his way out.

"Send the eagles anyway. Damek will surely help us, and he is the only one who she would have trusted Kymir to in her absence," Favian ordered, not really believing that the spidery old advisor would do anything of the sort. Damek hated Astraeus and he hated Samirra. If he sent even a quiver of arrows to aid them, it would be a miraculous occurrence.

Hovard seemed to know what he was thinking but he nodded his head in compliance and they stood there a moment, regarding each other, both wondering if it was for the last time. Favian broke away first, hurrying back to the palace, trying to think how to staunch the flow of deserters. He rounded the corner and almost collided with the stooped figure of Astus. The former king was muttering to himself, twitching his arthritic fingers in agitation. He glared at Favian for being in his way then his face softened and he beamed up at the Guardian.

"Ahhh, my boy!" Astus exclaimed, trying to embrace him.

"No, no, it is me, Favian. I am not Astraeus," the Guardian protested, sidestepping the awkward hug and trying to move past him down the hallway.

"Eh? Favian?" Astus rubbed a hand over his balding pate, causing the remaining whisps of hair to flutter around his head like dragonfly wings. "Do you know what all the commotion is?"

Favian sighed, wondering if he should even bother trying to explain the dire situation old man. "The Fomori are on their way here to attack Iriellestra."

"Why are they attacking my wife?" Astus cried in a panic, his rheumy eyes growing wild and round.

"No, they are not attacking Irielle, they are coming here, to the city," Favian corrected him.

"Why is your hair so long?"

Favian groaned aloud. He should have known it was a waste of time. He tried again to move around the former king and this time Astus grabbed his wrist in a vicelike grip, surprising in its strength.

"You must take care of my grandson," the former king said vehemently.

Favian narrowed his eyes, wondering if the old man was having a lucid moment or if he had no idea what he was saying. "You stay with Aracellis. Keep him safe. If the palace falls, I will make sure that the two of you make it out safely. I give you my word."

Astus clapped him on the back and his age-spotted face split into a smile. "Thank you, boy! We will be in the library. Now go find my wife, she is supposed to be bringing me some tea."

23

I stared down at the cup in my hands, trying to empty my thoughts into the honeyed liquid but my mind refused to be silenced. After walking for what had felt like an eternity we had made it to Cafa, a sizeable town that housed several regent families, one of which had been quite eager to take us in. I was sure it would cost me greatly in favors later, but at the moment I was grateful for their hospitality. An older man and his portly wife, both white haired and quite jovial, they seemed kind enough and the lady of the house began clucking and fussing around us like a mother hen. She had attempted to wipe Blaise's face with her thumb, which she had swiped across her tongue for moisture, but he had caught her arm, the look in his amber eyes so hostile that she had backed away quickly with a nervous laugh. She had called her maid in to draw a bath for him and had taken me to another wing of the sprawling estate, tsk-ing repeatedly over the state of my dress.

"What were you doing out there?" she asked, seeming genuinely concerned, lifting the hem of my torn, dirty gown.

I stared up at her and wondered what she would say if I told her the truth, that I had killed a man I had once loved as a brother. Then a strange man with a belt of knives and a mangled dog that we had left for dead in a cave full of blooddrinkers had mysteriously reappeared and taken the orphaned child away from us, because he was more fit to care for her than we were.

"Oh, my dear," she fussed, petting my hair gently as tears started to fall down my face. "Whatever happened I am sure it must have been a terrible ordeal. You do not have to speak of it if you don't wish to. Come, let us get you bathed and in fresh clothes, you will feel much better!"

I had let her tend to me, helping me out of my clothes and into the bath, where she had gasped at the sight of the scratches on my neck and the two wounds on each of my palms. She did not ask how I received them, but I saw her eye the burned marks where Blaise had cauterized the wound with a knowing glance.

"He did not hurt me. The wound was bleeding, I asked him to do it," I said lamely. She merely nodded and started to scrub at my hair, chattering away about mundane things she knew I cared nothing about. When it was done she brought me a velvet gown in a deep bronze color, exclaiming delightedly at my restored appearance. I smiled wanly for her benefit, thanking her and promising that I would one day return her kindness. She had tittered happily like a plump little bird and then led me back to the long dining hall, where she sat me down and shoved a cup of sweet wine into my hands before hurrying off to see to our supper.

"You look quite beautiful, Earth Queen. Sad, but still beautiful," Blaise's rich timbre interrupted my brooding and I jerked my head up to watch him stride into the room. He was wearing a simple white tunic and dark leather breeches, his feet encased in new boots that looked supple and rich. The Fire Opal gleamed beneath the laces of the tunic, the stone only slightly brighter than his shining red curls. His handsome face boasted an easy smile, as if he had no cares in the world, and I wondered how he did it, how he could not feel the unbearable weight of it all.

He lifted his eyebrow when I did not respond and gestured at the cup in my hands. "Drinking your troubles away?"

I took a heavy sip from the cup, feeling the warmth of it burn down my throat and settle comfortingly in my stomach. "Perhaps it will help."

"Maialen, what happened was an accident, you did not intend to hurt him-" Blaise began, repeating the words he had already said to me a hundred times.

"But I did!" I cried back. "I did hurt him, and now he is dead!"

Blaise started to reach for me then stopped, his brow furrowing as if he were struggling with something. For a moment the only thing I wanted was to feel his arms around me, to have him hold me and comfort me. It was like an ache in my chest, but he remained aloof, throwing himself down in a chair and resting his booted feet on the table.

"The regent has offered us horses and an escort back to the Royal City. He would not agree to me taking his animals or his men to Veruca, so I assume once we get to your manor you can supply me with the things I need to get home." His tone was flat and matter of fact, as if the days between us had never happened.

"And then you will leave..." I murmured, feeling the sting of his careless words. "Just like everyone leaves."

He frowned, staring across the table at the hearth fire that burned on the other side of the room. He was silent for an eternity, then finally he said, his voice barely more than a whisper, "You have never asked me what it is like."

"What it is like?" I repeated, not knowing what he meant but hearing something in his voice that I had not heard from him before.

He dropped his feet from the table and sat upright, then lifted his hand and the fire danced in the hearth at his command, shrinking and swelling into fantastic shapes and whorls. Sparks sizzled in the air and I felt the room grow warmer, so warm that sweat started to bead on my forehead.

"My Element. Being the Keeper of Fire. I told your sister what it was like once, because I thought she would understand, but I don't think anyone can understand," he began. "It is like holding the sun inside of you. You can feel it burning every second of every day, a merciless and unending heat that never dissipates, only builds until I think I will die from it and all I can do is try not to let it consume me. The only time I feel better is when I can release it, when I can burn through something till there is nothing but ash and smoke. Sometimes I feel like I could burn all of Imbria to the ground and it still would not be enough."

He finally pulled his eyes from the fire and looked at me, his gaze so haunted and raw that it made my heart skip a beat. He went on, "You think I don't feel anything, that I am heartless and cruel, but I feel everything just like you do, Earth Queen, a thousand times more, perhaps. When I was a boy, my mother killed my younger brother, Bastion, because he was too great a burden to her. I loved him more than anything on Imbria and I hated her for it. I was so angry at her for taking him from me and she laughed about it. I pushed her and she fell. She died. So you see, I know what it is to take a life you don't intend to, and I know what it is to take the life of someone who is meant to love you."

"I... I did not know..." I said, feeling my cheeks flush at the inadequacy of my response. He was still watching me with a haunted gaze and I could see the tortured boy inside him, buried deep under the cynical and callous exterior.

He shrugged and the wall was back up, the boy hidden from sight, shoved back into the dark recesses of his mind. "You must find a way to live with what happened, or it will consume you."

I wanted to do as he said, to find a way to release the guilt that was lodged in my heart like a stake, but I did not know how I would ever be able to. It was like a festering wound that would never heal.

"Blaise," I began timidly, finding his name strange on my tongue. After everything that had happened, he was no longer just Blaise, as I had known him before, but an altogether different man. Saying his name was like meeting him anew, like I had never known the man who sat across from me before this moment, despite all that we had shared. I wanted to say more but the words did not come and he seemed to understand, to know that whatever I had wanted to say to him was there, left unspoken in the air between us.

We did not have another chance to talk that night, for our hosts had joined us and gabbed delightedly with nonstop enthusiasm throughout the meal. I was grateful for the food, and I hoped that they were not offended by my short responses or the lapses of melancholy I found myself drifting into as they spoke. They completely ignored Blaise, the lady of this house still bristling from his hostile attitude towards her good-intentioned ministrations. She threw him distrustful glances that seemed to amuse him, and he insisted on switching plates with her, a notion that seemed to offend her greatly. For a moment I thought she would refuse, and that perhaps they had poisoned his food, but then she capitulated, thunking his plate down in front of her and taking a huge bite to prove it was edible. She then turned back to me and continued her long-winded tale, barely stopping to chew her food.

That night we had slept in chambers at opposite ends of a long hallway, though any actual sleep I would have had was interrupted by nightmares that left me trembling and drenched in sweat. I kept seeing the dark, wet hair of the creature that had been trapped in the cave, Gideon sprawled on the ground with blood seeping into the dirt beneath his chest. Sometimes the two intertwined and I saw the Fomori swarming over Gideon's corpse, the haunted shape of his daughter, Eolande, watching from far back in the forest, her flowered necklace clutched in her hand. The flowers that had matched the one Gideon wore on his tunic.

I was grateful when morning finally came. The regent and his wife bid us a fussy goodbye, sending with us a stable hand and his grown son, and ensuring us that the sagging, grey-muzzled horses they plodded out of the stables were the finest they had and would get us home swiftly.

Home.

It seemed that my whole world had changed since last I had been there. Would it feel the same? Comfortable and safe, the shadows of the past clinging to the edges of the forest, or had the shadows spread too far, the darkness swallowing everything around me.

As we neared the Royal City, the elderly horses moving at a pace that was barely faster than a snail, the roads grew more familiar and I could not help but smile up at the towering treetops that soared above us. It was like seeing old friends and I stopped my mount, sliding down so that I could walk on the side of the road to be nearer to them. The stable hand paused and looked back, thinking there was something wrong with the horse that had caused me to dismount, but Blaise gestured for him to carry on.

The Fire Keeper leaned forward in his saddle, watching me with a grin and saying to the other men, "The Earth Queen is merely greeting her loyal subjects."

I turned my smile on him, pleased that he understood, as I ran my fingers along the rough edges of bark. We walked on, following a bend in the road and as we rounded the curve, I saw a shock of white hair and the skinny limbs of my nephew as he perched on a rock, watching the road with unblinking diligence.

"Oh, for the love of Imbria," I muttered. I had sent the child back so that he would be safe in my manor, not so that he could roam the countryside unaccompanied. I called out to him, "Kaeleb! What are you doing out here?"

He came darting forward, like an arrow released from a bow, skidding to a halt in a cloud of dust in front of us. Our two escorts looked quite surprised and Blaise was watching the boy carefully with narrowed eyes.

"So, you are not dead, despite your weak, Kymirran blood," my nephew said, folding his arms across his chest and eyeing us accusatorily.

"You are such a sweet child," I replied sarcastically.

He made a face at me, then turned to Blaise. "You lost your army?"

Blaise raised an eyebrow and grinned at him, chuckling at his impudence. "It appears that I did."

Kaeleb grunted as if he had expected that outcome all along. "It is good that I came to escort you back, then. Come along. Why are your horses so old? Could you not find any better than that? They are disgraceful. You look like you are riding to your own burial."

He continued to ramble on about the miserable state in which he had found us, including the ineptitude of our escorts who, as he put it, looked like they could not fight off a one-legged flea. I apologized to them profusely, and they seemed nonplussed by the child, throwing him wary glances as if he were quite mad, which I was starting to think he was. Blaise, however, was quite entertained by the boy's sharp wit, and was even encouraging him, much to my annoyance. I could not help but wonder if the fond tolerance he seemed to show for my nephew was because he was my sister's child and I felt the long ties of jealousy pulling at me.

"What would you have done differently, my boy?" Blaise was asking him after Kaeleb had begun to berate the Verucan's loss to the Fomori.

Kaeleb snorted as if it should have been obvious. "I would never even have bothered with the Fomori. I would have just killed the Samirran King."

"Kaeleb!" I exclaimed, shaking my head in admonition at his boldness. "You cannot say such things!"

"But he asked me," Kaeleb countered.

"He is right, I did ask him," Blaise chuckled.

I glared at the Fire Keeper. "Stop encouraging him."

"Come now, Maialen, do not be cross," Blaise placated. "It has been a rough time for all of us, the boy's humor is a welcome distraction."

"Perhaps for you," I said, miffed. "I find him quite offensive."

"That is probably because of your weak, Kymirran blood," Blaise teased, laughing heartily. Kaeleb snickered with mirth while he walked beside him, looking up at the older man for boyish approval. I felt another stab of jealousy, wondering how my nephew did not hate the Fire King, for surely Alita would have taught him that sentiment. Watching them walk beside each other, I could not help but see the vision of what might have been had Orabelle never fallen in love with Tal, and if she had married Blaise as intended. Perhaps they would have had a child that looked like Kaeleb, walked together and laughed together. I felt a queasy feeling in my stomach at the image I had conjured and I grabbed my amulet, taking a deep breath and using the calm, grounding energy of my Element to soothe my raw feelings.

Our reception in the Royal City was not the warm welcome I had anticipated, and I supposed that by then I should have stopped expecting people to be happy to see me. We had barely approached the manor when Damek came rushing out in a swirl of black robes, his agitation humming from every pore on his body. Behind him I saw a group of gathered men and women, regents and some of the officers from my legion. Vayk was among them and I flinched at the sight of him, for I knew that I would soon have to explain what had happened to his brother and their mongrel dog.

"What kind of mess did you make up there?" Damek practically shrieked at me. I startled, blinking at him in surprise and opening my mouth to reply but he hurried on, not giving me a chance to speak. "The Samirrans claim that they are being overrun with Fomori. They sent eagles here to ask for Archers to help them fight but I fear it was a trick to divide our troops, to make us vulnerable. I have sent them back to their cursed kingdom and burnt everything they touched with their plague-riddled hands."

"The Legion of Archers is back?" I asked, trying to catch up to what he was saying.

"Yes, of course, they came across the Verucan army, what was left of it, and the two cavalrymen you sent back to warn them. We thought you were lost! Dead! The noble lineage of your father completely wiped out!" Damek wailed. Kaeleb winced at the shrillness of his voice and I hoped that the child would not try to stab the old advisor for being too loud.

"I am fine, there is no need to be upset. We were taken by the Fomori but we escaped. Damek, please, it has been a long journey and we are so tired-" I began but he stopped me with an abrupt gesture, seeing Blaise saunter up behind me.

"And this one is also alive? Your little friend Logaire will be quite disappointed to learn about that. My spies say she has fully ensconced herself on the Verucan throne, claiming that the Fire King is dead somewhere up in the snow."

"What did you say?" Blaise seethed, his eyes narrowing to slits and the easy grin slipping from his face.

"Your little whore cousin has stolen your throne right out from under you," Damek practically spat at him in disgust. "She has slaughtered anyone who was still loyal to you and I am sure that by now she has removed your adopted son's cantankerous head from his shoulders."

Blaise looked as murderous as I had ever seen him, and I worried for a moment that he would strangle Damek right then and there. He struggled to control his temper, turning to me and saying, "Give me men and horses."

"Blaise, please," I tried to calm him. "Let us think this through."

"There is nothing to think through, Maialen! I am the King of Veruca and if someone is sitting on my throne then I intend to go and remove them from it!" he shouted at me.

"She will be expecting you to come! She will kill you if you just go riding up to the gates of the castle in a rage. Logaire always thinks of everything, you must be careful and you need to outwit her."

Kaeleb tugged on Blaise's tunic, drawing the Fire Keeper's wrathful attention down to him.

"What?" Blaise snapped at the boy.

"You are talking about the red-headed lady? The one who always smells like flowers?" Kaeleb asked. Blaise nodded and the boy went on, "Brother Kaden said to draw your enemy out you must entice them with something they are certain to take, something they will be unable to refuse. I watched her when she was here, because Verucans cannot be trusted, as you know because you are a Verucan yourself. She wants to be one of you, that is what she wants most."

Blaise stared down at the child, contemplating for a long moment. "Maialen, you are going to call a meeting of the Council."

24

The Fomori attacked Iriellestra in the darkest part of the night, in the hour just before the sky would begin to lighten in anticipation of the dawn. The moon was obscured by thick, bloated clouds that churned overhead, making the blackness complete, and Favian thought how ironic it would be if rain finally fell in Samirra that night.

There were thousands of them, more than they had anticipated, and Favian had mounted his defenses as best he could with the meager resources they had. He was still hoping and praying to the gods that the Kymirrans were on their way, flying to help them on the eagles they had dispatched with a desperate plea.

The outer walls held for a time, the darkness melting into morning with the Fomori battering repeatedly at the gates and searching for any weakness. The Samirrans lined the top of the battlement, reigning down arrows and throwing anything they could find at the fearsome creatures who were trying to claw their way in, but there were too many, and they kept coming. Some of them carried huge blocks of stones that they tossed in piles against the walls so they could scrabble their way over the barricade. Others built massive fires, hurling burning bundles of dried grass and twigs over the wall into the overcrowded city so that great swathes of it caught fire and burned like tinder.

"The outer wall will fall soon, we must let the people behind the second wall," Favian said urgently to his King, who stood on his balcony, useless as ever and staring at the massive plumes of smoke that wafted around them.

"We cannot risk them bringing the plague with them," Astraeus answered with a shake of his head.

"Then you are condemning them all to a horrible death."

Astraeus rounded on his Guardian, his face like the statue of one of the gods, glorious and cold beneath the dark sweep of hair. "We will all die a horrible death if plague enters the palace. It cannot be helped. Seal the inner wall."

Though he hated it, Favian knew he had no choice but to obey, and he sent a man with orders to Hovard, who was charged with holding the main gate of the inner wall. He hated even more that it had come to this, that his King had let it come to this.

"We should be out there, fighting," he said quietly, his fingers tugging at the end of his braided hair. Above all he was a warrior and cowering behind the safety of the palace walls while women and children were slaughtered was shameful. There was no honor to be found in hiding from the enemy.

"There is nothing to be done out there that is not already being done, and I need you here, protecting me. You are, after all, my Guardian and that is your purpose," Astraeus said darkly. He was clutching the Sapphire in his hand and Favian wondered if he still tried to conjure his Element or if he had given up completely. If they had the Element's power then perhaps they could stop the fires that raged below, repel some of the Fomori, or at least make it more difficult for them.

"If you could use the amulet to-" Favian began but this time when Astraeus rounded on him, he struck him physically, the shock of the blow startling the Guardian into stumbling back.

He stared at his ruler with wide eyes, touching his jaw where the King's fist had smashed against his narrow face. Favian could have killed him in seconds, with barely any effort, and for a brief moment the thought crossed his mind, but he could not bring himself to do it. Astraeus, however flawed, was his King and Favian had sworn an oath to him.

Astraeus seemed vexed by what he had just done and he reached out, but Favian stepped away from the gesture of apology. He continued to rub his jaw and annoyance flashed across the King's face.

"It is your fault I had to do that. I am the King, you should not question me!" Astraeus told him. Just then there was a loud rumble, like peals of thunder echoing in the sky, and part of the outer wall disintegrated in a shower of dust and rubble. Favian watched in horror as the Fomori swarmed over the wreckage like ants, spreading into Iriellestra with wild abandon.

"Your kingdom is dying and all you are concerned for is your vanity," the Guardian said through clenched teeth, backing away further, unwilling to look at what was happening below them. He could hear the screams of the Samirrans, the howls of rage and delight from the beasts and he turned his head, sick from it, retreating into the palace and away from the carnage.

Favian walked blindly through the hallways, making his way out to the outer courtyard, to the main gate where Hovard and his men stood atop the walls, watching what was happening with pale, drawn faces. Below, at the gate, a crowd had gathered, pleading to be let in, banging on the locked gates in panic.

"Do we let them in?" Hovard called as Favian approached, even though he already knew what the answer would be.

"The King has ordered that it remain closed and sealed. We cannot help them."

"If we live through this I do not think I will ever sleep well again," Hovard muttered as the Guardian came to stand beside him. "There must be something we can do."

"Our only hope is that the Kymirrans will come to our aid," Favian responded, once again praying to the gods that Damek would do the right thing, or that Maialen would return safely from the north, for surely she would not abandon them. Favian drew a deep breath and took his friend's hand in his, squeezing it. "I will not let you die at their hands."

Hovard looked at the wiry Guardian, at his narrow face and earnest expression, and he pressed his hand back. "Nor I you."

They stayed at the wall together for hours, waiting, watching as the crowd at the gate grew larger. Favian could not imagine the horror that they would witness when the Fomori reached them, herded out there together like cattle. He heard the screams of terror before he saw them, and the people pressed tighter, crushing each other in their panic to get away.

"Samirrans!" a woman's voice rang out over the cacophony. Favian squinted through the smoke-filled air, trying to see where the throaty sound had originated from. A murky figure was striding into the outer courtyard, the Fomori streaming ahead of her and flanking her from either side so that they formed a protective wall of their own, shielding her as she moved.

"This can all end, none of you have to die!" Her voice rang out over the marble and the crowd began to quiet, stopping their inevitable press forward and distracted by this new thread of hope they so desperately wanted to cling to. "All I need is for your King to surrender. His life, for all of yours."

"Who is that?" Hovard whispered.

Favian shook his head. "I do not know."

She continued to move forward, the Fomori forcing the crowd to part with gasps and cries. She stopped some distance back from the wall, throwing off the hood that she had draped over her head and staring up at the wall defiantly, a short sword in her hand. She was not a Fomori, he realized, at least not a full blooded one. Whatever she was, she was painfully exquisite. Even from a distance Favian could see the fine lines of her long nose, the full, wide mouth and dark eyes ringed in a heavy fringe of lashes. Her skin was dark ebony, shining and smooth like glass, and her hair cascaded down her back, glossy and thick. She wore a grey robe lined in fur and did not seem at all bothered by the oppressive heat, though the sun still hid behind the thick blanket of clouds.

"Did you not hear me?" She called up to the wall and Favian felt her black gaze fixate on him. "Are you the Keeper? I must tell you, I expected more of a fight. This was quite...pathetic."

There was something strange about her voice and the way she spoke, an accent that he had not heard before.

"I will not tolerate disrespect!" she shouted suddenly, anger distorting the painful perfection of her face. She motioned with her arm and one of the Fomori grabbed a man, dragging him to where she stood and forcing him to his knees in front of her where she slit his throat in one quick movement. When she motioned for another Favian yelled out for her to stop and she smiled.

"So, you do hear me? Then answer my questions."

"I am Favian, the Guardian to King Astraeus."

"Guardian," she laughed the word. "You are nothing but servants to their whims, a meaningless life to be sacrificed for theirs. Where is your King?"

"He is safe, behind these walls. We will not let you past this gate."

"As if you can stop me. Go, peasant, and get your King. I will speak to him," she commanded, her voice so sure of its authority that he found himself wanting to obey. "For every hour that you are gone I will kill one of your people so you may want to hurry."

Favian looked at Hovard. "Hold the wall. I will be back soon."

He raced to the palace, yelling for the King, shoving people aside in his haste. How ridiculous it all was, he thought bitterly as a man went by with an incense censer, swinging the gilded and lacquered bowl filled with fragrant smoke. How could they just pretend that what was happening outside the gate was not of any concern?

Favian finally found the King, reclining in one of the parlors on a plush bench, his hands pressed to his temples while a woman massaged his tense neck. The sight of it filled the Guardian with so much resentment that he had to stop for a moment, counting and tugging on his braid, before he could enter the room. Even then he could hear his voice wavering with emotion though he tried to stifle it.

"They have reached the inner gate," he said.

Astraeus waved the woman away with an irritable shake of his hand and she bowed quickly, scurrying out of the room. "The gate holds?"

"For now, but a crowd has gathered there and they are surrounded by the Fomori. There is a woman with them and she has asked for a parlay with you," Favian told him, not bothering to add that she had asked for his life and his surrender. Astraeus would never risk himself if he knew. "If you do not come she will kill them, one each hour until you do."

"A parlay?" the King perked up. "So, they wish to surrender?"

Favian just stared at him, lounging there in his glittering robes, the worthless Sapphire hanging from his neck. How was it possible that he could be so completely unaware? *If only Irielle was still alive.* She had been the only one in that entire family with a drop of good sense.

"I do not think they are in a position that requires them to surrender," Favian pointed out. "They have us surrounded. We do not have the food or water stores to withstand a siege. We must find out what she wants, perhaps there is a way that we can stop this before more innocent people have to die."

Astraeus sighed heavily. "I am tired of dealing with women. You go and see what she wants."

"She does not wish to speak to me, she insisted that it be you," Favian countered.

"This could all be a trick just to get to me. I cannot take the risk, I must be here to protect Samirra. The people need me." Astraeus pushed himself up from the cushioned bench and began to pace the room, his hands clasped behind his back. "Is there any word from Kymir?"

"Not yet."

"Then go, find out what she wants and find a way to put an end to this mess," the King commanded. He stopped his pacing to stare at a tapestry that was draped across the wall, the scene depicting the morning sun as it rose over the Samirran cliffs, threads of silver woven through the sky to represent the wind. Favian left him there, his heart sinking as he walked away. If the Kymirrans did not come, then it was over. They would lose his beloved Samirra.

25

Favian sat across from the woman in a room that used to be part of the city guard's barracks. Now it was the main camp of the Fomori. A single lamp burned on the table that stretched between them, the flame flickering as shadows crawled along the edges of the room. The meager firelight lit her ebony skin so that it seemed to glow from within and he found himself having to look away from the immaculate faultlessness of her face. She sipped from a goblet, watching him with a toying smile, and he could see the tips of her white teeth had been filed down to points.

"You were sent to bring me the Keeper," she said, her strange accent both alluring and unsettling. Her black eyes, flecked with yellow, were infinite as the night sky.

"He has asked me to parlay on his behalf."

She laughed, a throaty sound that echoed around the room. "I see they are still cowards. I have no wish to parlay with you, peasant, or with your spineless King. I want his surrender, and to see his head on a spike. That is the only parlay you will get from me."

The Fomori had pushed back the crowds from the gate, herding them into penned up areas where they could be easily killed. She had been true to her word, leaving a bloody corpse at the gate every hour until Favian had come out to meet her, sure that this would be his death. Hovard had begged him not to go, suggesting they slip out at night with the other deserters and leave Astraeus to clean up his own mess. For a heartbeat Favian was tempted, but in the end he had gently declined. His life and his duty were to Samirra and he would not leave until he had done everything he could to save the kingdom. It had been then that the eagles had come soaring back into the sky, heartbreakingly riderless. He and Hovard had watched as the Fomori raced along the rampart of the outer wall, hurling spears at the great, winged creatures. The eagles had shrieked in panic and without riders to control them they had veered away, soaring off to hide in the safety of the cliffs. Favian had watched it all with the last vestige of hope dying in his chest, feeling as if his heart were being turned to stone and pressing down on him. He had taken one last look at Hovard, telling him to get out if he still could, then he had gone out to meet the mysterious woman who led the Fomori.

Favian watched her now as she sipped, the liquid thick and crimson as she darted her tongue out to lick the drops from her lips, and he wondered if it was Samirran blood that she was drinking. She seemed to intuit what he was thinking and her smile widened, showing off the pointed teeth, now colored pink.

"Diluted pigs' water, really," she said, swirling the cup. "But then, it has been generations since the Gods chose to abandon you."

"The King will not surrender," Favian told her.

Annoyance flashed across her glittering eyes. "Why is he bothering to pretend like he can win? We have taken your city. We have your people. You are trapped in your shining palace and from what I have been told, it does not appear that you will last very long on the supplies that you have. Those birds, they were meant to bring help, were they not? How sad. It appears your King does not have any friends that are coming to his aid. Does he not see this?"

Favian considered for a moment, then shook his head, deciding that there was no point in lying or trying to pretend. She was the one with the power here and they both knew it. "He is a fool. He will never surrender because he loves himself more than anything else, it does not occur to him that he will lose."

She seemed to appreciate his honesty, nodding her head in approval. "A true Keeper, through and through. You, however, seem to care greatly about the people of Samirra. Perhaps you and I can come to an understanding."

"Why are you doing this?" Favian asked suddenly. Maybe it was the utter exhaustion of the last days, or the mental turmoil he had undergone, but he felt a compulsive need to know why it was all happening, why the city was burning, why the Fomori had come for them, why she wanted Astraeus dead. He needed to know because without that knowledge he felt like he would break inside at the futility of it all.

She raised her arched brows, causing a faint wrinkling on her forehead, the only blemish he had seen on her perfection and even that was fleeting, smoothing away as she settled herself back in her chair. "So you wish to know my story? Are you stalling for time?"

"No," Favian responded honestly. "I just need to know."

She began to tell him and as she spoke he felt his eyes growing rounder, not sure whether he believed her or not, but what other choice did he have but to believe.

Her name was Chaote. She had been born in the time of the first Keepers, when the gods still roamed across Imbria at their whim. Her parents were unknown to her, one Fomori and one Tahitian. Back then, the Fomori were a formidable tribe of warriors, known and feared across Imbria for their ruthlessness. They raided town and villages, took what they wanted, and did not care who they left for dead, for anyone who was not Fomori did not matter to them. The world was chaotic then, the elements uncontrolled and the furies and tempers of the gods always a threat. Chaote had been raised in Tahitia, by a family who had known what she was, but who had not cared and had kept her secret so that she would not be treated differently because of it. She had loved them, and she had been happy there on the island. Her father was proud and stern, but humorous and quick to smile, and her mother was a renowned warrior, brave and wise and protective of her daughters. Her sisters had been kind, gentle souls, more suited to the task of healing and mending than to the practice of war. Chaote, on the other hand, had followed in the footsteps of her adopted mother. She was strong and fierce, driven by ambition and the need to achieve more. She trained with the other warriors, winning every competition until she was revered by her people for her skill.

"Then the Keepers were created," she said to Favian, her voice lowering with emotion. "The Gods had become bored with this land, they could no longer be bothered with humans and their petty troubles and so they left their power in the hands of a few, to absolve themselves of the guilt for abandoning this world."

The Keepers had called for all the tribes to send a delegate to pledge their loyalty. The Tahitians had bristled at this, for they were a proud people and had always governed themselves, but rumors of the Keepers' immense powers made them reconsider. Chaote had been restless, Tahitia had always been too small for her great ambitions, and so she had volunteered to go. It was there that she met the first Keeper of Water. Rilian.

The land had not been called Kymir then, that name came later with a different king. As Chaote walked through the forest she had marveled at the soaring trees, reaching so far into the sky that it was almost painful to look up at the tops of them.

There were people from all over the land, all of the tribes, and the vibrancy and thrill of life swelled within her. This was what she had been missing in Tahitia.

"Is this your first time in the forest?" a man asked. He was just as tall as she was, with golden skin and pale grey eyes that tilted up in the corners, and his hair was long and white. She had never seen anything so beautiful and for a moment she just stared at him, unable to speak.

He had slipped his arm through hers, guiding her through the maze of trees and telling her stories of the fantastical places he had visited that she must see. She found out later that he was Rilian, one of the chosen ones the gods had deigned to bestow their powers upon. They had fallen in love, and she had believed him when he told her that they would rule the island kingdoms together. As they lay in bed one night, their bodies intertwined, he had asked her about her family. Foolishly, she had told him the truth. That her family had taken her in as a baby and that she was part Fomori. Rilian had been shocked, furious with her that she had not told him sooner and disgusted that she had the barbaric blood of the Fomori in her veins. She did not know at the time, but he and the other Keepers had been devising a plan to stop the Fomori, to be rid of the threat of them forever. Rilian believed that by being with her, he would lose the favor of the gods and his new power mattered more to him than anything else. He had her beaten and bound in chains and she remembered with such intense clarity the pain of that moment, when she realized that he had never truly loved her. She was dragged out to where the Keepers had ambushed the Fomori, thrown in with them as they were sealed away in a cave, the land around them stripped of everything that would give life, should any of them ever escape.

She paused in her telling, closing her eyes, as if reliving the agonizing moment all over again. Favian waited, and eventually she shook herself from the depths of her memory and went on.

The Fomori tried to kill her at first. She was not one of them, and they would not tolerate her existence, but she was strong and she fought them back, over and over. Bloody and exhausted she fought and kept fighting. She eventually earned their tolerance and then their respect. They began to listen to her, to obey her commands and accept her decisions. When it came time that they would die of starvation if they did not eat, it was she who decided which of them would live, and which of them would sacrifice themselves for the others. They began to call her Mother.

She told them where to look for water and where to dig, feeling the passageways with her fingers outstretched, seeking the merest movement of air that could mean a way out. It was a long, excruciating process, using the bones of her sacrificed brethren as tools, but one day there it was, the tiniest pinpoint of light. She had wept at the sight of it, and it had taken months for them to widen it enough so that she could squeeze through, months of having to choose who lived or died, of eating the flesh of her companions to stay alive. But finally, she was free. She made her way through the desecrated land, the southern wastelands that the Keepers had created as part of their prison, and she found the ocean. It took her days to build a boat, but she had learned patience in the caves, and she did not rush.

When she arrived on Tahitia they did not recognize her. She had been gone for so long, and the gaunt, thin woman who climbed out of the rickety, makeshift raft was not the brave warrior that had once championed their tournaments. She hurried to her parents' home, tears streaming down her face, wanting nothing more than to feel the warm embrace of her family, to know that she was still loved despite what she was.

"There was nothing there. It was just dirt, an empty mound where our home had been," she said to Favian, her black eyes sparkling. "I began to ask what had happened, demanding that someone tell me. It was then that they realized who I was, and I could see from their faces they were ashamed. Rilian had come and murdered my family and torn down our home. He was showing everyone what would happen if you harbored a Fomori."

"I am sorry," Favian murmured, sincerely remorseful for the depth of pain that he saw reflected back at him in her gaze.

She had been furious with the Tahitians for letting it happen, that no one on the island had tried to help her poor family. She screamed and cried and beat the dirt with her fists, unable to stop herself from picturing the deaths of her proud parents and sweet sisters. Her mother would have fought, she was certain of that, and she could not stop imagining the defeat, the moment when the warrior woman must have known she had lost, and that it was all because of Chaote. Had her mother cursed her with her last breaths? Had her loving family hated her for being the reason their lives ended too soon? Had her sisters cried out for her to help them? She could not bear her own thoughts and she turned on the other islanders in a fury, not caring who she hurt, wanting to kill them all, but she was too weak. They took her down to the beach and threw her into her boat, shoving it back out to see and warning her to never come back. She had been abandoned by everyone on Imbria, everyone except the Fomori. And so she had gone back to them.

Her grief was overwhelming and relentless. She had fallen on her knees one night, in the darkness of the caves that she had tried for so long to escape from, pleading to the gods, whoever was left, to help her, to give her the vengeance that she deserved. She stayed there on her knees for days, not moving from the spot, not eating or drinking or sleeping. Finally, one of them heard her pleas and granted her mercy. He, too, was an outcast amongst his own kind, feared by them, distrusted because he was powerful. He came down and listened to her story, and he had created the Warding Stones, a way to absorb the power of the Keepers, to keep them from running rampant. She had snatched the stones, taking one and carving a long line in her chest, shoving it under the skin there, where it would always be safe. Then she had taken the Fomori back out into the world and gone after Rilian, destroying everyone and everything in her path.

"I almost had him," she told Favian wistfully, a dreamy look floating over her ephemeral features.

The other Keepers came to his aid but they were weak without their powers in the presence of the Warding Stones and by then Chaote had realized that the divine blood made her even stronger, that by consuming it in great quantities she was practically immortal. The Keepers would have fallen, but the god who had given her the Stones returned to the world, angry with her for her murderous rampage for it had caused him to be punished by the other gods. Her actions gave them the justification they needed to be rid of him and he was cast down, sent to dwell for eternity amongst the humans, to make sure that she stayed locked away forever. Fenris. He was the one that helped them to bind her in her prison, denying her the one thing she wanted most, the death of Rilian.

"So you see, Guardian, I intend to finish what I have started, to destroy the Keepers and rid the world of the abomination they are," she explained, spreading her hands elegantly as if she were bestowing a great gift upon him.

"You are killing innocent people just like your family was killed," Favian countered with a shake of his head. "And this Rilian is dead, he has been dead for centuries."

"The Keepers are all the same and your people are not innocent!" she snarled. "Do you know how many of your kind watched as I was dragged away in chains? Do you know how many of them spat on me? Kicked me? Beat me? Look what you have done to my poor children, forced them to live in caves and hide from the world, to become more beast than human. Your kind does not deserve mercy but I am willing to grant it, in exchange for the Keeper. My terms have not changed, this is the only thing that will save you. If not I will kill everyone who is left alive in this wretched city while you are forced to watch and after that I will rip your King's head off with my bare hands and you, Guardian, you will die last so that you can watch it all with the futility of knowing you could have stopped it but you chose not to!"

Favian once again felt like the world was falling away beneath him. She was right, there was no way to stop her other than to give her what she wanted.

"Go, now. Go back to your palace and wait with your precious King to die. I will come for you both soon enough," she dismissed.

"Chaote," he began as one of the Fomori moved towards him. He would not have another chance, he could not leave there without any hope, he had to find a way. "You want the amulet, to destroy it. What if I can get him to give it to you? Astraeus will not sacrifice his own life, but I may be able to convince him to give up the Sapphire, especially if you promise to let him live."

"Bring me the Sapphire and we will see how forgiving I am feeling," she said with a laugh, knowing that he had no other choice.

26

I felt a dull ache beginning to manifest behind my forehead as Damek rattled on and on about the cost of what he was now calling our frivolous war in the north. The table we stood over was littered with parchment and scrolls but try as I might, I could not force myself to focus on his words or the march of characters across the pages he waved under my nose. I stared out the open window, feeling the cool breeze that shifted through the trees and wishing that I were anywhere else. I had been so eager to return home to Kymir, but I was realizing that neither Kymir, nor I, would ever be the same.

"Are you listening?" the old advisor snapped, snatching a paper from my hand in his spidery fingers.

"I, er.. I am sorry, Damek, I am just distracted today," I apologized.

"You have been distracted since you returned," he said with an unconcealed look of hostility thrown over my shoulder to where Blaise had just entered the room.

I felt my cheeks redden and I glanced up to see the Fire Keeper smirking at us, his arms folded over his chest as he leaned casually against the doorframe. I had barely seen him since we returned. He had stormed off after I agreed to send hawks calling the other realms to Council as he wanted, bait that Logaire would find impossible to resist. Kaeleb was right, and the one thing she yearned for most was to be acknowledged by the rest of us. A Council meeting where she would be recognized as the new ruler of Veruca was not an opportunity she would let slip by. I had expected Blaise to be pleased that I had granted his request, but he had neither thanked me nor even acknowledged the gesture, and he continued to shut himself away from me and everyone else. Everyone except for Kaeleb. Blaise seemed to have plenty of time and tolerance for my sister's wicked child, and a bond was forming between them that I found greatly disturbing.

"I see you have stopped your brooding," I remarked flippantly, wishing that the sight of him did not still cause my breath to catch in my throat. I wondered if he knew that part of me was secretly pleased by what Logaire had done, because it kept him close to me.

He arched an eyebrow. "Did you miss me, Earth Queen?"

"Oh, for the love of Imbria," Damek muttered in exasperation. "Whatever ridiculous game you two are playing at, do it out of my sight."

My face flushed even deeper scarlet, causing Blaise to chuckle as he pushed himself into the room. He walked over to the table, his amber eyes scanning the pieces of parchment with interest. Damek cursed under his breath, snatching up the scrolls as quickly as he could.

"These are Kymirran affairs, not Verucan," the advisor glowered. "Though I suppose you no longer have to worry about Verucan affairs since you lost your kingdom to a trussed-up strumpet."

"Very amusing," Blaise said, though I noted the hard edge to his voice. I reached for my amulet and attempted to soothe the tension in the room.

Damek paused a moment, seemed to hesitate, then dropped the armful of papers back down on the table with a thud.

"Since you are both here, I suppose there is something we need to discuss."

"How to remove my thieving cousin from my throne?" Blaise asked.

"Not hardly. I could not care less which of you imbeciles sits on that barbaric throne, as long as whoever it is, they honor their agreements to Kymir. No, what I wish to speak to you about is Lehar."

"Lehar?" I repeated, surprised.

"Yes, Lehar," Damek said impatiently. He waved his arms around him, his black robes shivering over his skeletal frame. "You may not have considered this, but Logaire has the Warding Stone, and the only place she could have gotten it was from that usurper you so eagerly put on the Leharan throne. It is obvious that the two of them have formed an alliance and I fear for what their conniving intentions are for Kymir."

"Logaire would not do anything to hurt Kymir," I started to say, interrupted by Blaise's incisive burst of laughter.

"Darling, my cousin would slit your throat from ear to ear if she thought it would get her what she wanted."

"But she is my friend," I protested lamely, the words sounding pathetic even to my own ears.

"Since you have mentioned throat slitting," Damek interjected. "That brings us to the point of this vexatious conversation. I have found evidence that it was the Leharan usurper who had Alita killed."

I let the words sink in and I had to close my eyes for a moment, feeling slightly faint.

"Maialen?" Blaise reached out and grasped my arm, his fingers hot against my skin.

"I am fine," I lied, smoothing down the folds of my skirt. I wanted more than anything for it not to be true, for someone connected to my family to be a decent, compassionate person. We were like the plague in Samirra, no better than the blooddrinkers in the north. Savage and ruthless and bloodthirsty for power. Even the child, my sister's son, the boy who thought he would save the world, showed the promise of becoming a monster. How could he not when he had our blood running through his veins?

Damek fluttered a hand around my face, fanning me, his mouth turned down in a frown of sympathy. "I know this is upsetting, my dear, but it must be dealt with. I found the guard who was supposed to be watching Alita. The only thing he confessed to was that a Leharan had rewarded him handsomely to leave his post. Sadly, before we could question him further, he took his own life."

"Convenient," Blaise quipped.

"A Leharan does not mean Thyrr," I pointed out.

"No," Damek conceded, "and that is why I began to ask the other men who they had seen this Yosef fellow speaking to in the days before the incident. Several of them claimed to have seen him with the Leharan, Orabelle's supposed brother. I know this is hard for you, my child, but we must have a plan to deal with him when he comes to Council. This vile act cannot go unpunished!"

Blaise was watching Damek with an unwavering intensity, a smile playing at his lips. "And you want to punish him by removing him from the Leharan throne?"

Damek lifted his hands as if it were not his choice, but the only thing to be done. "Murder in Kymir is punishable by death."

"No!" I swore vehemently. "I will not kill anyone else!"

Damek gave me a sharp glance. "Anyone else? What does that mean?"

"Nothing, she is still traumatized by the ordeal with the Fomori. The battle in the north was enough bloodshed for her to endure in one lifetime," Blaise said smoothly.

"Then he should be banished to the wastelands," Damek suggested.

Blaise grinned. "And Lehar is once again back under Kymir's control."

"Better that than some murdering commoner who is aligning himself with other usurpers. I warned you all about him and about that heathen she-demon you call your cousin. He and Logaire have likely already made plans to steal Kymir out from under us! It is no coincidence that Thyrr promised to send help to the north, and not one ship was seen leaving the Leharan harbor! He left you both for dead!" Damek cried, his voice rising shrilly.

"Calm yourself, advisor. I have no love for the Leharan, and if it is as you say and he has aligned himself with Logaire, then that makes him my enemy. You are telling us this now because you want to ensure that we will go along with this plan before you bring it up in Council?" Blaise once again guessed correctly.

Damek gave him a shrewd glance. "We should all be in agreement. I have studied the Edicts and even though you may not have a kingdom, you are still a Keeper and you hold sway at Council."

Blaise watched him for a long moment, the advisor glaring back at the unseated King with barely veiled hostility. It would have been clear to anyone, even a blind man standing in that room, that those two were not allies. When Blaise finally spoke again, his amber eyes glittered with intent and I felt a shiver go down my spine.

"If I do this then you will also agree to help remove Logaire from my throne so she can join Thyrr in the wastelands. I help you get rid of Thyrr, you help me get rid of Logaire."

Damek smiled at him and patted his shoulder with all the warmth of a venomous snake. "I will do whatever I can to help.

I told you before, I care not which of you rules that pile of rubble."

The spindly old advisor once again snatched up the mountain of parchment and hurried from the room, his black robes billowing out behind him like a sail. I watched Blaise watch him go, wondering how on Imbria we were going to put right everything that had gone wrong.

"I cannot believe it was Thyrr," I murmured.

Blaise scoffed, sitting on the edge of the table that Damek had cleared off. "I doubt that the man had anything to do with it. Damek is just using this as an excuse to get Lehar back under Kymir's control and if Thyrr had no intention of ever coming north, then he is right to do it. You put him on that throne and he betrayed you the first chance that he got. Thyrr gave the Warding Stone to Logaire, he is vulnerable right now, it is the perfect time to correct that little mistake."

"That mistake? But he... if he..." I trailed off, feeling the dull ache in my head growing stronger. I could not keep up with it, the constant backstabbing and lying and betrayals. I remembered being in the forest, riding beside Thyrr and watching his arresting young face as I warned him not to come to Kymir. I had tried to stop him, to tell him that once he was part of us it would be a nightmare he could never escape from. He had refused to listen.

"Maialen, you had to know this would happen. Thyrr has no real power. He was never going to hold that throne, there are too many others who want it," Blaise reminded me.

"I know. I just... I just wish that it was different. That everything was different." I turned to him, feeling his proximity like the warmth of a fire, remembering the feel of him beside me. "Blaise, I-"

Kaeleb came tearing into the room then, in a flurry of white hair and apple fritter. He shoved the pastry into his mouth and ducked under the table, pressing himself back into the shadows behind the Fire Keeper's legs. I bent down to try and drag him out and he kicked me soundly on the forearm then shushed me with a frantic gesture of his hand. Out in the hall one of the cooks came barreling through the manor, yelling and cursing the Leharan brat soundly and vowing revenge.

When he was gone Blaise bent over, peering under the table with a grin. "I think you can come out now."

"He kicked me!" I was indignant, rubbing at the tender spot on my forearm. "He is completely out of control!"

Kaeleb crawled out from his hiding spot, having the decency to at least look somewhat chagrined. "Apologies, aunt. Last time he caught me he hit me with a wooden spoon that left a mark for days."

"Because you deserved it!" I retorted. "Go away and stop terrorizing everyone in the manor!"

The boy looked down at his feet and plodded for the doorway, his shock of white hair falling over his eyes.

"Kaeleb," Blaise called after him. "Next time take one for me too."

The boy's crestfallen face split into a grin and he nodded, bolting out the door. I pressed my hand to my forehead. The ache had become an insistent pounding.

"Why must you encourage him?" I asked Blaise once the boy had gone.

"He reminds me of myself at his age."

"It does not bother you that it is their child? Her and Tal's?" I asked, my jealousy causing me to needle him with that reminder, for his affection for the boy was a constant and painful reminder to me of his affection for Orabelle.

Blaise frowned, his eyes seeming to look through me, at something far away. "I know what it is like to be alone, to have everything taken from you until all you are left with is a destiny that someone else has forced upon you. What Alita did to him, it was very much like what my mother did to me. Whoever's child he is, he does not deserve the burden they have made him carry."

"You would still care what happened to him if he were not Orabelle's son?" I pressed, hating myself for it but wanting something from him that I could not explain. A word, a phrase, a gesture, anything that would make me believe that he did not still love my sister, that he cared for me the same way I cared for him.

He toyed with the edge of the Fire Opal, considering his next words carefully. "I took Akrin in, and he was not Orabelle's son, just a boy who needed guidance. Though I see now that I was not the best one to give it to him, not back then. I was so consumed by my own needs that I barely saw his and now there is a bitterness in him that has taken root and cannot be plucked out. I told you once before that you knew nothing about Alita and her family, but perhaps you should know so you can understand what Kaeleb must have gone through being raised by that woman."

He told me what he knew of the night Alita had left Veruca with Orabelle. Akrin had not wanted to go, was afraid of the water, and so he had gone to the castle and told one of the soldiers what was happening. They had come that night to stop the girl from leaving, thinking she must be someone important if the Water Keeper was trying to take her, and that their King would be displeased. In the confusion a little boy was killed, their brother, Aron. When Blaise returned to the castle and found out what had happened, he punished the man who ordered the attack on the children, and he had taken Akrin in, telling himself that it was so he could discern the importance of this random waif of a girl that Orabelle had risked lives to abscond with. In truth he felt a kinship and a pity for the boy, and he hoped that by raising him as his own son, Blaise could fill the void in his own life that had been hollowed out by the death of his brother, Bastion.

"But Akrin was not Bastion, and I was not ready to raise a son. I made him sullen and vengeful, shaped into something that was just on the edge of darkness but loyal to me," Blaise admitted, his voice soft and tinged with regret.

Blaise had learned much later on about Alita and who she really was. Her father had not been the innocent torch lighter of her stories, who had been caught stealing bread to feed his starving family. That whole tale was a farce, a ploy for sympathy. Her father had been a member of the Harbonah in Veruca, and when he had been killed, it had not been for stealing bread but because he had attempted to assassinate the King. Blaise had thwarted the attack, learning of it from one of the participants who found silver to be more inspiring than their religious dogma. Blaise had rounded up all of the conspirators, everyone involved, and fed them to the blooddrinkers.

"I could not allow what they had done to go unpunished," he said, seeing my grimace at his admission. "The Harbonah are poison and the moment they think they have gained any power, they will scurry out of the shadows like cockroaches. I made an example of them, all except the girl."

He had forgotten the name of the young girl who had also been part of the plot against his life, the one who had gone to the old, wizened woman in town and gotten the herbs they would try to use to poison him. He believed then that she was being manipulated by her father, she must not have understood what she was a part of. He remembered his commander, Caranor, warning him that they should kill her too, that once she had believed the doctrine of the Harbonah, she would always be a threat. Blaise had refused. He had looked down at her big, brown eyes and warned her that this was the one time her life would be spared, that he would not grant her leniency again. She nodded, tears falling down her face as she threw herself at his feet, thanking him for his mercy. He had dismissed her and completely forgotten about her, not piecing together the puzzle of who she was until long after Orabelle was dead.

"Everything she told your sister was a lie. When I heard the rumors that she had taken the child, I started to search for them, but every time I got close to finding them they slipped away," Blaise told me.

"Did you have her killed? As punishment for what she had done?" I had to ask him.

He laughed, a bitter sound. "No, it was not me, Maialen. Though I know how all of you like to blame me for every untimely death."

"I did not mean-"

"You don't have to explain yourself. I am not innocent, I have done my share of killing, just not the ones that I have been credited with," he muttered darkly.

"The Harbonah, what else do you know about them?" I asked, wanting to comfort him but afraid to try, afraid that he would push me away.

Blaise shrugged, shaking off the melancholy that had settled over him. "Before Alita brought Kaeleb to Council it had been years since I heard anything of them. Since then, rumors and whispers from zealots spreading the seeds of discontent. The end of the Keepers is imminent, prophecies of the Solvrei, things of that sort."

I thought back to my conversation with Kaeleb, remembering the odd way he had spoken of it. "When I asked Kaeleb about them, he once referred to the Harbonah as a he, as a person. I had thought maybe at the time the boy was just confused, or had mixed up his words, but perhaps he meant what he said. Could the Harbonah be a single person, leading the others against the Keepers?"

"It is possible, every sheep needs a shepherd. And the boy did not learn the ancient language from Alita or Kaden, someone taught him. There are not many who could have done that," Blaise mused thoughtfully.

"He said they lived in Samirra for a long time, it had to be someone there," I surmised.

Blaise seemed amused. "And what will you do to the Harbonah once you learn who they are, Earth Queen?"

"They want to kill us. I will kill them first." I lifted my chin, staring boldly back at him. He laughed and pushed himself up from the table, taking a strand of my hair and tucking it behind my ear, his breath warm on my cheek.

"You are not the timid mouse you once were. I pity your enemies, Queen Maialen. I will see what else I can find out from the boy," he said before turning and striding from the room, leaving me staring after him, breathless.

27

The beat of drums echoed over the sand dunes as Cossiana stared out over the vast expanse of blue sea that surrounded Tahitia. As the Elder of her people, it was she who would decide what would happen next. So many long years had led to this moment, enough so that she had begun to think the Samains had been wrong in their prophecies. She had hoped fervently for them to be wrong, but those hopes were gone now. She had known the truth of the legends the moment she had seen the two identical brothers step off the ship with the Earth Queen. She had known that this was the beginning of the end.

She was a young woman when she first heard the stories, vibrant and proud, full of a fervent zest for life and possessing a natural talent as a healer. It had been a night much like this one, a jubilant ceremony full of music and dancing. She had sat cross-legged on the cool sand, the moonlight bathing the island in its ephemeral glow while she clutched her baby in her arms. Her sweet baby boy, Damian.

The Samain had hobbled his way into the center of the circle, glaring around at the happy, festive faces that surrounded him. He gestured for the islanders to silence their drumming, and there was nothing celebratory in the look he had given them.

"The time of peace draws to an end," he began with a warning. Cossiana had felt her smile falter, holding her baby tighter against her as the Samain foretold the coming of the Solvrei and the return of the wolf-god who would herald the end of the world, the Fenris.

The Samain said the Fenris was an ancient god who had been banished to their realm as punishment, for he had gone against the will of the others and created the Warding Stones, but the truth was that the other gods feared him. The gods had their own legends and prophecies and one of them foretold that it was the Fenris who would bring about their destruction. He became known as the harbinger of doom, the bringer of death. The other gods hated the sight of him because they hated to believe that anything bad could happen to them, and so they had taken the opportunity when it presented itself, and accused him of wrongdoing so they could banish him, trapping him on Imbria where he would be forced to dwell, immortal but not invulnerable, until he found redemption.

Cossiana drew herself out of the memory and looked at the man who now stood beside her at the edge of the sea, unremarkable in every way except that he existed at all. She said to him, "You are not as I expected."

He seemed undisturbed by her comment. "We are what we are."

"Is there no way to stop what is coming?" she asked him.

He glanced down at her face, lined with age and worry and wisdom. "You took in the child. You knew what would follow."

"You speak of Tal." Cossiana felt the ghost of a smile tug at her lips at the memory of the quiet boy they had found wandering outside in the rainstorm. Her heart still ached for his loss, even to this day, for though she had never told him so, she had loved him as if he were her own son. Damian's birth had been difficult, her womb not strong enough to carry any more life in it afterwards, and she had resigned herself to never having more children, though her heart ached at the thought. She had always wanted a large family, to give brothers and sisters to her first-born son, allies with the unbreakable bond of blood to see them through this life. But it was not to be and she accepted it. Then one day she was down at the beach, sweat beading along her forehead beneath the scarf that held back her long, black braids, cleaning fish while her young son splashed in the surf. The Samain had come hobbling across the sand, leaning heavily on the twisting piece of driftwood he used to supplement his aging legs. His beard was dense and white, hiding most of his face, and his hair was shaved close so that the sun glared off his skull like a halo. She had inclined her head, thinking he was merely passing her by, but he stopped in front of her, regarding her closely.

"You show promise as a healer," he had commented.

"My thanks to you," she replied, feeling her face warm with his regard. It was rare for the Samain's to speak to anyone but the island elders, rarer still for them to bestow compliments. She was pleased by his attention, proud that he had noticed her hard work.

"Your sons will be important in what is to come, as will you."

She was startled by this admission and eyed him cautiously, wiping the bloody fish guts on her apron. "What do you mean, Samain? I have but one child, and sadly I am unable to carry another."

The elderly man had looked past her to where Damian was frolicking in the water, trying to catch slippery fish with his bare hands, the dark umber of his skin glistening with saltwater. He watched the boy for so long that Cossiana began to feel apprehensive, not caring for the vagueness of his words and his ominous tone in regard to her son, the boy who meant everything to her.

"You will have another," the old man finally said, turning his gaze back to her. The whites of his eyes were yellowed with age and there was a cloudiness over the dark pupils, but still they were sharp with knowledge. "It is customary for our people to raise orphaned children as their own, despite where they come from. In ancient times, before the peace the Keepers brought, we would take in the babies of our fallen enemies, raise them as our own, train them to be warriors of Tahitia. You want more children, do you not?"

She was afraid to tell him that she wanted it more than anything, for she did not want to seem ungrateful for the gifts the gods had already bestowed on her. She simply nodded her head.

"When you find him, you must take him in and raise him as your own, in the tradition of our people. Raise your sons to be warriors, Cossiana, for they will need their strength to fight what is coming."

She felt a chill run down her arms at the Samain's use of her name, strange to hear on the lips of the revered elder.

"What is coming?" she had asked, her voice barely a whisper.

"The time of the Solvrei is at hand and the gods will return. Take the boy when you find him, all of Imbria depends upon it." He had glanced once more at her young son who was proudly holding aloft the wriggling silver fish he had finally managed to catch. Damian called for his mother to look and the fish slipped out of his hands, smacking him wetly on the face before escaping back into the safety of the cool, deep water. Cossiana could not help but smile at him, and the Samain hobbled away down the beach, never speaking another word to her again.

She had done as he asked, knowing the second she laid eyes on the somber boy who had been wandering aimlessly through the rain, that this was the son she was meant to have. Tal had been quiet and gentle, his grey eyes always watching. At first, she had been unsure that the other families would accept the Leharan boy as one of them, but the Samain had been right, and the Tahitians had remembered the old custom, welcoming the boy as one of their own with open arms. He and Damian were so young when they began training to be warriors, their tiny bodies still thin and spindly with youth, but they fought hard, and always side by side, one with a spear and one with a sword. There was never any dividing them. Cossiana remembered a time that someone had stolen an extra saltfish she had been drying. She knew the boys were hungry, and that hunger was part of their training, that they needed to learn to be clever and quick and to fend for themselves. She hated to punish them for simply eating a small saltfish, but she knew that she must. She had brought them in to the round hut they lived in, dragging them by their ears. Damian had winced and wriggled in her grasp but Tal had walked silent and proud, his face not giving anything away.

"Who took the fish?" she had demanded of them, pointing to the conspicuously empty spot where the morsel had been.

"I did," they both claimed at once.

She tried to hide her smile. "You both stole and ate one tiny saltfish?"

"No, it was me, not Damian," Tal said in his quiet way.

"It was not him!" Damian insisted, stomping his foot. "I am the one who did it!"

Cossiana had sighed but inwardly she had swelled with pride, pleased that the boys would defend each other, that each was willing to take the punishment for their brother. "This is your last chance, tell me who really did it."

They both stared at each other, their jaws set, and she knew they would not say another word. She had punished them both, then that night she had slipped a tiny bundle of saltfish wrapped in banana leaves under the woven grass door of their room.

They had continued on like that, thick as thieves, both determined to protect the other no matter what. She had watched them grow into young men, watched their muscles fill out and their faces lose the roundness of childhood. They were incredible warriors, their skill unchallenged by anyone but each other. She had watched them fight, coming to every tournament, marveling at their skill and grace and clapping her hands and hollering wildly when they won. She had taught them to read and write, had spoken to them in the ancient language, borrowing words and phrases from the elders to share with them. She taught them about the realms of Imbria, about the Keepers, learning everything she could so that she could pass it on to her sons.

Then that fateful day happened. Chronus summoned a healer for his wife, and it was Cossiana who answered the call. She had left her beloved sons and gone to Kymir to attend to the Leharan Queen, Ursula, who lay wasting away in her bed. She had known the signs of the blooddrinkers bite, recognized the sickness, but she could find no mark on the woman, no reason why she should be ailing. She had told Chronus that if she could take the Queen back to the islands, she could save her. She needed time to find out what had happened and what was causing the illness. Chronus had refused, dismissing her back to Tahitia with a flick of his wrist. He had brought her there as a pretense, a way to pretend that he cared what was happening to Ursula, believing the islanders were nothing but savages and would not be able to cure her. Cossiana had been angry, and she considered telling the next Council gathering what she suspected was happening, that Chronus was poisoning his wife, but the clever Earth King was too quick for her. The banishment occurred, orchestrated by Chronus, and the Tahitians were suddenly isolated from all of Imbria, even

Lehar, the realm they had pledged loyalty to and protected for hundreds of years.

Cossiana had gone back to her sons and known then that Tal could not stay with them, not if he was to have the life he deserved, and so she sent him to Lehar. Damian had been devastated, begging her not to do it, not to send his brother away from him. After Tal was gone, Damian coped with the loss by going to the wastelands to complete his training as a warrior. When he returned, he had come to terms with what had happened, accepting that his mother was right and that Tal was meant to go, but he had never stopped wishing for his brother to come home. Even on the rare times when Tal made it back to Tahitia, telling them of his new life and of the beautiful and wonderful Water Keeper he had become Guardian to, still Damian wished for things to be as they had been, for his brother to come back to them. But it was not meant to be.

"I had hoped the Samains were wrong," Cossiana said, coming back to the present and shaking off the heavy shroud of the past.

The man beside her frowned, the moonlight glistening off the long scar that cut through his eyebrow. "The Samains repeated what we told them to. You doubted us?"

"I simply hoped, Fenris," Cossiana answered, spreading her weathered hands in a gesture of supplication. There was a low whine and she looked down at the mangled dog who lay in the sand at her feet, its one eye fixed on her. Seff seemed to accept this answer and they both returned to watching the sea, waiting. Behind them the musical rhythm of the drums continued to fill the night air, mingling with the sounds of laughter and excitement. Tonight was a full moon, and the Tahitians were celebrating, a joyful and exuberant dedication to the gods for the gift of light in the darkness. She saw the tiny figure of the girl, Eolande, spinning in a circle, her arms thrown wide as she contorted her small body to the rhythm of the drums, mimicking the movements of the Tahitians with innocent glee. It was good to see the girl smile for a moment after what she had been through. It was the children who would suffer the most in what was to come.

She remembered her own boys dancing in the light of the full moon, so many years ago, one dark as night and the other golden like the sun, with hair that was as pale as the moon. They had spun around each other, waving their arms wildly, pounding their small feet into the sand until they were panting with exhaustion. They had grinned at one another, gulping down water from the jug she brought to them before taking her arms and dragging her with them to go and dance some more. They had stayed until the sun came up, laughing and spinning in circles, twirling around her as she showed them the proper steps.

Cossiana closed her eyes, losing herself in the memory for just a moment, until the sweet, impossible ache to hold her children once again became unbearable.

A long while passed, nothing breaking the monotonous ebb and flow of the waves against the shore. Seff sighed, folding his arms over his chest, his placid face bland as he suggested to her that maybe the person they were waiting for was not coming.

"He will be here," she said with conviction.

A deep, heavy baritone rumbled through the sound of the drumbeats. "Your belief in me is unwavering as always, mother."

Cossiana turned to find herself looking up at the stoic and proud face of her son, Damian. The glittering moon threw shards of light against the silver hooks that pierced his ears and he wore dark blue fisherman's pants, tucked around his hips and tied at the waist. He was older, his long dreadlocks sporting the merest hint of grey at the roots, and he seemed a little thinner than she had remembered, though he was still a tower of heavy muscle and sinew.

"My boy," she said, her smile engulfing him in its warmth. She spread her arms and he hugged her tightly, breathing deeply of the scent he remembered so vividly from his childhood, of the ocean and herbs. "I wish that we were meeting under better circumstances."

"Has the time come already?" Damian asked, stepping back from her with a frown. The dog gave a low growl and Damian turned his black eyes on the beast, regarding him thoughtfully.

It was Seff who answered him. "The Earth Queen has the boy, and Chaote has been released from her prison."

Damian seemed surprised. "Maialen has the boy? Is that wise? Why did you not take him from her?"

"I told her to kill him, but she refused. She will protect the boy," Cossiana said.

Her son turned his dark gaze on her, his brow furrowing. "You told her to kill him?"

"A test," Cossiana explained. "There is much for you to catch up on, my son."

"It was a wise ploy," Seff said, giving Cossiana an appreciative glance. "The Earth Queen now believes that the Tahitians wish the Solvrei to die."

Damian shook his head, grinning in the moonlight and teasing his mother. "I did not know you could be so devious."

Cossiana shrugged her shoulders that were starting to curl inward with age. "The Keepers are not the only ones who can hide things."

She watched her son as they stood there on the beach, bathed in silver light. He was her pride and joy, her legacy, all that she would leave behind in this world when she had gone, and she had hated being apart from him all these years. She remembered when he had left Tahitia for good, after Orabelle had died. He had been inconsolable then, dark and brooding and tormented by his failure, convinced that the Queen's death was his fault because he had failed to protect her. Cossiana had gone looking for him one night, the instincts of a mother telling her that he needed her. She found him standing at the edge of the shore where the water caressed the sand, tears streaming down his strong face. In the distance she could see the faint shimmer that was Lehar.

"Oh, my boy," she had murmured, laying her hand on his massive shoulder.

"I loved them both," he whispered, "and I could not save either of them."

"Your brother's death was not your fault, my son," Cossiana had said sternly, turning his chin and forcing him to look at her. "He would not want you to think such things."

"He would not have wanted me to let her die. All of my training, all of my strength was worth nothing when it mattered."

Cossiana had not answered, but stood beside him in silent tribute, her hand on his shoulder, connecting him to the living, reminding him where he had come from. Together they stared out at the sea, at the beautiful blue-green forms that wavered in and out of sight along the waves, a high-pitched keen carried on the wind. She had known then what he had done with the Pearl, and she approved, for no one would guard the amulet better than Orabelle herself, and what were the Sirens if not part of her.

"I must leave the islands," he had said, breaking the silence after what seemed like an eternity. She felt her heart swell with grief at his words but she forced herself to remain impassive, waiting for him to explain. "I have to protect their child; it is the only thing I can do that will atone for my failures. If I stay here they will find me, and I cannot take that chance."

She wanted to argue, to assure him that he did not need to carry the burden of guilt, that the choices Tal and Orabelle had made were no one's fault but their own, but she knew he would not listen. Her son was stubborn and proud, and his honor meant everything to him. She had felt such overwhelming love for him then, for the good man that he was, that she had nearly choked on the emotion.

"Do what you must, my boy. I will always be here waiting when you return," she told him.

He hesitated, his eyes still searching the sea, filled with a longing to reclaim what was lost and could never be recovered. "Do you believe that there is a chance this child could be happy?"

Cossiana had considered his question for a long time. She knew the old legends better than anyone, and she knew the prophecies and the promises of the ancients. She recited them in her head, knowing that if any of it was true, then the answer would be no.

"I hope so," was all she said. Damian had embraced her then, breathing deeply, feeling the unequivocal comfort of a mother's love one last time before he had left forever.

She watched him now, her joy at seeing him again dampened by the reasons he had come. The Warding Stones had been recovered, the Fenris had returned, the half-breed was released from her prison, and the fate of their world rested in the hands of one little child, the child her son had sworn to protect. It was Damian that would be in danger now, for she knew without a doubt that he would willingly sacrifice his own life to save the rest of them.

"The Earth Queen has sent a summons to Council," Cossiana told them. "I received it today. I will go and represent Tahitia, and find out what the rest of them know. When I return, we can decide together what we should do next."

"Find my brother while you are there and bring him back with you," Seff beseeched her, the first hint of emotion she had ever heard from him creeping at the edges of his voice.

"I will do what I can," she promised him.

"You must be careful, mother," Damian warned. "They are all snakes that would swallow themselves whole if they thought it would give them more power. Especially the Fire Keeper."

She smiled at his concern. "I will be fine. I will convince the Earth Queen once again that the Tahitians wish the boy to die, that we want nothing to do with the Solvrei. It is the safest way."

"Do not be too convincing, we do not want her to kill him," Seff offered, absently stroking the mottled brown fur along the dog's neck.

Cossiana chuckled and took Damian's hand to lead him back towards the circle of drums. She would dance with her son one more time. "I have no concerns there. Maialen is too gentle a soul, she would never harm a child. He is safer with her than anywhere else on Imbria."

28

Favian tugged on his long braid of hair, his lips pressed into a thin line as he tried to remain calm and speak slowly and carefully. His eyes burned from the smoke and ash that filled the air, and as the Fomori gathered outside the inner gate in greater and greater numbers, the smell of rotten flesh had permeated the palace. Favian had not seen Hovard since he told him to leave, and he prayed that his friend had made it out safely and was far away from the horrors that taken over Iriellestra.

Chaote had been true to her word, the bodies piling up as she waited for Astraeus to surrender the Sapphire. Favian had not been to see her again, though he watched her from the battlements as she slid her knife across the throat of another pleading Samirran. The black eyes glittered with hate and her lip curled in disgust as she dropped the dying body onto the heap of corpses. She had seen Favian there, and she had shaken her head as if disappointed in him, walking away until it was time to kill again. She had found new clothing, changing the fur-lined robes of the Fomori for dark leathers, a gleaming silver breastplate over her chest. He wondered which of the Samirran soldiers it had belonged to, and he hoped they had not suffered too much before she had taken it. He wanted to shout at her, to implore her to stop every time she looked up at him, but there was no need, because his King refused to accept the reality of what was happening. It mattered little to Astraeus that his people were being slaughtered at his doorstep, as long as he remained safely inside the palace walls.

"My King, I mean no disrespect," Favian began, trying once more to reason with his obstinate ruler, "but the amulet is worthless to us if you cannot use it. The Fomori are gathering and the men are deserting. Soon there will be no one left to defend the wall and it will fall. If you would just give up the Sapphire-"

"I will not say it again!" Astraeus practically snarled at him, the statuesque face distorted into something feral.

"But people are dying!" Favian shouted, the last of his resolve finally breaking. "Your people are dying! And it is you who are sworn to protect them! The wall is going to fall, you are not going to stop it, all you are doing is prolonging the inevitable. I believe that this woman will keep her word, and we have no other choice."

"You cannot trust a Fomori! Or anyone aligned with those miserable beasts. I will not surrender, Samirra has stood for hundreds of years, it will not fall now," Astraeus insisted with unwavering confidence.

Favian was about to say something more when the ground began to shake beneath them. He reached out, grabbing the King instinctively to protect him, shielding him with his body as a great roar like a thousand peals of thunder filled the air. Then as suddenly as it had started, it stopped.

"Is it Maialen?" Astraeus asked, hope springing joyfully upon his face.

"I do not think so," Favian answered, making his way to the window to look out at the cloud of dust and debris that was billowing out from the spot where the inner gate had been.

The gate that was now a pile of rubble. "They have broken through."

Astraeus stared at him as if he were mad, unable to comprehend what Favian was saying for in his mind it was still impossible.

"Do you hear me? They are coming!" Favian yelled at him, grabbing him by the collar and shaking him.

"The wall..." Astraeus muttered, his face paling and his eyes growing round as it finally dawned on him what was happening. "Get me to the clearing. I have an eagle there."

Favian shoved him towards the doorway. "Go, I will get Astus and Aracellis and meet you there."

Astraeus turned and fled down the hallway and Favian ran the other way, towards the library. Already he could hear screams from the courtyard and he tore through the palace until he reached the ornate doors, trying to shove them open but they were barred from the inside. He pounded on the carved wood with both fists, shouting for Astus.

"Who is there?" the old man asked timidly from the other side of his barricade.

"It is Favian! Open the doors, Astus, we need to go now!" Favian yelled. He heard the bar slide back and the click of the mechanism as it was released, and he shoved the doors open, toppling over the old man in his haste. He reached down and grabbed his tunic, hauling the old man to his feet while he looked around for the child. Aracellis was folded against the door frame, his face white and terrified and his bottom lip trembling with fear.

"Come with me, your father is taking you from here," Favian told him, grabbing the child's hand and shoving Astus out ahead of them.

"Where are we going? Is Irielle coming?" Astus demanded.

"Irielle is already there," Favian lied, not having time to try and reason with the mad old man. Astus flapped his hands in agitation, the whisps of his hair floating straight up from his head as they hurried through the corridors. More screams floated in with the smoke and ash and there was an insistent thumping sound, which Favian assumed was the Fomori battering at the palace doors.

"Faster," he snapped at the old man, shoving him along rudely. He would never have been so callous to the former king of Samirra, but manners could be apologized for, being ripped apart by a vengeful Fomori could not. He scooped Aracellis up in his arms, feeling the boy's cheek press into his neck, wet with tears.

They burst out into the clearing between the domed minarets, the air enveloping them in a thick, yellow haze. The eagle was hopping from foot to foot in agitation, its head darting back and forth and jerking at its tether as the handler tried to sooth it. Astraeus stood beside the great bird, buckling his helmet and saying something Favian could not hear to the handler.

"My King!" Favian boomed out across the clearing. Astraeus ignored him, swinging himself onto the great neck of the beast. Favian set Aracellis down and sprinted forward as the handler began to loosen the tether.

"Wait, I have brought your son," Favian said, pointing frantically at Aracellis, who was trying so hard to be brave despite his abject terror.

Astraeus shook his head. "The eagle is only equipped for one rider."

"At least take your son!" the Guardian countered in disbelief.

"Keep them safe, Favian. I trust you will do all that you can," was the King's reply.

Favian was dumbstruck. For a moment he just stood there, watching as Astraeus adjusted himself on the eagle, wrapping the tethers around his gloved fists. This was the man he had served all these years. This was the man he had defended, the man he had refused to betray, the man whose life he had saved over and over again. This was the man he had given his life to, given up everything to protect.

It was too much to bear and he jumped, hurling himself at Astraeus and sending them both tumbling off the other side of the feathered creature, the eagle screeching in protest as they hit the fragile, hollow bones of its wing. Astraeus rolled beneath him, shoving the Guardian off of him and kicking out with his booted foot, hitting Favian in the thigh. The Guardian got to his feet, grabbing the back of the gilded jacket and throwing the King to the ground before he could clamor back up onto the protesting bird.

"I will have you killed for this!" Astraeus snarled. "Traitor!"

"We are all going to die anyway," Favian said darkly, straddling the King and pressing his forearm against his throat.

Aracellis let out a wail but his grandfather shushed him, pulling the boy into his arms and pressing his face into his shoulder so he could not see.

"Astus, get on the eagle," Favian said, trying to hold down the struggling King who was writhing furiously beneath him.

"But I-"

"Get on the eagle!" Favian commanded, his voice echoing over the polished white marble. Astus shuffled forward, the boy still cradled against him, and they clamored ungracefully into the saddle on the feathered back.

"Release them," Favian told the handler who was watching the whole tableaux in shock, his mouth gaping open. He pulled the tethers loose from the thick, silver rings that held them.

"No! Do not leave me here! Father!" Astraeus shoved Favian's arm aside, breaking the Guardian's hold with the strength of his panic.

"Save him if you can," Astus said to Favian. He gave his son a last, sad look, his drooping face sagging with regret, then he flicked the tethers and the beast leapt into the sky.

Astraeus roared, throwing Favian completely off him and sending the wiry Guardian rolling across the floor. He bolted after the eagle but he was too late. The massive creature dipped over the edge of the clearing, soaring into the space between the minarets and arcing into a slow curve around the palace. Favian could see the Fomori, thick as ants, crawling over the battlements of the inner wall. They saw the eagle and howled and then she was there. Chaote. Her dark hair streamed behind her as she ran, the Fomori parting around her to let her through, a spear clutched in her hand. He realized what she was doing, that she was running to intercept the eagle. She was magnificent, a deadly valkyrie bent on destruction.

"It is not him!" Favian bellowed, knowing that she would assume it was Astraeus escaping, but the din of the battle around her ate away at the sound and she could not hear him. His heart felt like it would beat out of his chest as he watched the eagle, praying for it to soar higher, to lift itself out of her reach. He saw it struggle, the wing that he and Astraeus had fallen on unable to extend fully. Then Chaote leapt into the air, throwing her spear just as the eagle curved around the palace above her. It screeched, the spear piercing its undamaged wing in a burst of white feathers before it plummeted towards the ground.

Favian pushed himself to his feet, his breath ragged, his eyes filled with smoke and tears. Astraeus was barreling down on him, his face a mask of rage.

"What have you done?" he cried, hitting the Guardian under the chin and throwing him backwards.

At first Favian just lay there, watching what was happening as if it were happening to someone else. Astraeus kicked him in the ribs and he felt the breath leave him, struggling to gasp for air. He deserved it. He deserved to die. He could have stopped it, he could have listened to Magnus and stopped all of it before it started. At least if Astraeus killed him it would be over soon. He could feel the blows of the King, tasting blood on his lips. Then he saw the blue flash of the Sapphire beneath the jacket. The amulet of a Keeper, of a man whose responsibility was to protect the people of his realm. Favian could not give up, not yet. Not while he could still save some of them.

He coughed, blood and spittle foaming from his mouth as Astraeus kicked him again and again. He reached out, grabbing the booted foot and twisting it so that the Air Keeper lost his balance, toppling sideways. Favian scrambled across the ground, wrapping his arms around Astraeus's neck and pulling the King against him, almost in an embrace. Favian held him there as he struggled, blood and tears mixing as they ran down the Guardian's face. He closed his eyes, tightening his hold on the other man's neck, feeling the warmth of the body in his arms, the man who had been his entire life. He remembered the first time he had seen him, how glorious he had seemed, and how strong and brave, how full of promise he had been. A thousand lifetimes ago.

"It is the only way," Favian whispered, his voice raw and tears still streaming down his face as he grieved for the man that might have been. The booted feet stopped scraping against the marble and the dark sweep of hair fell across the Samirran King's forehead as the last of his breath left him.

29

I stood beside Blaise on the docks as grey storm clouds churned overhead, watching the Leharan ship as it approached and feeling my stomach knot in anticipation. Damek was near us, the scroll he had prepared rolled up in his hands and he was frowning with all of his might, the aged lines of his face folded down in bitter disregard.

"We should be doing the same for my cousin," Blaise muttered under his breath, referring to the scroll which listed Thyrr's accused crimes.

"Your cousin is not some impetuous boy," Damek snapped at him. "Something you should have realized and dealt with long ago. It is not our problem that you are a sentimental fool."

Blaise glared at him, his amber eyes glistening with anger. "Perhaps I should deal with the problem of an advisor who does not know his place."

"Please!" I interrupted. "Please, stop fighting. This... this is bad enough."

I waved a hand at the approaching ship, once again feeling a wave of guilt roll over me. I tried to shove it down, telling myself that I did not owe Thyrr anything, that perhaps he really did kill Alita, but I knew in my heart that it was wrong. I also knew that we needed Lehar, now more than ever, and that

Thyrr had proven he could not be trusted as an ally. I wished he had just listened to me that day in the forest, that he had walked away from us and never looked back.

I glanced back at the men behind me, waiting to take the young man into custody and keep him locked away until the Council was officially convened. I wondered if Astraeus would come, if he would send someone in his place, or if he would just ignore us completely, still seething over our invasion of his lands. I remembered the burned bodies of the plague victims, the smell of the charred corpses that littered the field, and I prayed that my husband would stay far away. I did not think I could bear to look upon him after what he had done. I also had no doubt that this time there would be no dissuading Blaise from killing him, not after all that had happened in the north, and with the Fire Keeper's temper already on edge thanks to Logaire.

I felt another pang of guilt at the thoughts that burdened my mind. I could not help but consider that keeping Logaire in power in Veruca would keep Blaise here in Kymir, with me. We had been through so much together that I felt a panic in my chest at the thought of being so far apart from him. It was his consolation that made the overwhelming pain of Gideon's loss bearable, and it was his strong presence that made me believe we could stop whatever was coming from the north. I shuddered at the thought of those black, bottomless eyes staring up at us in the cave, hissing the word *Fenris* from her hoarse throat. Whatever she was, and whatever she wanted, I did not want to face it alone.

The ship had tied off to the docks, the ramp lowered so the Leharans could disembark. Bacatha was first, the titan of a woman striding down the pier, eyeing us warily. There was the distant rumble of thunder and the air felt heavy, laden with unfallen rain.

"Earth Queen," Bacatha said, bowing slightly to me, her icy gaze wandering across the gathered men. Her hand rested on the hilt of her sword. She was no fool, she knew something was amiss. "We did not expect such a robust greeting."

Behind her a stream of Leharans were following her path towards us, a line of regents brought up by the shining soldiers of the Leharan Guard. Damek frowned harder, if such a thing was even possible, clearly displeased at the number of islanders that had come. His black robes flapped in the rising wind like the wings of a crow.

Bacatha noticed his discomfort and smiled. "Your invitation was for all of the islands to be represented. Did you not believe that we were so united?"

Damek ignored her, tapping the scroll in agitation as he searched for Thyrr. The young man came last, Colwyn walking beside him. Blaise chuckled softly and Bacatha threw him a sharp glance, which he returned with his careless grin.

"Thyrr of Lehar!" Damek sang out, his shrill voice causing the others to stop and stare curiously.

Thyrr sauntered up to us, his arresting countenance looking anxious but friendly. He grasped my hands and my stomach churned again, my face flushing as he said," Queen Maialen, I am glad you are safe."

"No thanks to you," Blaise pointed out, his voice harsh though the smile lingered on his chiseled features. "Your promises to send help turned out to be rather empty."

Thyrr gave him a crooked smile though I could sense his discomfort. "There were mitigating circumstances that delayed our departure. By the time we were able to sail, there was word that the Kymirrans had turned back. We assumed that the war was over. I must say, I was surprised to learn of your defeat."

"Did you learn of it from my cousin?" Blaise sneered.

Thyrr's face flushed and I was surprised to see the anger that washed over his features. He was about to respond when

Damek pushed his way forward, unrolling the scroll and reading the proclamation aloud that accused Thyrr of the murder of Alita.

"This is absurd!" Bacatha spat, her sword half-drawn from her sheath. The men behind me moved forward to surround Thyrr and the rest of the Leharan Guard looked to Bacatha, their hands on their sword hilts, waiting for her command.

"Stop!" Thyrr ordered. "There will be no bloodshed on my account. These accusations are preposterous. What proof do you have?"

Damek sniffed in annoyance then began to recite the testimony that he had gathered against the new Leharan King. The wind flapped against the scroll, the advisor struggling to keep hold of it as he read. Thyrr listened with narrowed eyes, and I saw that Bacatha was still clutching her sword with a white-knuckled hand, ready to sever the heads of all of us should the young man deem in necessary. My thoughts flashed to my own Guardians, both of whom had abandoned me willingly, though Gideon had tried to protect me from Blaise in the end, and I wondered bitterly what it was about Thyrr that inspired such loyalty. Orabelle had possessed the same quality, inspiring the same all-encompassing devotion, and I had never understood how or why.

"You have already decided, haven't you?" Thyrr asked when Damek had finished. He was looking at me, his blue-gold eyes full of hurt. For a moment he looked so much like my sister the last time I had seen her that I was unable to speak.

"I..." I let my voice trail off. There was nothing that I could say that would make it better, and there was no going back now. "I told you that you did not want this life."

"I never thought it would be you," Thyrr murmured.

I felt a stab of guilt so intense that I nearly gasped aloud from it, hating him for the way I felt. I had told him how it would be, tried to warn him and he had not listened. No one ever listened to me. Thyrr had made his own choice and he had chosen poorly, trusting Logaire instead of me, and that was his own fault.

"You are Orabelle's brother, not mine. I owe you nothing," I said to him, hardening my heart against the pain in his face. I had to do what was best for Kymir and for all of Imbria. "Take him away."

"No!" Bacatha protested but Thyrr lifted his hand, calling for her to be calm.

"Now is not the time," he said to her, gesturing to me and Blaise. She would never be able to defeat two Keepers and to try would only result in a pier littered with Leharan bodies. The men took Thyrr with them, heading to the cells where Alita had been held. Bacatha and given me a look so cold that it stung, then she spun on her heel and stomped back to the ship, refusing to be part of anything else that went on.

Rain began to fall, not much more than a mist at first, then gathering in intensity as the restless grey sheets of clouds molded themselves to the horizon. We turned back towards the forest, the wet droplets soaking my hair and gown. I looked at Blaise as he walked beside me, the rain glistening off the planes of his face and dripping from his crimson hair. He felt my gaze and glanced over, his amber eyes bright in the dull greyness of the storm, and I wondered what he was thinking. The rest of the delegations were due to arrive soon, and the Council meeting would convene the next morning. The meeting that would decide the fate of Veruca. I wanted to reach out and touch him, to take his hand and tell him that no matter what happened, he would always be a Keeper and he would have a place there with me, but I held my tongue, not wanting the others to hear or see.

When I first heard it, I thought it was the wind. The rain had become a torrent and the storm was rumbling in from the sea. Blaise stopped abruptly, his amber eyes growing wide at the sound, the high-pitched keen that I had not heard in more than ten years. He looked at me, as if to confirm that he was not mad, that I heard it too, and I nodded my head imperceptibly, the barest of movements as a vice closed around my heart.

The Sirens.

Blaise spun around, sprinting back in the direction of the pier and I stood helpless, watching him go, the rain making his form hazy as it disappeared into the fog that was rolling in with the storm. I would never forget the look on his face, the desperation and the hope. It was like he had ripped my heart from my chest when he ran to them, leaving bloodied pieces of me trailing after him. I would never forget that one unguarded moment when I had seen the truth, a truth I had known all along but had not wanted to accept. He still loved her. He still loved Orabelle, and he always would.

I heard shouting near the pier, then a scream of pain. The shrieks of the Sirens filled the air like the cries of a banshee and I wanted to go, to see what was happening, but I could not move. I was rooted to the ground, frozen in my fear, the fear that she would be there, that my sister was still alive. It dawned on me in that moment how much I hated her for all that she had done, and for all that happened because of her. I squeezed my eyes shut, pressing my hands over my ears, not wanting to see or hear the horrible sound of their wailing any longer.

"Maialen! What is happening?" Damek's spidery fingers gripped my arms, jerking me out of my stupor. The rain had plastered his thin hair to his forehead, his small eyes darting over my shoulder in panic at the sounds that floated through the storm.

"I do not know," I whispered.

"Call the guards! Get down to the docks!" Damek screeched at another man who stood near us. I saw a flash of white and Kaeleb was there, squinting up at me as the rain pummeled his tiny face. I stared down at him, hating him too, wishing he would go and find his mother and she would take him away forever.

"Why have they come?" Kaeleb asked me, his tone accusing.

I shook my head. He gave me a withering glare then he went hurtling down the path, disappearing into the misty ether. There was another scream, this time in the direction that the men had taken Thyrr, and I realized that he must be what the Sirens had come for. I finally broke out of the paralyzing grip of my shock and lifted my skirts, running down the path after the boy. I had seen firsthand the fury of the Sirens and what they could do when they had ripped Raynor apart right in front of me. I could not let them loose on Kymir.

When I reached the docks the storm had released its full fury upon the sea and the waves rose and fell in great swells, battering the piers with showering arcs of sea water. I saw Bacatha there, facing Blaise with her sword drawn, blood smeared on the corner of her lip and dripping down her chin with the rainwater. Blaise had Kaeleb shielded behind him, one arm thrown back protectively over the boy.

"He is one of ours, you should let me take him!" Bacatha was shouting. The Fire Keeper was shaking his head. Then the hideous sound once again pierced through the storm and the keening of the Sirens rose like the waves. They were with Thyrr, flanking him as he ran back to the ship, and my heart pounded in my chest at the sight, my eyes searching the mist around them for her.

"Where is she?" I screamed at them and the creatures slowed down, moving away from Thyrr and coming towards me, their keening growing softer, more melancholy in its tone. "Is she here?"

They approached me almost timidly and I stared at their awful, beautiful faces, so amorphous, like liquid barely holding its shape. One of them tilted its head and made a mournful sound, reaching out to touch my face. I slapped its hand away, my fingers slipping through the seawater body and making me shudder in revulsion. They backed away, one of them pulling Thyrr to the ship and the other watching me sadly over its shoulder as the wind whipped the seaglass colored hair around its head.

"I hate you!" I screamed at them, and the ground shook beneath us, the land beginning to crack beneath their feet. I wanted to swallow them up, to crush them, to destroy something of hers to make her pay for all the pain she had caused the rest of us. The ground shifted before they could reach the pier and the Sirens tumbled into the crevice, shrieking in protest, their liquid bodies pooling out over the dirt and rising up again, safely away from where I had tried to swallow them. I screamed again in frustration and then they were gone, out into the sea where I could not reach them.

Bacatha was still facing off against Blaise, her sword ready. I anticipated the hot burn of fire, to see sparks dance over her sword, to see the ship burst into flames, but Blaise did nothing. He nodded his head at Thyrr, taking a step back and lifting his hands, yielding. I saw his lips moving, saying something I could not hear. Thyrr gave him a grateful look and then sprinted down the docks with Bacatha. I was breathing heavily, the knot in my throat choking me, my eyes burning with tears. Blaise swung the boy into his arms, walking towards me, his jaw set in stern lines, water pouring off of them.

"Your sister is dead, Maialen, I told you that before," he said, his voice barely discernible over the sounds of the storm.

"But the Sirens..." I began, choking back the sob that threatened to engulf me.

"They live despite her death," he answered flatly. There was a shadow on his face beneath the sheen of rainwater that coated his ruddy skin. I could not stop seeing the look he had given me when he had first heard them keening, the mere second before reason had set in and he had hoped more than anything that she could be alive.

"You let him go," I said lamely, waving at the Leharan ship that was shoving away from the dock. It would be a miracle if they even made it back to Lehar in this storm.

Blaise watched me carefully, so virile in the grey of the storm that it made my heart ache even more. "It was the right thing to do."

"You don't care about the right thing," I said with a bitter laugh. "You did it for her."

He searched my face. "I told you before, Maialen, I cannot be what you want me to be."

He walked away, still holding the boy, leaving me standing alone in the rain as the guards Damek had yelled for finally came rushing towards us.

30

Logaire trailed her long fingernails along the edge of the iron bars, smiling delightedly at the sullen young man who crouched in the dark cell. She turned to Magnus who stood behind her, waving her hand at the dungeon around them.

"See, darling? This is so much better than that silly tower," she said with a laugh.

Magnus grinned at her. He had shaved the thick beard he had grown in captivity, and a dusting of grey coated his chin. She preferred him with the beard, without it he looked so Samirran, but it was not of consequence. As far as she was concerned, Magnus could waltz around in a ball gown and she would not say a word, for the former Guardian had served her well.

He had done as she asked, dispatching her enemies methodically and with brutal efficiency that fateful night after she had claimed the throne. The next morning Veruca had known they had a new Queen, and one that would not tolerate insurrection. Those that did not respect her now feared her, and her power within the Kingdom was nearly absolute. She had called another meeting of the regents and this time no one walked out on her, all of them taking the knee so willingly that she barely had to ask. She sat on her cousin's obsidian throne, a vision in copper and gold lace, feeling satisfaction swell within her as they each pledged their devotion to her once more.

"Tell me, Akrin, do you think he will come and save you? Will he sacrifice himself for you, his supposed son?" she taunted. Akrin glared at her from the darkness of the cell. The bowl of gruel he had been given was untouched and she motioned to it with the toe of her slipper. "You should eat, darling. You need to keep up your strength for what comes next. I am afraid that I need something from you that you are not going to want to part with. But don't worry, it is not your head."

"I will give you nothing!" Akrin seethed, his face murderous.

"You do not have a choice," Logaire gloated. She had to admit to herself that she was enjoying his captivity thoroughly. She had always disliked him, and part of her had always feared him. There was something dark and twisted in the boy's mind, and she could not help but recall the mangled bodies of small rodents she had found littered in a shadowy corner behind the castle years ago. She had been horrified by the sight, and turned to flee from it, nearly colliding with the sulking boy who stood watching her.

"Akrin! What are you doing here?" she had asked, trying to turn him away from the grotesque display of little bodies.

"Do you like them?" he wanted to know, blinking up at her, an eager look on his face.

Logaire's stomach had turned with revulsion. "You did this?"

The boy shrugged, a slight smile touching his lips, as if he were proud of what he had done but did not want to brag. He did not seem to notice that she was completely disgusted.

"Does Blaise know that you do this?" she asked him.

He shook his head and she swept past him, immediately going to find her cousin and tell him that his new son was a deranged little monster. She never had the chance though, for as soon as she had found Blaise she was confronted with a new horror.

"Ahhh, Logaire, just who I was looking for," her cousin had said, and the way his amber eyes sparkled with delight made her wary. "It is time that we see you married, don't you think?"

"Married?" she repeated, caught off guard.

"Yes, dear cousin, you are now betrothed to Lindonivis, the silver merchant. It is a worthy match and I am sure you will be quite happy," he had announced expansively, as if bestowing a great gift upon her.

Her head reeled and she tried to think quickly, to find some way to object. The last thing she wanted was to be married and enslaved to a man, any man, and especially not the walking corpse that was the aging Lindonivis. "A merchant? That is the best you could do for me?"

Blaise chuckled, sitting on the edge of the desk and looking quite amused. He was enjoying this thoroughly. "He is quite wealthy; you will be well cared for."

"He is ancient!" she had protested, picturing the doddering and miserly old man they spoke of.

"Then you will not have to suffer the marriage for long," Blaise remarked.

"You are doing this for you! Because you need his coin to rebuild your stupid castle that you nearly lost over a woman! How much did he offer you? How much did it take for you to sell me off like cattle?" she accused. He had not bothered to deny it, dismissing her from the room with a wave of his hand. She stormed away, seething with anger, but there was nothing she could do, and she married the old miser, suffering through his elderly ministrations until she could take no more. Lindonivis had died suddenly after a meal, his poor old heart giving out while his wife watched him thrash about on the floor, lifting her skirts out of the way so that he would not soil them with his passing.

Blaise had been furious when he found out, destroying several pieces of furniture as he raged at her. Lindonivis had been a constant source of support for the King's costly endeavors to rebuild and without him he would be forced to find another way. To punish her he had married her off again, this time to a disgusting man he knew she would despise. She once again rebelled, this time by administering her deadly herbs at the wedding feast, watching the man drop dead at the table across from her with half of the regents of Veruca in attendance. She had smiled sweetly at Blaise and lifted her cup of wine, tilting it towards her cousin in tribute. He could do nothing to her in the crowded room and that night she fled to Kymir, seeking refuge with the Earth Keeper, determined to make herself so indispensable to the Kymirran Queen that she would never have to marry again.

Now she watched Akrin, thinking of the disgusting feel of Lindonivis's hands on her beautiful, young body and knowing that she would never have to suffer that fate again. She had the power now, the ability to decide fates, and she would die before she gave it up.

"Magnus," she said, motioning for the Guardian. He pulled a knife out of his belt, not a combat knife but a heavy cleaver used in the kitchens. She saw the flash of fear on Akrin's face and set her resolve against it, remembering the tiny, tortured bodies that had littered his secret copse. She would not pity this monster, and she was merely inflicting a fraction of the pain he had inflicted on others.

"Give me your hand, boy," Magnus ordered. Akrin shrunk back away from the bars and Magnus sighed in annoyance. "Do not make me call for others to hold you down and witness your cowardice. Be a man and come over here and let us be done with it. I will only take the small one if you do not make this difficult."

Akrin ground his teeth together, giving them a look of such hatred that it almost made Logaire flinch. He pushed himself to his feet, coming forward and standing close to the bars. She could see the spots on his skin, the dark hairs of his brows where they knitted together over his eyes.

'We need a little gift to bring to your so-called father at the Council meeting," Logaire explained. "The Earth Queen has summoned the realms but we know that he is there with her, and will be all too happy to see me dead. We need to provide him with some...motivation to hold his temper, and pieces of his adopted son should do the trick nicely."

"He will burn you to ash," Akrin snarled.

Logaire laughed, the musical sound echoing in the dank chamber. "Oh, I doubt that. My darling cousin has grown soft and you are one of his weak spots. You see, he still thinks there is hope for you, but you and I both know better. You and I know what you really are."

"Then I will kill you myself," the young man ground out. "I think about it sometimes, when I am here in the dark, alone. I think about how I will kill you, how I will carve you up and listen to you beg for mercy, the things that I will do to you before I let you die."

"Enough!" Magnus boomed, grabbing Akrin's black jacket through the bars and jerking the young man against them. "Give me your hand."

"You are going to kill me? You silly fool, you rode right in here, battle-weary and blind, and practically threw yourself in this dungeon. You are no threat to me," Logaire retorted.

Akrin stuck his hand out through the bars, his eyes fixed on Logaire, the cruel half smile still teasing at his lips. Magnus took the hand and pressed it against the iron door frame, cutting off the smallest finger in one quick motion. Akrin cried out, hurtling himself back into the corner of the cell, wailing in pain. Logaire tossed him a rag to use as a bandage and Magnus grimaced in disgust, holding the severed pinky finger up to examine it.

"This should do the trick," Magnus said. "Stop sniveling, boy. It could have been worse."

He followed Logaire's glittering trail of lace out of the dark chambers, taking the sloping tunnel back up into the castle.

"You should kill him while you have the chance. He is a sick man," Magnus warned her.

"I know that," she said, "But I need him breathing. The threat of harming him will keep my cousin in check. For now."

"Or we can ignore the summons to Council," Magnus suggested, not for the first time. It was a dangerous tactic, answering the summons, and he was not entirely sure they would make it back alive. He also doubted the wisdom of leaving Veruca so soon after laying siege to the throne.

Logaire rounded on him, her golden eyes flashing. "If I do not go I am practically admitting that I am an illegitimate ruler. I will go, and I will be recognized as the new Queen of Veruca. I have just as much power as they do, now that I have the Warding Stone."

"Any word from Samirra?"

She knew he was asking after Favian and she frowned at him in sympathy. "No, I have sent hawks but none have returned. There has been no word since my cousin went north. If not for Akrin crawling back here with what was left of the army, we would not even know that they had lost in the north. I would think Astraeus would be gloating, but perhaps he is saving it for Council?"

"Perhaps," Magnus muttered, his concern apparent on the stark lines of his face.

"Why couldn't Blaise have just died in the north like he was supposed to?" she asked rhetorically. She remembered the moment she had found out he was alive, the shudder of panic that had wracked her body. She had been sure that he was dead, murdered by the Fomori, leaving her path to the throne clear. Then Maialen's message had come. *Council is summoned. Blaise and I are safe and have returned to Kymir. We convene the day after the new moon.*

Logaire still was not sure why Maialen had told her that Blaise was alive. Was she warning her out of friendship? Could she just be so naive that she did not understand what was happening? The Earth Queen could have sent the summons without that bit of knowledge and Logaire would have walked right into their trap. So why had she told her? Frustration welled up within her. She hated not knowing, and hated the feeling that she was not one step ahead of everyone else.

"I am tired," she told Magnus with a sigh. "I wish to rest for a while, then we will prepare to set sail at first light."

"We are sailing to Kymir? Is that wise?" the Guardian questioned. Being on unfriendly terms with the Leharans was not ideal when they would have to sail right past them in a very conspicuous Verucan ship.

Logaire made a pinched face, thinking of the last time she had taken the overland route to Kymir, bouncing along miserably in the wagon before being set upon by Thyrr and his henchmen. "We will sail."

She took her leave of Magnus, going to the chambers she had chosen for her own. She had not cared for the Fire King's personal rooms, that was a little too familiar for her tastes, and she had thought he was dead, making the idea of sleeping in his bed quite morbid. Instead, she had chosen the rooms beside his that had been locked for years. Orabelle's rooms. The Water Keeper had only been to Veruca once, forced to stay while Gideon recovered from a blooddrinker's bite. Logaire had been surprised at the time, not seeing the Water Queen as one to put herself in harm's way, but Orabelle had done it willingly for Maialen, so that her younger sister would not have to feel the pain of losing her Guardian. Logaire was surprised when she had found the rooms exactly as they had been all those years ago, and she wondered if that was where her cousin went to nurse his grief.

Logaire trailed her fingers over the objects in the room, touching the silver handles of the pearl inlaid hairbrushes. Thoughtful items, and she felt a pull of sentiment towards her cousin, imagining him choosing the gentle, feminine things he thought the Water Queen would like. He might have been so different had his mother not been the heartless shrew that she was, or if his father had lived just a little longer. Logaire could still see his boyish face under the mop of red curls, his brow furrowed as he stuck his nose in a book and Maritka, his mother, looming over him in judgment, never pleased enough to utter even a kind word. If not for his younger brother, she did not think Blaise would have ever known what love was.

Her own childhood had not been easy either. Her mother was Maritka's sister, beautiful and gentle, but with a weakness of spirit that made her easy prey for cruel men. Logaire's father had been one of those men, foul-tempered and heavy handed. One of her first memories was of her mother clutching her face, a bruise darkening around her eye while her father raged drunkenly, toppling furniture and staggering into the walls. Logaire had hidden, tucking herself under her bed and squeezing her eyes shut, praying to the gods that he did not remember she was there. Her father had not stayed long after that, one day taking his things and tossing them into the rickety wagon led by the only horse they owned. Her mother begged him not to go, crying pitifully and stumbling after him as the wagon lurched away from the house. He had not even glanced back.

At first Logaire had been glad to see him go, happy that they were free of his cruelty, but she had not known then that there were worse men than her father and that her mother would be quite adept at finding these men. She had not known then just how weak her mother was, but she had soon learned the hard way. Her only escape from the bitterness of her life at home was when she went to see her cousin. She would convince him to sneak away from his endless studies and they would take Bastion when Maritka was not looking, running through the dark mountains of Veruca, wild and free and unfettered by the binds of their parents. The little boy would climb onto Blaise's back when he could not keep up on his twisted feet, and her cousin would carry him for the entire day without a word of complaint, Bastion laughing delightedly at everything they did.

Logaire let the memory wash over her and for a moment the nostalgia was so intense that it was almost painful. It was hard to believe that they had once been those sweet, happy children, running to escape the life that threatened to dampen the fire in their hearts. Poor babies, she thought, they had not run far enough or fast enough.

She kicked off her delicate slippers and laid down on the bed, careful not to muss her gown but not wanting to bother with the endless hassle of undressing. She wondered if Blaise ever thought of those children, if his heart ever ached the way hers did in these unguarded moments for the innocence they had lost. If it did then perhaps he could find a way to forgive her for what she had done, and she could forgive him.

Logaire did not know how long it had been since she had closed her eyes. The sun was still slanting through the window, so night had not yet fallen. There was an insistent tapping at the door that had woken her from her nap and though she was annoyed at being disturbed, she knew that there was much to do and she should not waste any more of the day sleeping.

"One moment," she called to whoever the imbecile was who was still tapping at the door. She had replaced most of the staff in the castle, for she knew the power of gossip and the source of it, and she wanted people that she could trust to be close to her. Whoever this was, she would make sure that they never set foot in the castle again.

The tapping continued and she flung open the door irritably, ready to give them a scathing reproach, but her words died in her throat as she looked upon the sullen face of Akrin. He was holding a bloody finger in his bandaged hand, using it to tap on the door. She took a step back in shock and he took advantage of the space she had made to step into the room with her, blocking the entry so that she could not slam the door shut again.

"You look surprised," he said, wagging the severed finger at her. "Guess whose this is? I will give you a hint, it is not mine."

Her mind was reeling and she tried to think, choking back the panic and the hysteria that were her first instincts, her mind going to back to that place it had gone when she was a girl, when she needed to survive, be more clever than the men who came for her.

"How...how did you..." she began to stammer, trying to take a moment to assess the situation. There was blood on his black coat, she could see the shimmer of crimson liquid in the swathe of light from the window, and it was splattered across his face. In his other hand was a cloth bundle, the bottom soaked in blood and dripping along the stone floor. Was Magnus close by? If she screamed, would he come in time to save her?

"I have brought you a gift," Akrin said, lifting the bundle and shaking it at her. Droplets of blood splattered on the hem of her golden gown.

"What is it?" she whispered hoarsely.

"Who is it, you mean," he laughed. He tossed the bundle at her and she slapped it away, the cloth coming open and pieces of someone scattering across the floor. "Say hello to Magnus."

"By the gods," she croaked at the gruesome sight, turning her head as the bile in her stomach rose into her mouth. She breathed in deeply, willing herself not to be sick, to think and to think quickly. "I did not know he was so weak."

Akrin's predatory grin faltered slightly. He was surprised by her comment, but like all cruel men, he reveled in the disparagement of others. "He was weak! He cried like a baby as I carved him up."

"Pathetic. How did it happen?" she asked, knowing that he would be delighted to retell the tale. His sort always enjoyed talking about their evil deeds.

"He did not know his place, for starters. You told him I was not to be killed, but he thought he knew better than you," he began.

Logaire forced herself to laugh. "Imagine a Samirran thinking they know what is better for Veruca."

She kicked at one of the severed ears with her bare toe, sending it flopping over in disdain as she prayed to the gods that her stomach would not lose its contents. Akrin seemed to warm to her contempt, continuing on, "He came to the dungeon and told me he was there to kill me, that I was evil and could not be left alive. I told him that you would not be pleased but he had no regard for your wishes. So I cowered in the corner, clutching my hand like an injured animal. He was so arrogant, waltzing in there with me without even bothering to think that I might be pretending."

"A fool," Logaire agreed scornfully.

"When he reached for me, I broke his wrist. I think he was more surprised than hurt. He dropped the knife. After that, it was just a matter of taking my time. I wanted him to beg but he would not. If he had, it would have been quicker," he said, gesturing to the body parts that littered the floor.

"You have shown me his weakness, and that is good. We need to be strong to hold Veruca."

"We?" Akrin asked, his eyes narrowing at her. "There is no we. You threw me in that dungeon and cut off my finger!"

"And look how you have returned! I doubted you, but you have proven me wrong, you have proven your strength. You defeated the great Magnus, champion of Samirra. With me to help you, we can make you a legend of Veruca. People will fear you, all of Imbria will fear you," Logaire said, her tone purring and persuading. "But without me they will not listen to you, they will think you are just a soldier, a nobody, they will not respect you. But if you are by my side, then together we are undefeatable."

Akrin frowned his surly frown, considering what she was saying while shaking Magnus's severed finger thoughtfully. She forced herself to keep breathing, to not collapse in fear or scream or run because she knew men like him, and it would be the end of her. All she could do now was hope that she had been convincing enough. Her heart pounded in her chest as she waited for him to decide whether she would live or die.

31

The storm had been so severe, raging throughout the day and night, that the next morning the Royal City was littered with fallen debris and caked in a layer of mud. A fine mist clung to the forest, stretching down to the sea, coating everything in a glistening embrace. The sky was still heavy with clouds, but they had thinned and flattened to long, grey sheets, no longer bloated with rain. The storm had rolled in from the south, moving north, and I wondered if it had finally rained in Samirra.

I had pulled on tall boots that morning, pinning up the edges of my gown so that it would not drag in the mud. I tried to carefully set my hair, but the damp weather made it frizz around my head in an unruly halo and I gave up, pulling it back severely in a knot at the base of my neck. I could have called for a maid to help me, but I wanted to be alone, to do things on my own. I stared at myself in the mirrored glass, my face stark without the soft waves of chestnut to soften it. I looked tired, my eyes large and solemn above the smattering of freckles and my lips pressed into a thin line. I tried to smile, to soften my troubled appearance, but it only made me look worse and I glared at the doll-like face in the mirror who was grimacing back at me.

I walked down the winding paths that snaked through my dense gardens, holding my amulet and using my power to soothe the land the storm had ravaged. Stems that had been uprooted crawled back into the ground and the bare limbs that had been stripped of leaves sprouted new growth. I felt the life growing around me and I breathed it in, relishing the simplicity of it, the ease with which it ebbed and flowed with the seasons. If only all of life was so simple. I stopped near a sprawling stretch of dogwood blossoms that were tangled amongst wild blackberry bushes, white petals scattered across the ground like fallen snow. Orabelle and I had played here as children. I could see her so vividly, it was as if her ghost had come back to haunt this place. White hair ruffling in the wind, her golden skin glowing in the sunlight, and her pale eyes flashing. She was laughing, a handful of blackberries clutched in her hand while the dark juices dripped down her arm, staining her dress. She had pointed to the ripest ones.

"These are the ones you want, Maialen," she had said. I held out my hand, waiting for her to pluck it for me with her quick, delicate fingers. I popped it in my mouth, a grin splitting my face as the tart juices exploded on my tongue.

"You are a good sister!" I announced, in my mind bestowing a great honor upon her with my praise. She had laughed and looked back to see our mother watching us, their eyes meeting in a tender embrace over the distance. Ursula was like a beautiful statue, and looked so much like my sister that I felt a pang of jealousy towards them for sharing something I could never be a part of. Ursula called to Orabelle that it was time to go, and my sister had wiped her stained hands on her pretty white dress, pulling me against her and kissing my cheek before skipping off to join our mother, her hand sliding into hers with ease as they walked away. I had stood alone in the garden, watching them go, wondering what it was like to be like them, to be part of the islands and the sun and the sea and each other.

I reached out a hand in the present, caressing the storm-damaged branches of the blackberries, watching the fruit swell and ripen, glossy in the misty air. I could not help but wonder if my mother had ever loved me the way she loved Orabelle, if she had ever looked upon me with the tender affection that she heaped upon my sister, or if I had been too much like my father. It was his face I saw in the mirrored glass, his features that were so unlike theirs. Did she hate him? Did she hate me because I had been his?

A roar of laughter drew me out of my reverie and I looked around for the source of the sound, following the path until it opened up in the clearing before the docks, the great expanse of the sea diminishing the horizon beyond. Blaise was there, dressed in loose cotton pants and a tunic, covered in smears of mud, and looking so completely common that I was taken aback. In that moment he was not a Keeper or a King, but just a man, dirty and laughing, his head thrown back and his amber eyes sparkling with mirth. I felt a smile pulling at my lips, a genuine smile this time, then I saw the flash of white hair as Kaeleb darted forward, flinging a large glob of mud directly at the Fire Keeper.

"Kaeleb!" I shouted. "Stop that this instant."

Blaise had dodged the mud easily and jogged over to me, grinning his easy grin. "Relax, Maialen, the boy is only playing."

Kaeleb waved his hand at me boisterously, the fingers caked in mud and splatters of dirt covering him from head to toe. I felt my smile falter, and I could feel the same tug of jealousy that I had felt thinking of my mother and sister. I had wanted to keep Blaise here with me, not to keep him here with the boy, with Orabelle's son, the constant reminder of my lost sister. It angered me to see them playing together, laughing easily as if they had not a care in the world, when the world around us was falling apart and Orabelle had been the cause of it all.

"The Tahitians have come," Blaise said, waving a hand at the docks where the ship was anchored. "Damek explained about the Leharans, of course making it sound completely different than it was, as Damek does, and conveniently leaving out the part about the Sirens."

"Were they upset?" I asked, my brows drawing together with worry. We were bleeding allies and the last thing I wanted to do was to enrage the fierce island warriors. I was glad Damek had not mentioned the Sirens, I did not care to see any more people chasing the memory of my sister.

"Cossiana herself came. The old woman seemed to take it in stride. Vayk stayed to speak with her after Damek had gone. He is on the ship with them now."

Our eyes met and I knew we were both thinking the same thing, wondering what she and Vayk were saying, and just how angry the man was that we had lost his brother. When I had tried to tell him what happened, leaving out the part where I killed my Guardian and orphaned his daughter, he had silenced me with a slash of his arm through the air.

"So, my brother is gone and you do not know where he has gone to?" Vayk had asked me pointedly, his normally bland face filled with ire.

"I... he just left us in the woods..." I muttered lamely, the explanation sounding weak even to myself. I had not been able to tell him the truth though, I could not utter the words aloud that would tell him what I had done.

"And the dog?"

I shook my head. They really loved that damned ugly dog. "The dog went with him."

Vayk had nodded, staring out over my head into the forest, then he abruptly turned and walked away. He had not spoken to me since, taking very deliberate care to avoid me. I had a sinking feeling in my stomach that he knew I was lying, that he suspected there was more to the story, but Blaise and I had both agreed as we stood in the forest watching the cabin burn that we would never speak of what had happened there.

I turned to Blaise now, as he looked out at the ship that rocked gently against the pier, and murmured in an admonishing tone, "Perhaps this is not the time to be playing games."

He let out a short, bitter laugh, the brilliant amber eyes sliding back to me, the look in them so intense that I felt my heart skip a beat. "Do not think that I ever forget who I am, Earth Queen."

I opened my mouth to soften the sting of my words, but he had already walked away, Kaeleb running to keep up with his long-legged stride.

I made my way back along the path, needing to prepare for the Council meeting that was fast approaching. I could not worry that I had hurt Blaise's feelings. My sister had done nothing but throw scathing remarks at him, and he had doted on her, so his feelings could not be all that delicate, I reasoned bitterly.

Damek was waiting at the manor for me, scurrying back and forth over the lower terrace like a spider guarding its web. He saw me coming and rushed out to meet me, demanding to know where I had been.

"I went for a walk."

He frowned at my lack of apology but hurried on, "The Tahitians are here and I have spoken to their elder about the Lehar predicament. At least there is one person on that island with some manners. She claims Tahitia does not wish to be involved in such affairs. I told her that Colwyn was still here with us, the Leharans having sailed off like cowards without their own people, and he can represent Lehar at the Council. We never should have let that usurper take the throne. Colwyn has been a fine leader there for years and he was much better suited to the task than some murderous bastard."

"You mean Colwyn does what we tell him to do," I corrected him.

Damek sniffed in umbrage. "He does what is best for Imbria."

"Is there no word from Samirra?" I asked, changing the subject. "Or the Verucans?"

"No, and my spies have been quiet on both fronts. Logaire probably rooted them out in Veruca when she went on her little killing spree, that damned witch. She is too clever by far. We need her on our side, perhaps your message should have been more clear," the old advisor sanctioned. We had argued over what to send, and he had finally submitted to my insistence that Logaire would understand the meaning behind my words. I had told her Blaise was here in Kymir, my way of telling her that I was on her side, that she would not be walking into a trap. It had also been vague enough that if the message were intercepted no one would think more of it. I felt a flush on my cheeks, a manifestation of the wave of guilt that I felt for betraying Blaise, but it was the best option. And it kept Blaise here with me, something that I had selfishly wanted. I had pictured a future together for us here in Kymir, and I had believed it possible until I had seen his face yesterday as he stood in the rain, listening to the mournful wail of the Sirens. I felt like a fool for believing that there was something between us. I was still married to someone else, and he would always be in love with my sister. But despite all of that, I could not help still wanting him.

"Then we will begin the Council without them, with Blaise remaining as King of Veruca for now," I said, hoping that I sounded firm and decisive. Inside, I was trembling, overwhelmed. Blaise would be furious that Logaire had not been drawn out of his kingdom, especially since I had assured him that our plan would work. Besides that, we had agreed to tell the Council today what had happened in the north, about freeing that creature from its prison and the horrible things the Samirrans had done that had led up to it. We would be asking them to unite with us against Samirra, to take that land back so that we could make it fertile again, keeping it a vassal of Kymir until my son was old enough to rule. It did not help our cause that we had just attempted to oust the new Leharan ruler and failed, and I could only pray that Thyrr's short time on the island had not been enough to garner the loyalty of the proud islanders. He no longer had the Warding Stone, and without it all he had was a weak blood tie to the former Queen, a claim that he could not prove and we could deny if we had to.

I took my leave of Damek, changing my muddied gown for a finer one, long and velvet green, trimmed with brown lace. I left my hair in the severe knot, there was no helping it, and my fingers touched the Earth Emerald that hung above the low neck of the gown. I closed my eyes, trying to settle my nerves, to stop the ever-present and insistent desire to flee from everything and everyone.

The doors to the underground chamber were already thrown open when I reached them, and I paused, seeing the carved sigils of the Elements, the harmony they represented as they intertwined with one another. I shook my head. There was no harmony among us, we were always fighting, always scheming, always trying to take something from someone else. I hated it. I longed for the days when I had been so blissfully naïve, thinking that everything would be fine just because I willed it so. I was about to cross over the sacred threshold into the chamber when a shadow slanted across the ground and I looked up to see the graceful swoop of an eagle overhead. My stomach turned and I felt a rush of panic at the thought of facing Astraeus after all that had happened. Several more eagles filled the sky, crying and screeching in agitation, circling each other and dipping through the trees. I peered through the mist that still hung over everything, trying to see who all had come, wondering if perhaps he had brought Aracellis with him.

The first eagle circled lower but instead of going to the stables where they normally alit, they were heading straight down towards me and I flattened myself against the carved door, trying to move out of the way of the giant winged beast. I saw the long braid of hair trailing out from underneath the helmet. Favian. The eagle settled on the ground, dipping its wing to let the Guardian slide off his back. Several people stopped on the path, the eagle blocking their way. I saw the dark ebony skin of the Tahitians, Cossiana leading them, wrapped in a deep blue swathe of cloth, her long, grey hair trailing in braids almost to the ground.

"What are you doing?" I asked Favian, trying to maneuver around the huge bird. "I have handlers ready at the stables."

He lifted his helmet off and I nearly flinched at the gaunt appearance of the wiry Samirran Guardian, so startling was the change in him. He was thinner than I had ever seen him and I could tell that he had not slept. There were dark circles under his eyes and his skin looked waxy and pale. I took a few steps back. "Are you ill?"

"Maialen," he said, his voice catching on my name and there was such a tumult of emotions that poured out of him in that one word that I felt my heartbeat quicken in anticipation. Something was very wrong. He took a long breath and shook his head. "I am not ill; it is not plague."

"What has happened?" I demanded to know. "Is it Aracellis?"

He gave me a look so pained that I felt the strength in my legs falter, and I gripped the edge of the door to keep from falling to my knees on the ground.

"Where is my son?" I asked again, my voice rising with trepidation.

"Queen Maialen, I am so sorry," he whispered. "He is gone."

The world went black for a moment and I could no longer hold myself upright, my knees hitting the muddy ground.

"What happened?" I practically screamed at him, digging my fingers into the dirt, trying to stop the horrible, crushing ache that was gripping my heart. "What happened to my son?"

"The Fomori came, Samirra has fallen. They are all dead. I am so sorry, I tried..." his tortured voice trailed off, unable to go on.

"My Queen," one of my guards took a tentative step towards me, clearly unnerved by what Favian had just said and un-equipped to deal with whatever was happening. "What should I do?"

I just stared up at him. What should he do? There was no one to go to, no one to call for. There was no one else. I closed my eyes, feeling as if the world were spinning beneath me. They were gone, my son was gone, and I was alone once again. Even though I had not been able to love him the way I wanted to, Aracellis had been something for my heart to hold onto, someone to keep me from being utterly and completely alone. I should have protected him, I should have kept him with me, and not been so afraid of being his mother. I let out a sobbing cry, crushing the dirt in my hands, hating everyone and everything that had made my life what it was, the constant pain of my existence that I had done nothing to deserve.

"Maialen!" Blaise's deep voice cut through my hysteria but I could not force myself to look at him. "Maialen, what has happened?"

"They're dead," I cried, waving a hand at Favian as if he should ask him, then warm arms wrapped around me. It was not Blaise's strong embrace, but the comforting, weathered hold of a mother, smelling like the sea. Cossiana was there, petting my hair and pressing my face against her shoulder.

"There, there, child," she murmured and I hugged her back, sobbing incoherently, knowing that I would never be able to be that kind of mother to my son. I had not been there to comfort him, or to protect him. I had failed him since the day he was born, and now he was gone.

"What on Imbria happened up there?" Blaise growled at Favian, snatching the Guardian by the front of his jacket and shaking him. The Verucan had donned his usual black attire for the Council meeting, no longer the carefree man playing in the mud, but looking like the wrathful Keeper we had known all these years.

Favian shoved his hands away. "You tell me! It was after you came north that the Fomori attacked us!"

"When I left they were still hiding in their caves," Blaise snarled back. "You must have done something to provoke them."

Favian shook his head. "We did nothing. They just came, thousands of them, led by a woman-"

"A woman?" Cossiana jerked her head up, letting go of me and standing up to face the Samirran. "What woman?"

"We let her out," I confessed. "They made us do it, I was going to tell you at the Council. She was trapped in a cave-"

Cossiana stopped me with a shake of her dark head. "Not here. Let us go to the Council chamber where we will not be overheard. Maialen, child, can you walk? Can you come with us?"

"Get everyone out of there!" Blaise roared at the poor guard who was still standing by, helplessly watching. The man fled across the threshold and down the stone steps, ushering out the gathered regents and merchants who flooded past us with curious stares. I could hear their whispers and I kept my face turned, not wanting anyone to see my grief. Blaise came and stood in front of me, blocking me from their sight, and helping me to my feet. I started to lean into him and he stopped me, his hand firm on my wrist, setting me away from him so that I stood on my own. I flushed dark crimson, and tried to stop the tears that were coursing down my cheeks, wiping at them with angry strokes of my hands, feeling more alone than I had ever felt in my entire life.

The guard returned, telling us that the chamber had been cleared. The smooth, marble table sat solid and unyielding, as it had sat for hundreds of years, for generations of Keepers. I looked at my chair, the chair of my father, of every Earth Keeper that had come before me, the chair Gideon had stood beside, the chair that Orabelle had sat across from, and I felt the overwhelming urge to run from it all. I wanted to turn and flee into the darkness, to run and run and run until I collapsed and there was nothing left of me for anyone to take.

"You may as well sit there," I muttered to Favian, motioning to the place that was normally reserved for the Keeper of Air. The Guardian also seemed haunted by the chamber, looking around him as if seeing the ghosts of the past gathered together at the sturdy block of marble.

Cossiana sat in Orabelle's chair and I saw Blaise's gaze linger on the carved lines of pale teak wood that cradled the islander. I had not removed it this time, hoping that we could move on from her memory, but I now knew that he couldn't. I stared down at my hands, refusing to look at him again, not wanting to watch him remember my sister.

Cossiana's warm voice broke the stillness. "Tell me everything."

"We let that woman, that thing, out," I said miserably, focusing on Cossiana so that I would not shatter into a thousand pieces. "The Fomori took us in the north, they would have killed us if we did not do as they asked. We managed to escape but it was only after we had been forced to free her. I tried to seal her back in her tomb, I thought perhaps I had... I am sorry,

I should have told you sooner. I wanted to tell you, I was going to, at the Council."

The Tahitian elder looked sympathetic and she patted my clenched hands with her weathered fingers. "What is done is done. It was foretold."

Blaise snorted in derision. "You and your Samains, with your ridiculous prophecies. She is one of you, did you remember that in your little story telling parties? I saw her, she was Tahitian. This is your mess as much as it is ours."

"Be calm, Fire Keeper. We are not here to quarrel with you, though you do not deserve such grace," Cossiana warned.

"And what makes you say that, old woman? Something your son told you?" Blaise countered. "Where is Damian these days? Hiding behind his mother's skirts?"

Damek came rushing in then with a flurry of black robes, waving his arms in distress, nearly toppling his skeletal frame down the stone steps in his panic and drawing everyone's attention to him.

"Is it true? Tell me it is not true! Not Aracellis!" he lamented.

I felt a flash of anger. Damek had no love for Aracellis, whatever he was crying over, it was not my son, though I was glad that he had interrupted the argument that was about to ensue between Blaise and the Tahitian woman. The last thing I needed was to hear them yelling and accusing each other.

"He is the last of the line of Chronus, if he is gone then the greatness of that bloodline is gone," Damek went on, the reason for his agitation becoming clear. He was still so devoted to my father that he could not bear the thought that something had befallen his heir.

"Enough!" I snapped harshly, causing everyone to startle. "If you cannot sit and be silent then I will have you removed!"

Damek's mouth fell open but he quickly shut it, hurrying over to sit in the first row of benches and folding his arms over his chest and I could practically feel him frowning at the back of my head. I did not care. In that moment, I did not care about any of it, or any of them. All of Imbria could be crumbling into the sea, and I would not have cared. All I cared about was knowing what had happened to my son.

"Tell us what happened in Samirra," I said to Favian, surprising myself with the forcefulness of my voice.

The Guardian took a deep breath and let it out, gripping his hands together with white knuckles. "The Fomori came, thousands of them."

He told us how they had come in the night, how quickly the outer walls had fallen, how Astraeus had hidden himself away in the palace, doing nothing to save his people. He told us how he sent the eagles to Kymir for help, and we had sent them back, riderless and hopeless.

Damek let out a bewildered moan, interrupting the Guardian. I had not been there and it was Damek who had sent the eagles back to Samirra, refusing to help, thinking it was some trick that Astraeus was playing at. He collapsed himself into a ball of grief, realizing the part he had played in what happened next.

"Oh, for the love of Imbria," Blaise muttered irritably. "Guard! Get him out of here!"

The same guard who was standing watch at the threshold came hurrying in, hauling out the wailing old advisor unceremoniously. We waited until he was gone and his cries had stopped echoing over the stone before urging Favian to go on.

He told us about the woman who called herself Chaote, who led the Fomori. He told us how she wanted to destroy the Keepers and how she claimed that she would leave the Samirrans unharmed if Astraeus surrendered and gave up his amulet. Favian explained how Astraeus had tried to run away like a coward, refusing to take Astus or Aracellis with him as the palace was overrun. I saw Blaise's fingers twitch across the table from me and I wondered what he was thinking, if he was as sorry as I was that he had not killed Astraeus before now. We should have killed him and I should have taken my son back with me, away from that cursed place, and left the Samirrans to rot.

Favian told us how he had thrown Astraeus from the eagle, trying to send my son and his grandfather to safety instead. Then he told us how the injured eagle had tried to fly and almost made it past the palace walls, but she had come. Chaote, the half-breed creature that I had helped unleash upon the world. She had thrown the spear that brought down the eagle that carried my son.

I rolled the thought of her over and over in my mind, seeing the dark head in the cave, the inky black eyes. The thing I had freed from her underground prison. I could not stop the thought from repeating in my head, that I was the one who released her, I was the one who freed the woman who killed my son.

"Maialen," Cossiana said gently, touching my hand. I jerked away from her and realized that the ground was trembling above us, dust raining down to dull the shine of the marble table. I took a deep breath, trying to calm myself, and the quaking subsided.

"Astraeus was... he was beating me. He was furious at me," Favian went on. "I knew that he would never do the right thing, and I had to try to save Samirra, or what was left of it. I... I had no other choice. I killed him, and I took the amulet."

Blaise leapt from his chair, slamming his hands on the table. "Tell me you did not give it to that thing!"

"I had no choice!" Favian cried. "There was nothing else that I could do, she would have killed everyone."

"So you just handed over one of the strongest weapons on Imbria to her?" the Fire Keeper bellowed in rage.

"You weren't there!" Favian shouted back at him. "You do not know what it was like!"

Blaise kicked his chair back and lunged over the table at the Guardian, jerking him forward by the collar of his jacket. "I know what it was like in the north, when you and your coward King sent your own people to die and infect us with plague! You did not care about their lives then!"

"That was not my doing, I was against it!" Favian argued, trying to pry the Keeper's hands off of him. Sparks sizzled in the air and Favian cried out in pain.

"Stop this!" Cossiana interjected, slapping Blaise soundly across the face. He blinked and stared up at the elder woman, his amber eyes round with shock. They faced each other for what felt like an eternity, neither of them flinching from the other, and I almost laughed at how ridiculous it was, the old woman and the raging Fire Keeper. Abruptly, Blaise let go of Favian, sliding back across the table and throwing himself in his chair.

"What happened after you gave her the amulet?" Cossiana asked the Samirran.

He had taken the Sapphire to the edge of the clearing, calling out for Chaote. The Fomori had stopped their attack and the chaos had parted as she had strolled through the courtyard below, her smile dazzling as she laughed with pleasure.

"Well done, Guardian. Bring it to me and your people stop dying," she had yelled back to him. She noticed his hesitation and added, "There are so many children here, it would be a shame to have to cut their tiny heads off, but if you need more persuading, it can be arranged."

He had taken the amulet to her, the Fomori standing aside and letting him pass, their death smell overwhelming his senses as he tried not to stare at the bodies and blood that were littered throughout the palace halls. He crossed the courtyard and Chaote held out her hand, grasping the blue stone in triumph.

"You have pleased me, peasant," she said, and Favian had looked away from the exquisite face, unable to meet her exultant gaze in his shame. She clutched the amulet in her fist and he watched in horror as the color faded from the stone, leaving it a dull grey orb. Choate squeezed tighter, concentrating all of her power on crushing the stone. Her hand trembled with the effort and tiny cracks splintered through it, but it would not shatter. She gave a cry of rage and then stopped, taking a moment to regain her composure.

"The pigs' blood your people have given me is weak, I need better. I have heard there is one descended from the divine who walks Imbria. Do you know who I speak of?" she asked the Guardian curiously, as if they were discussing pastries and tea.

Favian shook his head and she watched him for a long moment, deciding whether she believed him or not.

"I will find them, with or without your help," she told him. "Go now. I will keep my word, unlike your lying Keepers. You have one day to get your people as far away from here as you can, then we will follow and whoever is left I will feed to my army. Samirra belongs to me now."

"But-but you said you would spare them!" the Guardian protested as she started to turn away.

Chaote spun back to face him, her perfect features twisted with wrath and the black eyes glittering with malice. "I am sparing them, and allowing them to leave, which is more than they deserve! If you do not wish to go, by all means stay. I will enjoy tasting you."

"But where will we go?" he asked helplessly. How could he possibly evacuate an entire realm in one day? They would starve on the road, if they could even get far enough away to outrun the Fomori. It was not possible.

She once more relaxed into her disarming smile.

"To Kymir of course. I believe that is what you call it now, the Earth realm. We will follow behind you so you should make haste, Guardian. Take one of the birds and go ask the other Keepers for help. See what they do for you," she sneered derisively and then she had strolled away, the broken Sapphire still clutched in her hand. She called over her shoulder, "Tell the Earth Queen I will be seeing her again soon, to express my gratitude to her for releasing me."

As Favian finished recounting what had happened, Damek crept back into the chamber, looking weak but calm. He hesitated and I motioned for him to sit, not having it in me to argue. Blaise shoved himself once again from his chair but this time he did not try to attack the Samirran, pacing the room instead, crossing back and forth with long, agitated strides.

"You brought more eagles with you, why would she allow that?" the Fire Keeper asked, his mind racing.

"She didn't. The other eagles had fled from the violence in the city and were hiding in the cliffs. When I took off they followed me. Believe me, if I had known I would not have let them come riderless, I would have brought others," Favian explained, shaking his head.

"So where are the Samirrans going if they are fleeing Samirra?" Damek demanded to know.

"They are coming here, to Kymir."

Damek nearly fell out of his seat. "Are you mad, you imbecile? They are riddled with plague! And the Fomori come on their heels! Maialen, you cannot allow this!"

"I told you to get rid of that child," Cossiana chastised me. "She will come for him, and none of us are safe! It is his blood that she is after. I must go, I must return to Tahitia."

"The Samirrans will destroy Kymir! We will all starve!"

"You have to help them!"

I sat staring blindly down at the swirl of stone in the marble table, hearing their demands echoing around the chamber. It was too much. I could not think, I could barely force myself to keep breathing. All I wanted to do was make it stop. I recalled that moment in the woods with Blaise, listening to the sound of Gideon and his daughter singing their beautiful, sweet song, and wishing that it could have been like that forever. I just wanted that one peaceful moment to go on forever.

"Maialen!" Damek was practically screeching.

I shook myself off and stood up, walking out of the chamber without saying a word. I heard their voices behind me, someone calling my name, but I did not stop. I went to the manor, rushing up to the room where my nephew slept, banging on the door insistently. If I was going to do this, then I needed to do it before anyone could stop me.

"Who is it?" Kaeleb asked through the thick oak barrier, his light child's voice heavy with distrust. "I have a sword!"

"You have a stolen kitchen knife, not a sword," I corrected him. "It is your aunt. Open the door, I need you to come with me."

The door cracked a fraction and I saw his small face, grey eyes darting up and down the hall. Satisfied that I was alone he pulled the door open wide. He had bathed and cleaned the mud off of himself and he was fully dressed, even wearing his boots. His little knife was strapped to his side in a hand-made sheath that he had cut out himself from one of my leather archery vests, a bit of innovation that I had not been pleased by.

"What were you doing?" I asked him, noting the glassy look in his eyes and his tousled shock of hair.

"Napping."

"You sleep in your clothes?" I queried, looking at the rumpled bed. For a moment I felt a sliver of doubt at what I was about to do. He looked so innocent with his sleepy face that it nearly undid my resolve. I could not help but see my own son's face, kind and patient, asking me to come and see his new toy. Such a simple request, and I had been unable to grant it. I should have gone to see his new toy. I should have done a lot of things differently. Tears stung my eyes and I blinked them back quickly, not wanting Kaeleb to see.

"Of course, I sleep in my clothes, I am the Solvrei and I must always be prepared to fight," Kaeleb said, as if I were daft. The aura of innocence around him faded and there was the boy I had come to know, my sister's impudent child who wanted to save the world.

""Come with me. Get your jacket, we are taking an eagle and it will be cold."

"Where are we going?" Kaeleb wanted to know, hurrying to grab his brown leather coat and throwing it over his bony shoulders. I watched him with a painful ache in my chest, unable to stop thinking of Aracellis, of how scared my poor, sweet boy must have been as he had fallen from the sky, a swarm of beasts waiting below. I breathed in a ragged gasp, still trying to fight back the tears. There would be time for that later. Right now, I needed to stop the creature that was heading my way with an army of blooddrinkers. I forced a smile at my sister's child.

"We are going to see just how powerful a Solvrei you really are."

32

Dust and feathers showered around him as Astus rolled across the ground, tumbling off the bird who had stopped screeching and now lay still and silent in death, its bent wing crushed beneath it and its white feathers stained with blood. The old man pushed himself to his knees, wincing at the pain beneath his legs as his papery skin rubbed against the rubble that was strewn on the ground.

"Aracellis!" he called out, his voice thin and shaky. Around him was chaos, blooddrinkers growling and swarming over the toppled walls, people screaming and dying. "Aracellis!"

He heard a dry cough and crawled toward it, staying low to the ground so the beasts did not see him. Astus had pushed the boy from the eagle's back just before they had hit the ground, aiming at a pile of corpses, the only thing he had seen that could have softened the fall.

"Aracellis!" he cried happily, finding his grandson in the dirt at the bottom of the hideously stacked bodies. He must have rolled off of them, tumbling to the ground and sliding over the dirt before he had come to a halt below the shadow of a merchant's shop. He was bleeding from his nose and his arms and legs were scraped raw, but he was alive, his big, blue eyes round with fright as his grandfather clutched him tightly.

"Are you hurt, grandfather?" the boy asked, kind and worried about others, as always.

"No, no, my boy, I am fine. Your grandfather is tougher than he looks," Astus assured him. Aracellis noticed with surprise that the rheumy eyes were sharp and aware. "Come, Aracellis, we need to hide."

Astus pulled his grandson up, pressing them both flat against the outer wall of the merchant shop. The window had shattered and he motioned to it, sinking down on his knee so that the boy could use him to step up onto the sill. Aracellis tried to hoist himself up, but the shattered glass cut at his hands and he fell back with a cry, his palms bleeding. Astus told him to wait, hurrying over to the pile of bodies and yanking off a piece of torn clothing from the mound, struggling violently for a few moments to break the seams. Aracellis watched the bodies wriggle and slither across each other as the old man dislodged them, their open eyes staring right at him, and the boy turned away, horrified by the sight, pressing his hands over his eyes. Finally, Astus returned triumphantly with a long scrap of wool, tossing it across the windowsill to cover the shards of glass. He once more hoisted Aracellis up, and this time the boy crawled through, landing on the other side with a thud. Astus stood back up, his old bones creaking, and tried to jump up onto the opening, but he was not the young man he once was and his body would not allow it. He sank back down under the window, melting into the shadows as a group of blooddrinkers passed nearby, their putrid stench rolling over him like a smothering blanket.

"Grandfather!" Aracellis hissed, not realizing the beasts were so close. "Are you alright?"

Astus pressed his hand over his mouth, willing the boy to be quiet. He could not answer him for fear that the Fomori would hear. He closed his eyes, his mouth forming the ancient words of ritual as he prayed to the gods to keep the boy silent.

One of the Fomori had stopped, his ears pricking at the sound. He lumbered over towards them, swiping at the expired corpses like a cat toying with dead mice. Astus swallowed his revulsion, praying harder, trusting that the gods would save him. The beast turned its yellow eyes to peer into the shadows, and for a moment Astus thought it was looking right at him. Then it snarled, bit down on the pale arm of a dead woman, spitting the meat out and hacking in revulsion.

"They all taste like swine," the creature muttered, stalking off to find better prey. Astus let out the breath he had been holding, scurrying over to make sure they had gone. The street was empty and he could see the door to the shop, just a few feet away. He could make it without being seen.

"Aracellis!" he whispered, tapping on the door, his head swiveling back and forth to make sure that no one was coming. "Aracellis open the door, let me in!"

He heard sounds from inside, like something being dragged and he pushed on the door again, but it was still locked. "Aracellis, hurry!"

The smell was growing stronger again, the reek of decay that told him the Fomori would soon be there. He begged the child to hurry, his voice barely a whisper. Finally, he heard the metallic slide of a latch and the door fell open, sending him sprawling into the dark room. He wriggled his legs out of the way and Aracellis pushed the door shut, climbing back atop a teetering stack of crates to reach the lock.

"Well done, my boy," Astus panted, his breathing coming in heavy gasps and his chest aching from the exertion. He wondered how much of this his old heart could take.

It was dark in the shop, the pungent smell of tea filling the room and Astus thanked the gods for their good fortune. The strong smell of the herbal brews would mask their scent from the Fomori. They would be safe here, for a while at least. Astus motioned for Aracellis to follow him, moving to the back of the room. Tea also meant casks of water to make the tea with, and he was desperately thirsty, their throats parched from the heat and dust.

He found a half-filled cask and two clay cups, opening the plug and filling the cups with water. Aracellis gulped his gratefully, liquid dribbling down his neck. He sat back, shaking his dark hair from his head in a gesture so like his father it made Astus wince. He did not want to think of his son right now.

"Grandfather," Aracellis said quietly, as if reading his thoughts, "Do you think father will come for us?"

Astus shook his head sadly. "No, dear boy, I do not believe he will. You and I are on our own."

"What will we do?" the boy asked, with the trusting innocence that only children had, believing that an adult would make everything better for them.

"We will wait for nightfall, then we will go to the tunnels that run beneath the palace. We can use them to escape the city."

"There are tunnels beneath the palace?"

Astus nodded his wispy head. "There are tunnels all over Imbria, left from a time long, long ago when the air was too foul to breathe. You only have to know where to find them."

"And you know where they are?" Doubt threaded its way through the boy's voice.

"I do," Astus said firmly to reassure him. "And I know people who will help us once we have escaped."

Aracellis looked pensive, his little face pinched with worry. He glanced at the broken window, the sky outside growing dark under a threatening blanket of clouds. "What if you start to go mad again and you forget who they are?"

"There is something I need to tell you, my boy," Astus began, wondering where to start. He had known that one day he might have to explain things to his grandson, but he had thought it would be when the boy was older, when he could better understand the choices that had been made. Aracellis filled his cup again, his solemn blue eyes watching the old man patiently, waiting for him to go on.

Astus began to tell the boy the story he had not told anyone in more than thirty years. How long ago, he was the Keeper and controlled the Air amulet, and how he hated the Element, hated how the power made him feel. He detested the feel of it, and he could not help but think that this was not what the gods had intended for their chosen children. He came to believe that the power of the amulets had been corrupted, that the Keepers had distorted their gifts into something dark and twisted. He wanted to be rid of it, but he was supposed to pass it to his son, and how could he wish that fate upon his own progeny? He also could not admit to the other Keepers how he felt about their power. He had no doubt that Chronus would have him killed the instant he spoke out against the amulets. So he was forced to live in misery, always feeling the pull of the amulet's power like an evil demon whispering in his ear. He began to pray every night to the gods, praying for them to spare him, to spare his son. He would use the tunnels beneath the palace to sneak out at night, leaving offerings to the gods outside the city walls. It was on one of those nights, when he was gingerly placing an offering in a shallow pit he had dug, that the two men had approached him.

They were twins, dark skinned and ordinary, identical in every way save the scar that crossed through one of their eyebrows. Each had a belt of knives slung around their waist and between them was a massive, terrifying creature, a wolf, mangled from years of conflict, his one eye staring right at Astus as if he knew him.

"They were the Fenris," Astus told his grandson. "The god who had been sent to the world to dwell forever as punishment for his disobedience. They gave me a task, telling me that the Solvrei would appear in my lifetime and that they would need my help. I was to gather people together, people who would be willing to rise up against the Keepers when the time came, people who would be willing to help the Solvrei unite the Elements and destroy the amulets forever. They said one would come to lead the Fomori, that she would bring great power, and it was her power, her blood, that would allow the Solvrei to do what they needed to do. They said the two could not exist without each other, but they could also destroy each other, and in doing so destroy our world."

Aracellis was watching him with round eyes, absorbing the knowledge in the open, trusting way that children do, never believing that what they are told might be impossible. Astus was suddenly grateful to his grandson, relief flooding his weary chest at finally being able to tell someone.

"I had to keep the secret, but I needed time to learn all I could, and to help them do what must be done, to teach the child, the Solvrei. So, I pretended to be mad and everyone left me alone, leaving me to do whatever I wished and never be questioned," Astus admitted. "That is why I will take us out of here, because the gods are on my side and I am their vessel."

"So... you are not mad?" Aracellis wanted confirmation, still looking wary as he peered through the darkened room at this new grandfather he had never known before. There was a distant rumble and he heard the soft spatter of rain falling on the roof.

"No, my boy, I am not mad. I am the Harbonah."

33

I stood with my hand shading my eyes, staring across the open stretch of land that was banked by the giant white cliffs of Samirra. The eagle rolled its great eyes and hopped uncertainly on its feet, sensing a threat approaching. Kaeleb petted it absently, making cooing sounds to try and soothe it while he glared into the distance.

"Are you sure they are coming?" he asked me, leaving off his comforting of the eagle and standing at my side.

"They are coming," I assured him. "They are coming for you."

He nodded, his small fist gripping the handle of the knife at his belt. Such a tiny, ineffectual weapon against what was coming. I started to feel a stab of pity for him and I shoved it down, burying it in my hatred for his mother. This was all Orabelle's fault. Everything that had happened in the last ten years had all been because of her and her selfishness. Kaeleb existed because of her. She had destroyed my life, and the lives of so many others, and then she had left us to try to clean up the mess.

Dust swirled on the horizon and I lifted my finger, pointing. Kaeleb saw it and nodded, taking deep breaths. I wondered if his heart was pounding as hard as mine, or if Alita and Kaden had taught him how to harden it, how to stop the fear from overwhelming him. His small hand slid into mine and I forced myself not to jerk away, gripping his fingers tightly. We stood, watching and waiting as the Samirrans drew closer, a long swathe of desperation. Some of them were running, others crying, their backs laden with everything they could carry. It was a pitiful sight, the refugees streaming towards us from a war they had not asked for, a war that had begun hundreds of years before they were even born.

I waited until they were close, close enough that I could see their eyes, praying there was another way, but my prayers were unanswered. The ears of the gods were as deaf to my pleas as they had always been. I knelt, letting go of Kaeleb and spreading my hands on the land. My land. I had to do it for Kymir, and for the rest of Imbria. I had no other choice.

The ground trembled beneath us and I closed my eyes, concentrating all of my power. I heard the terrified cries of the already petrified Samirrans as this new horror reached out to them, the land quaking beneath their feet.

I thought of my sister then, of that moment we had laughed in the shade of the blackberry bushes, our faces stained with juice. I had been so happy. She had destroyed that happiness. She had betrayed us all, left us without the Pearl, left Samirra to dry up into a wasteland, left me to carry the burden of her bastard son, left us to try to go on without her.

It started as a small fissure, a tiny crack in the dirt that snaked out from my hands. It grew, spreading, widening, growing longer. The Samirrans gasped and fell back as the earth beneath Imbria began to rip apart, a huge crevasse opening like a wound. I pushed it wider, farther, my scarred hands curling with pain and my arms aching, but it was not enough.

I stopped and stood, brushing off my gown with trembling hands, glancing at Kaeleb who was watching the people on the other side of the fissure with a stony face.

"Go back to Samirra!" I shouted across the scar. "You cannot cross into Kymir!"

I heard the terror, the wails and cries and I closed my eyes. I had to do it. I could not let them come. The crevasse was still not big enough, they would find a way across. I had to keep going. I heard the screeching cries of more eagles and I knelt again, trying to push the opening wider.

"Hello, Earth Queen." The strange voice floated over the emptiness between us and I stood, staring at the most magnificent creature I had ever seen. She was so perfect that it was almost painful to look upon her as she sat astride the eagle, at the other edge of the deep scar. She was wearing silver armor that gleamed even in the dull, grey light that sifted through the thick clouds overhead. Her dark skin was like polished marble, her features so perfectly formed that they did not seem real, like they could only have been sculpted by an artist's hands. The Samirrans were fleeing in panic as more Fomori dropped down beside her, lining the rim of the canyon I had carved out between us. She called out, "You know I will kill them, don't you?"

"You killed my son."

Kaeleb glanced up at me sharply, his eyes narrowing at this news, for I had not told him of Aracellis's death.

She shrugged, sliding off the feathered back of the eagle and walking to the edge, peering over curiously. I gripped my amulet, willing the ground to crumble beneath her feet, to send her tumbling into the abyss, but nothing happened and I felt the emptiness of a Warding Stone wash over me. She smiled. "I have killed a lot of people in Samirra. If your son was a casualty, then perhaps you should not have started a war."

"Your kind started this!" I retorted angrily.

"Did we?" she asked, arching her perfect brows above her glittering black eyes. "That is not how we remember it. Did you not come north to attack us? Had the Fomori not left you alone for years, only attacking when one of your kind demanded it? You could have let them be, but no, Keeper, you were greedy and you wanted the land that you had yet to destroy, needed it to fill your gluttonous bellies with food."

"You want my amulet, why don't you come over here and take it from me?" I asked her, wishing that she would, not caring if I would not survive, knowing I probably wouldn't.

She laughed, a throaty sound that floated lightly on the air. "I am tempted to. But I have underestimated the Keepers once, I will not do so again, and you have made it difficult for me to get my army across. We only have a few of the birds, the rest were lost when we destroyed this pathetic realm."

"Come and fight me yourself, you do not need your army," I challenged her.

"You are braver than I thought you would be, little mouse," she said, clearly amused. "Perhaps I will."

She motioned to one of the Fomori and he ran forward, leaping over the crack in the ground and rolling onto the other side. Kaeleb dove at it with a cry, grabbing its long hair and spinning himself onto its back, stabbing his knife upward beneath the creature's snapping jaws. A flash of irritation went fleeting across Chaote's face.

"Whatever that little demon you have there is, he will not save you." She moved her hand again and more Fomori started to run, leaping across the ravine. I felt panic rising in me. I knew it was not wide enough. I grabbed my amulet, holding it so tightly that I felt the edges cut into my palm, using all of my strength to will the earth to move. The Fomori on my side of the crevasse stumbled, roots tangling around their legs, but it was not enough, not with a Warding Stone so close. I needed more power.

"Kaeleb!" I shouted to him. He looked up from where he had just stabbed one of the beasts through the eye, jerking the knife back and sprinting towards me. All down the edge of the ravine the Fomori were lining up, ready to leap across, their jaws snapping hungrily, and more were coming. They were streaming towards us through the fleeing Samirrans, the smell of them washing the landscape in death.

Kaeleb came to stand beside me, using his tiny body to shield me and once again I felt a sharp sting of guilt.

"I am sorry," I whispered, and then I gripped him around the neck, snatching the knife from his hand. He struggled, caught off guard, and I backed away from the edge of the abyss, away from the Warding Stone, feeling my power start to return, trickling back to me in a weak flow. Gnarled roots crawled up out of the ground, wrapping around the boy's legs, snaking up his small torso and holding him in place.

"What are you doing?" He was screaming at me, his pale, grey eyes wide with fright as he whipped his head back and forth between me and the approaching Fomori.

"I have to stop them. I am so sorry," I told him again, then I grabbed his arm, slicing it open. He screamed and I thought I would be sick, glancing up at the beasts that were running towards us.

"Maialen!" Blaise's voice boomed over the cacophony and he leapt from the eagle he had taken, rolling on the ground in front of us and facing the onslaught of coming Fomori.

Tears were streaming down my face. I did not want to, but I had to try. I kept remembering what Vayk had told me, about the blood of the divine strengthening the Warding Stones. If I could use Kaeleb's blood to make my Element stronger, then I could beat them. I could stop her. I lifted his arm and pressed my lips to his skin, tasting the coppery tang of his blood in my mouth.

"Maialen, what are you doing?" Blaise was shouting at me. He lifted his arms, an arc of fire flaring ahead of him, dying off as it reached the barrier of the Warding Stone's power. The Fomori within his reach screamed, flames licking their grey skin, but they were undeterred and kept coming. I dropped Kaeleb's arm and grabbed my amulet, once again willing the ground to open. The abyss widened a mere fraction, the ground trembling, but it was not enough. I screamed in frustration and grabbed the boy again, ignoring his pleas for me to stop. This was his mother's fault not mine. I had not done this to him, she had.

"It isn't him!" Blaise was bellowing at me.

I pushed Kaeleb's neck to the side, looking at the warm beat of his pulse beneath his skin. Maybe I just needed more, maybe one sip was not enough. I lifted the knife again, laying it against his delicate throat and Blaise slammed into me, throwing me off my feet, the knife flying from my hand as I skidded across the ground.

"It isn't him," he said again, shaking his head and I would never forget that moment, the look on his face as he stared at me, as if I were the monster. Whatever had been between us was shattered in that moment, I had destroyed it forever, and I felt a sob wrack my body as my mind grasped what he was saying.

It isn't him.

I went back to the forest, back to the cabin in the woods where Gideon had been, the words he had said as he had brought his axe down in a rage.

You will destroy her.

They had not been talking about me.

"It was her, wasn't it?" I cried, great hiccupping sobs shaking my whole body as the Fomori bore down on us. "It was Gideon's daughter. He took her from Orabelle, that was why he left, all those years ago, to protect her child. He owed Orabelle for saving his life. You lied to me! You knew, you knew this whole time! You all lied to me!"

Blaise turned away, reaching over to rip the vines away from Kaeleb's body and swinging the boy onto his back. Kaeleb clutched him around the neck, his face pale and blood streaming from his arm. Then Blaise went towards the Fomori, lifting his hands, and I could feel the hot rush of his power flow past me. He let out a cry of rage as he released it all onto the beasts, calling forth every ounce of strength that he had. The abyss I had opened rumbled and shook, and fire spewed out of it, the liquid center of the world flowing out over the Fomori in long arcs of molten lava. I saw Chaote running back to her eagle, her eyes flashing with anger. Smoke filled the air and then I was blind, the world shrouded in darkness. I closed my eyes, feeling the utter blackness of my existence swallow me whole.

It had been her the whole time. Eolande.

COMING SOON

BLAISE: THE KEEPERS OF IMBRIA
BOOK 3

Jenna Barrett is an award winning author who writes fantasy novels and is currently at work on the Keepers Of Imbria series following the release of her debut novel, Orabelle. She weaves complex emotional dichotomies and breathes life into strong female heroines and villains that you love to hate. Jenna is a recent breast cancer survivor and currently resides in Texas with her three-legged dog, Artemis. When she is not writing, she spends her time doing freelance photographer and is avid adventurer who enjoys anything outdoors, especially rock climbing and mountaineering.

Visit her on the web at www.jbarrettauthor.com
on Twitter and Instagram @jbarrettauthor
or on Facebook J Barrett Author

AFTERWORD

My name is Jenna Barrett and my debut novel was *Orabelle*, the first book of *The Keepers of Imbria* series. I wrote *Orabelle* twelve years before having the courage to publish it, the idea blossoming from a writing exercise I was doing with my sister. My decision to publish and share my work came after my mother was diagnosed with stage 3 colon cancer. She was extremely ill and was not given a very high chance of survival. My younger brother and I became her caretakers and though it was a long journey, she is now thriving and cancer free. *Orabelle* was something that my mother helped me bring to life, brainstorming ideas and proofreading my many attempts, and I knew it would be special to her to see it in print, so I decided to go for it. Six months after it was published, I was diagnosed with breast cancer. Being young and healthy, it completely caught me off guard. I was overwhelmed, knowing what my mother had gone through and now facing those hardships myself. This year has been one of the most difficult trials of my life, and when I was unable to work, unable to do the things that I love most, and unable to express how I was feeling, I once again turned to writing. My second book, *Maialen*, was the perfect distraction. Instead of focusing on my own anxiety and illness, I could get lost in the world of Imbria, forgetting about medications and surgeries and doctors for a few beautiful moments. I hope that my books offer you that same escape, that whatever is happening in your life can be forgotten for a brief time while you lose yourself in an exciting new world. Thank you so much for reading and I would love to hear your thoughts on *Maialen* if you could please take a moment to leave me a review.

Printed in Great Britain
by Amazon

33602077R00179